EMPATHS
A Pyreans Novel

S. H. JUCHA

D1737193

Published by Hannon Books, Inc.
www.scottjucha.com

ISBN: 978-0-9975904-8-7 (e-book)
ISBN: 978-0-9975904-9-4 (softcover)

First Edition: September 2017

Cover Design: Damon Za

Acknowledgments

Empaths is the first book in the Pyreans series. I wish to extend a special thanks to my independent editor, Joni Wilson, whose efforts enabled the finished product. To my proofreaders, Abiola Streete, Dr. Jan Hamilton, David Melvin, Ron Critchfield, Pat Bailey, and Mykola Dolgalov, I offer my sincere thanks for their support.

I wish to thank several sources for information incorporated into the book's science. Toby's bone replacement (BRC, pronounced brick) originated from the website of EpiBone and commentary by CEO Nina Tandon.

The El car diamond-thread cable concept was borrowed from Penn State Professor John Badding and Dow Chemical Company senior R&D analytical chemist Tom Fitzgibbons, who isolated liquid-state benzene molecules into a zigzagging arrangement of rings of carbon atoms in the shape of a triangular pyramid — a formation similar to that of diamonds.

The shielding of ships with boron nitride nanotubes (BNNT) was borrowed from NASA. The experimental material is thought to be useful as a key structural and shielding material in spacecraft, habitats, vehicles, and space suits that might be destined for Mars.

Despite the assistance I've received from others, all errors are mine.

Glossary

A glossary is located at the end of the book.

CONTENTS

1: Murder

Aurelia sat on the edge of the bed, waiting in trepidation. Her hands were deeply entwined in the coverlet to prevent tugging on her short robe, which didn't begin to cover her slender legs. She jerked reflexively when the room's door opened and her tormentor, Dimitri Belosov, strolled in, his eyes sparkling in anticipation, and his mouth formed in a lascivious sneer.

"You know I don't like it when you're not ready when I enter," Dimitri snarled, when he spotted Aurelia in her robe. "Strip," he ordered.

Aurelia fingered the robe's tie, but anger smoldered deep inside her, and she attempted to fan its flames.

"Reluctant, are we?" Dimitri said, a cruel smile twisting his lips. "I was going to be generous today, but it looks like you need another lesson, cousin. Get the ropes."

A shudder went through Aurelia at the prospect of being tied up again. Numb to the sights and sounds around her, she walked to a bedroom nightstand and opened a drawer containing Dimitri's favorite devices. For several months, she'd suffered unimaginable abuses at the hands of her cousin. Dimitri was the governor's nephew, and Aurelia was trapped in the governor's home and made Dimitri's personal companion.

Thoughts of suicide crossed Aurelia's mind many times, but she feared her mother and sister, who were also prisoners, would pay a price for her act. Worse, the thought of leaving her younger sister, Sasha, to the likes of Dimitri revolted her.

Anger, frustration, and humiliation welled up inside Aurelia, swirling together, brewing a storm, and overcoming any fear she had for herself and her family. Pushed one step too far, Aurelia desperately grasped the growing courage that insisted she fight back. She focused her power, released her controls, and pushed the terror at Dimitri that she'd suffered at his hands.

The seventeen-year-old Dimitri eyed his cousin, waiting for her to turn around with the ropes he'd requested. He ached to see the shame on her face. His hunger was nothing personal — any girl would have satisfied what his darkness demanded.

Markos Andropov, the Pyrean governor, had two children with Helena Garmenti. Markos had given Dimitri Helena's eldest daughter, Aurelia, as a companion to his nephew, with the strict admonition that the relationship was to be strictly platonic. Dimitri obeyed the restriction for two weeks. His first furtive attack on his cousin released the blackness that grew inside him since he was a child. With each encounter, Dimitri promised greater acts of revenge against Aurelia's mother and sister, if Aurelia ever said anything to anyone.

"I'm waiting," Dimitri announced. "You know what happens when I'm kept waiting." Suddenly, his pulsing anger was overridden by unfounded doubt. He glanced hesitantly around the room but saw nothing untoward. He considered ratcheting up his threat to Aurelia, but his anxiety, instead of fading, escalated into unreasonable alarm. Dimitri swung around, searching the room for danger.

Unable to locate the source of the creeping nightmare, Dimitri backed toward a point where he could observe the entire bedroom at a glance. His body broke the sensors of the double doors, which led to the balcony, and they slid aside. Dimitri's heart raced in panic, and he broke out in a cold sweat. Swinging his head to and fro, he was frantic to spot the source of his impending doom.

Backing onto the balcony, Dimitri glanced overhead, ensuring the attack wasn't launched from overhead. Hundreds of meters up, the dome's transparent panels filtered Crimsa's weak pink light.

Aurelia sensed her tormentor's full-blown dread. A small voice inside her mind screamed at her to stop, but there was no turning back once she'd started. Instead, Aurelia pushed, sending the horror created by sensing creatures crawling over the skin. Dimitri wouldn't receive her imagery, but he would be overwhelmed by the unsettling and unreasonable feeling of his skin under attack.

The more Aurelia saw Dimitri swipe at his arms and face and heard him whimper, the harder she pushed. She was desperate to end her torture and had no thought for the outcome of her actions.

Dimitri wailed and pleaded for the terror to cease, but the more he cried, the worse it got. His heart pounded in his chest, and sweat rolled down his face. An overwhelming desire to end the nightmare engulfed him. Relief lay only meters below. Succumbing to the sweet temptation, Dimitri leaned against the railing and tumbled over. As he fell to the rocked walkway below, he thought with relief: *Now, it will end.*

Aurelia ran to the balcony and stared at the body below. Blood from Dimitri's crushed skull splattered the walkway. Her eyes darted around the grounds, searching for witnesses. Spying none, she raced back through the bedroom into the corridor beyond. In her panic, she could think of only one place of sanctuary, her mother's quarters, one floor up. She ran down the corridor, accessed the disguised actuator, and dashed through the hidden panel as it opened. She raced up the servants' back stairs, which ended at the third floor. Tripping the hidden catch to open the door to the family's quarters, she burst into the room, crying.

Aurelia's mother, Helena, was brushing the hair of her younger daughter, Sasha, and Aurelia's distraught emotions were broadcasting so strongly that Sasha broke into tears. Helena hushed Sasha, sending her to the girls' bedroom, and hurried to embrace Aurelia.

Through tears and sobs, Aurelia told her story, her entire story — the months of sordid transgressions by Dimitri, despite the governor's admonitions, and the nephew's perverse intentions only moments ago that had caused her to rebel.

"Mother, I pushed with all I had," Aurelia wailed. "All the darkness he ever visited on me, I returned tenfold. He cried and screamed and begged, and still I didn't stop. He backed into the balcony railing and fell over."

Helena held Aurelia, miserable at the thought of what her beautiful and sensitive daughter had endured. "How badly is he injured, daughter?"

"There was blood everywhere, mother. It came from his head, and his skull was oddly shaped."

Cold fear struck Helena's heart, and she fought to prevent her emotions transmitting to her daughter. Both of her daughters were sensitives, empaths, as was she. Young Sasha had already exceeded her mother's power, and Aurelia surpassed her capabilities by the time she was nine. Thereafter, year over year, her older daughter only grew stronger.

The governor had hoped that Aurelia could attenuate Dimitri's darkness and promote a sense of well-being, but neither Helena nor the governor imagined the nephew possessed the deviant proclivities Aurelia described or that he would employ blackmail to silence her.

"You must run, Aurelia," Helena urged her daughter. "No good can come of this. Dimitri belongs to one of the domes' premier families. They will demand justice, and the governor will be forced to offer them a sacrifice in hopes he can keep his secret. Your only hope is to run. You must make it to the El and escape to the station, but don't go to security. Trust no one until you reach Harbour aboard the *Honora Belle*."

While Helena raced to open a hidden panel, artfully concealed inside a clothing closet, sixteen-year-old Aurelia stood frozen. She had fled to her mother for safety but was being told that there was none to be had in her arms. She closed her eyes, and her thoughts faded into hopelessness only to be buoyed by waves of love. Aurelia opened her eyes to find her mother standing before her, pushing with all her strength. Aurelia dropped her mental guards and let her mother's affections wash through her mind.

"Here, daughter," Helena said. She shoved a c-chip ring into Aurelia's hand. "Wear this. There's not much coin on it, but it might help. And take these," she added, handing Aurelia a hand-drawn map and a set of instructions. "Use these to guide you to the El, but you must get clear of our dome as fast as you can without attracting attention. The governor's people will be hunting for you. Once you exit our dome, you can study the remaining details."

Aurelia slipped the c-chip ring on a finger, while Helena ran to the bedroom, calling to Sasha, "Come daughter, hug your sister goodbye. She's leaving." When Sasha hesitated, Helena projected strength, saying, "Your sister is in trouble and must flee for her life. Hug her, return to your room, and crawl into bed. You must appear to be asleep, and you never saw your sister return to our quarters. Now, go, say your goodbye quickly."

The two sisters fell into each other's arms. Sasha was in shock at the thought of losing her sister, but streams of love overrode her fear. Tears stung her eyes. Her sister always sensed her darker moods and lent her strength. This time, rather than play the passive and enjoy her sister's mental ministrations, she pushed back with her love.

"Enough," Helena announced sternly, breaking into the sisters' farewell. "Sasha, go to your room and remember what I said."

As Sasha waved goodbye at the bedroom door, Helena shoved clothing into Aurelia's arms. She could see her daughter mentally struggling and sought to break her out of her daze. "Come, Aurelia, there's no time to waste." She tugged on the robe's belt, and Aurelia mechanically stripped the garment off. "Dress in these," Helena instructed. "You must appear as a privileged Pyrean."

Aurelia required her mother's help to don the unfamiliar fashions of a wealthy, young, Pyrean girl. The dress, what there was of it, draped and clung, with hidden fasteners to artfully reveal swaths of young skin. The shoes defied description. Impractical was the first thought that occurred to Aurelia. They were flamboyantly delicate.

Once her outfit was complete, Aurelia turned to a viewer, dutifully turning in a circle, and a set of lasers translated her image into a 3D projection. Aurelia scarcely recognized herself, and she turned a questioning look at her mother.

"I have tried to prepare for this day, child of my heart," Helena said. "My plan was that one day all of us would escape together, but you must go now. When you reach the El, you must change into these."

Helena opened a stylish shoulder bag, which matched the fabric of Aurelia's dress. "There's a cap, to disguise your hair, coveralls, and ship shoes. You must take on the appearance of an El tech and that means, when the gravity disappears, you remain relaxed, as if you've done this many times before. The instructions I've given you will tell you how to board the El. Ensure you hide the clothes you're wearing when you change into these."

Aurelia felt her mother pull her around and lay a mist mask over her face, activate it, and study the application of preprogrammed makeup on her face. Aurelia turned back to the viewer. The face of a young, pretty, privileged Pyrean girl stared back at her, subtle shades of color and glitter flowed across her face in rivers. The youth of Pyre loved artful camouflage. Her mother grabbed Aurelia's long, straight hair and twisted it into a knot on the top of her head, shoving two trans-sticks through the knot to hold it in place. The bright, glowing trans-sticks, which constantly shifted colors, hid their function, which was to relay a person's comm-dot.

"Place this in your ear," Helena instructed, handing her the comm-dot. "The device isn't active, but if you're approached, and, daughter, looking as you are, you will be, wave them off with a finger and pretend you're conversing with your sister. Remember, you're one of the elite. You choose who will receive your attention."

With Aurelia's transformation complete, the two women hugged, pushing enduring love at each other. Then Aurelia slipped out of the room into the third-floor corridor. She navigated down two flights of back stairs to reach the ground level. She slipped through the side garden and past decorative gates to reach a ped-path.

Aurelia found balancing on the delicate shoes a challenge. *I'm running for my life and I might as well be hobbled,* she thought angrily.

Helena was right about one thing. Aurelia had little time to study her instructions and set out in the right direction before three young men in an e-trans glided silently up behind her.

"Hey there, pretty one," one youth said, running his hand down the back of Aurelia's thigh.

If Aurelia hadn't dealt with Dimitri for the past few months, she might have jumped out of her skin. Instead, she turned a cold eye on the youth, pointed a finger at her comm-dot, and imperially waved her fingers, shooing the youths along.

The boy in the control seat of the e-trans said, "Resume," and the vehicle accelerated to its usual speed. None of the threesome reacted blatantly to Aurelia's dismissal. Her manner of attire indicated she was someone of importance, and they didn't dare anger the daughter of a powerful family.

Luck was with Aurelia. An empty e-trans passed her, responded to its programming, and turned around to crawl beside her. Recalling the actions of the youth, who had been in the other transport's control seat, Aurelia climbed in behind the screen. She opened her instructions but couldn't find anything about how to order the vehicle.

Mother, I guess you weren't any more knowledgeable about the grounds outside the governor's house than I am, Aurelia thought. It hit her that Helena was only a year older than she was now when she was kidnapped. One moment, her mother was topside, enjoying her teenage life, and, the next, she woke up in a bedroom in the governor's house downside. It occurred to Aurelia that Helena must have gathered snippets of information throughout her adult life on Pyre to put together her plan. *Thank you, mother,* Aurelia thought, wishing she was hugging her one more time.

"Destination, miss," Aurelia heard, snapping her out of her reverie.

"The El, please," Aurelia said, with all the authority she could muster.

"Yes, miss. Travel will be through four dome connections and take approximately twenty-eight minutes," the voice said.

A smile plastered across Aurelia's face. For the first time since Dimitri fell to his death, she felt hope. But, it was quickly vanquished by a rush of guilt *He didn't fall to his death, Aurelia; you pushed him. Maybe not with your hands, but you pushed him, nonetheless,* she thought.

Aurelia's thoughts scared her for more than one reason. Her mother had repeatedly admonished her that she was an empath with tremendous power, but Aurelia had no means of measuring and comprehending her strength. The only people she'd openly shared her power with were her mother and sister, and then it was rarely a negative emotion. Even when Sasha attempted to infuriate her, she was careful to be patient and return her sister's dark emotions with calming support.

Dimitri's actions had broken her control. Where she was normally fearful in his company, there was a sudden uncontrollable anger and a desire for revenge. Her mother's repeated warnings came back to her, "Aurelia, child of my heart, you've no idea what you can do with your mind. You must be careful. I wish I could train you, but I was never taught, and I have little concept of how to teach you. All I can tell you is that you must minimize your emotions. Never push with even half your strength."

Before recriminations could grow, the e-trans slowed, as three Pyrean youths in bright, colorful clothing skipped through the front gate of an elegant home, and one of the boys stepped in front of the transport to stop it.

"Where you going?" a girl asked Aurelia.

"The El," Aurelia replied.

"Great," the girl replied. "Jump in," she ordered her companions.

The moment everyone was seated, Aurelia, said, "Resume," and was relieved that the e-trans proceeded on its way.

The boy in the front seat with Aurelia said, "E-trans, destination dome five, block three."

"Understood, sir," the voice of the e-trans replied.

When the boy turned to eye Aurelia, she abruptly laughed and said, "Oh, Sasha, you say the funniest things." The entire trip with her companions, Aurelia kept up an imaginary conversation with her sister. In her mind, she was repeating a conversation they had a few days ago. Then, it had been funny, but repeating it made her stomach clench at the thought she might never see her sister again.

After transiting several domes, the car stopped, and the threesome climbed out. Aurelia waved her fingers brightly at the girl who'd asked her destination, and the teenager signaled back with a hand motion Aurelia couldn't translate. Instead she ordered the e-trans to continue.

While the transport was navigating the next interconnector, which was designed to isolate the domes from each other in the event one of them was breached, Aurelia hurriedly reopened her instructions. At the far end of the transparent tunnel, the sign on the upcoming hatch read "Dome 8, El Transport," and, soon after entering the dome, the e-trans came to a halt.

Aurelia anxiously looked up. She hadn't finished reading her instructions, but a group of people were approaching a growing line of empty e-trans, and her transport had joined the line. She stuffed the instructions into her bag, continued her charade of conversing with Sasha, and climbed out of the vehicle.

Close to panic, Aurelia angled away from the massive landing pad of the space elevator. A line of Pyreans was waiting to board the El for transport to the station, and Aurelia wasn't ready to put her mother's plans in action.

A stack of crates seemed the perfect hiding place, and Aurelia casually walked behind them, despite the pounding of her heart. When no hail or shout of alarm followed her, she breathed a deep sigh of relief and opened her instructions. She read carefully. Many of the steps were foreign to her, since she'd never been off the governor's grounds. At the end of them, her mother had written, "I love you, Aurelia, memorize these instructions and dispose of them. If you make it to the joss and security questions you, they must not find them on you."

Mother, couldn't you have told me what the joss was? Aurelia thought. She read the instructions twice more and then knelt to unpack her next disguise. She glanced around to see if anyone was watching her. Confident she was hidden from view, she yanked out the trans-sticks, the colorful hair adornments. Then she opened a small container and pulled a single mist wipe out. Following her mother's instructions, she pressed it to her face and felt the tingling sensation she was told to expect. When it stopped, she examined her face in a small mirror, and removed the little amounts of makeup that were missed.

Next, Aurelia stripped out of her frilly clothing and silly shoes, grateful she didn't have to walk anymore in them. She unpacked the tech clothing and slipped on the coveralls. The legs and arms ended past her ankles and wrists, and there was room in the body for her little sister. The poor fit reminded Aurelia that her mother was desperate to accept any clothing she could procure to fulfill the family's escape plan.

Aurelia twice folded the ends of the voluminous coveralls' arms and legs until they ended at her wrists and ankles. She tucked her long, auburn hair under the cap and yanked it down on her head. Thin socks and some light shoes, which had a quick close and an odd coating on the bottom, completed the outfit.

The El had yet to return from its last trip topside, and Aurelia was forced to wait. As time passed, she grew more nervous, sure she would be discovered. To occupy her mind, she practiced walking, as per her mother's instructions. She wasn't an elite anymore; she was a tech. Techs don't appear proud and are careful to pay deference to privileged downsiders.

Twenty minutes later, Aurelia breathed a sigh of relief. The El car was transiting the dome's airlock, which kept Pyre's heavily laden air, contaminated with noxious gases and ash, out of the dome. When the El settled onto the landing pad, there was another excruciating waiting period for Aurelia, while the passengers exited the upper level and the cargo crew dropped a ramp on the lower level and began offloading passengers' personal items and freight. Aurelia recognized that the crew wore similar clothing, except much nicer and better fitting, to the coveralls Helena had given her.

Aurelia waited until the line of passengers, who were traveling topside, had dwindled to a few stragglers, and the cargo crew's trips down the ramp seemed to be ending before she left her hiding place and walked toward the car's lower bay. Aurelia was near the ramp when she heard a demand by an angry voice, "Where you been? Grabbing a nap or something?"

"Sorry, sick to my stomach," Aurelia replied, holding her lower abdomen and playing true to her mother's ruse.

The cargo chief took in the ill-fitting coveralls worn by the teenager, and his demeanor softened. "Newbie, huh? You'll get used to it. It always hits the newbies hard, if they've never left the station. But, hear me, newbie, admin might have hired you, but you work for me now. If you haven't checked in with me and you're not wearing a badge, you're not earning any coin. Am I clear?"

"Yes, sir," Aurelia replied, quickly bobbing her head.

"And another thing, newbie, as soon as you collect some coin, purchase a decent pair of coveralls. That pretty face of yours will only get you so far. Once the downsiders get a look at those coveralls, they're going to start complaining about the service. So, don't embarrass me. Now, get aboard."

Aurelia nodded and hustled up the ramp. The freight crew was seated and strapped in, and Aurelia took an empty seat at the end of a double row and fumbled with her straps and buckle before she got it right. She could hear the snickers of those around her at her ineptitude, and she reined in her anger. *Try being in prison all your life, and let's see how well you get on in the world,* Aurelia thought.

The cargo chief walked by Aurelia and handed her a bag. "If you're going to be sick, newbie, use this instead of spraying my deck, and after this lift, come see me. You're supposed to report to me first. Not start work, unless maybe you don't want to be on the rolls. In which case, you'll be working without earning any coin," he admonished before he took a seat and connected his harness.

A senior crew member leaned over to the chief and said, "I don't think that one is going to make it."

The cargo chief grunted in reply. *A shame,* he thought, *the girl looked like she could use a break.*

A red light flashed for five seconds, and Aurelia felt the car move. For a while, there was little sensation other than the car's stopping and starting as it transited the airlock. But, after that, and the higher the car rose, the lighter she felt. Soon her stomach seemed to want to climb out of her throat. She gagged, swallowed, and tasted bile.

A boy across from Aurelia, not much older than her, motioned holding the bag tight to her face and taking short, quick breaths. His pantomime didn't make much sense to Aurelia, but she did as he indicated, since she sensed compassion and sympathy from him. Keeping the bag tight to her mouth made it difficult to breathe. Within thirty seconds, the dizziness and nausea she was experiencing subsided, and Aurelia realized she'd been hyperventilating, dragging in huge gulps of air, as the weightlessness accelerated her anxiety.

Slowly, Aurelia gained control of her upset stomach and calmed down. She pulled the bag from her mouth and smiled crookedly at the boy across from her. Around Aurelia, the crew, including her sympathetic helper, underwent various reactions, indicating that Aurelia had driven their fears too, and now they were recovering. That realization alone jarred her, and she concentrated on sending soothing calm. The last thing she needed was to have the cargo crew suspect she was a sensitive.

Finally, the El car decelerated and came to a stop. Aurelia determined the best course of action was for her to pay close attention to the boy across from her. He picked up on her intention after tapping the release for his harness and noticing that she did the same thing and waited. He exaggerated placing his shoes firmly on the deck, picking up one, and placing it back down before he picked up the other.

Aurelia felt a tacky sensation from the soles of her shoes when she walked across the decking after climbing aboard the car. Now, she understood why. She nodded to him, and, when he stood, she did too.

"Look, best you stick with me," the boy said to Aurelia. "I'll operate the e-cart. You stand by. I'll signal you when I have the load secured. Then, you unlock it from the deck. Okay? And, the name's JD."

Aurelia smiled shyly at him, thanking him for his kindness. It seemed best not to encourage him, but she couldn't help sending the smallest amount of appreciation.

JD used a hand signal to tell Aurelia to wait, and he left. The thought of being weightless made Aurelia giddy. She wanted to shove off the deck and fly, but she noticed that around her the crew were walking with a fixed gait, placing one foot solidly before lifting the other. *Once you leap up, silly girl,* Aurelia admonished herself, *just what are you going to use to guide yourself around ... wings?* The thought of having wings made her snicker, which drew a few glances her way, and she cleared her throat and tried to look as if she belonged on the crew.

When JD returned, driving an e-cart, he pointed a device at the crate in front of him. A red telltale flashed, and he read something on a handheld device screen and then stuck the unit to the front of his coveralls.

Aurelia stepped away from the load, noticing the e-cart's wheels were covered in the same material as the bottom of her shoes. She glanced down at the pallet that JD hooked to his cart and saw a clamp attaching it to the deck.

"Got it," JD said. "Release the load."

Thankfully, for Aurelia, the clamp had a square, red button, which was labeled "load release," and she happily mashed it, watching it spring free of the pallet. She stood and smiled at JD, who gave her a silly grin and shook his head. "Both sides, newbie," he said good-naturedly.

Aurelia mimed "oops" to him, flashed her best smile, and then hurried to the other side. She could sense JD's reaction, and it gave her mixed feelings. They felt similar to the emotions Dimitri emanated when he looked at her but without the ugly darkness. She released the second lock and gave JD the thumbs-up signal she'd witnessed the other assistants giving their e-cart operators.

When the belly of the El car was empty, Aurelia followed behind JD's last load. After exiting the El car, he turned toward an airlock that would accommodate his e-cart and load, but Aurelia spotted a sign that directed people to the El car's passenger access level, and she followed the sign up the ramp.

2: Secrets

A stationer, Phillip Borden, who rotated planetside for three weeks of each month to tend the grounds of many of the dome's wealthier families, finished checking the beehives in the rear of the governor's home.

Every inch of the grounds under the domes that wasn't covered by environmental control buildings, houses, ped-paths, walkways, patios, or other small sundry items was planted with small fruit trees, herb gardens, and flowering shrubbery to satisfy the bees' desire for pollen. Crimsa's light, which was filtered by the hazy atmosphere, required the bioengineering of every plant species brought from Earth to thrive. No plant cuttings were ever wasted. Each house had several composts.

The domes tended to be as self-sufficient as they could be for food, but they still depended on an exchange with the orbital station, which contained extensive hydroponic gardens and protein culture vats.

Phillip was carrying a collection of honeycombs to the house when he spotted Dimitri's body. A weaker person might have dropped the precious container, but, like most stationers, Phillip had seen his share of death. After witnessing a fellow human killed by explosive decompression, there's little that can disturb an individual about a dead body.

Despite the gruesome circumstances, Phillip obeyed rule number one of his employment: Never enter the house, no exceptions. Setting the honey container on the patio, Phillip pulled his comm unit and contacted Giorgio Sestos, the governor's head of security. Sestos was the kind of man, who when he laid down rules, Phillip, having a sensible head on his shoulder, knew better than to disobey any of them.

"Sestos here, go ahead, Phillip," the voice on the gardener's comm replied.

"Sir, Dimitri's on the back patio. He's dead."

"Dead? Are you sure? Did you check for a pulse?"

"It wasn't necessary, sir. I think he fell from the balcony. His head looks squashed."

"Anybody in sight when you approached the body?"

"I didn't see anyone, sir."

"Stand by the body, Phillip. On my orders, no one is to touch the body. I want the evidence preserved. I'll be there in five."

"Understood, sir." Phillip barely finished when the comm signal cut off. He stared at Dimitri's blank eyes and the darkening pool of blood. *Couldn't have happened to a better kid,* Phillip thought, but he was careful to keep his expression neutral. At this point, caught smiling over the body of a household member could make him a suspect.

In short order, Giorgio Sestos and a second security man came through the patio doors. They were careful to step in a wide circle around the body.

"Did you or anybody else touch the body after you discovered the boy?" Giorgio asked Phillip, drilling the groundskeeper with cold eyes.

"No, sir," Phillip replied evenly. He knew Giorgio was a dangerous man, but he was too old to be intimidated by him.

"Sniffer scan, then body temp," Giorgio ordered the second man.

Pulling a sniffer from a case, the man leaned over and traced the body at about 8 centimeters above it. While the sniffer analyzed the intake, he inserted a digital thermometer into Dimitri's ear. When the sniffer beeped, the man checked the results. "Negligible results on the scan, Mr. Sestos. No significant DNA contamination here. Body temp suggests the boy died within the last hour."

"Where were you during that time, Phillip?" Giorgio demanded.

"Pruning fruit trees and then at the beehives, sir," Phillip replied, pointing to the container of honeycomb near his feet.

"And you heard nothing?"

"I thought I heard an argument or, at least, Dimitri's voice from an upper floor. But, I've often heard him raise his voice. So, I didn't think anything of it. If you're asking if I heard anyone else or if I heard Dimitri scream as he fell, the answer is negative."

Giorgio regarded the misshapen skull. *The impact must have been head first,* he thought, and he stepped out to look up at the second- and third-floor balconies. "Stay with the body," he ordered his man and ran back into the house. Giorgio didn't wait for the lift but ran up the back stairs instead. In the private bedroom reserved for Dimitri, he searched for signs of a struggle, but there was no evidence of any. A drawer was open, revealing Dimitri's sex toys, and Giorgio closed it, thinking he should get rid of the items before the household or, worse, the governor discovered them.

Carefully checking the railing, Giorgio found no marks or scuffs. It looked as if the boy had gone over the rail without a struggle. Except Giorgio knew Dimitri wasn't the type to commit suicide. "I knew this day would happen," he muttered. "You had to play domination games with a powerful teenage bender, didn't you, you little idiot?"

In a foul mood, Giorgio took the stairs one floor up to Helena's rooms. She and her daughters occupied half the house's top floor, where their isolation could be easily maintained. Giorgio didn't bother knocking, hoping to catch the family by surprise.

"Mr. Sestos, how rude of you," Helena said tartly. She was busy preparing a meal, and the small table was set for three people. "I didn't make enough for four if lunch is what you're after."

"Where's your daughter?" Giorgio demanded.

"Which one?" Helena retorted, turning to face the man she'd come to despise even more than the governor.

"Don't play games with me, woman. Where's Aurelia?"

"She's with that psychopath. It's where she is every week, at this time." Then Helena smoothly switched roles. "Why are you asking? Did something happen to my daughter?"

Not getting the expected reaction, Giorgio stomped across the sitting room and opened the girls' bedroom.

When light spilled into the darkened room, a sleepy-eyed Sasha raised her head from a pillow, saying, "What's wrong?"

Giorgio turned on the lights, and Sasha sat up quickly, calling, "Momma."

Helena ran to the doorway and called out, "Stay in the bed, Sasha. The governor's dog is searching for a bone."

Giorgio checked the girls' room thoroughly, and then he searched the rest of the accommodations. When he was done, he faced Helena squarely, hands on hips, and said, "I'll give you this last chance to tell me where Aurelia has gone."

"If that creature has hurt my daughter and done something with her, I'll make you and your master pay. One way or the other, I'll make the two of you pay."

Giorgio wasn't scared of Helena, she didn't have the power, but when he felt fear creep up his spine, he eyed Sasha, who was standing in the bedroom doorway, a coverlet around her, glaring at him.

"Don't, kid," Giorgio warned Sasha, "or I'll be happy to juice you." He patted his injector pistol for emphasis. Immediately, the unnerving sensation disappeared.

"Benders," Giorgio said, with disgust. "You're a bunch of abominations who should never be allowed to exist." He didn't wait for a reply but left in a hurry. It took him a few minutes to search the house and discover Aurelia was nowhere to be found. Then he went to a small room on the first floor located at the back of the house and unlocked a door to which only he knew the key code.

Using a palm scan and a second code, Giorgio activated the monitors of the house's surveillance. He rolled back the recordings to an hour and a half ago, focusing first on Dimitri's private bedroom. He slowed the file to normal speed to watch Aurelia undress and don her short robe before he fast-forwarded to Dimitri's entrance. Activating, the audio, he listened to the exchange.

Giorgio discovered he didn't need the audio. He could tell by the change in Aurelia's body language and facial expressions that when she turned from the drawer the girl had had enough of Dimitri's depraved attentions. He watched the boy's fear escalate until the terror that was etched in his face totally consumed him. Aurelia stalked him, and, driven by desperation, Dimitri deliberately leaned backward over the balcony's railing.

The scene gave Giorgio chills. The girl was untrained, completely unaware of her tremendous power and how to control it.

"And thanks to you, Dimitri, she's loose in the domes and mad at the world. I pity the next poor slob she meets and who doesn't know enough to shock or juice her first and ask questions later," Giorgio said, addressing the monitor, which showed an image of Aurelia's face contorted in anger.

Searching surveillance footage, Giorgio found a good closeup image of Aurelia, which he loaded into his comm unit and sent out to his network. The accompanying message said, "Report the location of this girl. Don't approach. Reward offered. DNS." The acronym, which ended the message, meant the recipients weren't to share the information with others. It was for their eyes only. It also said this was a high priority request and the reward would be significant.

Throughout the domes, hundreds of people, who had done business with Giorgio at one time or another, raced to be the first to provide the information to the governor's head of security. It was an El tech, Gerald, monitoring the cams focused on the landing pad and the airlock, who spotted Aurelia. He had loaded her image into his system and ran a face recognition comparison on the passengers, who boarded the most recent car to lift. When that search returned as negative, the tech widened the program's input to include the pad and surrounding freight areas.

The recognition program returned a 72.8 percent match, and Gerald zoomed in to study the girl, in ugly coveralls with a cap jammed down on her head, who was climbing the car's ramp. The El car's cargo chief seemed to recognize her, which made the tech doubt he'd found the target. However, the possibility of earning coin drove him on, and he selected the widest cam view of the pad and freight area. Locating the girl talking to the cargo chief, Gerald reversed the recording. He watched her walk backwards to hide behind a stack of crates.

Gerald found the girl had waited and watched the landing pad from a hiding place, which made the tech suspicious, and he reversed the recording at high speed, pausing when he caught her changing clothes. "Got you," he whispered, snatching up his comm unit.

"Mr. Sestos, this is Gerald at the El pad. I've found your girl."

"Don't approach her, Gerald. We'll be right there," Giorgio replied.

"Sorry, Mr. Sestos, she's gone. She snuck aboard the El as cargo crew. She'll make the station in another half hour." When Gerald heard nothing, he was tempted to ask about the reward but thought better of it. Shortly thereafter, the comm went dead.

"Well, the day's not been a total waste," Gerald whispered, an ugly smile on his face. He accessed a back door in the monitoring system and sent the recording of Aurelia changing her clothes to his comm unit.

Giorgio's comm unit was tucked against his chin, as he thought. Gerald would get his reward, but he had more to worry about than that.

An eighty-year-old agreement regarding empaths was broken when Giorgio helped the governor kidnap Helena. At the time, it was a calculated gamble on his part. He was a new hire on the governor's security detail. But assisting the governor with his dangerous and foolish action placed Giorgio in a position of power and confidence, and he'd reaped the reward every year since then.

However, Giorgio knew that the governor and he were lost if their crimes were discovered. It wasn't only the kidnapping and illegal incarceration. There existed a delicate truce between topsiders and downsiders about empaths, after a series of ugly incidents surrounding their mistreatment. A binding agreement was signed by all parties, stating that when an empath was identified, he or she was to be sent to Harbour aboard the *Honora Belle*, the old colony ship, to be trained. When she certified their training period was successfully completed, they could choose to live on the station or aboard the *Belle*.

Since the initiation of the agreement, not a single identified empath had ever returned to the station. They'd stayed with Harbour. Coincidentally, not a single empath had ever been born to downsiders, and it was those in the domes who had transgressed against sensitives before the agreement was in place, which is why it stated that no empath could reside downside, under any circumstances.

Giorgio tried one last tactic to reacquire Aurelia before he contacted the governor and sent a coded signal to a contact on the station's security force. When he received a reply, he shook his head in disgust and commed Markos Andropov.

"In a meeting, Sestos," Markos replied tersely.

"Apologies, Governor, but you have a priority one at the house," Giorgio replied.

"Handle it, Sestos. That's what I pay you for. This meeting's important," Markos replied testily.

"Wish I could, Governor, but one of your private birds has flown the coop ... all the way to the station."

The comm was silent, and Giorgio waited. He could imagine the turmoil roiling through the governor's mind. He heard, "Coming," before the comm abruptly ended.

* * * *

When Governor Markos Andropov arrived home, he found Giorgio had moved Dimitri's body to a private room and had his man clean up the mess on the patio. The security chief's briefing to Markos was terse and to the point.

"No doubt about it, Governor," Giorgio said. "The girl mentally pushed him. The recording shows Dimitri was terrorized."

"How can that be, Giorgio? Helena is an extremely weak empath. Why would her daughter be so strong?"

"I've no idea, Governor. There was no indication of it prior to this point," Giorgio replied evenly, keeping a neutral expression on his face, even though he was lying.

"What about Sasha?" Markos asked, with concern.

"That's a good question, Governor, but I wouldn't be sure about how to go about investigating her strength. Right now, we need to think about Aurelia." Giorgio needed the governor to focus on the bigger problem and to drop any inquiry into how Aurelia was capable of pushing Dimitri to his death. The last thing Giorgio wanted was to have the governor discover his secrets.

"You reached out to your contact on the station?" Markos asked.

"He's been warned, but he was across the station, investigating a mining ship. She'll probably have exited the El before our agent gets there."

"Appearing as she does," Markos said, examining the image of Aurelia on Giorgio's comm unit, "and knowing nothing about the orbital platform, she'll be easy to spot."

"But what if she runs afoul of station security before our man recovers her?"

Markos stared at Giorgio, while he thought through his options. He couldn't believe that this day had arrived, and he damned his sister for being unable to control her son. "I'm going to have to call a meeting and warn the others."

"And tell them what, Governor?" Giorgio asked.

"I need their station assets, if we're to recover Aurelia before she's discovered or makes it to the *Belle*. And, if they're going to help, they'll want to know why they should. This thing could blow up in our faces and undo the delicate balance of power between us and the topsiders."

"The family heads could throw you to station security as a sacrifice."

"They could, Giorgio, and they know that we could do the same to them."

* * * *

Markos Andropov fumed, fretted, sat down, jumped up, paced, and sat down again. In minutes, the dome's power elite would descend on his home, and his secret that he'd kept for nearly two decades would be exposed. Worse, it was the type of explosive revelation that would endanger the Andropov dynasty that had governed Pyre's domes since their inception.

The original patriarch, Andrei Andropov, wasn't the greatest contributor to the construction fund for the North American Confederation's (Sol-NAC) last colony ship, the *Honora Belle*. He was the third, and his credits guaranteed seats for his family. Andrei made his fortune as a brilliant building engineer. It was he who designed the domes of Pyre, which kept the ash-ridden, sulfur-polluted air at bay. His inventive metal-silica transparent plates resisted the bombardment of the mild volcanic eruptions that still plagued Pyre, nearly three centuries after the colonists achieved orbit.

The Andropov family held the governorship of the domes ever since Andrei was first elected and now Markos was about to place the dynasty in jeopardy because of a rash decision to kidnap a young girl. He had been on station to see to the death ceremonies of his wife and brother-in-law, who were killed in a decompression accident, while they were inspecting a terminal arm.

The Andropov adults were engineers. That was the Pyrean discipline in greatest demand, and it kept the family in the forefront of society. In the case of Markos' wife and brother-in-law, they were simply in the wrong place at the wrong time. Construction on the space station's shipping arms was a dangerous business.

Deep in misery, Markos found comfort in the attentions of a young, seventeen-year-old girl, Helena. She was a sensitive, a late-maturing empath, her powers so weak that she wasn't aware of her capabilities and hadn't been identified as a sensitive. People would characterize her as a girl whose personality lit up a room.

Helena was attracted to Markos' power and position, but she refused his offer to return downside with him, and mired in his grief, Markos committed a singular act of stupidity. He kidnapped her.

Helena was hidden in the Andropov house, where only a few, trusted, and well-compensated servants had access to her. Markos and his wife had chosen to put off having children until later in life, and left without an heir after his wife's death, Markos hoped to have a son with Helena, but she'd given him two daughters.

When Markos' sister, Liana, approached him, complaining again of her son's destructive and dark nature, Markos conceived the idea of making Aurelia a companion to his nephew. His hope was that Aurelia's capabilities could soothe Dimitri's provocative nature.

Although Dimitri wasn't told the nature of Markos' relationship to Aurelia, it didn't take the shrewd nephew long to discover the Andropov family's dark secret. He kept his knowledge from his uncle, but not from his cousin, Aurelia. Dimitri threatened her at every opportunity to enforce her silence.

That Aurelia possessed the power to push someone into killing themselves scared Markos, and he wondered again about Sasha. Worse, if Aurelia had that capability, she could easily convince station security of the veracity of her story of being held captive downside. While Markos ruminated on his choices, Giorgio knocked on his study's open door.

"Your guests are here, Governor Andropov," Giorgio announced formally.

"Show them in, Mr. Sestos," Markos replied. He crossed the room to warmly greet three more powerful family heads. Together with the Andropov family, they formed an unshakeable cabal that ruled the domes. "Friends, good of you to come on such short notice," Markos said. He tried to make them comfortable, offering seats and drinks.

"Let's dispense with the amenities, Markos," Rufus Stewart said, and remained standing as did the others. "Your comm said urgent."

"There's been a tragedy in my household, my friends. My nephew has been murdered," Markos replied, dutifully hanging his head.

Condolences came to Markos, as was expected, but he knew better. None of them were his friends, especially Lise Panoy, who pretended to be.

"Who did this?" Idrian Tuttle asked.

"A young woman in my household," Markos replied.

"Do you have her in custody?" Rufus Stewart asked.

"No, she escaped topside."

"Then station security will have her soon," Lise said. When she witnessed a pained expression cross Markos' face, she asked, "Markos, you did report her to the commandant?"

"I can't," Markos admitted, "and that's why I called this meeting. I need your help. More specifically, I need your assets on the station to help me recover the girl quickly and quietly."

Rufus scowled at Markos. The details weren't fitting together, and he became suspicious. "What's the servant's name?" Rufus asked, reaching for his comm unit.

"Don't bother looking, Rufus," Markos admitted. "She's not in the domes' registry."

"How can she not be registered?" Idrian asked loudly.

"She's a sensitive," Markos said.

"Markos, I thought you said she was a member of your household?" asked Lise, frowning and attempting to piece together Markos' disjointed comments. "You implied she's a downsider. Now, you say she's an empath, who, by the way, shouldn't be planetside."

Before Markos could reply, Idrian pointed an accusing finger at him and declared hotly, "You kidnapped this girl, didn't you?"

"No, I didn't. I kidnapped her mother. Aurelia is my daughter," Markos said quietly. It felt as if his world emptied out of him — his secret, his future, and his family's dynasty.

"When ... when did you do this, Markos?" Lise asked quietly.

"Nearly eighteen years ago," Markos replied. "Helena's her name, and she's given me two daughters, Aurelia and Sasha,"

Markos' three guests stared at him in horror. The ramifications of what the governor had done and what it meant to the domes' elite families were too far-reaching to predict.

"Did Aurelia kill Dimitri physically?" Rufus asked. He was always the detailed-minded one.

"No. She's an extremely strong sensitive, unlike her mother. She terrorized Dimitri, who killed himself to end his torment."

"Wonderful, Markos," Idrian ground out. "You kidnap a woman, who gives you two daughters. Then you raise the girls in captivity in your house, without training and without realizing their powers. Now that the engine's red hot, you throw in plasma and introduce this powerful, untrained empath to someone we all know is rotten to the core. Then you're shocked and saddened when the girl retaliates against that piece of discharge you call a nephew."

"How could you be so stupid, Markos?" Rufus railed.

"Stop, all of you," Lise said into the noise. "Shouting isn't going to get us anywhere. What's done might be one of the greatest mistakes ever committed, but it's done, and we have to think about what it means to all of us and what we need to do to direct the outcome."

"Please, friends, I need your help," Markos pleaded. "Employ your assets on the station to find Aurelia and return her downside before station security locates her."

"I agree that's our priority," Lise urged, but Rufus and Idrian looked unconvinced. "If station security gets to Aurelia first, what's the commandant going to believe? That this was just the governor's doing ... that for two decades we visited and dined at the governor's house without knowing three women were held captive here? Damage control first, sirs. Then we can figure out what the families should do about this."

Rufus and Idrian reluctantly agreed to Lise's reasoning, and all three committed to Markos to use their station assets to locate Aurelia and secretly return her downside.

Lise briefly hugged Markos, assuring him that the families would work to mitigate the issue, and, as Giorgio led the three family heads from the house, Markos sat at his desk and wept.

At the door, Rufus and Idrian passed through first, and Lise spared a knowing glance for Giorgio, who tipped his head by the smallest increment.

Out on the ped-path, the three family heads caught a passing e-trans, and Rufus entered a priority code that would keep the transport from stopping along the way to their destination.

"Well, that certainly wasn't the meeting I was expecting," Idrian said from the back seat.

"Me neither," Rufus acknowledged. "I thought you had Giorgio on the coin?" he asked Lise.

"I thought I did too," Lise replied. "Just goes to show you that some secrets cost you more than you're paying."

"What's the plan, Lise? Don't tell me we're going to help that idiot. We've got him right where we want him, and we can finally unseat the Andropov family from their lofty perch," Idrian urged.

"I'm with Idrian, Lise," Rufus agreed, "as long as the plan doesn't get us in trouble with station security along with the Andropov family. What you said about what the commandant might think made sense to me."

"Yes ... I was thinking about that," Lise said, staring ahead at some teenagers laughing and cavorting on the ped-path and forcing the e-trans to navigate around them.

One of the girls in the group of teenagers flashed a rude hand sign at the passengers of a transport that slowed to ease by them, and she was prepared to do the same to the next one. But, at the last second, her hand froze when she locked eyes with Lise Panoy's cold, blue stare. She yanked the boy on the outside of the group from the e-trans path and hissed a warning. The seven teens hurried to the side of the ped-path and managed to look as guilty as they could when the family heads passed. Of course, since they were teenagers, they were laughing and giggling about it moments after the e-trans, with its preeminent members, got out of hearing distance.

"I agree with Idrian," Lise resumed. "This is our opportunity, but we have to protect ourselves, which means the commandant has to be made aware of the circumstances. He and I have a solid relationship, coin-wise. If I tell him what's going on, he'll let the investigation go forward as a hunt for a murderer, nothing more."

"Then we help station security get ahold of Aurelia and discover she's an empath. Then the wrath will fall on the governor," Rufus reasoned.

"That means we keep our assets out of this, right?" Idrian asked.

"Absolutely," Lise replied. "That fool gets no help from us, whatsoever."

"What about the governor's man, Sestos?" Rufus asked.

"He chose to keep this secret from us, which we could have used nine years ago when I recruited him on the coin," Lise replied. "I say let him go under with Markos." She grinned at Rufus and Idrian, who returned their own evil smiles.

* * * *

When Markos heard a soft knock at the door, he quickly dried his eyes and blew his nose. Having composed himself, he called for Giorgio to enter.

Giorgio could see that Markos was an emotional wreck, but events were moving too fast to let sentiment stand in the way of planning.

"What do you think they're going to do?" Markos asked Giorgio, when his security chief plopped down in a chair across the desk from him.

"I think they'll use this against us, Governor."

"But they'll have to be worried that their families could become embroiled too," Markos protested.

"I agree, which means Lise will take steps to protect the other families, while we take the heat from station security."

"Then you don't think they'll use their assets to find Aurelia and bring her back to me? What then? They find her and keep her for themselves so they can blackmail me?"

"That's too soft an approach, Governor. Admittedly, Rufus and Idrian are the type to want to blow things up, but Lise is the strategist, which is why she offered me coin nearly a decade ago."

"And now she knows you held out on her, Giorgio," Markos said, with regret.

Giorgio quirked his mouth in reply, knowing that it was only a matter of time before this day arrived.

"What are our options, Giorgio?" Markos asked.

"You can be sure that Lise will activate her plan, whatever it is, shortly. It's my bet that she'll probably involve the commandant. She'll find a way to engage station security to find Aurelia before our asset does. If she's successful, then I think its game over for us."

"If your asset gets to Aurelia first, then what?" Markos asked.

"Then you and I have to think about what to do next."

"Meaning?"

"The three women have always been liabilities, which we sought to minimize. Now, our secret has been outed to the family heads, and we have to mitigate our exposure."

"You're saying we have to get rid of Helena and Sasha," Markos said, appalled.

"You have to choose between them and your governorship, which includes your family and me, by the way."

"If we recover Aurelia first, we can decide what to do then, but, if station security gets her first, then there's nothing we can do," Markos replied.

"Think it through, Giorgio. If the commandant gets Aurelia in custody, he'll have this powerful empath telling him this wild tale of being raised in captivity. But, because of what Lise will have told him, according to you, he'll know that Aurelia's story is true. The commandant will have to investigate, and he won't come alone. You can bet Harbour will be accompanying him and his security force. Then it won't matter if Helena and Sasha aren't here. We can't make the household disappear, and once the interviews start with Harbour in the room, she'll perceive every little lie they tell. And don't think you or I can hide from a trained and powerful empath like Harbour."

Giorgio stood abruptly and headed toward the door.

"Where are you going?" Markos asked.

"To contact my asset with on-station security and see if he can enroll others to help him without spilling the entire story. It looks like the only way out of this mess is to spend as much coin as it takes to keep Aurelia out of the hands of station security."

3: The JOS

By walking slowly from the cargo level of the El, Aurelia stalled her approach to whatever waited at the end of the exit ramp. Eventually, two cargo crew members passed her, and she kept pace with them. The three of them joined a short line. The taller and older of the two boys recognized Aurelia, turned around, and said to her, "Look, newbie, don't you get sick when we get twisted. I just had these coveralls cleaned."

The boys laughed harshly at the joke, but Aurelia kept her temper under control. She had no desire to hurt anyone else, despite the hostile treatment she was receiving from these strangers. She glanced down to avert her eyes and noticed, for the first time, footprints etched into the deck. From the line's front to her, the prints were green and numbered six pairs. Behind her, a man stood on a red pair.

A rush of air emanated from in front of Aurelia. It brought her head up, and she looked past the front of the line. A protective hatch slid aside, and then a polished metal door rotated aside to reveal a small car. Six people poured out of the car, and Aurelia's line hurried forward. By now, Aurelia, who was a quick study, was learning to observe and imitate. The people on the green footprints went; she was on green; and so, she went.

Inside the car, people pressed against a padded backrest and pulled a pair of restraining bars down to brace their shoulders, and she copied the action. When they snapped a wide belt around their waist, she did too.

When all six positions were occupied and restraints in place, green lights lit over the passengers' heads, and Aurelia felt the capsule accelerate. As the speed increased, the car rotated 90 degrees, dropping Aurelia's body forward. She swallowed bile to keep from staining loudmouth's coveralls, who was strapped opposite her. When the boy realized his jest might become reality, fear crossed his face, and that helped Aurelia maintain control of her stomach.

In less than a minute, the car stopped moving, the lights turned white, and passengers pushed up bars and unsnapped belts. Where there had been no gravity, now Aurelia felt her weight firmly on her feet.

Glancing down at his feet, the shorter of the two boys commented to his friend, "Luck is with us. Our deck shoes are still clean," and he gave Aurelia a nasty smile. She was tempted to drive his taunt back at him, but she settled for ignoring him.

Aurelia exited the capsule into a corridor and was immediately brushed aside by six people rushing to enter the car. She glanced back and read a sign's three lines: "JOS Translation Capsule, El Cargo Area, Authorized Personnel Only." It dawned on Aurelia that this device was how the station handled the transition from gravity to weightlessness and back again to access the El.

Aurelia followed the short corridor to a much broader one, her eyes attracted to the statue of a man in the center of the corridor. She stopped at the edge of the corridors' intersection. Crowds of people flowed constantly in both directions, and Aurelia, who had lived her life in near isolation, found the crush of people incredible.

Standing still, unlike everyone else, Aurelia found she became the focus of those passing by. Most people eyed her curiously, some sympathetically and some with disdain, and she closed her mental gates for protection. It was obvious to Aurelia that her tawdry tech coveralls were a striking contrast to the close-fitting, decorative outfits of the stationers.

Aurelia made her way through the throng to eye the statue more closely. A plaque at the base read, "Stephen Jenkels, Designer and Chief Engineer of the Jenkels Orbital Station." *JOS,* Aurelia thought, recognizing the three-letter anagram, and a soft smile crossed her face.

Despite Aurelia's attempt to shut herself off from the impressions of the crowds, who numbered in the hundreds, their emotions were getting through to her. She'd never encountered this many individuals at any time, and it felt like everyone was screaming their feelings at her. Aurelia clamped her hands to her ears, as if that would block out the transmissions, and she glanced around for a place of solitude, anywhere where there weren't people.

Walking briskly with hands tightly against the sides of her head, Aurelia crossed to the other side of the wide corridor, passed shops, dodged people, and dived down a smaller corridor. It was still busy, and she kept twisting and turning, seeking an even smaller passageway and some peace.

Within minutes, Aurelia was lost, but she didn't care. The noise in her head had quieted to a murmur, which her mental gates could control. She stopped and eased her hands away from her ears.

"You okay?" Aurelia heard a small voice ask. To her right sat a young boy in a wheelchair with a cast on his leg from thigh to ankle.

"Fine," she said. "The crowds made me a little jumpy."

"They do that to me too. I like it quiet," the boy replied. "The name's Toby," he said, extending a hand.

"Rules," Aurelia replied, using the nickname given her by Sasha. It was a common complaint of her little sister, "Aurelia, you have too many rules," Sasha would say. Aurelia briefly shook Toby's hand.

"What happened to your leg?" Aurelia asked, leaning against the bulkhead next to Toby.

"Accident. It was shattered in too many places to fix properly, so I'm waiting for my BRC," Toby said, pronouncing the acronym as "brick."

"What's a brick?" Aurelia asked.

"A bone replacement copy ... a BRC," Toby replied. "You know you're wearing cargo crew coveralls, but you don't talk or act like a stationer, and you certainly aren't a downsider. Are you from the *Belle*?"

"Actually, I need to get to the colony ship. Do you know how to do that?"

"Sure, it's in section H. You take the *Belle*'s shuttle from terminal arm six, gate four. How come you don't know that?"

"I've had some problems recently," Aurelia replied, shaking her head slightly to intimate it had something to do with her memory.

"Oh, I'm sorry, Rules. Looks like you and I aren't having much luck lately."

"Could you show me the way to the shuttle, Toby?" Aurelia said hopefully.

"Yeah, it's a long way around the ring, but I can get you there. You have coin, right?"

"I have some," Aurelia said, holding up the hand with the ring on it.

"A c-chip ring. Haven't seen many of those around lately. My mom has a couple of old ones in a drawer. How much you got?"

"I don't know," Aurelia said quietly.

"Touch it to your comm unit, and it'll tell you," Toby said helpfully.

"Don't have one."

Toby gave Aurelia a look like he was talking to an alien. He pulled out his device, tapped the screen a few times, and said, "Touch it to mine, and I'll tell you how much is on it."

Aurelia was unaware of how the coin could be transferred from the ring, and she was loath to lose what little she had by doing as Toby requested. She opened her senses and pulled from him. She felt apprehension, sympathy, and gratefulness, presumably the latter for the opportunity to talk to someone. Toby seemed safe to her, so she tapped the ring to the top of the device he extended toward her.

"Sorry, Rules, it doesn't have near enough for a shuttle ride. You could buy some new coveralls," Toby said, eyeing Aurelia's tired and ill-fitting pair, "or you could get a few shriek lunches."

"Shriek lunches?"

"Yeah, shriek, as in what the heck did I just eat?" Toby replied, holding his hands above his shoulders and imitating a person freaking out.

Aurelia laughed quietly at Toby's antics. He reminded her of Sasha, who was the boisterous one of the sisters. She could sense Toby's jitters, and she thought through his emotions. "What are you worried about, Toby?"

"You know ... the usual things," Toby replied absentmindedly, but he pulled his arms protectively toward his body.

"Such as ..." Aurelia pressed.

"Mainly, it's the bone replacement. I don't know if it will hurt or if they'll get it right. They usually do, but sometimes it doesn't take. I could be crippled for the rest of my life."

The more Toby talked, the more Aurelia was moved by the worries that haunted him. His pain reminded Aurelia of hers. She closed her eyes and pushed, replacing Toby's anxieties with confidence and hope.

"Oh," Toby sighed in relief. "You're from the *Belle*. You're one of those people, Rules."

"Shhh," Aurelia replied, holding a finger to her lips. "It's our secret, Toby." She enjoyed the conspiratorial smile that crossed Toby's face. It smoothed the remaining frown lines on his forehead.

Aurelia debated asking the question on her mind. If her predicament weren't so dire, she might never have said anything, but her circumstances called for boldness. "Toby, you don't by any chance have enough coin to buy me a shuttle ride. I could pay you back."

Toby's immediate answer was a snort. "I'm eleven. How am I supposed to have that much coin?" When he noticed Rules deflate, he did what most eleven year olds do to help. "Hey, Rules, you want to have some fun? We can go to a terminal arm and play freefall. My mom took my deck shoes, but you can help me through the cap."

The mention of a station's arm and learning how to access one intrigued Aurelia. It would take her one step closer to seeking Harbour. "Sure, Toby, lead the way."

Toby gave Rules a grin and took off in his motorized chair.

Aurelia ran to keep up with Toby. She could hear his laughter, as he swerved around people. Some stationers turned to remonstrate with Toby for his unsafe behavior, but mouths were abruptly closed when they spotted his full leg cast and youthful face. Aurelia kept her head down and murmured "Sorry" to the many she darted past.

Starting to gasp for breath, Aurelia was grateful when Toby turned down a short corridor labeled "Section S, Terminal Arm 2."

"Mining captains dock their ships here, Rules, so the arm has little foot traffic. The crew gets downtime, and they don't return to their ship until the last minute." Toby locked his chair and set the alarm sequence, which would send a signal to station security if it was moved without his approval. "Help me up, Rules," Toby said, extending his arms to her.

Toby's excitement was infectious, and Aurelia dearly wanted to help him enjoy his freefall. For her, his emotion was liberating after the months spent with Dimitri. The images of her cousin's body on the patio started to intrude into her thoughts, but she pushed them away. She bent down and Toby threw his arms around her neck. Standing the boy up with his cast was trickier than she expected, and Aurelia was in danger of losing her balance.

Silently and swiftly, a pair of powerful arms reached around Aurelia and gripped Toby's shoulders to steady him. With the stranger's help, Aurelia was able to help Toby stand upright. Their rescuer was a shaved-headed woman, who had more mass than the two of them combined.

"Thanks," Aurelia and Toby mumbled together.

The woman smiled, and bright teeth flashed white against her brown skin. Then she joined her companions, who were waiting for her.

"Spacers," Toby whispered.

"How can you tell?" Aurelia asked quietly.

"You notice how the stationers always wear skins?"

"Hmm," Aurelia replied. She assumed that skins were the names of the body-hugging unitards that she'd seen. Some were a simple black, some were colored, and some were expensively decorated.

"Yeah, well spacers wear skins and something else ... almost anything else."

The woman's companions, including her, wore the strangest collection of clothing over their skins that Aurelia could imagine. She could swear one individual, who had disappeared from sight, was a man, who was wearing a colorful skirt.

"C'mon, Rules," Toby urged. "I got to hop, and you have to balance me." Toby switched to a single hand on Aurelia's shoulder, leaned his heavy cast behind him, and, as Aurelia took small steps, he hopped on one leg.

Toby signaled a translation capsule with his comm unit and tucked it deep in a pocket. Within seconds, the dual doors slid open, one after the other, and the two made their way into the capsule and secured their positions with shoulder braces and belts.

"Do we have to wait until the car fills?" Aurelia asked. She saw Toby give her the look that said she was a creature with two heads.

"It'll time out. Be patient," Toby replied. He'd no sooner spoken, than the lights over them turned green and the other positions went dark.

Aurelia experienced the same effect when she transited to the JOS from downside, only this time she was rotated onto her back because of her position in the capsule. And in contrast to her previous translation, there was no longer any weight on her feet. Remembering her newly learned lesson, she kept her deck shoes firmly planted.

When Toby threw off his restraints, he held on to his belt. "You have to come get me, Rules."

Belatedly, Aurelia caught on to Toby's needs. She gave him an apologetic smile and crossed the narrow capsule to hook an arm around Toby's waist.

"Great, isn't it?" Toby announced, absolutely ecstatic. "My cast weighs nothing. Okay, Rules, walk me over to the cap's doorway." When Aurelia positioned him in the opening, Toby said, "See those rails overhead that extend down the arm. Push me toward them. Not too hard though."

Toby felt the gentlest of motions on his waist, and, as he floated slowly upward, he broke into laughter. "Rules, you'd think you've never played freefall. It'll take me forever to reach the rails. You need to bump me."

"Bump you?" Aurelia asked. She had no more uttered the question than the capsule beeped alarmingly, and she realized she was standing in the opening, impeding the closing of the doors. Experienced stationers would simply have stepped onto the terminal arm and allowed their shoes to grip the deck. But, being a novice, Aurelia panicked and launched herself upward. Luckily, she flew past Toby, who grabbed her leg. Toby's action slowed Aurelia, and enabled the pair to reach the overhead.

"Grab a rail, Rules," Toby yelled. He latched on to the same rail as Aurelia did. Toby couldn't help the giddy laugh that escaped. "You really are a newbie to freefall, aren't you?"

Aurelia used her hands to turn around and face Toby. "Does it show?" she asked, with a straight face. Her comment cracked Toby up so hard, he started snorting.

"Okay, Rules," Toby protested, when he could regain his breath. "Seriously, you can hurt yourself playing freefall if you aren't careful. When you push off hard, you'll hit the next surface hard, and you'll need to have your feet under you to handle the impact. Understand?"

"Understood. One question, Toby: Aren't we in danger from radiation out here?" Aurelia asked, with concern.

"No way, Rules," Toby declared. "The terminal arms are like the JOS, the *Belle*, and every ship. They're built with double hulls and filled with hydrogenated boron nitride nanotubes. The tiny BNNTs are made of carbon, boron, and nitrogen with hydrogen filling the empty spaces between the tubes. They use boron because it's an excellent absorber of secondary neutrons, which makes it great for shielding material. And because it's strong even at high heat, they weave it into fabrics for space suits to protect against radiation. Everybody knows this."

"Yeah, I forgot," Aurelia said, and she discerned Toby's wave of sympathy for her supposed condition.

"Okay, Rules, I want you to watch me for a little while before you try this," Toby said, and shoved off the rail with both hands. He touched the deck and kicked off with one leg, somersaulting once slowly, before he grabbed an overhead rail.

During the course of several minutes, Aurelia watched in wonder, as Toby, despite the handicap of a full leg cast, performed acrobatic maneuvers up and down the length of the arm. His 8-centimeter long, light red hair waved over the top of his head, and his freckled face wore a dreamy expression.

Toby cycled back to Aurelia, who was in awe of the performance. "You're marvelous, Toby," she gushed, and Aurelia witnessed and detected his embarrassment.

"It's one of the reasons that I'm worried about the BRC, Rules. The only thing I want to be is a spacer. If the operation isn't successful, I'll never get a berth."

"I truly wish I could help, Toby ..." Aurelia started to say, but realized the uselessness of completing her statement.

"It's okay, Rules. Now, it's your turn," Toby said, brightening. Aurelia's earlier sharing of hope was still holding sway over Toby's worries.

"Remember, think where you're going next before you push off, and keep it gentle. If you don't reach the deck or a rail, don't panic. I'll come get you."

Aurelia nodded confidently, even though she could have used a little of the positive emotions she'd sent Toby's way. She shoved off, and it seemed to take forever to reach the deck. She was a little bolder on the next try, and then the next. As her confidence grew, she attempted some of Toby's simpler performances, and she laughed at both her failures and her successes.

Completing her first somersault, Aurelia was complimented by Toby, who steadied his perch with one hand, while he whistled his approval shrilly with his fingers in his mouth. Aurelia was struck by the realization that the boy was the first person she had ever played with other than Sasha, and the last time she'd enjoyed playing with her little sister was the day before she was placed in Dimitri's demented care.

Emboldened, Aurelia worked her way to the end of the arm. She faced backwards to Toby and declared, "Watch this one." Aurelia pushed off, intending to execute a backward double somersault at a shallow angle.

Toby watched Aurelia launch. Then, seconds later, he saw Captain Jessie Cinders exit the docking ramp from his ship. "Look out, Rules," Toby yelled. Belatedly, Toby realized he should have warned the captain, who looked up at him perched on the overhead rail with his cast.

Aurelia had completed more than a full revolution when she heard Toby's yell. She was upside down, halfway through her second somersault, when she smacked into a solid body, her legs splaying over a pair of shoulders. Her fear made her latch onto the stranger, her arms encircling his waist.

Jessie Cinders felt the impact, and, his reflexes, as a lifelong spacer, took over. Knocked forward, his deck shoes losing purchase, he curled his body, feeling what he suspected was a child gripping his back. When his hands struck the deck, he converted his forward momentum into an upward vector and executed a lazy somersault. He fully extended his hands to grasp the rails above him to protect the passenger he carried.

"It's okay," Jessie said gently, trying to shake the unreasoning alarm he felt. He slipped one leg of his passenger over his head to join the other and guided a hand from his midriff to a purchase on a rail. Much to Jessie's surprise, he stared at an attractive teenage girl, her auburn hair floating around her head, and, much to his relief, the anxiety he was experiencing disappeared.

Aurelia was aghast at what she'd done and angry for stopping to play when her life was in jeopardy. As soon as she was attached to the rails, she'd hardened her blocks, prepared for the customary male tirade. She barely heard the man's words when he asked her, "Are you hurt?" The stranger emanated concern, which caught Aurelia off guard.

"Sorry ... I was ... sorry, sir," Aurelia stammered. She wanted to explain what she'd been doing, but that seemed contrary to keeping a low profile. *As if playing freefall on a station's arm wasn't doing the exact opposite,* Aurelia thought, condemning her foolishness.

"Aren't you a little old to be playing freefall?" Jessie asked.

Aurelia heard the man's words that said she was in the wrong, but she detected no recrimination in his emotions. Luckily, she was saved from replying because Toby came to her rescue.

"Sorry, Captain Cinders. Rules was helping me, and I was teaching her some techniques," Toby said, after landing lightly beside the pair.

Jessie glanced at Toby's extended cast. "Waiting for a BRC, are you?"

"Yes, Captain, and I was getting awful twitchy sitting in my chair," Toby admitted. "Rules was kind enough to help me through the cap, but I don't think she's had much practice in freefall."

"I dare say she hasn't," Jessie replied, smiling. "You two be careful out here," he added, pushing off lightly and floating to the deck. His shoes touched gently, and he strode toward the arm's exit.

"Oh, Rules, you were so lucky," Toby gushed, when Cinders entered the translation capsule.

"Smacking into a stranger upside down and forcing him to wear me like a coat is lucky?"

Toby giggled. "You did look kind-a funny attached to his back like that." When Aurelia glared at him, Toby hurriedly added, "No, I mean, Cinders is about the only captain on this arm who wouldn't have chewed our butts off for that stunt of yours. That's who I'd like to work for one day," Toby said wistfully.

"Maybe we ought to end our freefall time for today, Toby," Aurelia said.

"Good idea," Toby replied. Then he grinned, shoved off, and yelled, "Race you to the cap."

Aurelia had to smile at that one. Toby and her sister were much alike.

4: Captain Cinders

Jessie Cinders exited the JOS translation capsule into the station's access corridor and turned right onto the main promenade. He was headed to the commandant's emergency conference, but his thoughts were still on the young girl, who bumped into him on the arm. Jessie considered himself a good judge of people. His instincts and ability to read applicants enabled him to build a profitable company with the help of the trustworthy group of spacers he'd hired.

Admittedly Jessie had no more than a minute or two to form an impression about Rules, but many things didn't fit. Her long hair said downsider, but her coveralls said stationer. The state of her clothing said impoverished, but her face and hands said privileged. Then there was her reaction to bumping into him. A downsider would have been politely apologetic, at best, or haughty, at worst, but Rules was frightened.

The *Spryte*, Jessie's ship, was nearing the JOS. He would have continued to the YIPS, the processing terminal, to deliver a shipment of high-value ingots, but he received the station's emergency security alert. Curious as to what constituted the commandant's broadcast to all captains, Jessie decided to dock the *Spryte*, give the crew twenty hours of downtime, and attend the briefing.

Before the crew exited the ship, leaving Buttons on dock duty, Jessie had a few choice words for them. "Don't get started on a binge and get detained by security," he'd said. "Your downtime is less than a solar day. Anyone not back aboard by 11:30 hours tomorrow is off the crew. Am I understood?"

A round of "aye, aye, Captain" had greeted Jessie's announcement, and he'd dismissed them. They'd filed past, wearing their usual assortment of spacer outfits — skins covered in all manner of odd clothing. In his days, Jessie had seen intricately decorated vests, brightly colored shorts, flower-printed shirts, and the odd skirt or two worn by both men and women. It was the manner in which spacers declared their independence from privileged stationers, who favored highly decorated skins.

On the other hand, Jessie's skins were covered by dress ship overalls, and his captain's stripes were prominently displayed on the shoulders. He took a seat at the back of the small auditorium, his deck shoes propped up on the back of a seat in front of him, while he waited for the commandant to take the stage.

When Commandant Emerson Strattleford marched with his short-man stride to the podium, he waited while security officers and stationers stood for him. The JOS commandant was elected-for-life and served until incapacitated or removed for cause. There was the usual pregnant pause, while Emerson waited for the captains to rise, but none of them did. He signaled the assembly to sit, and his briefing began.

"We have a serious security issue," Emerson said.

Cinders refrained from chuckling. Emerson inevitably tried for an authoritative manner, but his high-pitched voice and furtive habits betrayed him.

"A murderer is loose on the JOS," Emerson stated. "Early this morning, Dimitri Belosov, the governor's nephew was killed by a household member, and she's fled the domes to the station."

Suddenly, the commandant held the audience's attention, and Cinders launched upright. The murder of a governor's relative would mean trouble if the perpetrator wasn't caught soon.

"Security is searching for her, and, as of this moment, I'm ordering the terminal arm managers to withhold release of any ship in dock for a solar day until all ships are searched. We can't be sure where this culprit might be hiding."

The captains grumbled at the commandant's announcement, but it was limited.

"You're receiving a photo on your comm units of the girl, Aurelia, who killed Dimitri Belosov."

Jessie thumbed open his comm unit, pulled up the commandant's message, and opened the attachment. Rules' face stared out at him.

"I don't need to remind all of you, especially the captains, that harboring a criminal is a serious offense," Emerson said. "Add to that, we're attempting to apprehend a murderer of a son of one of the domes' prominent families."

"Commandant, a question please?" a captain asked.

"Yes?" Emerson replied, preening. He loved to be addressed by his title.

"There are no stats accompanying the photo I received," the captain said.

"There are none available."

"Well, what's the girl's last name?" another captain asked.

"We don't have that information," Emerson replied, the questions appeared to fluster him.

Jessie stood, so that Emerson could see him. "Commandant Strattleford," Jessie said. His words were formal, but it sounded more like he was about to dress down his third mate. "If this fugitive is a downsider, why hasn't your office received a complete history of her, which we know the DBs have on every resident? And who reported the crime to you in the first place? Finally, have the DBs provided you with any evidence of the crime ... vids, eyewitness statements, DNA sniffs, and so on?"

Emerson felt the heat rise up his neck, and he fought to appear calm. He'd told Lise Panoy that he needed more information about the crime to make a plausible presentation, but she said that would give away her identity to the governor, if he found out the details the commandant had been given. If anyone else, but Captain Cinders, had asked these questions, Emerson might have glossed over them. Unfortunately, Cinders not only ran the most successful mining company, he was one of the most respected captains.

"The investigation is ongoing, Captain Cinders," Emerson temporized, replying respectfully to Jessie. "We've only received the most cursory report and expect follow-up information shortly. Thank you." Emerson expected the captain to sit down, but he remained standing with his hands behind his back, and the audience's heads were twisting between the stage and Jessie at the back row.

"Did you have another question, Captain Cinders?" Emerson asked.

"Yes, Commandant. If and when the young girl is found, will she be held on station until the DBs present sufficient evidence of her crime before she's returned downside?"

Emerson nearly paled at the mention of the one question he didn't want to hear. Spacers tended to hold downsiders and stationers to a high standard of law and justice.

"Certainly, Captain Cinders. We'd insist on that."

Captains and security people glanced Jessie's way, and most of them caught the frown on his face. The captain didn't believe the commandant.

Rather quickly, Jessie left the small amphitheater when the briefing concluded, instead of staying to discuss the issue with the other captains. He was anxious to hear Rules', or Aurelia's, side of the story before he made up his mind what to do. He thought he might catch the two young people still playing freefall.

Thoughts tumbled through Jessie's mind, as he navigated the main promenade. Something didn't fit. The girl is accused of murder, but she stops to help a BRC recipient to a terminal arm so he can enjoy some weightless time. In addition, she escapes the domes and rides the El to the JOS, but why come to the station? The only place of refuge in Pyre's entire sphere was on the old colony ship, the *Honora Belle*, and Harbour wasn't going to protect a criminal.

The captain's final thought, as he transited the ring, was that the security briefing was the oddest one he'd ever attended. It generated more questions than answers. Jessie noticed the boy's chair was gone on the station's side, which meant he hadn't expected to find them on the terminal arm. Nonetheless, he made a quick scan for them. He didn't know whether to be happy or upset that they were gone.

At the arm's ramp to the *Spryte*, Jessie glanced around one more time before he made his way inside. Buttons was asleep on duty in the airlock, and the hatches were locked in the open position. Normally, that type of infraction was grounds for a captain's reprimand, but the old man was one of the last of Captain Rose's crew.

Buttons was past retirement age but resisted the idea of sitting out his last years on station. The aging spacer was wearing his downtime gear, even though he'd never left the ship. His skins were covered by a long vest that reached past his hips and every inch was festooned with buttons that he collected throughout the years from auctions. He was most proud of a fading yellow button with the peace sign in black ink, a symbol from Earth and more than a half millennium old.

Jessie didn't have the heart to wake the old-timer, but he did check a monitor to ensure the ship's portable cam, which had been placed at the end of the exit ramp and pointed down the arm, was functioning. Then Jessie made his way along the ship's axis to the gravity wheel and around to his cabin. He stripped out of his ship's overalls and opened a closet door to store it. Rules stared back at him.

"Come out of there, Rules," Jessie ordered. "Or is it Aurelia?"

"It's both. My little sister calls me Rules. It's her joke," Aurelia said, stepping from the closet. She stood with her arms at her sides. One hand tightly clasped the cap she had worn when pretending to be cargo crew.

Jessie took his time hanging up his captain's dress overalls and slipping on some work coveralls to buy some time to think. The girl, choosing to hide aboard his ship, had placed him in a tricky situation. Her DNA was all over the place, and there was no hiding it from a sniffer.

"They say you're a murderer, Aurelia. Is that true?" Jessie asked, when he closed the seal on his coveralls.

"I'm guilty. I did push Dimitri Belosov," Aurelia admitted.

Aurelia's confession wasn't what Jessie expected — a claim of self-defense, a story of an accidental death, or even an outright denial — but not an admittance of guilt. While Jessie considered his options, he felt a sense of calm settle over him and a desire to comfort the girl. He was ready to embrace the feelings when alarm bells tripped in his head, and a surge of anger stripped away the tender emotions.

"You're a bender," Jessie accused.

"A what?" Aurelia replied, alarmed at the reaction she'd provoked.

"A sensitive, an empath," Jessie clarified.

"Yes."

"But you can't be, or the story that's circulating about you is wrong. They say you were downside in the governor's household, is that true?"

"It's true."

Jessie couldn't believe his predicament. The one possibility no one would have considered was that the fugitive was an empath, who should never have been downside, much less working in the governor's household. Captain Corbin Rose, his mentor, had warned him about times like this when he said, "Stick to mining, kid. Space is safer than politics." Unfortunately, politics had knocked at his hatch, and, truth be told, Jessie, like most captains, had no love for Governor Andropov.

"Sit down, Aurelia," Jessie requested politely, intensely aware of the powers Aurelia possessed. "I need to hear your story. Start with when you first went downside, and, please, no more mind thing," he added, pointing to Aurelia's head, then his.

"No more mind thing, Captain, I promise," Aurelia replied, smiling shyly. She was relieved to have the chance to explain. Toby was right to admire Captain Cinders. She could feel his concern, and it gave her hope.

"I've never been out of the domes, Captain, until today. I was born in Governor Markos Andropov's house, as was my sister, Sasha. My mother is Helena Garmenti. The governor and one of his security people, Giorgio Sestos, kidnapped my mother from the station when she was seventeen."

"I remember the story of your mother's disappearance. Are you saying she was an empath who was never identified?"

"Her powers are minimal, Captain. Even she didn't recognize her capabilities, but they were enough to offer the governor solace when he was grieving over the loss of his wife and brother-in-law."

"Your influence nearly overwhelmed me, Aurelia, and you weren't touching me. Is that what happened when you said you pushed Dimitri?" Jessie asked, tapping his temple.

"Yes, Captain."

"Let's deal with the conversation about your family later. How and why did Dimitri end up dead?"

Jessie leaned back in a chair at his small meeting table and Aurelia sat at his desk, while she told the story of her time with Dimitri. Remembering the details of her abuse sickened her, but she chose not to hide them. She closed her eyes so she wouldn't see the captain's face as he listened to her tale, but she couldn't stop the tears that streamed down her cheeks. When she ended with the sight of Dimitri's blood splattered on the patio, she stopped. She felt a small towel pressed into her hands.

"There's a head there," Jessie said, indicating the doorway. "A bathroom," he added, when he saw Aurelia's confusion. While the girl was washing her face, Jessie ran to the bridge to check on the external arm cam. He didn't have a plan, but he needed to know if he still had time to execute one. He didn't. Lieutenant Devon Higgins of JOS security was exiting gate 1, accompanied by several subordinates. They were searching every ship on the arm. Jessie did some fast, mental calculations and figured he had about an hour or a little more to either come up with a plan or turn the girl over to security.

Jessie made his decision quickly and ran back to his cabin, yelling, "Aurelia, strip out of those coveralls. I need to hide you now. Station security is headed this way. They're searching the ships."

The key to hiding the girl was to beat the DNA sniffers, and Jessie thought hard on how to do it. When the answer occurred to him, he could have smacked himself in the head. It was simple. Jessie bolted down one of the ship's central hub corridors to a storage room where the vac suits were kept. He considered Aurelia's size and grabbed the vac suit of his navigator, Jeremy Kinsman, a slender, young man, not much older than Aurelia. He slung the suit's backpack over his shoulder and grabbed the accessory bag and helmet. Towing the vac suit behind him, he hurried back to his cabin.

Vac suit fabrics had improved greatly, and increased demand meant lower prices. Now, each spacer could afford to order one or two custom-fitted suits. The number of items a spacer wore was reduced to four — suit, helmet, gloves, and backpack.

Aurelia did as the captain requested, and she stood in the center of his cabin, her coveralls slipped through the arm of the desk chair to prevent them from floating free. She still wore her shoes to keep her feet anchored to the deck. With determination, she kept her hands at her side. It was the way Dimitri had requested she stand.

Jessie slung the backpack ahead of him through the cabin's doorway and staggered to a halt. "No skins?" he asked. When Aurelia shook her auburn curls, he said, "You truly are a downsider." Then he stuffed the helmet, accessory bag, backpack, and vac suit under his meeting table and ran to Jeremy's cabin.

Jeremy was a recent hire from the station's spacer training program. He graduated top of his class and had an extraordinary aptitude for navigation. Captain Sima Madigan's crew did their best to recruit Jeremy to the *Dauntless*, plying him with drinks and stories of opportunity for coin and advancement. Unfortunately for Madigan's crew, Jeremy was a bright boy, who did his research and spoke with other mining crews, including Jessie's. Hearing that the *Spryte* was forced to put its previous navigator on station, Jeremy applied for the position and was awarded the job.

Surveying Jeremy's cabin, Jessie was rethinking his decision about giving the boy a berth on his ship. The cabin was a mess, much as a stationer might keep his room. Dirty clothing was stuffed under the bunk, and several personal items floated free. The ill-kept cabin warranted a reprimand in the captain's log.

A crew member could be set on station for a second disciplinary note or for a dangerous first infraction. Fire, explosions, and sudden decompression could kill an entire crew. Even if some did make the lifeboats, it would be a race between rescue and the air running out. Space was huge, and Pyrean ship traffic was still in its nascent stages.

After a quick but thorough search of the cabin, Jessie did find a spare set of skins and slip boots. A quick sniff pronounced them serviceable, and he ran to his cabin. "Quick, Aurelia, put these on," he said, tossing the gear to her. To Jessie's lament, Aurelia searched for the opening in the skins.

"Oh, for the love of Pyre," Jessie groaned. He took the skins back, located the tiny tab at the rear of the neck, and activated it with a quick press. The motorized device traveled down the back of the skins, opening the suit from neck to buttocks. Jessie did the same with the tabs at the ankles and wrists before he handed the skins to Aurelia, saying, "They might be tight, but wiggle into them."

Jessie turned his back on Aurelia, while she dressed, and he readied the vac suit on the deck.

"Ready, Captain," Aurelia announced.

Jessie turned around, and his heart ached to see the gentle smile on Aurelia's face. She was pleased that someone, most likely in this case a male, was treating her with kindness. At that moment, Jessie would have enjoyed dumping Dimitri over the balcony.

"Turn around," Jessie said. He pressed the tab that now rested near the bottom of Aurelia's spine. The little unit traveled up the neck, sealing the skins and presenting a nearly invisible seam to the naked eye. Jessie repeated the action at each of the tabs at Aurelia's extremities to seal the legs and arms.

"I like these skins," Aurelia said, holding out her arms and then a leg to admire the form. She was looking for a mirror when the captain interrupted her.

"There'll be time for playing dress up later, Aurelia," Jessie said. "Take a seat at the table, pull off the deck shoes, and replace them with these slip boots."

Aurelia did as directed, remembering to keep one foot planted on the deck, at all times.

Smart girl ... catches on fast, Jessie thought. *She'd make a good spacer.*

"Now, come here," Jessie ordered. "Step into the suit."

Aurelia pushed her slip-booted feet into the vac suit's pants legs and down into the mag-boots. Then, Jessie helped her shrug the suit up in several movements until she could slip her hands into the arms.

Jessie was thinking furiously through his actions when he realized he'd missed something. Hurriedly, he grabbed Aurelia's clothes — coveralls, cap, deck shoes, and socks — and wrapped or stuffed them around her middle. Then he sealed the suit up the front.

"Brace yourself, using the table, Aurelia. Those mag-boots aren't active, and you'll float away." Then Jessie pulled the suit up to her neck and sealed it. Next, he motioned Aurelia to stand, and he strapped the backpack on. Then he added her gloves and slipped the helmet over her head, locking all three items to the suit. Finally, Jessie attached the backpack's hoses to the suit, powered the circulation and heating systems, and turned on her control and comm system.

Tapping Aurelia's hand to indicate she should release the table, Jessie grabbed the front of the suit via a safety ring and towed the girl behind him, as she floated off the deck. He exited the cabin, tugged the girl down the wheel's central passageway to a spoke corridor. After entering the ship's axis, Jessie hurried to the equipment and storage bays.

Part one of Jessie's hurriedly assembled plan was complete. Sealing Aurelia in a vac suit, which circulated her air in a closed environment, meant none of her DNA would be found along the path he was taking her. Inside an airlock, which led to a lower bay where a load of rare metal ingots was stacked, Jessie turned around to face Aurelia and held a finger to his lips to silence her.

"Captain's override ... identify," Jessie said.

"Captain Cinders identified," the vac suit responded.

"Identify name," Jessie requested.

"Frances," the suit replied.

Of course, Jessie thought, hiding his smile. *Young Jeremy keyed his vac suit to his mother's name.*

"Aurelia, any time you wish to command an operation on this suit, you look at your heads-up display and begin with that name. Now listen."

Jessie planted Aurelia's feet firmly on the airlock's deck, and said, "Frances, mag-boots on."

Suddenly, Aurelia felt her feet snap to the deck. She was still weightless, but it felt as if she was anchored in place.

"Walk for me," Jessie requested and observed Aurelia struggle to move her feet. "Frances, decrease mag-boot strength by thirty-five percent."

After the suit confirmed the change, Jessie twirled his hand in a circle, and Aurelia dutifully took a few tentative steps and smiled through her faceplate at Jessie.

"Frances, check suit integrity, systems, and air tanks," Jessie ordered. These items were available in the helmet's heads-up display, but it was too much information to expect Aurelia to absorb.

"Suit integrity at one hundred percent, all systems on line and functional, and air tanks at full capacity," Frances replied.

"Aurelia, I don't have time to hide you. You have to do this yourself. I'm going to cycle you through this airlock. After you enter the bay, go to the rear bulkhead ... to the right ... you'll see an equipment locker. Hide in there. You'll have to pull the door shut from the inside and remember to turn off your helmet lights. You can't have any light streaming out through the slots. These tanks have air for hours. As soon as I get station security off the ship, I'll come back and get you out. Do you understand?"

Jessie received a tentative nod from Aurelia. "Okay, now order your helmet lights on."

"Frances, lights, if you please," Aurelia said in a firm voice, as she focused on the glowing numbers in her helmet, which she hoped was her heads-up display.

Probably the first time this vac suit has ever been addressed so politely, Jessie thought wryly.

Jessie stepped out of the airlock and cycled Aurelia through into the bay. He watched via the viewplate long enough to see her turn right and work her way through the stacks of ingots. Then he raced through the ship's axis and wound his way around to the captain's chair on the bridge.

Jessie needed to put the last part of his plan into action. He accessed the ship's data log using a back-door sequence. It was illegal, but Jessie didn't know a captain, who owned a ship, who didn't have one.

The cam pointed down the arm and had been recording since it was placed out there. Jessie stopped the recording, erased the accumulated data, and then removed the entry log of the cam recording. When he exited the ship's data system, there was no record of the girl entering the *Spryte*.

5: Ship Search

Lieutenant Devon Higgins, Sergeant Miguel Rodriguez, and Corporal Terrell McKenzie were assigned to search terminal arm 2 in section S. On the JOS main promenade cams, security administration spotted Aurelia and an unknown boy in a leg cast entering the arm. The boy had later returned, but the girl hadn't.

After gaining the arm side of the ring, the lieutenant locked out the translation capsule. A notice was displayed at both the station and the arm side that the capsule was incapacitated due to a security emergency.

Of the four ships docked on the terminal arm, the first three had been searched by the security team when they made their way toward the last one. Their primary search tool was a portable sniffer operated by Corporal McKenzie.

Despite the commandant's pronouncement to the captains that no additional information about Aurelia had been received, he'd been forwarded a DNA profile from Lise Panoy. She'd collected the information from Giorgio Sestos, who cleared it with the governor before relaying it to Lise.

"Last ship, Lieutenant," Terrell announced. "She's got to be aboard the *Spryte*." Terrell's heart was pounding with excitement. The thought that he would catch the great Captain Cinders harboring a fugitive, a murderer at that, thrilled him to no end.

Jessie monitored the security team's approach, and, as they neared his ramp, he sauntered casually from the bridge toward the airlock. He covertly listened from the axis corridor and heard the security team comment about Buttons asleep at his post before he turned the corner and stepped into the airlock.

"Lieutenant," Jessie acknowledged. "I watched your search progress down the last part of the arm. Still no luck?"

"Cut the crap, Cinders, we know the girl is aboard your ship," Terrell snarled. He waved his sniffer as proof of his statement.

"That's Captain Cinders to you, Terror," Jessie replied coldly, using the nickname spacers and stationers had given the sadistic corporal.

"I'll handle this, Corporal," Devon Higgins said. "And you'll show proper decorum or you can wait for us stationside."

The thought that Terrell would miss out on the arrest was enough for him to curb his animosity.

The discussion woke Buttons, who struggled to his feet, glancing at his captain and the security team. He wondered if he was the cause of the excitement.

"Turn in, Buttons, get some rack time," Jessie said, patting the old spacer on the shoulder. "I got this."

Buttons would have apologized then and there to Jessie, but he had spotted Terror and wasn't about to give the corporal the satisfaction of hearing it.

"Is your cam recording, Captain?" Devon asked, pointing a thumb down the ramp at the arm cam.

"Nope, Lieutenant. Just monitoring the people approaching the ship. That's all."

"That's pretty sloppy, Captain, leaving only one man on duty and he's asleep at that," Miguel Rodriguez commented.

"Have to admit Buttons is getting along, but he was a faithful and longtime crew member under Captain Rose." The mention of the man, who did more than anyone to supply the metal that built the JOS, commanded respect, and Devon and Miguel acknowledged that with tips of their heads.

"Captain, station cams show the girl, Aurelia, entering this arm," Devon said. "She never came out, and the sniffer confirms she's been up your gangway. Now, I'm respectfully requesting permission to come aboard and search for her."

"I'm not one to impede a search for a murderer, Lieutenant. You and your sergeant are welcome, but Corporal Terror does not set one foot aboard my ship," Jessie replied, and he stared coldly at the corporal, as he spoke.

"Captain, Corporal McKenzie is my best DAD operator," Devon said, referring to the DNA analysis device or DAD, which everyone called a sniffer.

"She's been here, sir," Terrell insisted, hoping the lieutenant would fight for permission to allow him to step aboard.

"Lieutenant, I don't doubt Terror's ability to read his sniffer. But I haven't seen the girl, and I doubt either has my trusty watchman. However, as I said, you and your sergeant are welcome to search my ship, but it stays outside," Jessie said firmly, pointing a finger at Terrell.

"Corporal, hand the DAD to Sergeant Rodriguez," Devon ordered. "Captain, I'll ask you to remain here, while we search the ship."

"Be my guests," Jessie replied, waving them past him.

While the lieutenant and sergeant searched the *Spryte*, Jessie stood in the airlock and stared through the corporal, as if he didn't exist.

Corporal Terrell "Terror" McKenzie lived for the hunt and arrest of suspected felons. Most hadn't committed any serious crimes, but Terror didn't care. He loved catching them, and if they resisted arrest, so much the better.

Firearms were nonexistent throughout Pyrean society. It forced the harder felons to commit crimes with an edged or blunt weapon. It was Terror's hope that a suspect would pull his weapon when faced with arrest. It gave the corporal an opportunity to use his shock stick — not to stun them, at least, not until they were down. Terror liked to test his skill and use the weighted stick to block the attack and immobilize the suspect by breaking a few bones.

After a particularly harrowing arrest, Terror was on such a high that he sought relief in the sex services of a coin-kitty or coin-kat. In regard to the latter group, Terror enjoyed breaking in the new talent, as he referred to them. The better establishments had banned Terror, but the less-discerning operators simply charged him a premium fee for his business. It covered the occasional med costs for the service providers.

Terror's singular mistake was crossing the path of the *Spryte*'s crew. Dingles, a spacer for thirty-two years, first serving under Captain Rose and then for Captain Cinders, was forced to retire when he developed space dementia. Jessie gave Dingles a generous retirement payout and paid the rent on a small cabin on the JOS for six months. It should have given Dingles plenty of time to find gainful employment.

Instead, Dingles burned through his funds in four months and never searched for new work or bothered with checking out retraining opportunities. Desperate, Dingles robbed a store owner, but, in disgust, he threw the coin vouchers back at the owner when he saw the man's terrified expression.

Terror tracked Dingles down, gained access to his cabin with his security clearance, and accused him of robbery. The story was that Dingles yelled at Terror that he never took anything and tried to throw the corporal out of his cabin. That was all the excuse Terror needed. He used his shock stick repeatedly on the aging spacer, breaking Dingles nose, cracking a few ribs, and administering a host of bruises.

The JOS Review Board dismissed the robbery charges against Dingles, but gave him eighteen months incarceration for attacking a member of the security forces.

Unfortunately, for Dingles, his small, closed cell aggravated his dementia, but, as luck would have it, he was rescued soon afterwards.

Terror didn't fare so well. Dingles, whom Jeremy replaced, was one of the finest navigators. With little course correction, he could put a ship within a few hundred meters of a captain's requested destination, and the crews of the *Marianne* and *Spryte* loved him. They felt safe with Dingles plotting the courses.

One evening, after Terror ended his shift, he was using the maintenance passageways to return to his cabin, which was his habit. Suddenly, Terror felt a bag slip over his head from behind, and he was knocked to the deck and severely beaten. The attackers were careful not to strike his head, organs, or testicles, but they bruised half his body.

Terror was handed his comm unit to call for assistance. Before he could make his call, he heard a disguised voice whisper, "Leave spacers alone." The hissing of an aerosol can and the chemical smell that followed the voice, told Terror that his attackers knew enough to eliminate any trace of DNA they'd left behind. There were no cams in the station's maintenance passageways, so there was no record of the attack.

After slightly more than a half hour, the lieutenant and sergeant returned from searching the *Spryte*.

"The girl was here, Captain," Devon said. "According to the DAD, she passed through the airlock, while your man was asleep, walked down the axis passageway, entered the wheel, and made her way to your cabin, and, apparently, came out the same way. My guess is she was searching for something. Don't know whether she found it or not. You better check your cabin, Captain, and see if anything's missing. The point is that somehow we've missed her. My guess is the girl exited the arm disguised as a spacer."

"Lieutenant, that's not probable. If you let me search, I'm sure I can find where's she's hiding," Terrell insisted.

"Corporal McKenzie," the sergeant said in a hard voice, "I can read the DAD as well as you, and your inference that we can't is insubordinate. One more word out of you like that, and you're going to find yourself on report." The sergeant turned to follow his lieutenant and ordered Terrell to fall in.

Jessie could see the anger burning in Terror's eyes. The corporal was transfixed, unable to follow his sergeant. Jessie broke the corporal's contact with a snarky smile and a wave of his fingers. Terror threw him a rude hand sign and marched down the gangway.

That was stupid. Nothing says smart like antagonizing a sociopath, Jessie thought.

Jessie waited until the security team transited the ring via a cap to the JOS. Then he locked the outer and inner airlock hatches. He snatched a juice drink from the galley and settled himself on the bridge to watch. Jessie trusted Lieutenant Higgins. It was Terror who he suspected might double back, despite orders he might have received to the contrary.

After nearly an hour of monitoring, Jessie felt safe. He recycled his juice container in the galley, hurried to his cabin, and stripped off his coveralls. Once in the equipment room, Jessie traded his deck shoes for slip boots, donned his vac suit, shrugged on his backpack, attached the hoses to his helmet, and then locked it over his head. Once his gloves were on, Jessie ordered his suit, named Spryte, to turn on his mag-boots and run the integrity checks. He click-clacked his way to the hold where he had stowed Aurelia, his mag boots locking and releasing on the metal decking.

Jessie was worried for Aurelia. He'd placed a downsider in a vac suit and hid her in a dark bay. There was a high probability that she had panicked and hurt herself. He cycled through the airlock, signaled Spryte to turn on the helmet lights, and clumped his way over to the equipment locker.

Aurelia saw the light moving her way through the slots in the locker door. There was a moment of anxiety before she sensed Jessie's worry for her. She was surprised to realize that she could feel his emotions through an airless environment.

When Jessie opened the locker, he was greeted by Aurelia's radiant smile, visible through her faceplate.

"You needn't have worried, Captain Cinders. I found this suit and the dark environment comforting. More precisely, I felt wonderfully isolated."

Jessie was struck by the single purpose driving Aurelia. It wasn't so much that she was fleeing a criminal act, which she was, but the young girl truly sought refuge, a place she could feel safe, once again.

"Well, time to come out of hiding, Aurelia ... make that Rules, if you don't mind. No use waving your real name around."

"Rules is fine, Captain," replied Aurelia, as she grasped Jessie's gloved hand and emerged from the equipment locker.

They made their way to the vac suit storage room — doffed the gear, kept the skins, and added deck shoes, after which Jessie led the way to the gravity wheel.

"Captain, you provided these machinations to evade your security's sniffer, didn't you?" Aurelia asked. She smiled when she saw Jessie frown at her. "Don't look so surprised, Captain. My mother discovered when my sister and I were young that servants wouldn't speak around her but would chat happily in our presence. We became our mother's intelligence sources."

"It sounds as if your mother prepared you well for your flight."

"As best she could, I think," Aurelia replied. She dismissed thoughts of her family to focus on the question that had formed in her mind. "Captain, how do you suppose your security was able to use sniffers to try to locate me?"

Jessie started to explain the concept of a DNA-database and the secure means by which sniffers received that information and compared the profiles to the samples taken in by the devices when testing. Most important, the operator had no access to the profile information, at any time. But, despite Aurelia's youthful face, her eyes locked intensely with his, and Jessie paused to explore her question in depth.

"The commandant said this morning that security hadn't received any more details on you, other than your photo and the charge of murder," Jessie said. He had stopped by the galley and heated up a meal for Aurelia. Her stomach had grumbled several times, while they stripped out of the vac suits. They sat at a small table, and Aurelia dug into the food and drink on her tray. "I would presume the governor was the one who sent your DNA profile to the commandant."

"Don't presume that, Captain," Aurelia replied around a mouthful of food.

"Who else?" Jessie asked.

"According to the servants, there are many important families in the domes who would love to see Markos Andropov removed as governor."

"But, these people would need access to your DNA."

"My mother always said that coin is the lubricant of the domes, which I had always thought was funny when I was little. As far as I knew, the domes didn't move, which is why I wondered why they would need greasing."

"You believe that someone in the governor's household supplied one of these families with your sample."

"Not someone, Captain ... Giorgio Sestos, my father's head of security. He might have done it with or without the governor's approval." Aurelia finished the drink and regarded Jessie. "You have an intense dislike for the governor. Why?"

"Don't ..." Jessie warned, holding up a finger to stop her.

"Captain, you haven't shared much time in the company of an empath, have you?"

"Not if I could help it."

"Interesting response, but I wasn't referring to your personal preferences concerning empaths, I was speaking of your knowledge of how we work.

When I mentioned the governor's name, you broadcasted strong emotions. They were dark and angry, and those feelings are like a wave passing through me. I can hardly ignore them."

"Sorry, Rules, I didn't mean to imply anything about you by my comment."

"No need to apologize, Captain. I know my capabilities frighten people, and, now that I've killed someone with my powers, they frighten me."

"Well, I need to get you out of sight, while I figure out what to say to my crew, before they return from downtime."

"Speaking of your crew, Captain, I hope you won't be too harsh with your man who was guarding the entrance to your ship."

"You mean Buttons in the airlock?"

"Buttons, a colorful name for a kind man," Aurelia said. "He was awake when I peeked in the doorway to your ship. I hung on the rails above to be close without being seen, and I put him to sleep."

"You can put someone to sleep?" Jessie asked. A small thread of fear crawled up his spine.

"As I said, my powers are scary," Aurelia replied.

Jessie realized his apprehension was broadcasting, and he was angry with himself. Everything Aurelia had told him indicated that she was a young girl who had been victimized and was seeking shelter. She didn't deserve his innate, biased reactions.

"To answer your question, Captain: I can't put people to sleep directly, but I can make them feel warm and safe. It eventually leads to the same result. I've done this hundreds of times for Sasha. She hated being confined to the house, unable to join the world we witnessed from our window."

Jessie and Aurelia talked until she inadvertently yawned in his face, and he took her to his cabin to get some sleep. He chose to wait on the bridge for the crew to arrive. Later, Buttons came to the bow, apologized to him, and said he was ready to return to airlock duty.

"No need, Buttons. Do me a favor, and check the vac suit tanks. Some of them might need topping off."

"You want a list of the crew who failed to recharge?" Buttons asked, knowing it was SOP to refill tanks immediately after use.

"That's not necessary either, Buttons. The reason will be made clear, later."

"Aye, Captain," Buttons replied, touching a finger to the brim of his cap, which was plastered with small, metal, coat and shirt buttons that he'd collected.

Jessie waited in his captain's chair. He knew his second mate, Ituau Tulafono, would collect the crew and bodily haul them back to the ship, if necessary, to meet his deadline. With everything going on, the scuttlebutt concerning security's search would reach the spacers, and they'd probably choose to return early.

Thinking of Ituau made Jessie smile. Many people recommended that he not hire her. She was a bruiser, a brawler, they said, undisciplined and unmanageable. But that wasn't who Jessie saw when he interviewed her. Yes, she was a known carouser, who drank hard, enjoyed her stims, and chose her partners freely. But the heavy-built, Samoan woman, with brown skin and a shaved head, who sat before Jessie for their first meeting was composed, a no-nonsense spacer.

"You were put stationside from your last position as second mate, Ituau. Care to explain?" Jessie had asked her.

"The report will say, Captain Cinders, that I was insubordinate to the first mate," Ituau replied.

"Actually, it said that you decked him and then you were insubordinate," Jessie said.

"I choose who I sleep with and when, Captain. No man should be foolish enough to force me, or I'll disabuse him of that notion."

"It's a good thing you're not my type," Jessie said.

"I'm every man's type, at one time or another," Ituau wisecracked.

"You interested in crewing for me?" Jessie asked.

"Yes, Captain Cinders, it would be a privilege. I'll take any position you have, and I'll work my way up."

"Your fitness reports prior to the incident with the first mate were excellent, Ituau. My first mate is retiring. You interested in the job?"

Ituau's broad face had split into a grin, and she'd offered her hand in the spacer's clasp. Jessie had gripped her hand, thinking he'd grabbed deck steel, and Ituau had smacked her other hand over his. The sting took a while to fade, but his decision that day had stood the test of time.

There was a little shaking out of the crew, who were keenly aware of Ituau's reputation during downtime. Jessie knew of only two crew members, who had made the mistake of thinking their liaison with Ituau, while on station, meant they had special privileges when back aboard ship. One young spacer was corrected with a quick smack upside the head and a few stinging remarks when his hand strayed to Ituau's prominent breast, while they were in the galley.

Jessie's hard-nosed second mate, Nate Mikado, decided he could push the issue, figuring Ituau would succumb to his amorous attentions. When that didn't work, the problem landed on Jessie's table. He gave them two choices. Both could be put on station, or they could settle the dispute in any manner they chose. They elected the latter choice, and Jessie officiated at the bout. Nate was outmassed by a good number of kilos, but he was confident he could take a woman. In fact, he was downright haughty about it.

Time came and the combatants covered their hands in safety gauze. Then the fight started. It quickly became clear to Jessie that he should have had the two fighters wrap their elbows, knees, and, perhaps, even their teeth.

The bout wasn't a pugilistic display of skills. It was a dirty, no-holds-barred, knockdown, drag-out attempt on each party's part to win. Jessie was ready to call a halt to the fight when Ituau caught Nate in the solar plexus with a knee by grabbing his shoulders and leaping into the air to deliver the blow to her taller adversary. It knocked the fight out of the second mate, who lay on the deck, sucking for air, and holding a hand up in submission.

Ituau raised both hands in the air in celebration of her win, but it was short-lived, as Jessie ordered Ituau to help Nate up.

"Crew, disperse," Jessie had ordered, "and you two, clean up this deck, and I mean spotless. I don't want security sniffers detecting a drop of blood. Then clean yourselves up before you go to medical. You'll have to drop some coin to ensure they don't report you. Make it an even split on the coin. Do you read me?"

"Aye, aye, Captain," had been the responses.

Jessie would have been interested to catch a brief part of their conversation, as the paired transited to the station.

Nate had said, "I could have taken you in a few more minutes, if you hadn't got that lucky shot in with your knee."

Ituau replied, "In your dreams, boy. You're a good lay but a terrible fighter."

6: Crew's Decision

Jessie woke to the bridge monitor's soft chime, indicating the ship's access code was being entered at the outer airlock hatch. The arm cam showed the tail end of a line of crew who were waiting for the hatch to be opened. Jessie waited for the inner airlock hatch to be accessed before he walked down to the axis passageway to meet the crew.

"Follow me, everyone," Jessie ordered and led the way to the wheel's galley. "Someone, at the rear, fetch Buttons and bring him here too."

When the crew was crowded into the small space, Jessie spared a moment to regard his people. They were a good group of men and women, and he wondered if he had the right to ask them to risk their careers and possibly their freedom.

"A huge problem has just been laid in my lap, and, if I'm not careful, it will affect my company and this crew," Jessie started. "I suppose you've picked up on-station chatter about the excitement."

"Yeah, Captain, security is trolling the station," Nate, the second mate, replied. "Story is that some girlie is on the loose in the JOS, and they're trying to return the goodtimer downside."

"Not even close," Jessie commented. "The girl is a downsider, and she's wanted for murder."

"How does this concern you or us, Captain?" Ituau asked, suddenly alarmed by the captain's opening comment.

"The girl transited out of the JOS onto this arm, snuck past Buttons, and hid in my wardroom closet," Jessie replied.

The crew turned hard eyes on Buttons.

"Don't blame Buttons," Jessie said firmly. "Our downside escapee put him to sleep."

Buttons mouth dropped open. On the one hand, he was happy to know he hadn't been derelict in his duty. On the other hand, he had no idea how the girl might have drugged him.

"Where's she now, Captain?" Ituau asked.

"Asleep in my cabin," Jessie replied.

"Captain, how did she put me to sleep?" Buttons asked.

"Buttons, the girl, who's called Aurelia, but who we will call Rules, is an empath and a strong one." Jessie had nearly said Rules was an *extremely* strong empath, but, judging by the crew's mixed reactions, which leaned toward unfavorable, he was glad he hadn't.

The well-to-do, who had the coin, sought out the *Belle*'s empaths to ease their fears, concerns, regrets, and all manner of mental torments, but most common people had a distrust of the sensitives, whom they had little contact with and, therefore, didn't understand.

"Captain, I don't get this. If Rules is an empath, how come she was downside?" Jeremy asked.

"Good question, Jeremy, and here's where the story gets strange. Rules says she has a mother and sister downside and they're all empaths. But, here's the tipper. Rules' father is the governor."

The crews' groans were strong and loud at the thought the governor had harbored empaths, breaking the long-standing agreement that prohibited such things. The fact that he'd gone further afield by having an empath bear his children only made his trespass greater.

"Why is Rules wanted for murder, Captain?" a crew member asked.

"Rules killed the governor's nephew, Dimitri Belosov. He was molesting her, and, according to Rules, he'd been at it for months."

"Captain, if Rules' father is the governor, that makes Dimitri her cousin," Ituau reasoned.

"It does," Jessie agreed.

"Damn, Captain, I'd have killed that little reject myself," Ituau ground out harshly.

"How did she do it, Captain?" Nate asked, and the crew groaned at the insensitive question.

"Rules said she pushed him over a balcony railing. He hit headfirst on the patio."

"Good for her," Ituau commented. She hadn't met the girl and didn't like that she was a powerful empath, but loved the fact that she fought her molester.

"This is supposed to be a teenage girl, right, Captain? How's she supposed to have gotten the better of an older boy by shoving him over a balcony? That doesn't sound right," Nate commented.

A couple of murmurs of chauvinist and misogynist origin followed Nate's words, but he ignored them.

"You're thinking she physically pushed him, Nate. She didn't. According to Rules, she mentally terrorized him to the point that he threw himself over the balcony."

Jessie watched itchy shivers crawl across the faces of his crew. The thought of that much mental power scared them.

"And she's aboard now?" Nate asked, wanting confirmation.

"She is, but this story gets more complicated." Jessie warned. "Station security came down the arm looking for Rules, while I was listening to her story, and I made the decision to hide her."

Now the crew understood the serious trouble Jessie was in, and, by extent of him being the company owner, it included them. Spacers acted as independent from the JOS, but, in reality, they depended on the station, as every faction of Pyre did, and the head of the JOS was the commandant. If an emergency security condition had been declared and Jessie had evaded security's lawful search, then he was in jeopardy of arrest and a possible lengthy conviction from the Review Board.

"How did you hide her, Captain?" Jeremy asked.

"Your vac suit, mister, and, by the way, you're on report for your cabin's condition. First mate, see that his domicile is properly squared away."

"Aye, Captain," Ituau acknowledged, glaring at Jeremy.

"You're also missing a set of skins, mister," Jessie added. "I dressed her in my cabin, floated her down to the ingot bay, and hid her in an equipment locker, while Lieutenant Higgins and Sergeant Rodriguez searched the ship. I made Terror stay outside."

The mention of Terror's name elicited a few growls from the crew, but Nate was chuckling. "I bet that turned Terror red," he commented.

"Gutsy on Rules' part," Ituau said. "I mean she's a downsider, probably never experienced weightlessness. She makes her way to the JOS, gets out on an arm, puts Button to sleep, gets discovered, and you stick her in a vac suit to hide in a dark hold. That should have scared her to death."

"I would have thought so too, but she came out smiling," Jessie replied. "She said she liked the peaceful isolation."

"That's a born spacer," a crew member said quietly.

"I guess this is going to sound like another foolish question, Captain," Jeremy said, "but why can't we march into the commandant's office and call out the governor. An investigation and DNA should prove Rules' story. I mean if the governor abducted some woman from the JOS, he broke the agreement. Worse, he let his nephew molest his daughter."

"I appreciate your sense of righteous indignation and desire to demand justice, Jeremy, but I'm sure you noticed not only station security, but a good many plain clothes, security types joining the search."

"Uh-huh," Jeremy affirmed.

"Personally, I don't think we'd make it to the commandant's office before we were intercepted. Then we'd either have to surrender or fight. If we fought, odds are we'd lose, get stunned, and be arrested for harboring a fugitive. But there's something I haven't told all of you. I attended the commandant's security meeting this morning. He told the assembly that security received only a photo and the claim of a crime. The commandant offered not a shred of evidence or one iota of statistic about Rules, not even her last name."

"Are you saying the commandant is playing footsie with the governor?" Nate asked.

"Make up your own minds after you hear this," Jessie replied. "When I saw security exit the first ship on the arm, I saw a sniffer in Terror's hand. The only reason for that is security had Rules' DNA on file. If she's a downsider, how did security get that information? Rules said the governor might have authorized his chief of security, Giorgio Sestos, to pass it to one of the other powerful families, who, according to Rules, hates the Andropov family.

"What a nest of creatures!" Nate said, spitting into the recycling chute.

Jeremy eyed his fellow crew members in disbelief of what he was hearing. Some eyes ducked away, embarrassed by the reality crashing in on the young navigator, or they stared back, urging him to accept the captain's version of the way things were in this world.

"Captain, I think I can speak for the crew that we're sympathetic to the girl's story. She's had a rough go of it, but what are you intending to do with her?" Ituau asked.

"Well, I have an idea, but I thought you should meet Rules before you decide to go along with me. Agreed?" Jessie didn't expect an enthusiastic response, but the hesitation was palpable.

"I'd like to meet her," Jeremy piped up. "That's the least we can do."

The crew grudgingly agreed with Jeremy, and Jessie went to fetch Aurelia. She was still asleep, and it was necessary to wake her. She woke with a start before she recognized Jessie.

"Come with me, Rules. I need you to meet the crew."

"Okay, give me a minute to make myself presentable, Captain," Aurelia replied, brushing hair from her face.

"No, I think you should come as you are," Jessie replied and led a sleepy, tousled-haired Aurelia around the wheel to the galley.

"Crew, Rules; Rules, crew," Jessie announced with a flourish.

Jessie worked to keep a smile off his face. The crew had bolted hatches in preparation for meeting a murderer, an empath capable of sending another person to his death with her mind. Instead they were looking at a sixteen year old, who was blinking, smiling shyly at them, and waving her fingers. Aurelia looked like any crew member's younger sister.

"Hey, I know you," Ituau said, suddenly. "You were helping the kid out of his wheelchair ... the boy was wearing a leg cast. What were you two doing?"

"Yes, that was me," Aurelia replied, happy to find a friendly face in the crowd. "Toby and I thank you for your assistance. I'm afraid I wasn't ready for the weight of his cast, and he might have fallen without your help."

"Okay, you're welcome, but why were you headed into this arm?" Ituau persisted.

"Oh, Toby was going to teach me freefall. It was his idea. I agreed because he was suffering anxiety about his upcoming BRC operation, and I wanted to help lift his spirits."

"You stopped to play freefall with a kid in a cast, while you're running from station security?" Nate asked dubiously.

"Admittedly, it wasn't a bright decision, but Toby needed me."

"Oh, for the love of Pyre," Ituau commented. She scooted a crew member off a seat and sat down heavily. "Sweetie, you're not much of a murderer," the first mate lamented.

"I didn't intend to be any kind of a killer," Aurelia replied, starting to tear up. "I just wanted him to stop."

Jeremy offered Aurelia a clean handkerchief, and she accepted it with a sad smile.

"I hate to play the role of prosecutor here, Captain, but we only have this girl's word that she pushed Dimitri Belosov with her mind. What if that's not true? What if she's not a bender ... a sensitive?" Nate asked.

"Rules, I want you to push, Nate," Jessie requested, pointing to the second mate.

"I was just saying what if, Captain. I didn't mean we should test her," Nate objected.

"Don't hurt him, Rules," Jessie cautioned, and watched the crew clear space around the second mate, as if Rules' power might splash on them.

Nate had a look of horror on his face, and his hands were held up in protest. Then before he could utter another word, his hands dropped to his side, and his face took on a relaxed appearance. His eyes softened, and he gazed adoringly at Jessie.

"Okay, that's creeping me out," Ituau commented.

"Enough, Rules," Jessie said.

Aurelia was focusing her power and failed to register Jessie's request. Jeremy, who was standing next to her, touched her arm to gain her attention. The contact snapped Aurelia out of her efforts, and she crowded next to Jessie.

"A might skittish," Ituau commented, watching Aurelia tuck close to Jessie and hold his arm.

Nate looked like he was going to be sick due to the emotions swirling in his mind about his captain.

Jessie glanced at Aurelia and nodded toward Nate. She held onto Jessie's arm, while she broadcast her power again.

A few moments later, Nate released the food counter and straightened up, declaring, "That's much better."

The crew laughed, but it was strained.

"Do any others require a further demonstration?" inquired Jessie, the hint of a smile on his face.

After gazing around, Ituau said, "I think we're all good here, Captain. How about you, Nate? You good?" Ituau asked. She couldn't keep the smirk off her face, and Nate glared back at her. "I think we're back to the part where you explain your plan, Captain," Ituau added.

"I can't remember a more potentially explosive political event in my lifetime," Jessie replied. "The circumstances of Rules and her family will seriously disrupt the domes and possibly expose the commandant as a downsider crony. I'm thinking that, as long as Rules is aboard and we're docked at the station, all of us are vulnerable. Security will not stop searching the JOS and the ships on the arms until they've found her. So, we've got to get her away."

"To a mining site?" Ituau asked.

"Not just any mining site," Jessie replied. "The *Annie*'s next assignment is to explore Triton. We park her out there until I can meet with Harbour, and see if she can hide Rules until we figure out how to expose what's happened downside at the governor's house."

At the mention of Harbour's name, Aurelia brightened considerably

"Captain, if the *Spryte* heads out to Triton, it's going to look suspicious," Jeremy said.

"That it would, Jeremy, which is why we won't be going out there. We've a hold full of rare metal ingots, which have to be delivered to the processing station," Jessie said.

"And *Pearl* will be delivering tanks there about the same time. Brilliant, Captain," Ituau declared.

"I intend to transfer Rules to the *Pearl* and then to the *Annie*," Jessie said. "We'll return to the JOS for some extended downtime, which would be our normal schedule."

* * * *

Jessie Cinders owned three ships, the *Marianne*, the *Spryte*, and the *Pearl*. His mentor, Captain Corbin Rose, had willed him the *Marianne*, which the crew affectionately called the *Annie*, and the *Pearl*, although the *Pearl* wasn't the ship's registered name. Rose became disgusted with the number of construction issues delaying the tanker's delivery, and he changed the name to the *Unruly Pearl*, but her present captain and crew refused to call the ship by that name. As for the *Spryte*, Jessie ordered that ship with the profits he generated from owning his first two ships.

Much of the metal and frozen gases that built the JOS, the terminal arms, and the domes below came from an asteroid belt sunward of Pyre. Recently miners had explored Minist, the first of three moons that circled Pyre, and they'd discovered that the pickings were slim.

However, Triton was Pyre's third moon. It was massive and farthest afield from the planet. Its size and possibly dense structure kept it swinging around Pyre, the two bodies attracting each other and inducing a subtle wobble in Pyre's orbit of its star, Crimsa. Triton was in a locked position, one side constantly facing Pyre, and that side had a deep crater. It was thought by geologists that the moon had been struck by an asteroid, and the debris had pummeled the planet, creating Pyre's volcanic activity.

Triton's distance and unknown composition had kept mining ships at bay. If the moon proved to be an aggregate of common compounds, it could be an economic bust for a captain, if he or she owned a single ship. Jessie's three-ship company allowed him to take the risk. While he would still be financially impacted, if the moon proved to be a bust, he could absorb the loss. But if the moon was a rich composition of rare minerals and frozen gasses, he and his people would reap tremendous rewards, and Pyre would have a springboard to the outer planets.

Jessie sat in his captain's chair with Ituau and Jeremy at bridge consoles. Aurelia stood behind Jessie's chair, her hands resting on the top. The crew had quickly learned not to approach Aurelia too close. The only person she was comfortable with in her sphere was the captain.

"Commandant Strattleford," Jessie said genially over *Spryte*'s bridge comm. "Have you found your wayward downsider?"

"If you're asking if we found the heinous murderess, Captain Cinders, the answer is no."

"Well, Commandant, as your one-day moratorium on ships sailing from the arms is closing in fifteen minutes, I was giving you a heads-up that the *Spryte* will be launching immediately afterwards."

"I'm sorry, Captain Cinders. I've only just informed the terminal managers that I've extended the emergency order for another day."

"I understood that all the ships in dock have been searched."

"They have, Captain. In fact, I've come to understand that you might be a witness yourself."

"Then you understand wrong, Commandant. Lieutenant Higgins detected the presence of the girl coming aboard, visiting my stateroom, and leaving by the same route. And, I'm sure you recall that I was present at your meeting during the time. By the way, have you received more details about the girl or the crime?"

"Only her DNA profile, as you well know, Captain. I've imposed the additional hold on the ships, while we search the terminal arms again."

"Commandant, I have a theory for you, if I may?" Jessie asked politely.

"Any information would be valuable, Captain," Emerson replied. He didn't believe Jessie could add anything, but he was willing to placate the man.

"This is stitching together several odd pieces of information, but it might help you in your search and what you could be dealing with instead of what you might have been told. First, a downsider, who's supposedly never been topside, escapes the domes, makes her way through the JOS, and visits a terminal arm. Pretty accomplished for a newbie. Second, my crewman on duty swears he was put to sleep; we ran a drug test and he's clean. Third, my navigator's skins are missing."

"Excuse me, Captain, I thought it was reported that the girl only visited your cabin."

"That's correct, Commandant. Jeremy complained to me that he hadn't received satisfaction when he complained to a store owner about a faulty seal on a new pair of skins, and I told him to leave them in my cabin and I would contact the vendor.

"I see. Proceed with your theory, Captain."

"My last point is that security was monitoring this arm from stationside, saw the girl transit the ring to this arm, but didn't see her exit again. Still, your security team with a sniffer in hand couldn't find her out here."

"Your point, Captain?"

"Doesn't this seem to be much more complicated than a wayward young girl who panicked about a killing and fled? The girls' ability to evade your security is much too sophisticated and smacks of help aboard the JOS. If that's the case, the death of Dimitri Belosov might have been a long-planned and well-supported strike against the Andropov family. Have you considered that the other families are making a strategic move against the governor?"

Jessie didn't receive a reply for a couple of minutes, and he returned Ituau's grin, who was lauding his twist on the story proffered the commandant. "Well, only trying to help, Commandant, I must get my ship underway."

"I just told you, Captain," Emerson said, his voice rising, "all ships are on hold for another day."

"Yes, that's what you said, Commandant, but I'm sure you're about to reconsider that order. I'm running a mining concern, and unless you're prepared to put up the coin to pay my dock fees, my crews' wages, and my lost company profits, I do need to get my ship to the processing station."

"You know we have no need to accommodate your loss of income due to an emergency alert, Captain."

"Commandant, consider two things. No one believes a search for a missing teenager to be a valid reason for a station-wide alert and a freeze of our ships. Now, in five minutes, I'll be contacting every captain on the terminal arms and proposing that we boycott the station for the unnecessary hardship you imposed on us."

"This is blackmail, Captain."

"No, Commandant, this is business, and you're hurting ours. In five, I'm calling the docking manager. She had better give me the okay, or you'll have a bigger mess on your hands than a missing girl. Enjoy your day, Commandant," Jessie said and closed the comm before Emerson could reply.

"Why did that feel so good?" Jeremy said, and Ituau's chuckle said she agreed.

Jessie reached up and tapped Aurelia's hand.

Quickly, Aurelia tightened her controls and ceased broadcasting her pleasure. "Sorry, Captain," she whispered in Jessie's ear. "I'm not used to being around new people, much less normals."

Jessie waited out the five minutes and nodded to Ituau.

"Terminal arm two manager," Ituau called on the comm. "This is the *Spryte*. Ready to begin undocking procedures."

"You're cleared to begin launch preparations, *Spryte*. I'm closing your docking fee account. Terminal crew has been dispatched. They'll be at your gangway in four."

"Much appreciate the service, Penelope."

"No problem, Ituau. You give my regards to that hunk of a captain of yours. Safe voyage, *Spryte*."

Ituau closed the comm and regarded Jessie, taking in Aurelia's protected position behind him. "Any particular manner that you'd like Penelope's regards delivered, Captain?" Ituau said, smirking.

"I've an idea, First Mate. How about you get your butt and some crew down to the ramp, and get us closed up so we can get out of here?"

"Aye, Captain," Ituau replied, smiling. She winked at Aurelia in passing, to let her know that her conversation with the captain was friendly banter. What Ituau didn't realize was that Aurelia was quickly learning how to close one aspect of her power and keep another aspect open. She was practicing the curtailing of her transmissions but keeping her reception open, and she was enjoying the warm emotions shared between the captain and the crew. It was a far cry from the environment in the governor's house.

7: Hidden Away

Lise Panoy shooed her servant away with an imperial wave of her fingers. She hated to be disturbed during a massage, but the commandant's call warranted interrupting the indulgence.

"I've been looking forward to your call, Commandant," Lise said, as she stood and shrugged into a robe. "I'm anticipating good news," she added, shifting from a congenial voice to a firmer one.

"I'm afraid it's not, Lise," Emerson replied. He tried hard to keep his voice from cracking, but he failed.

"Who has her?" Lise demanded.

"That's just it, Lise. No one has her. We can't find her. We've searched every meter of the JOS, the El's passenger and cargo levels, the terminal arms, and the ships that were docked."

"That's impossible, Commandant. The girl can't up and disappear. You'll have to search the station's storerooms, cabins, and maintenance areas."

"We've already done that, Lise ... twice. Are you sure she doesn't have help from people aboard the JOS, individuals who could hide her in plain sight?"

"What're you suggesting, Commandant?" Lise asked, wondering who had influenced the commandant's thinking.

"We know she has to be here, Lise. That's a given, but we can't find her either by cam monitoring, hands-on searches, or sniffers. So how can a slip of a girl, who's supposed to be a topside newbie, hide from us, if it wasn't because she was getting help?"

"I told you, Commandant, that's she an empath. What I might not have mentioned is that rumor has it she's a powerful one."

"How powerful?" Emerson asked, his anger rising to the surface.

"Aurelia is strong enough to kill Dimitri without touching him."

"And you didn't think I needed to know this?" Emerson demanded.

Lise sought to placate the commandant, but the more she tried to explain the decision to limit the sharing of information, the angrier Emerson got.

"Lise, you've overstepped yourself this time," Emerson said, cutting her off. "Once we catch the girl, her capabilities are going to be obvious, and you can bet the entire populace of the JOS and the *Belle* are going to want satisfaction from the domes, and I don't mean only the Andropov family."

Lise was trying another line of reasoning when the comm signal went dead. She eyed the bust of the family's founding patriarch and then loosed an obscenity at the walls. Her masseuse, alarmed by the shout, ducked her head into the room, and Lise screamed at her to get out.

* * * *

Giorgio thumbed his comm unit off and the projected screen disappeared. A smile crossed his face. He'd received two calls within twenty minutes, saying about the same thing. A little more than a day ago, he'd have wagered that both the governor and he stood no chance of evading the punishment of a Review Board. Now, there was a glimmer of hope. He walked up the back stairs to the second floor of the house to update Markos.

The governor beckoned Giorgio into his study when his security head announced himself. He was lying on a couch, a cold compress on his forehead.

"A headache, Governor?" Giorgio inquired politely.

"And why shouldn't I have one?" Markos grumbled in reply. "I'm about to see my family's legacy flushed to the recycling plant."

"Perhaps, I can ease your pain, Governor," Giorgio replied, smiling, and Markos sat up abruptly, wincing at the sudden movement, to listen.

"I received a call from Lise Panoy. I've never heard the woman so angry, and she's demanding my assistance. The lady wants to know who Helena might have pointed Aurelia to on the JOS."

"What? She wants to know who Helena knows aboard the station?" Markos replied, not following the conversation's thread. "Helena's parents are dead. She has no siblings, and it's been seventeen, nearly eighteen years, since she was on the JOS. For the love of Pyre, what is Lise talking about?"

Giorgio's grin got wider. "It seems Lise spoke with the commandant, and he told her they can't find Aurelia."

"How's that possible?"

"That's what Lise wants to know. The commandant put a bug in her ear about Aurelia receiving help. It's his thinking that's the only way Aurelia could have disappeared from sight."

"They can't find her?" Markos asked, looking for confirmation from Giorgio, who tipped his head in agreement. "They can't find her," Markos repeated, smiling and easing the cold compress from his forehead, suddenly feeling his headache lessen.

"Oh, it gets better, Governor," Giorgio added. "I've heard the same thing from my contact in station security, Corporal McKenzie."

"Yes?" Markos prodded.

"Aurelia was seen entering a terminal arm, and security sent a team to investigate. The corporal accompanied two senior security people, and they searched every ship with a sniffer. Turns out our girl walked onto the *Spryte*, visited the captain's cabin, and walked back out, according to the lieutenant who headed the team."

"The *Spryte*? Why does that name sound familiar?"

"It's Captain Cinders' lead ship."

"Well, now, isn't that a coincidence?"

"The corporal, who's supposed to be an expert with a DAD, swears the girl was probably still aboard the ship, but he wasn't allowed to board."

"Why wasn't the expert allowed aboard?"

"Seems spacers refer to Corporal McKenzie as Terror. The corporal has a tendency to become overzealous during arrests. He roughed up the wrong spacer one day, and it's believed his crew took revenge on the corporal."

"Do they know who attacked him?"

"It's not known. The attackers were careful to hide their identities. But the crewman, who the corporal put in medical, was from Cinders' ship. That's why the captain denied the corporal permission to board."

"So what proof is there that Aurelia was still on the ship?"

"None, whatsoever, Governor, but security, with a cam on every cap that translates to the arms, has no image of her ever exiting the arm into the JOS.

"Interesting, Giorgio. Where's the *Spryte* now?"

"Undocked and headed to the processing station with a load of ingots."

"And the commandant couldn't find an excuse to stop the ship?"

"Rumor is that Captain Cinders threatened the commandant with a ship-wide boycott for interfering with business unnecessarily."

"Even more interesting," Markos commented, leaning against the back of the couch and dropping the compress on the arm. "What's your thinking, Giorgio?"

"I don't think you and I are clear of this mess, by a long shot, Governor, but I think we've bought ourselves some time."

"To do what with?"

"I think the corporal was right. I think Aurelia was on the *Spryte*. The timing was right for Aurelia and Cinders to have crossed paths aboard the *Spryte* before the security team arrived. How long would it take Cinders to figure out that the alert for a downsider was about an empath, a powerful one at that, and she was standing in front of him? Plus, in contrast to Lise's story of a savage murderer, Cinders is looking at Aurelia — a shy, attractive, sixteen year old."

"Yes, I see what you mean, but it would be a huge leap to think Captain Cinders would risk his career and his company to protect one girl, a downsider at that, from the authorities."

"From what I've heard about Cinders, he'd do just that."

"So how does this benefit us?"

"Exactly how, I don't know. But, with time, all sorts of things can be arranged, any one of which might prevent Aurelia from falling into station security's hands," Giorgio said, smiling wickedly at Markos.

* * * *

"You're saying I'm to travel with this captain aboard the *Pearl*, and then go with the captain of the *Annie* to this far moon," Aurelia said, repeating Jessie's plan.

"Yes, Rules. Remember our story."

"I'm Captain Cinders' protégé. He's allowing me to experience working in space to see if I wish to have a career in mining and exploration," Aurelia repeated.

"Excellent. I must say, Rules, you're taking this well."

"I've known only a few men in my life, Captain, and each of them spoke words that didn't match their emotions. For many years, it confused me, until my mother was able to help me understand that this was lying. You're the first man I've met whose words match what he's feeling ... most of the time."

Jessie quirked an eyebrow at Aurelia, and she added, "When I discuss my empath capabilities, you speak nicely to me, but I sense troubled thoughts. I don't think these emotions are directed at me personally. I think you find the subject of sensitives disconcerting."

"Yes, well," replied Jessie, wanting to change the subject. Aurelia obliged.

"How long will I be out there, Captain?"

"That's hard to say, Rules. As I've explained, your situation is a great deal more complicated than you imagined. The first step is to contact Harbour and make her aware of your circumstances. She can be a powerful ally for us. I don't know if she's willing to risk having you aboard the *Belle*. That could cause her to find herself and her people at odds with station security."

"You're saying I must wait and be patient."

"Yes, I'm afraid so."

"Then I wish you to change our story to your captains."

"In what way?"

"You intend to tell them that I should be treated carefully, and I'm only to observe."

"Yes."

"But have you considered the possibility that Harbour and you will find no suitable solution to the charges against me?"

"I don't believe it will come to that, Rules."

"And now you've said one thing, but I perceive another," Aurelia said simply.

Jessie wondered briefly if Aurelia's sensitivity was the cause of her maturing faster than other teens. "You're right, Rules, I didn't speak what I thought. There's a good chance that we can't find a way to present your case to the commandant without getting intercepted or arrested. We could be shut down because of the influence of the domes' families."

"In which case, I would be sent downside with only a few people knowing what the governor had done to my mother, my sister, and me."

"Yes, that's the way it would probably turn out, unless we can garner the help of a great many people, who would be willing to stand up to the commandant and the families."

"Then I think I should be trained to become a spacer."

"Seriously?"

"Could you not tell that my words matched what I felt, Captain?" Aurelia said, with a straight face, with only the slightest twitch at the corner of her mouth.

"Very funny, Rules."

Aurelia broke out laughing. "I must practice that. Ituau does it so well, as do you, when the two of you speak to the crew. But, Captain, if there is the chance I might never find justice for what was done to me and excused for my crime, then the only life I might have, for the foreseeable future, is out here in space."

"In which case, you want to start your training as a spacer."

"It can do me no harm, and it might be my future livelihood."

"I would hire you, Rules," Jessie said, and he put belief behind his words.

Aurelia's eyes teared up, and, when the captain stood, opening his arms to her, she fell into them. Jessie Cinders was the first man in her life with whom she felt safe.

* * * *

"Captain, YIPS docking is secure," Nate reported. "Unloading will begin within the hour. I've commed Captain Hastings on the *Pearl*, as you requested.

"Thanks, Nate," Jessie replied, rolling off the unfamiliar bunk. He hadn't slept in a crewman's cabin for decades, and he was grateful that it wouldn't be repeated soon, but Aurelia had occupied his stateroom during the trip to the YIPS. Jessie cleaned up and met Leonard Hastings at the gangway.

"Safe voyage, Jessie?" Leonard asked.

"Easy one, Leonard," Jessie replied.

Leonard Hastings was hired by Captain Rose, but Jessie had sat in on the interview, and the old man later asked his opinion of the man.

"He strikes me as a tough but fair man, who'll be straight with his crew, and he won't suffer fools," Jessie had said.

Corbin had laughed and slapped Jessie on the shoulder, saying, "Good assessment, son. You go call the man, and let him know he's being offered the position. I'll send the contract over to him for review, shortly."

Jessie had never regretted Captain Rose's decision. Handling the tanker freighter was a dangerous job, more so than anything, except working outside in a vac suit. The tanker hauled mixtures of dangerous solid gases. The frozen gases were shoveled up and shot through a compressor to liquefy the slush, before transport and transfer to one of the *Pearl's* tanks, where the slush cooled and formed into a solid state again.

Much of the mineral ore that the crew of the *Annie* recovered was sent by sled, which were small, automated, cargo ships, to the Yellen-Inglehart Processing Station, called the YIPS. The sleds came to a halt relative to the station, which charged a small fee for recovering them, but the method had saved the *Annie* innumerable trips to date.

However, YIPS operations refused to have the compressed, solid gases sent by sled. There was too much of a chance of an errant sled of tanks taking out the station. This required the *Pearl* to fill up at the *Annie's* mining site, make the trip to the processing station, and recover the sleds, which could be attached to the ship's multiple outriggers.

"What is this JOS alert that the crews of the YIPS are talking about?" Leonard asked.

"Funny thing you should ask, Leonard," Jessie replied, hooking the older captain's arm and leading him down the gangway out onto the docking arm, where they would have some privacy from the platform crew. "I happen to have the source of the trouble aboard my ship."

Jessie spent a half hour catching Leonard up on the details of what had transpired downside at the governor's house, Aurelia's escape to the JOS, and her making it aboard the *Spryte*.

"I presume there's a reason why I'm being informed in great detail about this girl," Leonard said, when Jessie ended his story at the *Spryte*'s launch from the JOS.

"I'm requesting, Leonard, mind you I said *requesting*, that you take Rules aboard the *Pearl*, train her as a spacer, and when you rendezvous with the *Annie* hand her off to Captain Erring. She'll continue Rules' training, while she makes the journey out to Triton. During this time, only you will know Rules' real identity, and it would be easy for you to say you were told nothing else about her. You were simply following the request of the company owner."

"Except for one small problem, Jessie. If Yohlin and I were to behave as you suggest, then we'd be duty bound to request Rules' ID and register her as crew trainee in the log."

Jessie swore silently at the overhead. "Sorry, Leonard, things have been moving too fast. I've been focused on how to get Aurelia off our hands and prevent risking the company any more than I already have."

"That might be your problem, Jessie. If Rules' predicament is as you say it is, perhaps the girl needs our protection, and this is the fight that spacers have known was coming for generations. The outcome will depend on what side the people of the JOS and the *Belle* take ... whether they stand with us against the domes' ruling families or not."

Jessie regarded Leonard, whose face said that the choice was obvious to him. For Jessie, who carried Corbin Rose's legacy, he was torn. In Jessie's mind, Aurelia's delicate, downsider face was contrasted against his crews' faces, many lined and worn from their years of hard duty in space.

"My thought, Jessie, is that you allow Yohlin and me to join your fight."

"I wasn't aware that I had started a fight."

"What would you call aiding and abetting a girl who was branded a murderer because she fought against the governor's unlawful imprisonment, the same man who fathered her by a woman he kidnapped?"

"An impulsive act?" replied Jessie, squinting one eye at Leonard, knowing his response fell far short of the truth.

"Jessie, ever since I met you, the last thing I would consider you to be is impulsive ... hardheaded, demanding, a workaholic —"

"Yes, yes, point made, Leonard. I admit Rules' story made me angry. It wasn't another complaint to lodge against the Andropov family. It was a serious breach of the empath agreement compounded by a series of heinous trespasses against empaths. I think the days of registering complaints against the downside families are over, and it's time to upend their political leverage over the domes and the JOS."

"And that, Jessie, is what we call a hellacious fight, which Yohlin and I would be pleased to join. My suggestion, concerning Rules, is that you let us help the girl. We'll keep her safe, train her as a spacer, and there'll be no need to register her in our ships' logs."

Jessie reluctantly agreed to Leonard's help and counted on his advice as to Yohlin's opinion on the issue, and he brought the *Pearl's* captain aboard the *Spryte* to meet Aurelia.

Tapping lightly on his cabin door, Jessie waited until he heard Aurelia call for him to enter. When he stepped inside, he signaled to her with a finger to his lips, and Aurelia winked an eye in acknowledgment. Then Jessie stood aside and waited for Leonard to take in the young girl who stood in front of him.

Leonard looked at Aurelia and then Jessie in consternation. "Captain Cinders, we were discussing someone fleeing the domes with a charge of murder over her head, and I was expecting someone more desperate looking like ..."

"Like you or me, Captain Hastings," Jessie finished.

"Well, yes."

"But, the charge of murder applies nonetheless, Captain Hastings," Aurelia declared.

"Not as I understand it, young lady. Let's get this straight right now before you and I begin our association," Leonard declared, settling his fists on his hips, a sure sign he was about to lecture a crew member. "You might have been responsible for Dimitri's death, but, under the circumstances, we call that self-defense, not murder. So, I'll hear no more of that."

"Yes, Captain," Aurelia replied sweetly.

"I just lectured you, Rules. Why are you smiling?"

"Your words and your emotions ... they match," Aurelia replied.

"Huh?"

"I'll explain on the way to the *Pearl*, Captain Hastings." Jessie said. Turning to Aurelia, Jessie added, "Gather up your gear, spacer. You're transferring ship."

"Aye, Captain," Aurelia replied heartily, and Jessie and Leonard shared grins.

Aurelia picked up an oversized spacer's duffel bag and said, "Captain Cinders, please inform Jeremy that I appreciate his generosity in sharing his extra clothing with me."

"I will," Jessie replied. The clothing wasn't really extra. Jessie had ordered Jeremy to give up his skins, deck shoes, and coveralls, making the young navigator clean them thoroughly before bringing them to him. "I'll replace your gear when we're on the JOS, except for a pair of skins," Jessie had told Jeremy.

"Only two of the three pairs, Captain?" Jeremy had asked.

"If I buy three, you get written up for your cabin's condition, Jeremy. If I buy two, then you get a pass, this one time."

"Two sounds fair, Captain," Jeremy happily agreed, appreciating the opportunity to duck a reprimand in the ship's log.

Leonard led the way down the main passageway, and they picked up Nate at the airlock. The second mate carried Jeremy's vac suit gear.

Once on the YIPS arm, Jessie touched Aurelia's arm, and she stopped and turned to face him. "Captain Hastings and I have determined it's best that he introduces you to his crew. So, I'll be saying goodbye for now," Jessie said. He didn't know what to expect from Aurelia but guessed at protestations, tears, or something of that nature.

Leonard cupped his fingers at Aurelia, and she handed off her duffel. Then she smiled at Jessie, before she threw her arms around his neck.

"I'll always be grateful for your help, Captain Cinders," Aurelia said softly in Jessie's ear, "and I have no right to ask, but please see what you can do for my mother and my sister." She gave Jessie a quick kiss on the cheek and was pleasantly surprised that the simple sentiment initiated a wave of embarrassment from him that passed through her. She laughed, as she released him, and hurried to catch up to Captain Hastings and retrieve her duffel.

When Aurelia glanced back, Jessie was disappearing up the *Spryte's* gangway, and she thought: *Why couldn't you have been my father, Captain?*

8: Harbour

In the early morning, before the rays of Crimsa touched the *Belle*, Harbour woke to the chimes of her comm unit. She washed quickly, gulped a hot drink, and munched on a small breakfast snack. Shrugging into a set of skins, she pinched the tiny activator near the base of her spine, and it snugged the skins tight, as it closed up the back. She finished by closing the calf and forearm activators and slipped on a pair of deck shoes, which would be needed on the JOS terminal arm.

Harbour examined herself in the polished metal of the cabin's door. The skins were black with a silver motif that began at the sides of her neck and traveled along the shoulder lines to the wrists, up the insides of the arms, and down along the sides of the body to the ankles. She'd purchased two ordinary pairs of black skins on JOS, but one of the *Belle*'s artisans, Makana, insisted on decorating them. The lines of silver were delicate and drew the eye to their patterns, as they wandered along her body's outline.

When Harbour had tried them on in front of her friend, she was aghast. "Makana, your work is gorgeous, but they accentuate the curves of my body. The effect is practically indecent."

Makana had laughed at her, saying, "If I had your curves, Harbour, I would be parading them in front of every eligible man."

Harbour had frowned at her friend, who chose to make a more persuasive argument. "Harbour, you are the defacto representative for the *Belle*'s residents. We need your appearance to make a statement, especially at these politically charged, monthly meetings.

Many meetings later, wearing her new skins, Harbour came to appreciate Makana's words. The more obstinate men whom Harbour dealt with were willing to communicate with her in private. Standing in her company, their eyes wandered along the delicate silver filigree, and Harbour put her attractiveness to good use, pushing for additional considerations for the

Belle's residents. Those individuals who didn't hear her requests soon realized, to their regret, how quickly they were dismissed.

Harbour tied her dark hair into a ponytail. The length was a luxury allowed by the *Belle's* gravity. The old colony ship continued to spin, driven by its great engines, and deliver a 1g environment to the ship's outer ring. Harbour threw on a thermal coat for the walk to the shuttle bay. The coat would be left onboard the shuttle once she reached the JOS. The orbital station produced an abundance of power, providing heat even to the terminal arms. The *Belle* could afford no such luxuries.

Striking the hatch actuator, Harbour slipped through the doorway before it was fully open and smacked it closed on the other side to preserve her cabin's heat. It wasn't cold enough to fog Harbour's breath, but she could feel the chill, and she activated her coat's seal, which closed from chest to throat, as she hurried through the narrow corridors to the launch bay.

The *Honora Belle* was the last colony ship launched from Earth. It wasn't designed with the luxuries of the JOS and should have been abandoned more than two centuries ago. *Yes, and we would have all left this ship to journey planetside if we'd have made our original destination. Instead, we were forced to accept this excuse of a planet with its volcanic attitude,* Harbour thought with disgust.

Only the occasional early-rising tech or artisan passed Harbour in the nearly deserted corridors, but pleasantries were always exchanged. The *Belle's* inhabitants were a tight, well-knit community, who occupied a minor portion of the ship's cavernous volume. They depended on one another for the quality of their accommodations.

Empaths, artisans, engineers, and techs, who lived aboard the *Belle* and could earn coin, contributed a portion of their income to the colony ship's general fund. The fund paid for the *Belle's* upkeep of its generators, environmental systems, and stipends to residents who required support. This latter group was Pyre's disenfranchised — those people, who for one reason or another, were unable to earn a living to pay for accommodations onboard the JOS.

Occasionally, Harbour received coin transfers into her general fund account from donors. The gifts were always accompanied by a comm call, the donors anxious to curry her favor. *But not always,* Harbour thought. There was one donor, who remained anonymous, and his gifts were as regular as Crimsa breaking the horizon, arriving in her account on the first of every month. The deposits weren't eye-arresting, but, when you added the years of contributions, it was an incredible amount.

Harbour put aside thoughts of her mysterious benefactor, as she entered the launch bay and greeted her pilot, Danny Thompson. Every afternoon before the monthly meetings, the JOS commandant offered to send a shuttle for Harbour, knowing the *Belle's* shuttle was long overdue for replacement. And, every time, Harbour graciously refused. She didn't want to be beholden to the commandant, and, worse, she had no desire to be trapped aboard the JOS, unable to return to the *Belle* when she wished.

Harbour and Danny climbed aboard the shuttle, and she heard the steps of his prosthetics as he walked down the aisle after sealing the hatch. Like many of the *Belle's* inhabitants, he was the victim of an accident. In Danny's case, he lost both legs. His prosthetics meant the loss of his job, as a hull jockey, which required the dexterous use of four limbs to pilot the tiny vessel around the exterior of a ship under construction. Only forty-five, Danny sought work aboard the *Belle,* where he could afford to live on his reduced income as Harbour's pilot.

"Ready, ma'am?" Danny asked deferentially, after he ensured she was strapped into her seat.

"Onward, Danny, the privileged await my company," Harbour replied.

Danny grinned at her, but Harbour could feel his depression, which she knew stemmed from his sense of isolation. It was a common problem among many *Belle* residents, who had grown up on the JOS and led active lives that were cut short. Retirement aboard the colony ship required a period of adjustment, and the empaths did all they could to help.

Harbour had long been able to keep the emotions of others at arms-length until her gifts were needed, but, around her people, she kept her senses open to monitor their well-being. With clients, she used the trigger of holding their hands to allow a free flow of emotions between them.

The usual dings and clangs that accompanied Danny's prelaunch preparations of the shuttle brought Harbour's attention to the here and now.

Everything onboard the *Belle* was old, and that included half of its inhabitants.

Residents did what they could to earn coin, taking menial jobs downside in the domes or working as artisans and selling their wares. But it was Harbour's empaths who earned the majority of the ship's coin. That income kept water in the tanks, purchased minerals for the hydroponics, reaction mass for the engines and generators, and hundreds of parts the engineers and techs required to keep the colony ship operational.

Clients paid dearly for the attention of the empaths. Fear, depression, anger, and haunted memories built over time and preyed on the human mind. Downsiders and stationers, who had the coin, sought out the empaths to ease their troubled minds. Occasionally, an employer sent an employee who managed a critical job for them. However they came to the *Belle*, Harbour's empaths sat with them, sensed their emotional states, and delivered alternative states of mind.

Sitting with an empath required cooperation. The clients had to immerse themselves in their torture for the empaths to sense their mental state. Only then could the sensitive know what emotions to push. The method of helping another person wasn't granted an empath at birth. The gift was, but it didn't show until puberty. Someone had to instruct emerging empaths how to shield themselves from others, how to harness their powers, and how to direct that power only when access was granted.

All empaths were women. The genes, which had been identified as producing the sensitives' capabilities, required the double-X chromosomes of females. The empaths were a minor portion of the population, but they were slowly growing or, perhaps, they were more easily discovered.

The first woman to lead the empaths had been named Harbour. Thereafter, whoever led them took the name of Harbour, and each Harbour chose her successor, who became the virtual head of the empaths and the protector of the *Belle*'s inhabitants. As a ship's leader, every Harbour had been granted a seat on Pyre's council, which was attended by the domes' governor, the family heads, the commandant and his key people, and the preeminent captains.

Danny guided the shuttle onto the JOS terminal arm 4, gate 1 docking collar. Sam, the terminal arm manager, confirmed a solid seal, pumped air into the collar, and triggered the terminal side hatch open.

"Seal confirmed and air pressure at one hundred percent, Sam," Danny replied.

"Welcome back, Danny. You have time for lunch later?" Sam asked.

"Sure do, Sam. Harbour's given me a long list on this trip. It'll take time for the vendors to prepare their packages and deliver them to the shuttle."

"Your choice this time, Danny."

"Julia's at eleven hours."

"Works for me. See you there."

Harbour heard Danny announce that the docking was complete, and she ensured her deck shoes were firmly attached before she released her seat belt. Danny passed her in the aisle, a smile on his lips. Obviously, her extensive list of small supply items allowed Danny to visit with old friends and chat with the vendors. It was an opportunity for him to experience a slice of his old life.

As Harbour followed Danny to the exit hatch, she thought again about the circumstances of their shuttle. It was the last original *Belle* shuttle. Most of the colony ship's many shuttles were lost establishing the first dome. Their engines were ruined by the heavy volcanic ash of Pyre. The past three hundred years had seen a huge improvement in the air quality, but it still wasn't safe enough to send a shuttle through the atmosphere. During the build out of the first domes, several shuttles attempting to return from the planet failed to make space, with disastrous results.

The station's terminal ring and its arms were constructed in concert with the establishment of the first domes. With only a quarter of the ring in place, crews built the structure that would house the El car. Above it, they constructed the housing unit for producing the El car's diamond-thread cable.

Engineers used liquid-state benzene molecules, which consisted of rings of carbon atoms, to assemble into neat and orderly threads, which were merely three atoms across and thousands of times thinner than a strand of hair. The zigzagging arrangement of rings of carbon atoms in the shape of a triangular pyramid created a formation similar to diamonds. Then they wove the threads into ever-increasing sizes until they had the cable's final thickness.

One of the last three *Belle* shuttles guided the end of a half-inch thick thread from the terminal arm down to the dome. With incredible risk, downside engineers locked onto the dangling thread and pulled it through the airlock opening at the top of a dome and anchored it to a spooling mechanism. Then, oh so carefully, engines wound the spool to pull increasing thicknesses of thread from the terminal arm. It took nineteen days for the El car's cable to be anchored inside the dome.

The shuttle used to complete the cable delivery landed on Pyre and remained there. The engines were considered too unsafe to lift the ship. A decision was made by the *Belle*'s leaders that the final two shuttles couldn't be risked. With more than two hundred engineers and techs in the domes, the only way back up was via the El car, which made its maiden voyage to the planet nine days later, arriving successfully in the dome with five courageous engineers aboard.

One day, we'll lose our shuttle, Harbour thought. The general fund didn't have enough to order a replacement, and she doubted a donor would step forward and rescue them. Then the *Belle*'s residents would be completely at the mercy of the JOS largesse, specifically that of the commandant.

Danny double-checked his telltales at the hatch. With them showing all green, he opened the shuttle hatch for Harbour. "Send the commandant and the family leaders my warmest regards, Harbour," Danny said, his lips twisted in a desultory smile.

"And I'm sure you mean that with all your heart, Danny," Harbour replied, chuckling. She sent a wave of warmth Danny's way, and her pilot relaxed into the pleasant sensation.

Danny flew for Harbour for many reasons, and this was one of them. He couldn't afford her prices, and she knew it, but it never stopped her from helping him.

Harbour left her thermal coat onboard the shuttle, and she joined the flow of people down the arm, a collection of spacers ending work schedules on the YIPS and individuals flowing to and from the *Belle* aboard JOS shuttles.

Harbour was easily recognizable, and people tended to give way to her, most due to fear and some out of respect. She joined the line for the capsule, but, when it arrived, several individuals in front of her stepped aside, and Harbour entered the capsule with a group of downsiders. She kept her senses tightly closed against their emotions.

There was no conversation, as the passengers locked themselves into positions, lights turned green, and the cap latched onto the ring. The transition device rotated, came to a halt, the lights turned white, and the passengers exited into the station's main promenade.

When Harbour arrived at the conference, she took her usual place at the room's centrally located, round table, which enabled egos to be placated. Harbour eased open her shields then slammed them shut. *This isn't going to be the usual petty, argumentative meeting,* Harbour thought. Anger, violent anger, dominated the room. Harbour's quick peek at the room's emotional temperature told her the governor and several family heads were the source.

Belatedly, Harbour noticed that the room's chairs, which were located along the walls, seated many more captains and security officers than usual. *Sharpen your wits,* Harbour thought. *This is dangerous space.*

"Now that we're all here," Commandant Strattleford said, opening the meeting, nodding perfunctorily to Harbour, "let's begin. Governor Andropov has asked to be the first to address this council. Governor, the deck is yours."

"A heinous murder has occurred downside," Markos said. "Immediately afterwards, the perpetrator escaped to the JOS. We had hoped station security could apprehend the felon without alarming the public, but the murderer has been loose on the station for more than six days."

Harbour eased her senses open. The governor's anger was evident in the pulsing veins at his temples. But something was wrong. The room should have been in an uproar about the announcement, but it was abnormally quiet. The only person seemingly surprised by the news appeared to be her.

"Under these conditions, I have to insist the commandant make a public announcement and ask for stationers and spacers' help in locating this person." Markos finished and sat down.

"I seem to be uninformed of events, Governor Andropov, and I'd like to ask a few questions, if I may?" Harbour asked.

"Certainly, Harbour," Markos replied.

"Who was murdered and was there a witness?"

"It was my nephew, Dimitri, and we know who it was."

"I'm sorry for your loss, Governor," Harbour said respectfully, while thinking *good riddance.* "How do you know who it was? Witness, DNA, fingerprints ... any or all of these?"

"Be assured, we know who did this," Markos replied.

Harbour could detect the governor's animosity, which she assumed was directed at her. *You don't like my questions?* she thought. "I presume you have the evidence in hand, Commandant," Harbour said.

Emerson squirmed in his chair and replied, "We have the perpetrator's DNA."

Harbour could sense the commandant's fear, and she pursued the cause. "Taken from the crime scene by dome authorities unconnected to the Andropov family?" she asked.

"I'm not in possession of the details as to how the evidence was obtained, Harbour," Emerson replied. "We have vid footage of the felon sneaking onto the cargo level of the El, pretending to be crew, and then she disappeared once she reached the JOS."

"A she?" Harbour said, amazed. "Was this woman a stationer?" Harbour's sincere hope was that the female wasn't from the *Belle.*

"She was a sixteen year old who was a member of my household," Markos replied tersely.

It didn't take Harbour's extraordinary senses to tell her that the governor and the commandant dearly wanted her to shut up.

"So what weapon did this teenager use to kill Dimitri?" Harbour asked. Along the room's periphery, she saw the captains shift in their seats in expectation of the answer to the question.

"Because there was extensive damage to Dimitri's skull, we've yet to determine the weapon used," Markos replied.

Harbour focused on some of the other family heads, particularly Lise Panoy. It confused Harbour that she perceived frustration and not anger. The woman wasn't in emotional sync with the governor.

Now, isn't that interesting? Harbour thought. "Do we have a clear photo of this girl?" Harbour asked, and her comm unit beeped softly. "Thank you," she said pleasantly, holding up her device. Interestingly, the image was sent to her anonymously, and she sensed a spike in anxiety from the governor and the commandant. "A slight build," Harbour noted out loud. "I can't tell from this photo, Commandant, what distinguishing features would be announced to the public, if the governor's request is approved?"

Emerson glanced at Markos, who was struggling to control his temper. The two men had already agreed to the public announcement, but something of this magnitude, which involved everyone's cooperation, required approval from the council. "She has auburn hair, although that might have changed, and no decorations, markings, or tattoos," Emerson replied.

"A sixteen-year-old, downsider girl with no adornments," Harbour replied, in mock wonder. "I didn't think such a thing existed."

The lives of most downsiders had become quite comfortable. It was well known that the young of the domes indulged themselves in all manner of decorations, some temporary and some permanent.

"Security surveillance should have been able to track her every movement from the El car, isn't that so, Commandant?" Harbour asked.

"We lost her after she transitioned to a terminal arm," Emerson replied.

"How did a downsider know to do that?" Harbour asked. She discerned a spike in animosity from Markos immediately before his palm smacked the table for attention.

"We're getting off track here," Markos declared loudly. "My nephew's murderer is loose on this station or hiding aboard a ship. I demand a public announcement with her picture distributed. I'm offering a reward of twenty-five thousand in coin for information leading to her capture. Once she's in custody, we take her downside."

The last part of the governor's announcement generated a great deal of outburst from the captains, and the commandant called for order.

"Why downside, Governor?" Harbour asked. "By agreement, egregious crimes of this nature are adjudicated aboard the JOS by the Review Board."

"No need, this time," Markos replied. "It's a no-contest situation."

"According to you, Governor," Harbour replied. Her indignation called on her power, but she held it in check. Markos would know if she influenced him. "It's the right of every individual to a fair review of a murder charge by the Board. That's the appropriate place for you to present whatever evidence you possess and prove this girl's guilt."

Harbour sensed a strong wash of fear override the governor's anger. *No public trial. This is getting more and more bizarre,* Harbour thought.

The commandant got control of the meeting and presented the governor's request for a public announcement with a photo and an offer of reward, which was approved by the council. The meeting descended into minutiae, and Harbour opened her reception to better judge the mood of the room.

The occupants' emotions appeared to be the usual mix, except for one. Most empaths, barring the exceptionally strong sensitives, had little or no sense of direction for the source of an emanation. They could orient themselves in one direction and sense whether the reception was stronger or weaker. Yet, at the same time, a person's broadcasted temperament wasn't static. It strengthened or waned as his or her thoughts churned.

Harbour taught her trainees to observe face and body language to augment their readings. Following her own advice, Harbour scanned the room in an absentminded manner, searching for the source of the odd output. Most men cast admiring glances her way, which, over time, she'd come to tolerate. Enough individuals had proclaimed her beauty to her that she'd come to accept it as fact without celebrating it. Women's glances fell into three camps, envious, neutral, or admiring.

The sensation Harbour perceived and searched for intrigued her. She judged it as coming from someone who emanated desire for her, but it said need, not lust. Occasionally, Harbour locked eyes with an individual and within moments their eyes averted. However, one pair of dark brown eyes stared quietly back at her.

Harbour held Captain Cinders' stare, expecting him to glance away. The captain's reputation was well known and respected, and she didn't expect this forward behavior from him. Notably, to her knowledge, the captain had never visited the *Belle*'s empaths, although he would certainly have possessed the coin.

The sense of need Harbour detected grew stronger, the longer she held Cinders' gaze. Finally, the captain casually turned to talk to the individual beside him. There was no doubt in Harbour's mind that Captain Cinders was the source of the strong desire for her.

The meeting wound down, and Harbour considered her options. Normally, she would have picked up some personal items and returned to the shuttle, where she would have used her comm unit to communicate with her people. However, the fact that Danny's list was long gave her the excuse to peruse the more exotic shops and give Captain Cinders an opportunity to contact her.

Harbour was of two thoughts, if the captain did manage to seek her out. On the one hand, she thought that the young girl, who escaped from the domes, would be the subject of their discussion. Yet, secretly, she hoped that Cinders wanted to meet her for personal reasons. The life of an empath was lonely. No matter how hard normals tried, they couldn't eliminate their fears over an extended liaison with an empath.

But, on this latter point, Harbour had to admit she wasn't any ordinary empath. She was the strongest sensitive on the *Belle* and, according to her mentor, the previous Harbour, she was more powerful than any empath that woman had known. This created a great demand for Harbour's services from the wealthiest of the families and left her as the most isolated person from normals.

On the main concourse, Harbour wandered past bars, restaurants, sleepholds, and vendors offering a range of items from practical to fanciful. Harbour earned enormous sums of coin for her services, but she transferred the vast majority of it to the *Belle*'s general fund. Those contributions, combined with the services of the other empaths, artisans, and trades people, allowed the colony ship to accommodate its necessities.

Walking the concourse, Harbour felt like a small island in a stream. Most normals continually ducked around her or bumped into each other to make way for her, as they hurried to their next destination. The flow of people around her always left a little space. Only some downsiders and children occasionally ran into her, and Harbour found the contact of the latter group comforting. Sometimes, she would think back to the carefree, early years before her power bloomed. *Once, I was a normal,* she would often think.

9: Rendezvous

Harbour kept her senses open as she wandered through shops. It was annoying, enduring the lust, envy, fear, and other sordid emotions from the normals near her. At times, she'd smile and regard the more ugly-minded individuals until they realized they'd been read and then they would scurry away.

The fact that Harbour hadn't been approached by Captain Cinders immediately after the meeting told her that he preferred to keep their interaction secret. That thought disappointed Harbour. It implied the captain probably wanted to discuss the girl.

Eventually, Harbour grew tired of waiting and thought of lunch. Most eateries on the main promenade were too pricey for her frugal nature. But, before she could decide on a location, a shop of polished rare minerals caught her eye, and she paused to enjoy the display. That's when the desire, the need for her, returned, and she wandered inside, feeling the emotion grow in strength.

At the rear of the shop, an older woman was bent over her tool, polishing an intricate figurine of yellow green stone. She looked up at Harbour briefly, smiled, and tossed her head at the door behind her workstation before resuming her efforts.

Harbour glanced around, discovering the lapidist and she were alone. Moving quickly behind the workstation, Harbour touched the door actuator, stepped through the opening, and closed the door behind her. Polished stone figures, uncut rocks, and supplies filled the shelves of the cramped space.

When Harbour heard her name whispered, she followed the sound around the shelves. "Captain Cinders," Harbour said, finding that the man and she were crowded together in a small alcove.

"I apologize for the intrigue, Harbour, but I wanted you to know that the governor's story is as potable as effluent waste."

"That's hardly news, Captain," Harbour replied sarcastically. "What else do you know?" Her senses were open, but she wanted to touch Jessie to confirm what she was receiving. This close to the man, it wasn't really necessary, not with her abilities, and she questioned her desire. She sensed an element of fear from the captain, but his overriding emotion was one of anger.

"I have her," Cinders said, without fanfare. Unlike at the meeting, Jessie kept averting his eyes from Harbour's face. That Harbour was a beautiful woman was an understatement, but it was the warmth in her eyes, despite their cool gray color, that sought Jessie's attention, which he was working to ignore. His personal encounters with women had always been fleeting and confined to station downtime. There were reasons for that, but the most significant one was that he hadn't found anyone who held his attention for longer than a night.

"You have her ... the girl who killed the governor's nephew?" Harbour clarified.

"That's one story," Jessie replied. "Another is she fought back against Dimitri in self-defense. She admits to pushing him, but she didn't touch him." Jessie lifted an eyebrow to emphasize what he'd said.

"If she didn't touch him —" Harbour started to say, before the captain's words sunk home. She leaned close to Jessie, forcing him to lock eyes with her, and closed a hand over his. "Are you saying she's an empath?" Harbour whispered. Harbour felt a spike of desire from Jessie, but it was quickly masked.

"Yes," Jessie replied. He would have stepped back from Harbour, but the little alcove he chose gave him no room.

"How did she get downside?" Harbour whispered harshly, her gray eyes flaring. The captain's story was explosive. A murder perpetrated by an empath could destroy the tenuous balance among the *Belle*, the station, and the domes.

"She didn't get downside," Jessie hissed, and the vehemence he exuded caused Harbour to release his hand and pull back. "She was born downside.

Her mother's an empath and so's her sister." Jessie watched Harbour's hand fly to her mouth, and she stood that way, her gray eyes reflecting the thoughts flying through her mind.

"The governor?" Harbour asked.

"The same," Jessie replied. "According to Aurelia, her mother was kidnapped by the governor when she was seventeen years old. Aurelia and her sister, Sasha, have been secluded in the governor's house their entire lives."

"How was this even possible?" Harbour asked.

"I'm sorry, Harbour, I don't have the time to bring you up on all the events that Aurelia shared with me. By the way, I recommend you and I refer to her as Rules so that we're never overheard mentioning her name." Harbour started to say something, but Jessie waved her off. "The important thing, and the reason for me meeting you, is that I need you to take her off my hands. Security is already suspicious that I might have her."

"Are you suffering from space dementia, Captain?" Harbour hissed, and Jessie drew back from the fear and anxiety that washed through his mind. "Sorry," Harbour apologized, tightening her controls. "We're talking about kidnapping, rape, illegal incarceration, murder, and breaking the accord, no less, and you want me to hide the girl who's at the center of all this?"

"What am I supposed to do with her ... add her to my crew?"

"Where's she now?"

"She was on the *Spryte*," Jessie admitted, but he didn't say more.

Harbour felt Jessie's emotions wink off like a light being doused. *Interesting control*, she thought. *You don't trust me if I'm not going to take the girl off your hands.*

"How come security wasn't able to sniff her out? The governor must have given the commandant a DNA profile."

"That's a secret," Jessie said, flashing a quick grin. "And, by the way, Rules thinks it probably wasn't the governor, but Giorgio Sestos, his chief of security, who might have passed it to an ambitious family head."

"Sounds like a bright girl," Harbour admitted.

"You have no idea ... a good kid too."

"What do you intend to do with her?"

"The safe thing would be to turn her over to security."

"From what I've heard about you, Captain Cinders, you don't tend to play it safe when it comes to a matter of justice, especially for one of this scale."

"Screw my rep, Harbour. I'm in danger of losing my company for aiding and abetting a fugitive."

Jessie was sending again, and Harbour detected a mix of emotions. The anger was still there, but the emotion didn't answer the why.

"Does your crew know?"

"Know what?" Jessie challenged, and his eyes narrowed, daring Harbour to follow through on her question.

The sensations Harbour received were white hot anger and indignation. The captain was known for his tough leadership, but his reputation said he handled his people with an absolute fairness, which engendered their loyalty. Now, she sensed her questions had crossed an invisible line with the captain. *Obviously, your crew knows, and they're backing you, but you'll not admit to their complicity,* Harbour thought.

While they were talking, security's announcement came over the speakers of the JOS public monitors. Harbour and Jessie could hear it sounding over the one located outside the shop in the main concourse. Harbour's comm unit chimed and Jessie's unit vibrated, and they both checked their messages.

"Not a flattering picture," Harbour commented.

"If you're trying to hide your crimes by recapturing your runaway daughter, what type of photo would you distribute of her?" Jessie commented bitterly. "Well, I think we're done here. Safe trip back to the *Belle*, Harbour."

When Jessie moved to edge past her, Harbour grabbed his shoulders, and said, "Wait. What are you going to do?"

"What does it matter to you? You can't or won't help, and I've got to get back to my ship," Jessie replied.

Harbour was crushed by the accusation, and, whereas, at the start of their conversation, the captain had barely glanced at her, now his brown eyes were hard, and they drilled into hers. "Give me your comm unit," Harbour demanded.

Despite Jessie's reluctance, he handed the device over after opening its security lock with his thumb, the unit sniffing his DNA.

Harbour entered a comm code and tagged it as "HB." Handing the unit back to Jessie, she said, "That's a private, untraceable line to me. It routes through a security backdoor without logging the calls."

"A favored client, perhaps," Jessie replied.

"That's none of your business," Harbour replied hotly.

"Fine," Jessie replied, equally unhappy with their final exchange. He edged past Harbour, activated the storeroom's rear door, which exited into a maintenance corridor, and paused. "One last question, Harbour," Jessie said. "Can you put a man to sleep at a distance of four to five meters without him knowing it was being done?"

"That's quite a specific question, Captain."

"Can you?" Jessie persisted.

"Yes, I can," Harbour admitted, thinking the conversation with Jessie had gone horribly wrong. Now, it looked as if she would have to scare away a man who she hoped might have been interested in her. "And, as far as I know, I'm the only empath strong enough to do that."

"Not any more, Harbour," Jessie replied. "That sixteen-year-old, untrained empath, who I'm protecting, did that to gain entrance to my ship."

Harbour could sense the conviction behind the captain's words, and she was stunned by the revelation, but before she could reply, the maintenance access door slid closed, and Jessie Cinders was gone.

Leaning an elbow on a shelf, a hand against her forehead, Harbour considered the ramifications of the captain's story. She was sickened by her refusal to help, but the girl's presence on the *Belle* would endanger the entire community.

Besides, Harbour told herself, the commandant's announcement was now stationwide. However Aurelia had managed to board the *Spryte* undetected, she wouldn't make it down a terminal arm and traverse the main concourse to another arm without being reported, if not immediately apprehended. Twenty-five thousand in coin was an enormously tempting reward.

Harbour had no doubt that if Aurelia was caught by one of the families' agents she would disappear downside in the next minute, and the governor would immediately cover up any evidence of his crimes, which meant all three women were vulnerable. *Whatever you do, Aurelia, stay with Cinders,* Harbour thought. She smacked a palm on the shelving in annoyance, exited the storeroom, and left the shop via its front doors.

* * * *

Harbour considered walking in station, to find a local food vendor who might offer fair-priced, if simpler, food, but her comm unit chimed, reminding her of an appointment. She muttered an oath and hurried to meet with Lieutenant Devon Higgins to review the most recently incarcerated individuals. Using her skills in an interview enabled Harbour to determine the difference between the dangerous and the unfortunate.

Incarceration of criminals was expensive for station security, and work details required oversight, which stretched security personnel thin. Despite the fact that the domes had the space, the governor and the families were dead set against taking convicted felons downside. As the governor repeated incessantly at council meetings, "Most criminals are stationers and spacers. Why should we host them when we aren't contributing to the problem?"

No one believed the domes had no crime, but evidence that crimes occurred never came to light. Somehow, the families policed their people and dealt with the troublemakers.

One of Harbour's predecessors had worked out a deal with the commandant, who held that position, at the time. The deal enabled Harbour to interview inmates, and if she felt she could help any of the recently convicted, she offered them an opportunity to work off their sentences aboard the *Belle*. They would have no supervision but would be expected to complete their work assignments well and on time.

Most individuals, who were offered the opportunity, readily accepted. The *Belle* received free labor, usually from accomplished and experienced individuals, and the colony ship's general fund received monthly coin for each individual transferred to her care. The amount was half of what it would cost security to maintain its incarceration, so the arrangement was a win-win for both the JOS and the *Belle*.

"Only three to review today, Harbour," Devon said, after greeting her. She'd interrupted him eating an early lunch, and half a sandwich lay on the tray. "Haven't eaten lunch, have you?" Devon asked, watching Harbour eye his food.

Harbour was about to deny the lieutenant's impending offer, but the growl of her stomach betrayed her.

Devon laughed good-naturedly, pushed the tray across his desk toward Harbour, and sent three files to her comm unit to review. In the meantime, he poured her a caf drink from his brew station.

Harbour pulled the tray to her, smiled, and sent a wave of appreciation to Devon. He was one of the members of the JOS security force she admired. A good-looking young man in his late twenties, he cared for his people and the rule of law, and he was unmarried.

Taking a healthy bite of the sandwich and washing it down with caf, Harbour opened the first file. Within minutes, she knew that the poor individual was long past rescue. He would be incarcerated for life for his crimes. She took another bite of sandwich and continued to the second individual. It was a middle-aged woman, who had claimed that she was innocent throughout the Review Board's hearing. The third man was an ex-spacer, who was charged with robbery, but that charge was dismissed. Instead, he was convicted of attacking a security officer.

Harbour was about to take another bite of the sandwich when she paused. She was curious to know which security officer the spacer had attacked. The answer disgusted her, and she placed the sandwich back on the tray and regarded the lieutenant. Tapping her comm unit with a finger, she said accusingly, "The spacer ... the corporal again."

"I know," Devon replied, holding up his hands in self-defense. "He walks a fine line, but, in his defense, the spacer shoved him first."

"Yet, the corporal put a retired spacer in medical for being pushed. He couldn't have stunned him? And what's with the original charges being dismissed?"

"The man started to rob a store owner of some coin vouchers, but instead threw them in his face and walked away. The owner called security anyway."

"And that was all that Corporal McKenzie needed as an excuse to force the man into an emotional corner where he would fight back."

Devon didn't bother answering Harbour. He knew she was right. If he had his choice, McKenzie would have been off the force after his second crossing of the line, as Devon considered it. But, the commandant saw it differently. He considered the corporal a "focused and diligent member of the security force."

"I'll interview these last two, Devon," Harbour said. "I'll finish your lunch, while you bring the woman to the interview room." She quickly devoured the remainder of the sandwich and chased it with the last of the caf before she hurried to catch up with Devon.

Five questions into the interview, Harbour looked up at Devon and shook her head. Devon called a female attendant to take the woman way, whose eyes smoldered at Harbour.

"I don't think Priscilla likes you," Devon said.

"That story of innocence is pure fabrication," Harbour replied. "She's pleased with what she did to her partner."

"Number three?" Devon asked, and Harbour nodded.

Minutes later, a male attendant brought the spacer into the interview room. He stood uncertain as to what he should do. An old frayed cap was held in his hands.

"Please, Mr. Bassiter, have a seat," Harbour offered.

"Ma'am, if you would, nobody calls me by my given name. I'm Dingles." He exhibited a spacer's walk, as he crossed the room and took a seat. Each foot was firmly placed on the deck, before the next one was lifted. It was a slightly halting gait.

"Well, Dingles, what do you think of me?"

"You're pretty."

"Thank you, Dingles, but do you know who I am?"

"Sure, everyone knows who you are, Harbour."

"Your file says you were put on station. Why was that?"

"The walls closed in," Dingles said simply, and Harbour could sense the spacer's deep regret and frustration.

"You wanted to continue to work as a spacer, Dingles, didn't you?"

"Oh, yes, ma'am! I'd still be navigating for Captain Cinders, if I didn't have this sickness."

"Are the walls closing in on you in your cell, Dingles?" asked Harbour, surprised that she missed the fact that Dingles worked aboard the *Spryte*.

"Yes, ma'am, it feels like I'm being crushed."

"I have an alternative for you, Dingles. How would you like to work off your sentence aboard the *Belle*?" Harbour expected Dingles to jump up and down with joy at the opportunity he was being offered, but the spacer sat there staring at the cap he kept twisting in his hand.

"Give me your hands, Dingles," Harbour requested.

Dingles laid his cap on the table and reached out to gently grip Harbour's hands. Instead, he felt strong fingers take hold of his hands.

"What are you worried about, Dingles?" Harbour asked.

"I don't see a difference between being locked up on the JOS and locked up on the *Belle*."

"You and only you would have access to your cabin, Dingles." Harbour felt a momentary lift in the spacer's spirits, but it sputtered out.

"What else bothers you, Dingles?"

"I'm a navigator, ma'am. I don't see the old colony ship going anywhere anytime soon, so I don't see how I can help you."

"You're a spacer, aren't you, Dingles?"

"Damn right I am," Dingles declared, "and a fine one, if I say so myself."

Harbour could sense the flare of pride, but it was fleeting too.

"And what else, Dingles?" Harbour waited, but Dingles remained quiet. She opened her powers fully to detect the emotions rolling off Dingles. Buried deep was bitter resignation. As an empath, she faced the usual question: What was the cause of the emotion? In Dingles' case, Harbour could guess it was the loss of his navigator's position.

"If I'm going to help you Dingles, you need to talk to me," Harbour persisted.

When Dingles glanced at the lieutenant, Harbour locked eyes with Devon, nodded toward the door, and Devon slipped out.

"Talk to me, Dingles," Harbour urged. The spacer released her hands and picked up his cap. It seemed to be his safety line to sanity.

"I appreciate the offer and all, ma'am, I really do, but what difference does it make? I work for you for eighteen months, and then I'm right back aboard the JOS. Then again, maybe I don't make it eighteen months on the *Belle*. Like I said, what's the difference? The walls are just going to keep closing in on me until there's nothing left of me."

"Give me your hands one more time, Dingles," Harbour requested, and the spacer dutifully complied. "I want you to think about the walls closing in on you, Dingles. I want you to imagine them shrinking and shrinking." Harbour could feel Dingles try to pull his hands back, but she held them tightly. "You know who I am, Dingles. Now, I want you to feel what I can do."

Dingles gave in to Harbour's request. It didn't seem to matter whether he let the walls get him now or later. He was tired of fighting every waking minute of every day to keep them at bay. Right now, he could happily lie down and let them take him.

Dingles closed his eyes and visualized his tiny cell. The light-colored walls and ceiling grew dark and began to move, and he didn't care anymore. *Let them come,* he thought. Then he did care. He felt some of his old confidence return and fuel his determination not to succumb to the encroaching, strangulating impression of the world trying to crush him. To Dingles' amazement, the walls stopped moving in, and they visibly lightened.

A shudder escaped Dingles, and he drew a deep breath. Miraculously, to the spacer, the walls retreated, and Dingles believed he was shoving them away. Relief flooded through him.

Harbour watched tears run down Dingles' face, and she sensed a brightening of his spirit. The relief wouldn't last, but it would buy the spacer a few days of freedom from his torture. Dingles would find his time aboard the *Belle* would have a dual purpose. The individuals released into Harbour's care helped her train the new empaths. The two groups shared daily sessions, which Harbour supervised, and the sessions prepared the empath trainees for the time when they would receive clients and earn coin.

When Harbour eased her push, Dingles grasped one of Harbour's hands with both of his. "If this lasts only a day, I thank you, ma'am," he said gratefully.

"It will last longer than that, Dingles, and, with time, it will last much longer. You might find that after you served your sentence, you'll want to stay aboard the *Belle*, in which case, you'd continue to receive the support of the empaths."

"In that case, ma'am, I'm ready to go to work for you anytime you say. How soon could this happen?"

Harbour tipped her head to Devon, who had been watching through the door's observation window and returned at her invitation. "Lieutenant, Dingles will be leaving with me, if the attendant could bring his things."

"We've prepared his duffel for you, Harbour. It's waiting in my office."

"Well, Dingles, I guess there's nothing to keep us here. Shall we go?"

"Yes, ma'am," Dingle replied, jumping and racing to stand by the doorway to allow Harbour to precede him. He stood erect, as if his captain was passing by.

"Thank you," Devon whispered to Harbour, when she passed close to him, and Harbour sent a wave of appreciation his way. The lieutenant's eyes fluttered briefly, while his mind absorbed the pleasant sensations.

10: Dingles

In the lieutenant's office, Dingles said, "If I could, sir, I'd like to change into more comfortable attire." He indicated his security prisoner overalls with a wave of his hand.

"Dingles, there's a head down the corridor," Devon replied. "Take your duffel and change in there. The attendant will show you the way."

Dingles acknowledged the permission with a short wave of his cap, slung his duffel over a shoulder, and followed the security personnel out the door.

"For your information, Harbour, Dingles hasn't been eating too well, and he was coming up on lunchtime."

"Thank you for that, Devon. I'll ensure he has a nice meal before we take the shuttle back to the *Belle*. Danny will be busy gathering packages for a while."

A few minutes later, Harbour heard behind her, "Ready when you are, ma'am." She turned around. Dingles stood in the doorway. He was wearing midnight black skins and a calf-length, pleated skirt decorated in a flower print of pinks, greens, and white.

"Yes, you are, spacer," Harbour replied, chuckling. She thanked Devon for his help and led the way out of security administration.

"I'm hungry. How about you, spacer?" Harbour said, with cheer. "Anywhere you want to go. Your liberation lunch is on me."

"Anywhere?" Dingles asked cautiously.

"Anywhere," Harbour confirmed.

A huge smile lit Dingles' face. "This way, ma'am," he said, taking a right turn at the next intersection. He paralleled the main concourse for about 50 meters before turning in station.

Harbour got a look at the back of Dingles' skins. *Marianne* and *Spryte* were woven into the fabric in an intricate pattern of raised black weaving. It was beautiful work.

"We're here," Dingles announced.

Harbour saw a small, neat sign, announcing the Miners' Pit, next to a doorway that resembled a ship's hatch. Beside the door was a palm-sized, red button, and, next to the button, was a sealed, hand-printed card, which said, "Spacers welcome. The rest of you can figure it out. C. Rose."

"Is this Captain Rose's place?" Harbour asked.

"Was," Dingles replied. "Now, it's Captain Cinders' place." He smacked the oversized actuator, and the door moved back from its seal and slid aside. It wasn't a painted door. It was an actual ship's hatch that had been set into the wall.

"Not a spacer," Harbour noted, pointing to Rose's note.

"You're with me, Harbour, and I belong," Dingles said proudly.

Dingles had no sooner stepped through the hatch than Harbour heard a woman cry out, "Dingles!" She saw a human arm and an animated prosthetic arm wrap around Dingles' neck. When Harbour stepped into the woman's view, the smile was wiped off her face.

"Ma'am," Maggie said politely.

"She's with me, Maggie," Dingles announced proudly.

"Welcome to the Miners' Pit, ma'am. Let me get you a table, Dingles," Maggie said.

The lunch crowd was in full swing, and the place was crowded with spacers, wearing skins and their colorful downtime accessories. Dingles was mobbed every step of the way by other spacers. By the time they were seated, the grin on Dingles' face couldn't get any wider.

"The usual, Dingles?" Maggie asked.

"Yeah, Maggie, but hold the alcohol ... water only. I'm working for Harbour."

"Good for you, Dingles," Maggie replied.

Harbour felt the emotions from the Miners' Pit hostess shift from cool to warm, as she regarded her.

"Water for me too," Harbour announced, "and I'll have whatever Dingles is having."

"That's fine, ma'am," Maggie announced and cued the order over her tablet.

Harbour took in the collection of individuals packing the tables and the long bar. They were spacers all, judging by the costumes. Nearly a third of them displayed some sort of prosthetic.

"I never really considered how dangerous space mining can be," Harbour commented.

"And those are the injuries you can see, ma'am. There are some here like me, struggling to keep their wits about them on a daily basis.

"Dingles, your skins have the *Marianne* and the *Spryte* on the back. So, you worked for Captains Rose and Cinders?"

"Yes, ma'am. I was on the crew of the *Marianne* with Captain Rose when he brought the boy aboard."

"You met Jessie Cinders when he was a boy?" Harbour asked, intrigued by this turn in the conversation.

"Yes, ma'am, but he wasn't Jessie Cinders then, just Jessie."

"I don't understand."

"You won't find any records for Jessie Cinders in the JOS personnel databases until the boy went to the spacer training program so that he could hold a mate's position. Jessie's parents and a bunch of others were killed in a terrible decompression accident while they were building a new terminal arm. The boy was an only child and traumatized from losing his parents. He didn't speak for more than a year, and the only reason anyone knew his first name was it was stitched, real nice-like, on his collar."

"How about DNA sampling to match him to his parents?"

"I imagine they tried, but, back then, a lot of station workers and spacers weren't registered. Now it's mandatory."

"Then how did Jessie get the last name Cinders?"

Dingles got a big smile on his face and started to chuckle.

"I suppose it's not a family name or something like that," Harbour said, smiling in return.

"Hardly, ma'am. When Jessie was a teen, he was working the ore hold with another young crew member. The *Marianne,* or *Annie* as the crew calls her, was still using the old method of scooping mineral dust from the surface and shooting it into a bay. A leveler, which traveled back and forth across the hold, was used to distribute the dust. Jessie's companion leaned too far out on the perch, and his safety line released. He fell into the dust, as the leveler was passing, and it buried him."

"Oh, for the love of Pyre," Harbour whispered, her hand to her mouth.

Dingles eyebrows rose in agreement with Harbour. He was in his element, telling old spacer stories and surrounded by lifelong friends.

"Well, Jessie hit the intercom, screamed for help, released the brake on his safety line, and dove in after his crewmate. The crew used Jessie's safety line to pull the two boys out. They were covered head to toe in dark, clinging ore cinders, and you couldn't tell them apart. Both were retching dust from their mouths and lungs. What was ironic was the young man Jessie saved had teased and tortured him since the day he came aboard the *Annie,* and yet Jessie hadn't hesitated to jump in to save his life."

Dingles smiled at the memories of that day. "Captain Rose eyed Jessie, shook his head at him, and said, "All cinders and courage, and no brains.""

They were interrupted, while a server delivered their water and lunch specials. The food smelled wonderful to Harbour, and she heard their stomachs grumble. She dug into her plate, and between bites she warned Dingles, punctuating her statement with her fork, "Don't you dare touch your food until you finish the story."

"Not much more to tell, ma'am," Dingles said, chuckling about the threat. "Captain Rose told his first mate to check the safety lines, and ordered the boys to clean up. As Jessie told me years later, Captain Rose reprimanded him for diving in after his crewmate, telling him that it was a foolhardy thing to do, but I know the captain admired the boy's selflessness. After that episode, the crew started addressing Jessie as Cinders."

"What was it like to work for Captain Cinders?"

"It was tough in the beginning, and, mind you, at the time, I wasn't a newbie. The captain asked for your best, every time. That can grind some people down, if you can't rise to the occasion, but, if you succeed, it can make you mighty proud to be a member of his crew."

"So how is it that you got into trouble stationside, Dingles?"

"It wasn't the captain's fault. He was real generous with me ... gave me rent for six months and severance pay. I blew it, ma'am. Squandered coin like a newbie on his first downtime, messed with a shop owner, and then I screwed up by pushing that little piece of space dirt, Terror." Before Dingles could say anymore, he grinned and threw his arms in the air.

Behind Harbour, she heard a woman's deep voice say, "Well, look who's out of confinement and having lunch with a hot coin-kitty."

"I've been called many things, but coin-kitty is a first," Harbour said, as the woman and her friends drew abreast of the table.

"Oh, call me a piece of waste ... I'm so sorry, ma'am," Ituau said, when she realized who was sitting across from Dingles.

"Harbour, this loud-mouthed woman is Ituau Tulafono, first mate of the *Spryte.* The scruffy looking one next to her is Nate Mikado, second mate, and that slip of a spacer on the end there is Jeremy Kinsman, navigator. Hey, Jeremy, you newbie, how come you can afford a hot new pair of skins?"

"Hook on, spacer," Ituau said.

"Aye, latched on," Dingles replied.

Harbour didn't understand the lingo, but the intent was clear, as were the emotional shifts. Dingles had inadvertently touched on some point he shouldn't have. Ituau had warned him off, and he'd received the message.

"How *are* you out, Dingles?" Ituau asked, with concern.

"I'm going to work out my sentence for Harbour on the *Belle*," Dingles replied proudly.

"That right?" Ituau commented, and her gaze shifted to Harbour. "Thanks, ma'am," she said, offering her hand to Harbour.

To Harbour's surprise, each spacer shook hands with her. The majority of normals avoided contact with empaths, unless they were clients, and then only during their sessions. Then it clicked for Harbour. This crew was already familiar with one empath, a young girl by the name of Aurelia.

The *Spryte*'s crew followed Maggie to a far table in the crowded cantina, and Harbour and Dingles returned to their meal. Harbour was happy to see Dingles' appetite restored.

"Keep going, Dingles. Jessie uses the name of Cinders when he registers for space training. I imagine he was an excellent student, being raised on shipboard."

Dingles laughed so hard he started choking on a mouthful of food, and he raised a hand to everyone to indicate he would be all right and slugged down some water to clear his throat.

"He was a terrible student, ma'am," Dingles replied, when he could regain his breath. "Captain Rose had to intervene several times to prevent him from being thrown out. The instructors claimed his argumentative attitude prevented him from learning the subjects, and Jessie accumulated several disciplinary reprimands in his file."

"What happened?"

"Captain Rose challenged the lead instructor. He proposed that if Cinders could pass the practical, then he could remain in the program, and the woman was happy to accept. I believe she was fairly certain Jessie didn't stand a chance."

"And?" Harbour urged, when Dingles paused. The retired spacer was enjoying the opportunity to spin tales for an attentive audience.

"He failed."

"Not possible."

"Yes, ma'am, it was, according to the instructor. But, see, they run vids on these practicals, so the students can review their errors. Captain Rose looked over the test with the instructor, and she pointed out to him all the places where she said Jessie failed. The story goes that the captain laughed so hard he tipped over backward in his chair."

"What happened? Did he fail, or didn't he?"

"It seems the program was primarily taking newbies from the station and teaching courses they designed a long time ago. Things change, equipment changes, and ships have new designs. Jessie was trained in the latest techniques and on the latest equipment."

"So how did Captain Rose settle the argument?"

"He brought in three other captains to review the practical. Every one of them said he passed, and, not only passed, but thought the boy made a damn fine spacer." Dingles smiled at Harbour, pleased to tell a story about a man he admired.

They finished eating their meal in silence, each left to their private thoughts. Dingles was curious as to why Harbour, of all people, was so interested in the captain. Harbour was thinking about the men and the women in the Miners' Pit, sharing meals and camaraderie, despite the hardships they had suffered before and would again.

Dingles was leaning back in his chair, patting a full stomach, when he leapt to attention.

"Rest easy, you old reprobate, before you fall over," Harbour heard a familiar voice say.

Captain Cinders wrapped his arms around Dingles and slapped him heartily on the back. Harbour thought the spacer was close to tears.

"Captain, you know Harbour, I take it?"

"From our monthly meetings, of course," Jessie said smoothly. "How are you, Harbour?"

"Quite fine, Captain Cinders. Discovering places on station that I never knew existed, listening to wonderful stories, and discovering a part of Pyre unknown to me."

"Sounds like you've been busy."

"You have no idea, Captain Cinders," Harbour said, smiling brightly at Jessie. She could sense a small spike of anxiety from him.

"Dingles, can I take it that you're sitting here with Harbour because you've been released into her custody?"

"Yes, sir, be aboard the *Belle's* shuttle when she undocks."

"That's good, Dingles. I'm pleased to hear that. How you feeling?"

"Much better, Captain. Harbour helped me with my problem over in security administration. She says I'll get regular attention from the empaths."

From Jessie's perspective, Dingles resembled his old self. He laid a hand on the spacer's shoulder to indicate he should take a seat. "I'm grateful for your help with Dingles," Jessie said to Harbour and extended his hand.

"It's my pleasure," Harbour replied, accepting the handshake. Warm, deep sentiments flowed into her, and she held the captain's hand a little longer than was usual to bask in the pleasant sensation.

"You keep your head on straight, navigator," Jessie remarked to Dingles. He touched the brim of his cap to Harbour and sauntered over to join his crew for lunch.

"Before we go, Dingles, I'd like to have a word with the hostess. Ask her to join us?"

Harbour expected a decorous invitation from Dingles, while he was face-to-face with Maggie. Instead, the spacer blew a two-tone whistle, which everyone ignored but Maggie, who hurried over to the table.

"Trouble, Dingles?" asked Maggie, a frown on her face.

"Harbour wants a word, Maggie. Take a seat."

"My apologies, Maggie," Harbour said, as the woman sat down. "I wasn't aware that Dingles would get your attention in that manner. He and I will have a discussion on the subject later."

Maggie cut her eyes at Dingles. "Spacers," she said. "They're not known for their manners. How can I help you, ma'am?"

"Dingles tells me that there are a good number of spacers who visit the Miners' Pit and are suffering from emotional issues.

"That's true."

"Do you have access to the schedule of the commandant's monthly council meetings?"

"Sure do."

"I'd like you to line up the ten spacers most in need of this type of help. Have them meet me here before eleven hours, and I'll transport them to the *Belle* for the afternoon."

"Ma'am, the spacers don't have the coin for your sensitives."

"There'll be no charge, Maggie, and I want you to know this is only a test. It might not work out, so don't make a big deal of it."

"Even if it's just one time, ma'am, these people will appreciate whatever you can do for them." Maggie extended her real hand, and Harbour received the same warm appreciation as she had received from the captain. *I've been dealing too long with wealthy stationers and downsiders,* Harbour thought.

"You ready to go, Dingles?" Harbour asked, after Maggie returned to her post at the Miners' Pit front door.

"Ready to undock when you are, ma'am," Dingles replied. He stood, and, with one motion, he waved Harbour to the exit with his cap, which ended on his head. The lunch crowd broke out in loud whistles, yells, and applause. Dingles half turned and touched his fingers to his cap in acknowledgment. Harbour could sense the pride rolling off the old spacer.

Why is it that the people who risk the most to build our world are those least cared for in retirement by the very people who benefited from their efforts? Harbour thought.

At the shuttle, Harbour boarded first and Dingles followed. Harbour took her customary seat after slipping on her thermal coat.

"Who's the pilot, ma'am?" Dingles asked.

"Danny Thompson. Know him?"

"Oh, yeah," Dingles replied, grinning. He made his way to the forward cabin. The hatch was open, and Dingles shouted, "So what piece of space dirt thinks he can fly this ship?" He threw a grin at Harbour, and she shook her head, smiling at the ex-navigator's antics.

"Dingles, don't tell me you've been rescued," Danny said, emerging from the pilot's cabin. "Harbour, I'm telling you this one is trouble. Throw him back before it's too late."

"Sorry, Danny, we're past that point. Guess we'll have to make the best of it." Harbour was enjoying their exchange, including the way the two spacers buoyed each other's spirits.

"Sorry to hear what happened to you, Dingles," Danny said, turning serious.

"Yeah, well, I knew better than to antagonize Terror, but I wasn't feeling too good."

"Don't you worry, Dingles, you'll be okay while you're aboard the *Belle*," said Danny, and leaned close to whisper, "Has Harbour given you any, you know?" He signaled by pointing his finger at Dingles' head, then his own.

"Yeah, in security's interview room," Dingles whispered back. "I never felt anything like that in my life. I think if a man had that every day, he'd enter dreamland and never want to come out of it."

Danny laughed and slapped Dingles on the shoulder. "Get strapped in, you old spacer, we're about ready to take off."

Dingles made his way to the main cabin, saw where Harbour was seated, picked up his duffel, and sought a seat several rows behind her.

"Did I suddenly become ugly, Dingles?" Harbour asked, as the spacer passed her by.

"Begging your pardon, ma'am?" Dingles said, stopping in the aisle.

"There's no one else aboard this shuttle but you and me, and there's a spare seat next to me."

"Sorry, ma'am, I didn't want to inconvenience you."

"Your manners are appreciated, Dingles, but, if you care to share more stories of Captain Cinders, I'd like to hear them."

"That would be a pleasure," Dingles replied.

While the spacer stowed his duffel in a bin and settled next to Harbour, it occurred to her that she was accumulating a team of experienced spacers — pilot, navigator, engineers, and techs — and she wondered what might be the possibilities for the *Belle* with the help of these people.

11: Anxieties

Captain Hastings called his first mate, Angelina Mendoza, into his cabin. The *Pearl* had undocked from the YIPS after unloading her tanks and was making for a rendezvous with the *Annie,* before she set sail for Triton.

"Angie, our orders are to train Rules to be a qualified spacer," Leonard said, after she sat down at his table. "No designated specialty yet."

"You want us to turn a downsider into a spacer?" Angelina asked dubiously.

"I don't ... Captain Cinders does."

"But, Captain, what if she doesn't like the training or the trainer, and she does that you know what?" Angelina protested, pointing a finger at each of their heads.

"Well, we do have a choice," Leonard replied good-naturedly.

"I like choices."

"Okay, we can either annoy a sixteen-year-old empath or Captain Cinders. Which would you prefer?"

"I say we risk it with Rules."

"Good choice, Angie."

"I'll start her training immediately."

"Belay that, Angie. I want Belinda on the vac suit work. Let her know that Rules is required to get a rating from you at training's end."

"Captain, that's either incredibly wily of you or suicidal, I'm not sure which." When the captain merely smiled at her, Angelina excused herself to share the news with Belinda.

"Why me?" Belinda protested, when the first mate broke the news to her. "We've got a freighter full of qualified spacers who could teach Rules the ABCs of vac suits."

"Captain's orders," Angelina replied. "And this isn't to be some sort of pretend. Rules must pass a rating's exam at the end of her training."

"Angie —" Belinda started to object.

"Don't Angie me, Kilmer. You have your orders."

"Aye, aye," Belinda replied sullenly. It crossed her mind that if something went wrong with the training and the empath decided to take revenge, the captain wouldn't have to set her on station, which was Belinda's present course.

* * * *

Early the next morning, Aurelia waited anxiously for Belinda to arrive at the vac suit room. The thought of beginning spacer training excited her. She was ready to embrace anything that supported an independent, free life.

"Morning, Rules," said Belinda, by way of greeting. "Let me tell you how this goes. I'm going to take you through the basic procedures of a vac suit ... commands, operations, maintenance, and emergency drills. I train you, and First Mate Mendoza will test you. You do well; I look good. You screw up your practicals; I look bad. You read me?"

"Your instructions are clear, Third Mate Kilmer."

Belinda shook her head, and Aurelia could sense the woman's exasperation and something else that resembled anxiety. "Rules, if a command or instruction is clear to you, you say aye, copy, or understood. If you're about to jump into action you can say aye, aye. And another thing, newbie, you're not a member of this crew. To you, I'm Belinda."

"Understood, Belinda. I'll be a good student. I promise you."

"Well, we'll see about that. Your suit is the one with the *Spryte* emblem on the sleeve. Do you know your suit's name?" Belinda asked.

"Yes, but I wish to change it."

"Okay, we'll make that your first command lesson, once we get through basic orientation. The most important lesson this morning is how to don a vac suit by yourself and do it quickly. If there's a decompression accident, fire, or some other emergency, how quickly you can get into your suit will be the difference between you living or dying. You copy?"

"Copy that."

Belinda regarded Aurelia for a moment. For a teen, the girl had a serious demeanor, which boded well for the potential to successfully train her. "One more thing, newbie, your exam is a combination of questions and demonstrations. I can teach you the answers, but when it comes to the practical, you'll have to demonstrate the skills. I'll show you the tricks of getting into a vac suit quickly, but you'll need to practice it until you can do it blindfolded."

"Blindfolded?" Aurelia asked.

"Emergencies can stir the air so thick with debris, sucking all sorts of loose items up, or maybe it will be thick with acrid smoke. The idea is the more you handicap yourself when you practice, the better you'll be in an emergency. And here's the truth of being a spacer, Rules. We depend on one another. You screw up getting into your vac suit and someone stops to help you, you might both be dead."

"Likewise, if I'm quick, I can help another or assist in emergency repairs."

"Yeah, that's right, newbie," Belinda replied, slapping Aurelia lightly on the shoulder.

Aurelia saw the third mate freeze, and she detected her fear, and Aurelia assumed a deep scowl. A few seconds later, Aurelia broke into a grin and said, "Teasing you, Belinda. I don't break," and she tapped the woman on her shoulder.

Belinda swore, before breathing a sigh of relief. "Don't do that, newbie," she said.

When Aurelia chuckled, Belinda joined in. "You might just fit in to this collection of space rats, newbie. Let's get started. We'll lay out the suit, and I'll take you through the basics."

The women worked up to lunch break before Rules tried donning the suit unaided. It took her more than six minutes.

Aurelia took in Belinda's frown. "Too long?"

"According to our practical's minimum time, you died three times."

"Only three?"

"Yeah, newbie. Actually, not too bad for a first time. I've seen trainees take fifteen minutes. It looked like a wrestling match that they kept losing. Before we take a break, let's rename your suit."

Aurelia tapped the power button on her chest, waited until she felt air flow, and then donned and locked her helmet. She ran Frances through the suit check. Receiving a report of 100 percent on the systems, Aurelia said, "Frances, name change."

"Vac suit rename. Please state name," Frances replied.

"Jessie."

"New name accepted."

"Power off, Jessie."

"Powering down. Please detach helmet."

Belinda hid her smile from Aurelia when she heard the vac suit's new name, but she forgot that her newbie could sense her mirth.

When Aurelia pulled off her helmet, she regarded Belinda, who was surprised at the intensity of the girl's stare. "I like the captain," Aurelia stated firmly. "He's the first man who cared about me."

Belinda held her hands up in surrender. "It's your suit, newbie. You can call it what you want. Okay, strip out of it, hang it up, and let's get some lunch."

After the women collected food trays and found a free table, Belinda decided to ask the questions that had burned in her since first meeting Aurelia.

"Does it bother you, Rules, that the crew constantly stare at you, but, when you look their way, they duck their eyes?" Belinda asked. "I mean because of what you are?"

"And here I thought they were staring at me because I'm considered pretty," Aurelia replied, straight-faced, as she bit into a roll stuffed with cooked, spicy peppers, onions, and protein-cultured beef.

"Seriously?" Belinda asked.

"No," Aurelia replied, grinning, but she quickly sobered. "I know I frighten them. They're probably wondering who I'm going to kill next."

"Rules," Belinda said, shaking her head in disbelief. "You've got a really strange sense of humor."

"Aren't you frightened of me, Belinda?"

"More this morning than now, but I've got bigger worries. C'mon, newbie. Lunch is over; back to training."

If there was one thing that Belinda emphasized repeatedly to her trainee, it was, "In vacuum, newbie, the integrity and performance of your suit is your life. Ignore it, and you're dead."

At the end of the first day of training, the women were in Belinda's cabin talking late into the night. Aurelia yawned, and she sensed a spike of fear from Belinda, and the empath wondered why the third mate would have a dread of the night. It wasn't the first time Aurelia had felt an underlying anxiety that would peak when the subjects of tomorrow or the next morning were mentioned.

"Bunk time, newbie," Belinda ordered firmly.

Aurelia heard her words, but her lack of emotional conviction belied the words.

The next morning Aurelia rose early and sought out the first mate and found her talking to a crew member. Aurelia waited patiently until their conversation finished.

"How can I help you, Rules?" Angelina asked.

"What's wrong with Belinda?" Aurelia asked, without preamble.

"What do you mean? Is the training going poorly?"

"I mean what's wrong?" Aurelia repeated, tapping her temple with a finger.

"Oh, that. Come with me," Angelina replied and led Aurelia to her cabin for some privacy. Once the door closed, Angelina said, "Belinda is showing early signs of space dementia."

"What's that?"

"Over time, but sometimes quickly, a spacer feels the bulkheads are closing in on them. The first indication of trouble is that they request more and more vac suit time. Being outside the ship and working the mining equipment on the moon's surface gives them some relief. But when the dementia gets bad, even that doesn't help. Then their outside work makes them feel ... I don't know ... unanchored somehow."

"What happens to them when the dementia gets bad?"

"The captain puts them off on the JOS, but the station isn't any help to them. They usually get worse and end up incarcerated for some offense. Once closed up in a cell, the end comes quickly, usually by their own hands.

Sometimes, they're fortunate and Harbour picks them up to work on the *Belle*. The tough cases have to remain with her. They need support from the empaths for the rest of their life."

"Why don't they go downside?"

Angelina stared at Aurelia, her eyes narrowing. "They said you didn't get out of the governor's house much."

"I never got out," Aurelia replied. "I wasn't a guest; I was a prisoner."

"Sorry to hear that, Rules. But, know this: The families who govern the domes are not fond of stationers, and they like spacers even less. There's no way the families would let a mentally unbalanced spacer, least of all, live downside."

"Why don't the stationers and spacers do something about that?"

"Rules, for a bright girl, you don't know too much. Tell you what, go talk to the captain about politics and power. Right now, you're late for vac suit training."

Aurelia snatched her comm unit, a gift from Captain Hastings, and checked the time. Then she excused herself and hurried to the vac suit room.

Belinda was waiting for her and gave her a jaundiced eye, and Aurelia mumbled an apology.

In what Aurelia considered disciplining for showing up late, Belinda timed her getting into and out of her suit ten times. With the ship underway, gravity had been returned to the ship's wheel, which held the operational decks, and Aurelia was overheated and close to exhaustion from the weight of the gear. She activated the neck tab on the skins, which separated the garment down the back, and then she peeled off the top half down to her waist.

"What are you doing? Are you trying to start a riot?" Belinda said aghast.

"What's a riot?" Aurelia asked.

"It's the fight among the men that's going to take place to be first to get to that youthful body of yours."

"And do you think any of them has the courage to bother me?"

"You have a point there, newbie. Suit up, anyway. I don't want to be placed on report for you walking around half-naked."

Aurelia was hot, and she did want to cool off, but her primary purpose in stripping was to distract Belinda, making it easier to influence her emotions. She'd done the same thing for Sasha, inventing techniques to get her little sister's attention and then using the opportunities to calm Sasha's anger.

* * * *

Seeking out the captain, who was on the bridge, Angelina was about to enter when she heard Aurelia's voice say, "I'm prepared for my first lesson in power and politics, sir."

"And you're requesting these lessons, why?" Leonard replied.

"I asked the first mate why spacers suffering from space dementia weren't allowed to move downside, and she suggested that I ask you about these subjects," Aurelia replied.

"She did, did she? I'll have to remember to thank Angelina for the recommendation."

On that note, Angelina hurried away from the bridge, wondering how this would play out.

"Well, we have several more days before we rendezvous with the *Annie*, Rules, but I need you to complete your basic vac suit training."

"I finished my first practical yesterday, Captain. Angelina entered the results in the ship's logs."

Leonard spun around in his chair, accessed his monitor, and requested the personnel log on Rules. On the screen, he saw:

Personnel: Rules

Crew Status: Trainee

Practical: Vac Suit Level I

Reviewer: Angelina Mendoza, First Mate, the *Unruly Pearl*

Result: Superlative

Systems Operations Test: No errors

Suit Test: Donned in 1.46 minutes, while blindfolded; done at trainee's insistence.

"Well done, Aurelia," Leonard said. "Meet me in my captain's cabin for lunch, and we'll start your lessons in Pyrean politics."

After Aurelia left the bridge, Leonard picked up his comm unit and called Angelina. "Keep Belinda on Rules' training."

"Turns out you were wily, not suicidal, Captain," Angelina replied. "We're seeing success on both sides."

Angelina stopped in Belinda's cabin to give her the news. "Captain has you continuing to train our newbie."

"Message received," Belinda replied.

"That's it? No objections; no fight?"

"The newbie's an empath, and the *Pearl* needs a qualified officer to ensure Rules is trained properly. With me in charge of her training, she's less likely to kill anybody."

Angelina stared openmouthed at Belinda. "I swear you're beginning to sound like Rules," she said, and left the cabin shaking her head in disbelief.

Once Angelina was out of sight, Belinda smiled.

* * * *

Toby listened to the commandant's public announcement about Aurelia, the girl he knew as Rules. Later, he played it several times on his comm unit. The more he listened to it, the more certain he was that he had to talk to Captain Cinders before his BRC operation. The problem was Toby was frightened that security would see him talking to the captain, if he waited on the JOS side of the terminal arm. So, he hatched a plan, which would start with the *Spryte*'s navigator, who was doing a great deal of shopping lately.

"Captain," Jeremy said, handing off a note to Jessie. "A freckled-face kid of about ten or eleven with a leg cast says he knows you and asked me to pass this note to you."

Jessie opened the note. Scrawled in poor handwriting, it read: "Need to talk to you about you know who. The Miners' Pit at noon."

There was still time to make the appointment, and Jessie thought there was no harm in having lunch at the Pit today. Ten minutes later, Jessie was striking the palm-sized actuator at the Pit's hatch and striding into the cantina.

"Captain, good to see you," Maggie said. "You have a table guest," she added, indicating a far corner table where Toby waited.

"Still waiting for your BRC?" Jessie asked, when he sat across the table from the boy.

"In two days, Captain Cinders."

"Good luck to you, son," Jessie said. "What did you want to talk to me about?"

"Security hauled me in to their administration offices."

"I imagine they offered you the reward."

"That was the first thing the sergeant said. That twenty-five thousand is a whole lot of coin. Do you think someone will turn her in to collect it?"

Jessie hid his smile. Toby glossed over the idea that he would be interested in the reward. "It's been days since the commandant announced the reward. If no one's come forward by now, then I think she's found a safe place to hide."

"I hope so," Toby replied wistfully, and then he added, "Captain, the lieutenant kept calling the girl Aurelia, but she called herself Rules."

"And what did you call her?"

Toby grinned. "I didn't call her anything. I told the lieutenant that she never gave me her name."

"Now, why would you do that, son?"

"The name's —"

Jessie cut Toby off with a wave of his hand. "Better I don't know your name, son."

"Understood, Captain. I didn't tell the lieutenant Rules' name because of that announcement. It doesn't make sense to me. They say Rules is a killer, but the girl who helped me and played freefall with me couldn't be the same one, could it?"

"You saw her photo on the announcement, right?"

"Yeah."

"Same girl, right?

"Yeah."

"Did you tell security that the girl who helped you into the terminal arm was the same one?"

"Of course, I did, Captain. I'm young, but I'm not stupid. They would have Rules and me on security vids."

"Yes, they would."

"Did you talk to her, Captain?"

Jessie wanted to allay Toby's concerns, but the details of his contact with Aurelia were too dangerous to share with a young boy. "Son, I think what's important in life is that we make our own judgments about the people we meet and don't accept the opinions of others about them. You often don't know the reason people say the things they do."

Toby thought that through for a minute and then nodded his head in agreement. "Aye, Captain," he said.

Jessie ruffled the boy's head. "Open your comm unit, son."

Toby thumbed his device open, and Jessie entered a comm number on the projected screen. "Let's say that you and I met, and I asked you to call me and tell me how your BRC operation went," Jessie said and winked at Toby.

"Aye, aye, Captain Cinders," Toby replied excitedly and returned the wink.

"You had lunch yet, son?"

"Don't have the coin, Captain."

Jessie signaled Maggie over to the table.

"You two ready to order?" Maggie asked.

"I can't stay, Maggie, but the boy is having lunch on the house. Anything he wants."

"Understood, Captain," Maggie replied.

Jessie touched Toby's head and winked at him again before he made for the exit.

12: Stalked

Corporal Terrell McKenzie haunted security's monitoring suite, spending hours each day tracking the *Spryte*'s crew the moment they exited the terminal arm where the ship was docked. He quietly cursed the screens when vid cams lost the crew, which frequently happened when they penetrated deeper into the station's interior or moved up or down to less-traveled levels.

The usual complement of monitoring personnel quietly ignored the corporal's whispered, angry comments and expletives, which littered his time in the suite.

However, Terrell's demeanor changed drastically one day. He'd tracked a young, *Spryte* crew member, he'd identified as Jeremy Kinsman, to a shop. That, in itself was nothing unusual, but Terrell recalled seeing Jeremy shopping the day before. While keeping an eye on the present cam, which was stationed outside a spacer's supply shop, Terrell ran a search for Jeremy from the previous two days. His search pulled up the navigator purchasing skins one day and deck shoes the next.

Rocking his chair slowly in anticipation, Terrell waited for Jeremy to exit the shop. When the spacer left, the corporal was sadly disappointed to see that the spacer carried nothing in his arms. Unwilling to let go of a niggling thought, Terrell jumped up and raced from the monitoring suite.

Minutes later, Terrell walked into the Latched On and approached the man behind the counter. From the disgusted look on the man's face, Terrell knew he didn't have to identify himself.

"You had a customer in here minutes ago," Terrell announced, showing the man Jeremy's photo on his comm unit.

"You have a warrant for our customer information?" Gabriel shot back.

"Not at this time. But I'm prepared to hang out at the front of your store until I'm ready to go on shift," Terrell replied, "which is in about four hours," he added, consulting his comm unit.

"You can hang by any part you want to, Corporal," Gabriel ground out. "Spacers won't be intimidated by you."

Terrell was about to retort when he felt a bump against his shoulder blade. Glancing behind him, Terrell found three spacers had closed in on him.

"Help you, boys?" Gabriel asked congenially.

"No hurry, Gabriel; you finish your business with Terror here. We're happy to keep the corporal company, while you see to his needs," said the largest of the spacers, and the group pressed a little closer to Terrell.

"Back off, unless you'd like a taste of this," Terrell snarled, and he patted the shock stick at his side.

"That's a pretty little thing, isn't it, men? I wonder what Terror would look like wearing it as an ornament in an inconvenient orifice?"

Terrell growled, shoved past the spacers, and stalked out of the store. His ears burned from the laughter he heard behind him.

Not to be defeated, Terrell returned to the monitoring suite early the next day and focused on the cam in the main promenade, which captured foot traffic entering and leaving the Latched On. He wasn't rewarded with what he sought until the following day.

"Yes," Terrell hissed, when he saw Jeremy enter the store. The corporal's eyes remained glued to the screen, confident he could play back his recording any time he wished. A half hour later, Jeremy pushed a cart of material out the doors of the Latched On, and Terrell froze the image. He expanded the shot, focusing on the goods on the cart. It carried a full vac suit — helmet, accessory bag, backpack, and suit.

Terrell jumped to the JOS personnel database and checked Jeremy's employment record. He found he'd been the navigator of the *Spryte* for less than six months. A vac suit would have been required day one before boarding the ship, and, typically, the captain would have lent the new recruit the coin to outfit his position, taking it out of his earnings over time.

"So why do you need a new vac suit, skins, deck shoes, and other gear, spacer?" Terrell whispered to the screen, and a nasty grin crossed his face, as an answer occurred to him. He searched the JOS logs of ship movements, which every captain was required to file. The *Spryte* had recently visited the

YIPS to drop off a load of ingots. Coincidentally, the *Pearl* was at the YIPS at the same time.

Terrell leaned back in his chair and stroked his chin. "The question is, Captain," Terrell murmured, "did you put Aurelia on the *Pearl* or is that a feint, and you have her hidden aboard the *Spryte?*" What nagged at Terrell was he couldn't figure out why Cinders would have wanted to give Aurelia a spacer's vac suit, if that's what he did.

Despite the questions, Terrell decided he had enough to push his superiors to act. The corporal caught up with Sergeant Rodriguez and presented his evidence, but the sergeant immediately jumped it up to his lieutenant. Recognizing the explosive nature of the request and the circumstantial but convincing details Terrell had collected, Devon took it up with his captain, Liam Finian.

Minutes later, Commandant Strattleford was listening to Terrell's recital. "That's it?" he asked when Terrell finished, and the corporal nodded enthusiastically.

"Admittedly, it looks suspicious, sir," Liam added, "but I can think of other reasons why Kinsman might have given up his gear. The captain of the *Pearl* might have hired a crew member off the YIPS and requested immediate supply from Captain Cinders. It might be a coincidence that Kinsman and Aurelia have similar builds."

Emerson thought for a moment before he made up his mind. "Request denied, Corporal. If you're wrong, and the odds are against you, then Cinders will be filing harassment charges with the Review Board. Simply put, Cinders is a much-too-popular captain to antagonize. Bring me some hard evidence, and I'll reconsider your request. Dismissed."

Terrell left the commandant's office incensed and made straight for his cabin. For his next call, he needed privacy. Closing his cabin door, Terrell opened his comm unit and selected Giorgio Sestos' number.

* * * *

"Captain, we've got a problem," Ituau announced.

"Talk to me," Jessie replied.

"I've heard from two sources that Terror is tracking our crew, and he's singled out Jeremy."

"How definitive is your information?"

"I've got a friend, who works in security's monitoring suite. She says Terror has spent days focused on cams to see where our crew goes when aboard the JOS. Then Gabriel at the Latched On said Terror walked into his shop minutes after Jeremy left. The corporal showed him a photo of Jeremy, heading into his store, and said he wanted to know what the customer bought."

"Your friend in security, is she reliable?"

"We're close, Captain, real close, many times," Ituau said, grinning.

"Spare me the details," Jessie replied. He sat down at his cabin's table to think and motioned to Ituau to take a seat. "Terror hasn't let go of his suspicion that Rules never left the *Spryte*. He's determined to find evidence of that."

"That's my guess, Captain. If Terror was watching the entire crew, he saw Jeremy buying a whole new set of gear, and he's asking himself why."

"I presume Terror got nothing out of Gabriel?" Jessie asked, chuckling.

Ituau smiled in return. She knew the captain's question was rhetorical.

"But, if that little piece of effluent didn't get what he wanted?" Jessie posited. "Then, he'd monitor or record that cam until Jeremy returned. What did the boy pick up? A vac suit?"

"Afraid so, Captain."

"This means Terror might have stumbled on to the similar builds of Jeremy and Rules."

"But Terror wouldn't know for sure that Rules isn't aboard our ship anymore," Ituau reasoned.

"Which means the corporal will be anxious to find out. I think Terror might target Jeremy," Jessie concluded. "From now on, crew members leave the *Spryte* in groups of two or more for safety, and, if they encounter Terror, they are under no circumstances to start an altercation with him. I want that clearly understood."

"Aye, Captain," Ituau replied. The tone in Jessie's voice said he would brook no disregarding of his order. "What about Jeremy? Should we keep him aboard?"

"No, that would only alert Terror that we're watching him, which would make him think he's on to something concerning Rules. Furthermore, I don't want any suspicion to fall on your friend in security, as a possible source of our information. We'll let Jeremy continue as usual, but he's always to be in the company of two other crew members."

"Understood, Captain. I'll occasionally mix up the crew to make the threesome look random."

"Do that, Ituau, and stress to those you assign to accompany Jeremy that if they slip up and let him out of their sight, it could be medical or worse for our navigator."

"Aye, aye, Captain," Ituau replied, rising from the table and exiting the cabin.

* * * *

When Lise Panoy finished her call with Giorgio Sestos, she drummed a well-manicured set of fingernails on the chair's arm. What had appeared to be a golden opportunity to overthrow the Andropov family was constantly and frustratingly attempting to slip through her hands.

To complicate matters, Lise was suspicious that Sestos wasn't bought, as she had first believed. She considered the possibility that he was playing a double game. For all she knew, the entire story of Dimitri's death by an enraged empath was pure fiction. She imagined for a moment that it was an elaborate trap by the governor. If the family heads took the bait and swallowed the story, they exposed themselves as enemies of the Andropov family.

Unfortunately, if the story was a trap, Lise couldn't figure an alternate move. A girl did exist, and she did run from the domes to the JOS. Unless she was a paid actress, they needed to locate that individual and find out the truth. Lise picked up her comm unit and placed a call.

"I hope this isn't another late revelation, Lise," the JOS commandant replied.

"No, Emerson, this is a complaint about the effectiveness of your security forces. How much time do you need to locate one girl on a station? It's not like she could fly away," Lise replied hotly.

"We had a solid lead, Lise, but it didn't develop."

"Would that be a sniffer detecting the girl aboard the *Spryte*?"

"You're remarkably well informed, Lise."

Lise ignored the commandant's attempt to gain information about her sources. She dropped the *Spryte*'s name to tell him that his actions were being monitored, nothing more. "I understand your best DAD operator wasn't allowed to investigate the ship. That was quite foolish of your senior people."

"Not much we could do about it. Captain Cinders did allow my lieutenant and his sergeant aboard, and they are qualified with a DAD."

"Not the same thing as an expert operating the device, is it though?" When Lise didn't get a reply, she pushed the commandant for what she wanted. "Is the *Spryte* in dock?"

"Wait," Emerson replied, while he pulled up the terminal arms statuses. "Yes, she's docked."

"Then I strongly suggest, Commandant, you get your expert over to that ship and prove once and for all that the girl isn't aboard. Otherwise, the families will be requesting the station elect a new commandant, who can handle these tragic situations." Before Emerson could respond, Lise severed the connection.

Emerson fumed for a half hour before he got control of his anger and called Major Finian into his office.

"Give Corporal McKenzie permission to carry out a DAD search on the *Spryte*."

"What's changed, Commandant?" Liam asked.

"Not a damn thing, but I'm getting pressure from downside to locate the girl, and I've decided to investigate every possibility, no matter how remote."

"Should I give Captain Cinders a heads-up?"

"Absolutely not. Make it a surprise visit. Oh, and Major, make sure that Terrell has support."

"Support?" Liam queried.

"Let's think of them as witnesses, in case the corporal's visit to the *Spryte* ends up creating more effluence than we can process. You read me, Major?"

"Understood, sir," Liam said, quickly retreating from the commandant's office. *Why can't I get a decent commanding officer?* Liam thought, as he made for Lieutenant Higgins' office.

Next, it was Devon's turn to inform Sergeant Rodriguez.

"Will you be accompanying me to the *Spryte*?" Miguel asked.

"It won't be necessary, Sergeant. You'll be sitting right here in my office when the corporal goes on his quest."

"I hate to be dense, Lieutenant, but could you explain this to me? Aren't we supporting McKenzie?"

"Yes, we're sending three privates to accompany him. As the major explained it to me, the commandant wants witnesses, in case the corporal makes a hash of his investigation."

"But he won't have a superior officer along? Isn't that asking for trouble, what with the corporal's reputation?"

"Let me ask you, Miguel," Devon said, leaning across the sergeant's desk. "Imagine these two scenarios. Aurelia is on the ship; Aurelia isn't on the ship. Now, also imagine that you and I have led the search of the *Spryte* for a second time. What do you think the outcome of the two scenarios would be for either of us?"

Miguel leaned back in his chair. He envisioned demanding access to the *Spryte* and requiring Captain Cinders to allow McKenzie to board the ship, per the commandant's orders. If they found the girl, he would have to take Cinders into custody, and he winced at that thought. If they didn't find the girl, he would have insulted the spacers' most respected captain. Both scenarios were lose-lose prospects. "You're absolutely right, Lieutenant. Your office is a much better place to wait out McKenzie's search."

"Right you are, Sergeant. Give McKenzie his marching orders.

* * * *

"This is the terminal arm manager calling the *Spryte*," Jessie heard over the bridge speakers. He flicked the link on his chair's comm board. "This is Captain Cinders. Go ahead, Penelope."

"You have inbound, Captain. Corporal McKenzie and three security newbies are translating through the ring. They're headed for your arm. And, Captain, be aware, Terror is wearing one effluent-eating grin."

"Understood, Penelope. Appreciate the heads-up."

"You want me to call anybody, Captain?"

"No, Penelope, we're fine out here."

"You be careful, Captain."

"Will do, Penelope. *Spryte* out."

Jessie jumped out of his chair, thumbed his comm unit, and called his three officers. The officers gathered every crew member, and the group met Jessie in the axis corridor next to the exit airlock.

"We have guests, Terror and three privates. No officers." When the crew started to grumble, Jessie growled, "Zip it. You follow my next orders explicitly, and you be good little spacers. Copy?" A rousing chorus of assent came back from the crew.

"We file off the ship, and you take an outward arm position and remain silent. I want neutral expressions on each and every face. I'll be the one greeting our guests."

If deck shoes would have allowed strutting, Terrell would have been doing that as he exited the cap and walked the length of the arm toward the *Spryte*. He felt redeemed and was determined to search every meter of the *Spryte* to prove to his superiors that he'd been right. *You can't hide from me now,* he thought.

Terrell's purposeful step faltered when he saw the crew of the *Spryte* flood out of the ship. That they took up a position arm outward leaving him open access to the gangway encouraged him, and he resumed his stride.

"Captain Cinders, I have orders —" Terrell stopped, when Jessie held a hand up to his face.

"I get it, Terror. You have an itch that you need to scratch. Be my guest, and search the ship. Mind you, I'm warning you in front of witnesses that you're not to touch anything electronic or any personal items. Furthermore, I'm giving permission for you alone to enter the ship. The three privates will remain outside with me.

Terrell regarded the looks on his security team. They appeared indifferent, and he tipped his head, saying, "Wait out here." To Jessie, he added, "I don't expect to encounter anyone aboard your ship, except the girl!"

"Enjoy yourself, Terror," Jessie said, standing aside, and sweeping an arm toward the gangway. That he continued to antagonize the corporal seemed childish. A better man wouldn't do it, but then he didn't aspire to be that kind of person.

After Terrell entered the ship, the *Spryte*'s crew and the three security privates mingled amicably. There were friends and acquaintances between the two groups, and none of them had any fondness for Terrell McKenzie.

Inside the ship, the corporal spent an hour checking the ship from top to bottom — bridge, cabins, galley, heads, wardrooms, vac suit rooms, and anything he could think of except the bays, which were in vacuum. In that regard, he wished he'd thought to bring a vac suit. But his belief that Captain Cinders had insufficient warning to put the girl in a vac suit and hide her in a bay made him feel confident that searching them was unnecessary.

When Terrell exited the *Spryte,* there was a quick reshuffling of people, as they separated into crew and security.

Jessie made a show of expectantly scanning the gangway behind the corporal. "Where's the girl, Terror?" he asked in mock seriousness.

Terrell bit his tongue. Anything he said now would put him in jeopardy with superiors.

A female private asked what Terrell found, and he snarled at the privates to fall in.

But before Terrell could take a step, Jessie commanded, "Halt," which brought the security detail up short. "Corporal McKenzie, you've been aboard a ship unaccompanied by a ship or security officer. Under the

Captain's Articles, I insist that you be searched to ensure you aren't carrying away any ship's items or crew's personal effects.

"That's not going to happen, Captain," Terrell snarled and turned to walk away, but his path was blocked by the privates.

"Sorry, Corporal," a male private apologized. "The captain is within his rights to insist on the search, and the three of us are in jeopardy of reprimands, if not a Review Board hearing, if we fail to comply. Better we get this over with. Please raise your hands."

"Don't touch me," Terrell threatened and backed away from his security team.

"If you prefer, Terror, I can have my crew conduct the search. But, one way or the other, it's going to happen," Jessie said, his eyes holding the corporal's.

Terrell watched the *Spryte*'s crew fan out behind his team, anticipatory gleams in their eyes. "Fine, but my people conduct the search," he said, and held his arms out wide.

The private, who had encouraged Terrell to submit to the captain's request, quickly searched him, turning out pockets for the captain's viewing.

When the search was complete, Terrell heaped all the scorn he could into his voice, asking, "Are you satisfied, Captain?"

"Oh, completely," Jessie replied with a bright smile.

The *Spryte*'s crew broke out into laughter, and Terrell turned red-faced. He didn't order his people to follow him. He simply turned and made for the arm's exit. The privates didn't bother to keep close with Terrell, which enabled the corporal to catch a cap by himself. He stomped his way to the commandant's office, where Major Finian waited for him in the outer vestibule.

Liam took one look at the corporal's face and heaved a sigh. "Let's get this over with," he said, knocking on the commandant's doorway.

"Come, Captain," Emerson replied. "Okay, Corporal, let's have your report."

Terrell noticed Major Finian ease toward the commandant in an attempt to distance himself from the coming fallout. "Nothing, sir," was all Terrell said.

"Elaborate, Corporal," Emerson commanded.

"There was absolutely no sniff of the girl's DNA. There should have been some residual pickup from when Lieutenant Higgins was aboard the ship. If I could have boarded the *Spryte* then, I'm sure I would have found her."

"Corporal, you've insisted Captain Cinders was involved with our suspect to the point that the families are clamoring that I support you. So, I gave you a chance. Now, you're telling me there's no proof whatsoever?" Emerson's voice took on the shrillness that underscored his anger.

"Sir, the only way this could have happened is by Captain Cinders opening his ship to vacuum to remove any trace of the girl's DNA."

"Corporal, do you not know that a ship's captain routinely opens his ship to space?" Liam asked. "He does it to clear out dust and fine debris that are fire hazards. The process also rids the ship of vermin. Then again, a captain could be practicing vac suit drills in the event of decompression emergencies."

Terrell felt the hard stares of his superiors, and, at that moment, he hated Captain Cinders with every fiber of his being.

"Thank you, Corporal, you're dismissed," Emerson said curtly.

"Please, sir —" Terrell began to plead.

"March, Corporal McKenzie," Devon ordered harshly.

Terrell left the commandant's office totally defeated, and anger simmered deep within him. Unfortunately, a coin-kitty or kat would need medical attention tonight when Terror finished with them, and another establishment would be placed off limits to him.

13: *Honora Belle*

After Harbour's meeting with Captain Cinders aboard the JOS, she had spent hours in her cabin. She was dismayed that she had refused his request to take Aurelia off his hands. She tried to excuse her actions with the thought that the commandant's announcement had negated that option. "Don't start lying to yourself," Harbour often remonstrated herself, as she sat in her favorite chair, one finger twisting a strand of hair. It was a habit of hers when deep in reflection.

For close to a century, a détente had existed among the various groups of Pyre. No one was happy with their lot in the arrangement, but, then again, a better alternative hadn't been found. Now, one empath accused of murder was about to destroy the delicate balance of power, and she'd undermined the only man in Pyre who could facilitate that. Not that Jessie Cinders might intend to do that. He was just the sort of stubborn, fair-minded individual who wouldn't back down from a fight.

"Time to pick a side," Harbour muttered. The thought frightened her. Safety lay in staying out of the way of the internal squabbles of the families, the commandant, the Review Board, and the demands of the spacers. But, underlying all her concerns was the realization that, whether she liked it or not, Jessie Cinders was going to force everyone to declare their allegiances. And Harbour was the pragmatic sort. In her opinion, the more difficult a decision, the sooner it should be faced.

One day, having made up her mind to take action, Harbour sorted through the options she might have and the obstacles facing each one. When an outlandish idea occurred to her, she laughed out loud. "Why not?" she said, slapping the arms of her chair. She grabbed her comm unit and pulled up a list of ex-spacers who were residents of the *Belle*.

Two hours later, Harbour met in a conference room with a group of thirty-plus ex-spacers. In concert with the previous Harbour, the *Belle* had collected a pilot, although not qualified on a colony ship, a navigator, an assortment of engineers and techs qualified on environment and propulsion systems, and a bunch of crew, all vac suit qualified.

"I apologize for the conditions of our meeting room," Harbour said, when she noted most of the people were dusting off chairs before sitting down. "Obviously, this room hasn't been used in a long while, but that might change soon."

The spacers, who had never been called to a meeting exclusive to their sort, went from curious to attentive.

"The residents of the *Belle* and I have appreciated what you've done and will do for this ship. Some of you are still serving out your sentences, and the rest of you have chosen to make this ship your home. Now, I have something important to ask of you. I need your experience as spacers. First, I want to know what conditions would hamper the movement of the *Belle*. Second, I want to know what materials and technical expertise we would need to prepare it for flight. And third, I want to know what additional people we would need to crew her."

"Pardon me, ma'am, but are you nuts?" Pete Jennings asked.

Harbour took no umbrage at Pete's manners. He was one of the empaths' lifelong cases. Heavily burned in an accident aboard the YIPS, medical had done wonders repairing his body, but he was left scarred with attenuated mobility. A brilliant engineer, Pete chafed when dismissed from his job, and he spiraled into a hole of depression. Due to uncontrolled fits of anger, Pete landed repeatedly in confinement. At the last Review Board, Pete was warned that one more incident would see him incarcerated for life.

Dingles, on the other hand, had no such reason to accommodate a fellow spacer, injured or not, and he growled, "Hook on, spacer."

"Aye, latched on," Pete replied sullenly.

Harbour realized the dynamics taking place. Dingles was the senior spacer, and, without a captain in their midst, the others deferred to him. From Pete, Harbour sensed anger at the reprimand, but she picked up something else. It was faint but warm, where so much of Pete's emotions typically were cold.

"You were saying, ma'am," Dingles said.

"You're familiar with Captain Cinders, even though most of you didn't crew for him on any of his ships. Well, the captain has gone and done something either incredibly foolish or brave."

"Knowing Captain Cinders, it's probably both," Danny Thompson called out, which started the spacers laughing.

Harbour could feel the renewed emotions circulating around the room. The men were galvanized by the nature of the meeting, spacers only, and the topics of conversation. Spacers, discussing the moving of a giant, colony ship and the actions of a popular captain, did wonders for their confidence and pride.

"Captain Cinders is sheltering the murderer who JOS security is seeking," Harbour said, dropping the statement into the room like an asteroid striking the planet.

Most of the spacers were stunned, but Dingles asked the simple question, "Why?"

It was what Harbour was hoping to hear. She needed the spacers thinking and questioning.

"The girl who security is chasing is sixteen years old. She admitted to Captain Cinders that she killed Dimitri Belosov, but it was in self-defense. But, the telling point of her story is that she told Captain Cinders she did the deed with her mind. She's an empath, and the governor is her father."

Angry shouts directed at the governor and downsiders, in general, followed Harbour's announcement. Dingles took a stance beside Harbour and shouted for order, and the spacers complied. Danny raised his hand, and Dingles acknowledged him.

"Word is that security has searched the *Spryte* twice and not found the girl," Danny said.

"That's what I hear, Danny," Harbour replied. "I don't know what Captain Cinders did with the girl, but I think it's important that you know that I've heard all of this directly from him. He hoped to pass the girl to me, but it was too late. The commandant's announcement and reward hit the public comm before we came to a decision." Harbour was grateful that the spacers weren't empaths. Surely, they would have detected her regret in telling the lie that she'd refused the captain's request to take Aurelia aboard the *Belle*.

"How far do you intend to move the *Belle*, ma'am?" asked Bryan Forshaw, who was the next to be acknowledged. Bryan was a propulsion engineer who'd lost his right arm and leg. His prosthetics facilitated most of his everyday needs but not the delicate work required for sophisticated engine maintenance. He'd adopted two orphans, a brother and sister, from the JOS and was often heard to say that in another two years the teens would be tech spacers, qualified to work under an engineering officer. Then he would often add, "Give me five years with them, and I'll make them junior engineers."

"How far do I need to move the *Belle* to make a statement to the rest of Pyre and keep the ship out of the reach of JOS security?" Harbour replied.

The spacers shared grins. This was the sort of challenge they loved, and they started arguing the merits of their suggestions among themselves.

Dingles kept an eye on Harbour, and when she looked at him for assistance, he shouted "Hook on."

"Aye, latched on," came a unified shout.

"Before you start figuring out the answers to my requests, I've got a few more to add," Harbour said into the quiet. "Some of you have general spacer backgrounds handling supplies for your ships. I need to know what it would take to maintain our independence for up to a year. That means food, water, and sundry supplies. I need a list."

"Ma'am, what's the aim of all these preparations?" Dingles asked.

Harbour could see and sense the spacers' anticipation ratchet up. "I think Captain Cinders has taken the first step in declaring war against the families by protecting Aurelia. I don't know whether he's thought it through to that point, but there's going to be major repercussions from his actions, once they're discovered. When that happens, people are going to have to choose a side."

"What's the expected outcome?" Pete asked.

Harbour hid her smile. Pete had raised a hand to be recognized by Dingles. It amazed her how quickly individuals fell back into their old habits, despite the horrific trauma they'd suffered. "My hope is that we can force a new agreement that gets Pyre a democratically elected government — no commandant, no governor, no family heads, and no Review Board. We return to a balanced, three-part system of elected representatives, judges, and a leader, but, before we get there, I expect a protracted fight."

"A fight with what, ma'am? Shock sticks?" asked a tech incredulously.

"If you had a ship out by Pyre's first or second moon, what would hurt you over time?"

"Oh, for the love of Pyre," the tech groaned. "Food, water, medical ... the very things you asked us to consider supplying the *Belle* with for at least a year."

"That's absolutely right," Harbour replied. "This could turn out to be a war of attrition. And, who do you think is best able to weather that type of conflict?"

An answer wasn't necessary, and the spacers didn't offer one. It was common knowledge that the downsiders held the upper hand. The domes sent their excess food topside to supplement what the JOS and the *Belle* could cultivate in their hydroponic gardens. In exchange, the JOS supplied the other parties with protein and hydroponic vegetables. In addition, the domes were the primary source of water, which they obtained from deep wells. The El car contained tanks below the cargo level, and every trip downside saw the car's tanks filled and then emptied once aboard the JOS. In the past half year, the YIPS had produced copious quantities of hydrogen, but oxygen was in short supply. Until there was a plentiful supply of that gas from production, the stationers and spacers would have to depend on the downsiders for most of their water.

"There is the option to stay out of the fight," Dingles said.

Harbour heard the spacer's words, but she sensed his humor. Dingles was asking the question to satisfy those individuals who might be thinking the same thing, even though he didn't believe it to be possible. "I'm afraid if we don't take Captain Cinders' side, the governor might become the defacto leader of Pyre — the domes, the stations, this ship, and every mining ship.

The spacers grumbled at the concept, and Dingles asked for more questions. When there were none, he turned to Harbour and said, "Ma'am, if you'll excuse us, we have some thinking and then some work to do. You'll be receiving your reports soon."

Harbour nodded her appreciation and turned to leave, when she heard Dingles shout, "Captain on deck."

The spacers jumped to attention, and Harbour turned to face them. They were grinning, and she was stunned.

"A ship in motion needs a captain, ma'am," Dingles said, touching the brim of his cap in salute.

Harbour was without words, and she left the spacers to get to work. Once in the corridor, she muttered, "What have I gotten myself into?"

* * * *

When Harbour had a moment to herself, she enjoyed a snack, while curled up in her chair. On her mind were the steps she initiated with the spacers. The one element that concerned her more than anything was her reading of Jessie Cinders. If she was wrong about how far he would go to protect Aurelia, then she would be making a great mistake to side with him.

It occurred to her that data was available to her that she hadn't investigated, which might help her understand the man. Harbour moved to her desk monitor and linked her comm unit. She accessed the JOS personnel database. As the defacto leader of the *Honora Belle*, she had a captain-level clearance. *And once this ship moves, I'll actually be a captain. A captain without experience and training,* Harbour thought. She wanted to laugh, but the idea scared her too much.

Harbour pulled up the contact list of her spacers and requested which ships they'd previously served on. Only three of them had crewed on any of Cinders' ships. The captain had close to one-fifth of the mining fleet, but less than one-fifteenth of the spacers, who had suffered injury of one sort or the other, were his.

Not sure what that factoid told Harbour, she queried for a list of retired spacers, within the past ten years, who were in active employment on the JOS. She matched that list to the last ship each spacer served on. This time,

Cinders' people were more than 40 percent. *So, captain, your people fare better in retirement and you have fewer injured than your contemporaries,* Harbour thought.

Resorting to her previous query, Harbour pulled up the ledger on the *Belle's* general fund. She eliminated every transaction but those of her anonymous donor and compared the dates of when the three spacers, who had served on Cinders' ships, first came aboard the colony ship.

"Will you look at that?" Harbour whispered, staring at her monitor. The first deposit occurred four days after the arrival of the first spacer. The donation doubled when the second spacer came aboard; and it was now three times greater than originally with the addition of Dingles. *Why, Captain Cinders, you're crusty on the outside and soft on the inside,* Harbour thought, smiling.

* * * *

Harbour organized a second meeting. It was with her empaths. They crowded into the space reserved for empath training. Harbour took in the faces of the individuals, who were so precious to her. There was only one woman more than twenty years older than Harbour, but there were nine young trainees, who averaged twenty years younger than her.

There were older empaths, who couldn't attend the meeting. One of the difficulties of aging sensitives was that at a certain point in their lives, they lost the ability to close their mental gates. Experience and capability grew with age, and then suddenly it was all useless, because of the loss of the control side.

Once laid wide open to the emotions of others, the older women felt constantly bombarded. They withdrew to quieter areas of the *Belle* and were visited only by other empaths, who could control the emotions they communicated.

The former Harbour had gone that way, while she was grooming her protégé, Celia O'Riley, who now stood in front of the assembled empaths.

"I've discovered the name of our anonymous donor. We've just adopted our third spacer from his ships and our donations have increased again. It's Captain Cinders."

"Do you realize, Harbour, that you're broadcasting when you mention the captain?" Yasmin asked.

If Harbour had a sister, it would be Yasmin, despite the fact that they looked nothing alike. The two girls had come aboard the *Belle* for training within months of each other and had bonded. Yasmin, who displayed the features of her East Indian heritage, was nearly as powerful an empath as Harbour.

"Is it possible, Harbour, you've recently spent some personal time with the captain?" Nadine, the eldest sensitive, asked. She made it sound casual, but she had a twinkle in her eye.

Harbour, feeling her skin flush, clamped down on her mental gates.

When the empaths sensed Harbour's broadcast shut off, they turned and smiled at one another.

"I think we can take that as a yes," Yasmin said to the group, and the women chuckled and tittered.

"It looks as if we've made a mistake servicing the stationers and downsiders, when we should have been servicing the spacers," Nadine said drily, and the group burst into laughter.

Harbour could understand the women's desire to vicariously enjoy a personal connection with a normal. None of them, including Harbour, had ever had a successful one. Communication between partners was difficult enough, without one side worrying that the other might be manipulating their emotions, and the other side sensing emotions from their partner that were never meant to be shared.

"Enough about the captain and me," Harbour said evenly. "Sooner than we might have wished, we've come to a critical crossroads. Captain Cinders has told me that the girl security is seeking is an empath, and she admits to killing Dimitri, whom she claims was abusing her. The weapon was her mind."

Unlike the spacers, who tended to be a boisterous lot, the women in front of Harbour sat quietly, mulling over the news, and formulating their questions.

"How does Captain Cinders know this?" Nadine asked.

"The girl, Aurelia, snuck aboard the *Spryte*. Captain Cinders found her and hid her before security searched the ships on his terminal arm."

"Now, isn't that interesting? A captain standing up for an empath, and Cinders at that," Nadine commented.

"I'm curious, Harbour, how could a young downsider sneak aboard a mining ship?" Yasmin asked.

"According to Captain Cinders, Aurelia lulled the airlock duty crew member to sleep by hanging on a rail outside the ship."

"That powerful," a young empath was heard to utter.

"Captain Cinders hid her the first time, but do we know where Aurelia is now?" Nadine asked.

"Security ran a second search on the *Spryte* and didn't find her. I surmise the captain has moved her somewhere else, but that's conjecture on my part."

"We don't know where Aurelia is hiding, and we've no proof that she killed Dimitri in self-defense. It doesn't sound as if there is any way we can help her," Yasmin said.

"Phrased in that narrow manner, I would agree with you, Yasmin, but I think there's a greater conflict looming. Aurelia is just the beginning." Harbour laid out the details of Aurelia's imprisonment with her family, the events leading up to Dimitri's death, Aurelia's escape to the JOS, and her contact with Captain Cinders.

"Judging by the emotions leaking from my sisters," Nadine commented, "we're all upset by the horrendous acts committed against Aurelia, but I, for one, am unsure of what you expect of us."

"Previous to this meeting, I gathered our spacers and asked them to determine what it would take to move the *Belle* and remain independent for a year," Harbour replied. She held her hands up to forestall questions and continued. "I have no idea what's coming, but I intend to play an active role in the outcome. To do that, we have to be capable of self-determination by virtue of this ship's movement and independence."

Harbour let the women absorb the concept of separation from their connections with the JOS for that length of time, and the knowledge that Harbour's plan would place them in direct opposition to the families who were their most lucrative clients.

"Each of you has a decision to make," Harbour said. "If you want to transfer off this ship, I can help you with coin from the general fund, and you can set up services on the JOS. I would speak to security and ask that they keep an eye on you. If any of you wish to leave before we depart, providing we can move this ship, then I must request you leave as a group so that you don't alert the JOS or the downsiders to my intentions."

Harbour took a breath, but Nadine held a hand up, requesting she stop. She turned to the other women and said, "Does leaving the *Belle* appeal to anyone in this group?" When everyone shook their head, she asked, "Does anyone want more time to consider it?" Again, the women shook their heads.

"Guess you have your answer, Harbour." Nadine said. "Tell us what we can do to make this grand plan a reality."

"For now, it's business as usual," Harbour replied. "The more clients we see, the greater the general fund's income. Most important, let's take care of our spacers. Our lives might depend on them in the near future."

14: *Annie*

"Samuels, I'm calling it," Captain Yohlin Erring said. She was ensconced in her bridge chair aboard the *Annie*. The ship was in orbit over Pyre's second moon, Emperion, and Tobias Samuels, the lead engineer, was supervising the processing of the previous days' excavation. "The *Pearl* is on approach with our package. Finish processing your backup, pack up your equipment, and recover your people. We're out of here."

"Aye, Captain. It'll take three, maybe four, days."

"Understood, Samuels. Get started." Yohlin closed the comm and thought on the message from Leonard. Per Jessie's orders, she was to take on a newbie, train her, and use an alias for her records. If that wasn't an odd enough request, Leonard relayed the girl's background. *What in Pyre do you think you're doing, Jessie?* she thought. *The planet's hot enough without you starting a fight with the families.*

Yohlin saw her retirement plans blowing out an airlock. As the captain of the *Annie*, she drew a good salary. But it was her share of the company's profits that would make her last years on JOS quite comfortable.

Each ship in Jessie's fleet was specialized. The *Pearl* was a tanker, which transported frozen gases. The *Spryte* was designed as an all-purpose ship. It had holds for shipping rare metal ingots; operated as the company's personnel transport; and enabled Jessie to travel between the mining sites, the JOS, and the YIPS.

On the other hand, the *Annie* was the company's primary mining ship. Yohlin was responsible for the prospecting, assaying, and excavating of new sites. She smiled at the memory of the first time Jessie called her his talisman. She'd had a remarkable string of luck, finding valuable deposits of metal ores that added to the company's ever-increasing profits. With another seven years, Yohlin intended to have saved enough coin to retire, if she chose to give up her captaincy.

Jessie hiding an empath, a murderer, put her plans in jeopardy, and this when Yohlin was about to take on her dream opportunity — to be the first miner to prospect Triton, Pyre's third moon.

* * * *

Leonard Hastings ordered the pilot to take up a position, 30 kilometers off the *Annie*. Once stationary, he retired to his cabin for a conference with his first mate.

"You called this meeting, Angie. Go ahead," Leonard said amicably, taking a seat at his table.

"Captain, I was wondering if you have any idea how long the effects from Rules last. I mean it's been almost two weeks that Belinda and she have been in contact. Do you think the changes for Belinda will wear off quickly or in days or what?"

"And you presume I have knowledge about an empath's work on a human's mind, why?"

"I'm just worried for Belinda, Captain. She's qualified for second mate and would have been there by now if it wasn't for her developing signs of dementia. With Rules, her rehabilitation has been amazing, but without Rules what's going to happen to her?"

"All I can tell you, Angie, is that according to discussions with other captains, who've known people who've had the coin to employ empaths, the conditions that determined the effectiveness of an empath's ministrations were the contact time of each visit and the frequency of the visits."

"Based on those variables, Belinda should be set for weeks, if not months."

"That's a strong possibility."

"Captain, what if we kept Rules and Belinda together?"

"And how do you propose to make that happen? My orders are to hand Rules over to Captain Erring."

"The way I see it, Captain, we're supposed to ensure that Rules is trained as a spacer, right? And Belinda has been doing a spectacular job at that. Rules already has three superlatives in her file for basic level competencies."

"Any qualified officer would be capable of delivering the same quality of training."

"Yes, Captain, but would Rules prefer someone else over Belinda? Remember, it was Rules who came to me and asked what was wrong with Belinda, and since then, the two have been thick as thieves. It's obvious that Rules wants to help Belinda."

"You make a good argument, Angie, but I can't force an extra third mate on Captain Erring."

"Maybe I can help you with that," Angelina said, smiling. "I mean here's this temperamental young girl who's a powerful empath and is responsible for the death of one man, and she's established a rapport with our third mate. Wouldn't it be for the good of the *Annie*'s crew that the pair is kept together?"

"Angelina Mendoza, that's close to fabrication."

"I ask you, Captain, do you know for sure that Rules is stable and able to mingle with the crew of the *Annie* without incident?" Angelina could see that she had hit on a touchy point with the captain. As an empath and downsider, Aurelia remained a mystery to them.

"Your argument is convincing, but that still leaves the problem of adding Belinda to Erring's crew."

"And for that, I say, we don't add, we exchange. Scuttlebutt has it that Captain Erring has filed several disciplinary reports on Schaefer, the second mate. According to my sources, the captain is about ready to put him on station if he doesn't straighten up. I say we offer Captain Erring a swap. She gets a third mate, who is due for promotion, and we take on Schaefer. Demote him to third mate, which is a great way to show him how close he is to being dismissed. If he doesn't work out for us, we set him on station."

"What's the status of Captain Erring's third mate?"

"A new officer recently promoted from engineering. He's too new to move up."

"Okay, that's one hurdle down, but I don't need a headache on this ship."

"Captain, Belinda deserves a break. She's been with us for twelve years, and, with Rules, she's got a fighting chance for more years and maybe a cure. And don't you worry about Schaefer. I'll handle him. We'll have Erring's reports. You warn Schaefer that he can't step out of line once for the next six months, and I'll ride him every step of the way, and I'll be there if he missteps."

"Okay, Angie, I'll try to sell this to Erring, but no promises."

Angelina smiled and closed on him, but Leonard held his hands up to ward her off. "No hugging or kissing, Angie. You know I don't like that."

"Aye, aye, Captain," Angelina said, delivering Leonard a big grin.

* * * *

Leonard enabled the transfer. Fact was, Captain Erring loved the idea of getting a seasoned third mate, who could be promoted, and ridding her ship of her second mate, who had failed to understand the extent of his poor attitude.

"Should I be concerned about this girl, Leonard?" Yohlin had asked.

"I admit I was, initially," Leonard replied, his feet up on a small footstool in Yohlin's cabin. "But I can tell you three things. One, Jessie wouldn't ask us to do this if he thought the girl was an immediate danger to us, other than we're hiding a murderer from the families, I mean. Two, the girl understands that she might be a permanent fixture out here, never to return to the JOS. In which case, three, she's adamant about becoming a spacer."

"I read her qualification reports. She achieved three superlatives in a short period of time."

"I believe that's due to her rapport with Belinda, my third mate."

"Leonard, my first mate tells me Belinda was showing signs of space dementia. Sounds like I might be trading one headache for another."

"Have you ever attended an empath session, Yohlin?"

"Nope, and I hope I never have need of their services."

"That's my hope too, but I can tell you I've never seen the likes of it. Belinda is her old self. She was always a hard-nosed, wise-cracking officer, who I wanted to promote, but there were good people above her. I thought that Jessie might build a fourth ship one day, and I would have great people to send his way to fill the officer positions."

"And you say that Belinda is a steadying influence on Rules."

"I think the two women have bonded for different reasons, and my first mate and I think it's a smart move to keep them together."

"Okay, Leonard, you've got a deal. You inform the women of the transfer, and I'll do the same for Schaefer. I have to admit, I'm looking forward to seeing him off this ship. I don't know if you can straighten him out, but maybe the transfer and demotion will manage to sink it into his hard head how much trouble he's in."

* * * *

Belinda and Aurelia sat aboard the *Pearl*'s shuttle. The seating was along the hull, with their gear strapped at their feet. They were ensconced in vac suits. Freighter shuttles were not premier transport service.

The pilot edged the shuttle onto the docking collar. It was located on the spine of the *Annie* between the equipment bays aft and the ship's gravity wheel toward the bow. He made a solid connection, and the collar mechanism sealed. Once the airlock was pressurized, the pilot announced to Belinda that they were free to exit.

Belinda gave Aurelia a thumbs-up, and, while she opened the collar hatch, Aurelia unhooked the gear. A spacer poked his helmeted head through the opening and announced, "Welcome aboard the *Annie*, I'll be your host during your stay at our extravagant resort."

"Well, host, stay right there, and we'll pass our gear your way," Belinda retorted.

"Aye, aye, ma'am," the spacer replied.

After the gear was sent through, Belinda gestured for Aurelia to go first, so she could dog the hatch behind them. Once both women were in the airlock with the gear, the spacer ensured they had a tight seal and then opened the hatch to the ship's axis, which extended from the bow communications antennas through the gravity wheel, aft through the equipment holds, and finally to the engine housing.

"Uh-oh," the spacer muttered. "I thought we'd clear the axis stem before our second mate boarded the shuttle. Careful, ma'am, he's mad enough to chew aggregate."

Schaefer stomped down the axis corridor, his mag-boots smacking the deck, while he floated his gear behind him. The *Annie*'s crew member stepped far aside to give him room, but Belinda had no such intentions. Unfortunately, Schaefer had mass and velocity. He slammed a shoulder into Belinda and unseated her mag-boots, floating her off the deck.

"Pardon," Schaefer said, with a dirty chuckle. Then he stopped in his tracks. Something forward of him, past the last spacer, gave him pause for concern. He stared down the axis corridor, and the harder he looked the more convinced he was that he had a right to be worried.

"Apologize and your fear will go away," Aurelia said.

The *Annie* spacer reached up and pulled Belinda down until her mag-boots clicked on the decking. She could see the worry in the young spacer's eyes. Obviously, Captain Erring had warned the crew who would be coming aboard.

Schaefer stared down the corridor and took a couple of tentative steps backward.

"The longer you look, the greater your dread will become. Apologize," Aurelia said, taking steps toward the man.

Schaefer's rancor over his transfer and demotion were swept aside by an increasing, unreasonable panic. He hung on the girl's words, which offered him a way out. He turned to the spacer he'd dislodged and mumbled, "Sorry."

"Not good enough," Aurelia said.

Schaefer dearly wanted the ugly darkness that was closing in on his mind to go away. "I'm so sorry, ma'am, for the insolent way I treated you. It won't happen again."

"Make sure of that," Aurelia said.

In an instant, Schaefer felt the distress disappear. His mind cleared, and he was his old self, once again, but without the hostility. The captain hadn't included him in the announcement of an empath coming aboard, so he was ignorant of whom he'd faced.

Aurelia pulled on her duffel and said, "Excuse me," when she came up behind Schaefer, who quickly stepped aside to let her past.

Schaefer would stand in the axis tunnel for several minutes after the others left, while he continued to stare aft down the corridor, expecting the darkness he feared to return. When nothing showed, he grabbed his gear and made his way to the collar airlock. It would be a while before his confidence returned, but without much of his old arrogance.

The young spacer led Belinda and Aurelia through the axis to the interlock transition to the wheel. Once they transited into the gravity hub, they deposited their gear in the vac suit room. Then they were led to their assigned cabins, gravity growing to 1g as they strode the spoke to the outer wheel.

Belinda glanced inside Aurelia's cabin and commented, "Hmm ... private quarters." As a crew trainee, Aurelia should have been assigned a cabin with bunkmates, but apparently the captain had other ideas about that.

"Probably just as well. I wouldn't want to kill anyone in my sleep," Aurelia said, so matter-of-fact that the spacer, who accompanied them, didn't know whether to be alarmed or laugh.

"She's kidding," Belinda said, ushering the spacer out the door ahead of her and frowning at Aurelia.

The crewman led Belinda to her cabin, and when she dropped her duffel on the cabin's deck, the spacer said, "If you please, ma'am, the captain requests your presence immediately. If you'll follow me, I'll take you to her quarters."

At the captain's door, the young spacer nodded politely and quickly disappeared. Belinda knocked and entered at the invitation she received.

"Third mate Belinda Kilmer reporting as ordered, Captain."

"I appreciate the formality, Kilmer, but you can relax. You'll find the same style here as with Captain Hastings and the same demands for job performance."

"Understood, Captain." Belinda was aware the captain was intently watching her. *She's probably looking for signs of space dementia,* Belinda thought.

"How you feeling?" Yohlin asked.

"Probably better than I've a right to expect, Captain."

"Sit down, Kilmer. You and I need a spacer-to-spacer talk," Yohlin said, taking a seat at her cabin's table. "I want to know how concerned I should be about this girl."

"Before we begin, Captain, I should tell you that Rules already used her powers aboard this ship." Belinda had to give the captain credit. She didn't flinch or bat an eye. "The second mate took the opportunity to express his displeasure at his demotion and transfer by knocking me free of my purchase on the deck in the axis tunnel."

"He did, did he? Do you wish to file a grievance, Kilmer?"

"Negative, Captain, no harm done, but Rules took umbrage of his treatment of me. While I'm not sure what she did, it resulted in the second mate frightened enough to apologize to me."

"I presume all of you were in vac suits, and the girl wasn't in contact with Schaefer."

"Affirmative on the suits, and her actions took place at about three meters distance. From the shoulder bump to the apology, I'd say no more than three minutes, if not less."

"I've never heard of an empath that powerful except for Harbour and Yasmin. By the way, was Schaefer's apology sincere?"

"Not at first, Captain, but Rules got him there."

"I missed it. I would have loved to have heard that. So, tell me, Kilmer, any incidents like that on the *Pearl*?"

"None, Captain. The only use of Rules' power has been on me, I'm pleased to say."

"What's it feel like?"

"I don't feel anything, Captain. I'm not sure when Rules starts or stops. I do know that after I started Rules' training, my anxieties occurred less and less, until they disappeared. I've been many days without any sign of my old symptoms."

"Sounds as if Rules and you have a solid rapport."

"I'd say we do, Captain."

"Excellent. Good to hear. Okay, Kilmer, let me lay out your duties. First, you'll be in charge of continuing the girl's spacer training. That's an order from Captain Cinders. Second, you're to keep that girl calm and under control. I want no more ad hoc empath sessions, except for you. Do you copy?"

"Loud and clear, Captain."

"Your ship's duties will be halved, and the first and third mates will pick up the slack." Yohlin noticed Belinda's subdued reaction to her last statement. "Cheer up, Kilmer. I laid it out for my officers, and they're thrilled. They were carrying baggage for Schaefer anyway, and, on top of that, they had to deal with his attitude. You're going to be a relief to them. Not to mention, by the time you and I finish here, everyone will have heard about the encounter with Schaefer. The entire crew will give you anything you want, so long as Rules is kept happy."

"I don't think she's a danger to them, Captain."

"Give them time to accept her, Kilmer. She'll earn their trust, and they'll earn hers."

"Understood, Captain."

"Good. Now, we have some cleanup work to do here on Emperion, and then we'll be setting sail for Triton."

"Triton, Captain?"

"That's right, Kilmer. We're going to be the first Pyreans to set foot on that moon. Maybe we'll figure out what made that great hole in it."

"Better yet, captain, maybe we'll discover a wealth of exotic minerals and rare metals."

"Now, that's the kind of thinking I like to hear, Kilmer. Get acquainted with my first mate, Darrin Fitzgibbon. In downtime, his friends call him Nose. He's waiting outside for you. Dismissed, Kilmer."

"Aye, aye, Captain," Belinda replied. She gave a quick salute and exited the cabin. Life had changed dramatically for her since she met Rules, and she thanked her good fortune and good friend, Angie, for the transfer that kept

Rules and her together. She smirked briefly, recalling how Rules handled Schaefer. It probably scared the *Annie*'s crew witless, but Belinda loved it.

* * * *

Jessie took a call from Yohlin. She was scheduled to break orbit from Emperion days before he arrived. Deliberately, during the conversation, he didn't bring up the subject of Aurelia, waiting until she did.

"For your information, Jessie, I've two transfers aboard, Belinda Kilmer and Rules," Yohlin transmitted. The two ships had nearly a second in transmission receptions, but the captains were used to handling the time lag with each other.

"Why the transfer of the third mate?"

"Leonard's idea, Jessie. Belinda and Rules have become tight. Good training pair ... Rules has three superlatives in basics so far. Remarkably, Belinda's dementia conditions have disappeared."

"You good with this, Yohlin?"

"Can't say I'm thrilled, but I like Belinda. If she does her job well, then I'll be as right as standing on a deposit of heavy metal."

"Speaking of fortunate finds, Yohlin. I wish you good hunting on Triton. Go be our talisman!"

"Got to say, Jessie, I've never been so excited about an opportunity since I first stepped aboard the *Annie* to crew for Captain Rose. Over and out."

Jessie had no more ended the call with Yohlin than Ituau indicated he had another call.

"It's Harbour, Captain. The call is originating from the *Belle*."

"Transfer it to my quarters. You have the bridge, Ituau," Jessie ordered, quickly exiting the bridge.

"Aye, Captain," Ituau acknowledged.

Ituau and a female spacer shared conspiratorial grins. "Now, I wonder what sort of discussion the captain plans to have with Harbour that requires privacy," Ituau said, and the two women laughed.

Jessie settled into a comfortable position behind his desk and tapped the comm light on his desk unit when it lit. "Hello, Harbour. How sure are you of this transmission's security?"

"This call is direct from the *Belle*, Captain. We aren't using the relay on the JOS. Things have been changing over here."

Jessie waited, but Harbour didn't continue. Then he twigged to the problem. "I take it, Harbour, this is your first call to a ship outward of the JOS. The *Spryte* has sailed past Minist. We've about a one-point-five-second comm lag. You can either say over when you're finished, or end on a question or a definitive statement."

"Oh, I guess my newbie status is showing, Captain."

Jessie heard Harbour's soft laugh and discovered he wanted to hear it again. "Not a problem, Harbour. When did you get the *Belle*'s long-range communications operational?"

"Turns out the system was always operational, Captain. I didn't have anyone aboard who could operate it until I asked my spacers to check it out. Over."

"Please clarify, Harbour. What do you mean by your spacers?"

"Did you know we've collected more than thirty of them?"

"I had no idea you had that many."

"Oh, yes, including your three."

"My three?"

"Come, come, Captain, let's not be coy with each other. There's too much transpiring to keep unnecessary secrets. I wanted to tell you that I appreciate your donations. Modest amounts they might be, but, coming as they do every month, you've been very generous to us."

Jessie made a snap decision. He couldn't say who was driving his ship at that moment — his logic or the memory of standing close to Harbour. "You're welcome," he said.

"Now, that wasn't so hard, was it, Captain?"

"I believe you called me, Harbour."

"Back to formalities so quickly, are we, Captain? Well, you better starting using my title then. It's Captain Harbour to you. Over."

"Are you planning to sail the *Belle* somewhere, Captain?" Jessie asked, smiling to himself.

"Planning to, Captain. My spacers are working on a feasibility plan to move the *Belle*. Over."

"For the love of Pyre, Harbour, why would you do that?" Jessie said, snapping upright. He focused on the desk comm station, willing a response.

"Do I detect concern, Captain?" Harbour asked. She had to admit to herself that she enjoyed listening to Jessie's voice and teasing him was better yet.

"You mean am I concerned about the lives you might be risking moving that ancient ship? Then, yes, I'm concerned."

"Does that mean you have no faith in spacers like Dingles? Did you know that I've collected some of the top engineers of Pyre? And I wouldn't risk the residents of the *Belle*, if my spacers didn't tell me we can do this, Captain. Over."

Jessie sat thinking about what Harbour was planning to do. He knew many of the spacers of whom she was speaking. They would tell her truthfully whether the *Belle* could be safely placed underway. The ship was basically operational, and, conceivably, there was no reason it couldn't be moved. The damage to the hull, which the ship had suffered, forcing it into this system instead of continuing on to its original destination, had been repaired. It forced him to consider what was likely to be his true concern.

Briefly, Jessie worried about interceptions of their comm signal until he remembered something Captain Rose told him. The colony ship's long-range communications dishes were highly directional, and there was little chance anyone could pick up on its beam, unless they were in line with him, which was possibly only the *Annie*. For a moment, he wondered if Yohlin was enjoying herself at his expense.

"I did say over, didn't I, Captain Cinders? Over."

"Yes, you did, Captain. My apologies. I was just thinking about what you've been saying. It's taken me by surprise. Over."

"And that's my intention, Captain. I want to take the families and the commandant by surprise. Over."

It hit Jessie how little credit he'd given Harbour. She was moves ahead of him. While he was struggling to figure out what to do with Aurelia, she was making plans to upset the balance of Pyrean power. "A bold move, Captain Harbour. My congratulations on your forethought."

"Thank you for that, Captain. By the way, this captain-captain stuff sounds too formal to me. Would you mind returning to calling me Harbour?"

"Certainly, Harbour, and please feel free to call me Jessie."

Harbour smiled and mouthed a yes. "How goes it with your ..."

Jessie picked up that Harbour was searching for a way to bring up the subject of Aurelia, but she didn't know if he had her and, if he did, how he would be hiding her.

"Our trainee, Rules, is doing fine, Harbour."

"Good to hear, Jessie."

"She's making great progress in her basics and winning some friends."

"Is she? I understand she's a very personable girl."

"Oh, absolutely. She's managed to make a powerful impression on one individual."

"And in such a short time."

"Surprising, isn't it, for an untrained spacer?"

"Tremendously surprising, Jessie. No telling how far she can go once her training is complete."

"If your spacers return an affirmative on moving the *Belle*, Harbour, where are you intending to move the ship?"

"Not sure, yet, Jessie. Still working out what might be strategically smart. If you have any creative ideas, feel free to call me."

"I'm sure you're considering the possibility of being cut off from the JOS if this trouble blows wide open. Are you considering supplies?"

"Yes, we are. I've people determining what it would take to be independent for up to a year. Over."

Jessie wasn't foolish enough to repeat with consternation what Harbour said. Her signal was loud and clear. But he couldn't help murmuring "one year" to himself. Obviously, Harbour was better prepared to foresee the fallout from one young empath's fight and flight to freedom.

"I don't think this over thing is working, Jessie. Over," Harbour said. She bit a fingernail between her teeth to keep from laughing.

"You remind me of one of my captains, Harbour."

"In what way, Jessie?"

"He spoke of my actions leading to a fight. I considered his opinion to be exaggerating the problem. Now you're saying the same thing and taking far-reaching steps to prepare. I think it's my turn to feel like a newbie. Over."

"I think many of us knew this day was coming. It was always a question of how it would arrive, and I, for one, couldn't have imagined it coming at us this way. But, I can't complain. It's probably the clearest and most definitive reason for breaking up the existing power structure and shaping a process to elect our government. Over."

Harbour waited for Jessie's reply. Too much, too soon, Jessie, she wondered, as the delay lengthened.

"Please keep me informed about your spacers' decision on the *Belle*'s flight worthiness, Harbour. Over and out."

Harbour was a little disappointed in the abrupt ending to their conversation. While she was reviewing it, she heard a familiar drumming of fingertips.

"Come in, Yasmin," Harbour called out. "Visiting or business?" she asked when Yasmin entered her cabin.

"Visiting," Yasmin replied with a smile.

"A green?" Harbour asked.

"Lovely," Yasmin replied, curling into a chair.

Throughout the decades, the engineers and techs aboard the *Belle* had made great strides, working toward self-sufficiency. The hydroponic gardens had been expanded to include flowering plants, and bees had been successfully resurrected. The air-scrubber systems were based on algae farms, and the excess growth was harvested. The green that Harbour offered Yasmin was a mixture of algae, honey, and flower petals. Empaths needed a diet rich in elemental compounds. Otherwise, they developed headaches.

Yasmin accepted her drink with a smile and sipped on it. The flower petals lent their aroma, and the honey gave the drink depth. "I was passing by, Harbour, and was surprised to find you broadcasting." Yasmin waited for her friend to deny it, but she wore a polite smile. "Let me guess. The spacers told you this afternoon that our long-range communications system was online, and they would keep techs on duty around the clock to operate it. So, you had to test it."

"Now why would making a comm call have me broadcasting?" Harbour said in dismissal.

"I don't know. Maybe because you called a certain captain," Yasmin replied, her cup paused at her lips and her eyes shining with mischief.

Harbour tossed her head, deciding not to acknowledge or deny.

"And what did the captain have to say?" Yasmin asked, driving right to the point.

Harbour laughed. Yasmin was the closest thing she had to family, and they often referred to each other as sister. Harbour was eight when her powers were announced by her parents to authorities, and, soon after, she was transferred to the *Belle*. She'd long forgiven her parents for the fear they felt about her. She had been a demanding child and learned early how to manipulate her parents to get what she wanted.

"I don't think our captain had considered the potential ramifications of his actions," Harbour replied. "It's dawning on him now."

"You mean to tell me the cold, expressionless, Captain Cinders rescued an empath without thinking of the consequences."

"He's not so cold," Harbour objected. Too late she saw the smile form on Yasmin's face.

"Finished your drink yet?" Harbour replied in protestation.

"Just getting started," Yasmin replied, grinning. "Tell me, what did you learn of our girl?"

"I still don't know exactly where she is, but Jessie does."

"Oh, so now it's Jessie."

"You can be worse than a bee sting, sister. Do you want the answers to your questions or not?"

"Yes, please," Yasmin replied demurely, as if she had been chastened, although Harbour knew better.

"Aurelia is on one of Jessie's ships. He tells me she's taking spacer training and is excelling. But, get this: Jessie hinted that she's already helped someone."

"We're still talking about a sixteen-year-old empath, who's untrained, right?"

"Remember, Aurelia told Jessie that she had a mother and sister downside. What if their confinement exacerbated the emotions of one or both of the other women?"

"And Aurelia became the moderating influence?" Yasmin guessed.

"My thought exactly. If so, she's predisposed to aid people she feels are emotionally struggling."

"Oh, for the love of Pyre," Yasmin said, sitting up abruptly.

"What?" Harbour exclaimed.

"Sister, can you imagine the anguish a teenager like that would be going through at being forced to kill someone to protect herself?"

Harbour thought of her conversation with Jessie, and she saw the faces of her own spacers pass before her eyes. "Perhaps, Aurelia is in the best place for her," she said, taking a long sip of her drink.

15: Downside

Giorgio Sestos glanced at the ID on his comm unit, and he requested silence from Markos with a finger to his lips. "Go," he said to Corporal McKenzie.

"The girl wasn't aboard the *Spryte*," Terrell said.

"So much for your idea, Corporal," Giorgio growled.

"Neither was her DNA. The sniffer picked up zero," Terrell added.

"Coincidence?" Giorgio asked.

"I checked Captain Cinders' logs for the past year that he has transferred to the JOS. He's a machine when it comes to routines, such as blowing out his ship to vacuum, running drills, and the like. If I extrapolate through this year, nothing should have been scheduled."

"Thoughts?" Giorgio requested.

"The *Spryte* crossed over with the *Pearl* at the YIPS. Thing is, the *Pearl* usually unloads within four or five days, but Captain Hastings was in dock for eight days. He sailed the *Pearl* within hours after Captain Cinders docked."

"Then you think it's likely Cinders transferred the girl to the *Pearl*."

"The evidence fits. Cinders shifts her to another ship, blows out the *Spryte* to get rid of the girl's DNA, and then politely acquiesces to a second sniffer search. The bastard was smiling at me all the time."

"Where's the *Pearl* now?"

"She set sail for Emperion where the *Marianne*'s been working."

"Will the two ships cross over?"

"It looks like they might."

Giorgio raised an eyebrow at Markos, asking if he had any questions, and nodded toward his comm unit. When Markos shook his head negatively, Giorgio signed off.

"Governor, I think we have to assume that Cinders bought the girl's story, whatever she might have told him. He's come to her rescue."

"Of all the possibilities, this one was so remote I never considered it," Markos said, leaning back in his chair. "The question is: What is Cinders thinking? Was hiding the girl a knee-jerk reaction, and he never thought past the first move, or does he have a plan?"

"What's the possibility of offering him coin?"

"Cinders?" Markos replied, breaking out in laughter. "I've listened to that man drone on endlessly in monthly sessions, talking about equal justice and responsible governing practices until I thought I'd spew across the table. He's the definition of straight."

"If that's true, what's our move?" Giorgio asked.

"I don't think we have one, unless we can buy a captain to go out to wherever and take her, but we don't know which ship has her. This is like some antiquated shell game."

"Even if we could buy a captain, it'd be a useless action of trying to board a freighter with shock sticks, at best. I wouldn't give them a hundred to one odds."

"At this time, I think we wait it out, Giorgio. Cinders has to make the next move, if he's prepared to make any at all."

* * * *

"Nothing?" Lise Panoy asked in surprise. "You're telling me the commandant has turned that station upside down three times, searched the *Spryte* twice, and he's got nothing?"

"That's the sum of it, Lise," Rufus Stewart acknowledged.

"How can that be?" Lise asked.

"One of my assets has been observing a Corporal McKenzie," Idrian Tuttle interjected. "He's one of security's expert DAD operators. The corporal is fixated on Captain Cinders. He led the second search on the *Spryte*. When that came up empty, he searched the logs of Cinders' ships, checking overlaps of his ships' meetings."

"So, the corporal is an idiot. What's the news there?" Lise demanded.

"A sniffer detected the girl aboard the *Spryte*, during the first search, Lise," Rufus explained, "But there was none detected the second time, and, according to the logs, a blow out of debris or decompression exercise wasn't scheduled."

"Interesting," Lise said, drumming her nails on her chair's arm.

"Add to that, Lise, my asset noticed the corporal's search included an extended stay for the *Pearl* at the YIPS. The ship stayed just long enough for the *Spryte* to arrive and then left soon afterwards," Rufus said.

"Lise, everything points to Captain Cinders hiding the girl," Idrian said excitedly.

"Wonderful, sirs, we know where Aurelia might be hiding, but we don't know exactly which ship has her, and we have no way of reaching her, if that ship is in the fields," Lise replied tartly. Her frustration drove her out of the chair, and she crossed the room to gaze out the window of her house at the beautifully maintained garden. "How could such a golden opportunity slip through our hands?"

"Could we expose Markos by alerting the commandant to the mother and second daughter?" Idrian asked.

"A couple of problems with that, my friends," Lise replied, rounding on the men. "One, we don't want to hand the commandant the means to attenuate our power once and for all, and, two, Markos would receive a warning of security's descent on the El in plenty of time to make arrangements for those two women."

"Do you think he'd dispose of them?" Rufus asked.

"It doesn't matter what he does with them, including hiding them elsewhere. Security would arrive, find nothing, and the household would say nothing. Once security came up empty at Markos' residence, do you think they'd search every house and maintenance building in every dome? Not a chance!" Lise reasoned.

"And, at that point, Markos would know one or more of us turned his secret over to the commandant," Idrian added.

"I don't think that matters too much anymore," Lise grumped.

"I thought keeping Markos thinking you were an ally was a key component of our strategy," Rufus exclaimed.

"It was," Lise allowed, "but based on the shift in communication with Sestos, I'm thinking that he's been Markos' man all along. I believe the governor has been working us."

"That means he knows we told the commandant about Aurelia," Idrian sputtered.

"Are you sure, Lise?" Rufus pressed.

"I'm not entirely sure. Call it a gut feeling," Lise replied, "and without Aurelia to prove our accusations, we are at zero, and we've probably exposed ourselves."

"Then do we have a viable option?" Rufus pressed.

"Markos is still vulnerable, as long as the girl is out there, and the mother and daughter are still in his house. More than likely, he's as stymied about what to do as we are. I think he'll be waiting to see what happens, and we're going to have to do the same thing. Have our assets keep an eye on any of Cinders' ships when they dock at the YIPS or the JOS. There's always the chance that one of the captains will slip up, and Aurelia will exit the ship. That could be our opportunity. Our assets should apprehend her and take her directly to the commandant's office."

"What if they encounter interference?" Idrian asked.

"Why would you ask that, Idrian?" Lise said, staring coldly at him. "They should use any force necessary against anyone who tries to prevent them from carrying out this directive."

* * * *

Sasha had been pestering her mother for days for news of her sister, but Helena thought it too dangerous to reach out to her contact. But, it had reached the point where Helena couldn't bear to be without news either. She eased her secret compartment aside and pulled out a comm unit. It was a child's device, often given to youngsters by their parents so they would always be in contact. In this case, it was programmed to couple with only one other unit.

"Hello," Helena said quietly into the comm, while Sasha listened with an ear at the suite's front door for the approach of any footsteps. There was no reply, and Helena moved to the suite's only window, which faced the rear of the house.

Phillip Borden, the groundskeeper, glanced briefly up at the window, as the curtains moved aside. He scratched his left ear and returned to pruning.

"I forget," Helena whispered to Sasha. "Scratching the left ear is how long?"

"Ten minutes," Sasha replied, and Helena hurried to hide the comm unit.

The two women busied themselves during the interim, as time dragged by, agonizingly slowly. They didn't worry about missing Phillip's call. He never would call them. That was part of maintaining their secrecy. Helena was the only one to initiate a call and only when she was confident they wouldn't be discovered.

Helena had contacted Phillip soon after Aurelia's first meeting with Dimitri. Although her daughter never said anything, it was obvious to Helena that Aurelia was suffering. It took time for Helena to cultivate Phillip's help. The groundskeeper was too scared to speak to authorities on their behalf for fear of losing his job and the governor's possible retributions against his family, but he was amenable to sneaking items to her.

Phillip buried his contributions beneath a cutting basket or honey-collection equipment. He would work toward the house, and, when he was beneath the suite, he'd tie the item to the line extended through a windowpane. It had taken Helena days to carefully remove the small pane and formulate a replacement, made of dried cooking dough, for the elastic caulking. Their transport line was made by sacrificing a few pieces of clothing.

"It's time," Sasha said, hurrying to the front door and taking up her post.

Helena fetched the comm unit and pressed send.

"I'm here," Phillip said.

"What news?" Helena asked.

"None," Phillip replied. "Your girl has disappeared."

"Is she presumed dead?" Helena asked fearfully.

Sasha glanced at her mother in horror, and Helena motioned toward the door, reminding her of her responsibility.

"No ... there's no indication of that. It's presumed she's in hiding. Someone must be protecting her."

Helena breathed a sigh of relief, and Sasha picked up on the visual and emotional cues.

"Can you tell us anything else?" Helena asked.

"There's nothing else to share," Phillip replied. "Do you need anything from me?"

"Not at this time," Helena replied. "There's no chance of Sasha and I escaping. We're being watched too closely."

"Be careful," Phillip replied and closed the comm.

* * * *

Enclosed in his security office on the bottom floor of the governor's residence, Giorgio selected Terrell from his contacts and called him.

"Corporal, you're to hire two teams of operatives. Station one group at the YIPS and the other group at the JOS. They're to monitor the docking of any of Cinders' ships, and I don't mean from a security suite. Find excuses for them to be onsite, where they can watch the spacers exit the ships. I want them on the spot if the girl steps from her ship."

"The teams should contact me if they spot her, so I can arrest her," Terrell replied.

"Listen up, Corporal," Giorgio snarled. "The teams will take her into custody. If they're on the JOS, they'll personally march her to the commandant's office; if they're on the YIPS, it's a shuttle ride and then security's offices."

"Does that mean they'll get the reward?" Terrell asked.

"Clean out your ears, Corporal. We're paying them. They'll get no reward."

"I still think I should be the one to arrest her," Terrell grumbled.

"You know what, Corporal, you're making a good case for me catching the next El lift and throttling you! The teams will make the capture, because they'll be authorized to use preemptive force. If you get involved, you'll be thrown off security, and you'll be of no use to us. In which case, that coin we pay you, which you lavishly spend on coin-kitties and kats will disappear. Of course, now that I think about it, that would probably make a lot of the service providers really happy."

"It'll be as you request, sir," Terrell allowed, even though he didn't mean a single word of what he said. "I'll need coin. These types will want something up front."

"I knew they would, Corporal. You'll receive a transfer to your private account."

"I'll make the arrangements immediately," Terrell replied.

"Before you go, Corporal, let me make one thing clear. Don't cross me on this. Hire the help, and stay out of it."

Before Terrell could reply, the comm connection went dead.

16: Triton

"Position achieved, Captain," said the pilot of the *Annie*. The ship was holding a fixed station out from Triton and was aligned with the edge of the crater. To act as the mining platform for the survey teams and later the recovery crews, Captain Erring was precluded from approaching the moon too closely, which would necessitate circling the body at a sufficient velocity to maintain orbit.

"Darrin, you're free to launch when ready," the captain sent over the ship's comm.

The first mate, Darrin Fitzgibbon, and the survey crew were in vac suits, loading the smaller of the ship's two shuttles. The *Annie*'s build was similar to that of the *Pearl*, except where Captain Hastings' ship had tanks for hauling frozen gases, Captain Erring's ship carried a collection of bays for the two shuttles and the mining equipment. Of all three of Cinders' ships, the *Annie* had the largest crew.

"You feeling lucky, Nose?" the assay tech, Hamoi, asked over the vac suit comm.

"It's itching," said Darrin, his grin displaying through his faceplate.

"We could help," Aurelia suggested to Belinda, but the second mate shook her head negatively, and the two women stayed back, while the survey crew moved gear. The loading of the shuttle could have gone faster with more hands, but each specialized mining crew preferred to work with the same team. In zero gravity, the equipment had no weight, but it still had mass. Once a piece was in motion, the crew had to be careful how that mass was directed onboard the shuttle and locked down.

Aurelia had asked Belinda to accompany the survey crew. Their excitement at being the first Pyreans to land on Triton was infectious, and she wanted to be part of it. It fell to Belinda to ask permission. When she spoke to Darrin, he decided to leave it up to the captain, which is where the two mates found themselves, moments later.

"Rules scores superlatives on every practical, Captain, and I admit I've been pushing her on the reviews," Darrin said. "She doesn't care either way. She performs well despite my pressure."

"That's because she knows what you're saying isn't what you're feeling," Belinda stated simply, as if it was common knowledge how emotions influenced Aurelia. But when Yohlin and Darrin stared at Belinda, she added, "It goes back to the ugliness that Rules experienced in the governor's house. She's delighted to find people, although they might be tough on her, whose minds evince concern for her. She's thriving in this environment."

"I can tell you, Captain, I've never seen the crew in a better mood," Darrin commented. "I'm comfortable putting Belinda in charge of the safety team and letting Rules work with her. It'll be good training for the girl, and it will keep our people in the right frame of mind ... or rather Rules will keep them in the right frame of mind."

"Belinda, do I understand that Rules' thing works in vacuum?" Yohlin asked, swinging a finger at each of their heads.

"It seems to work like any comm signal might, Captain. Hers is low strength, naturally, but it can penetrate most single layers of this ship and transmit through vacuum."

Darrin's mouth fell open before he could recover control.

"Okay, Darrin, add them to your survey crew, as you wish," Yohlin said. "Belinda, you take good care of that girl. I don't want to have to be the one who has to call Captain Cinders and tell him we lost her."

Darrin glanced at the two women standing far to the side, as the crew loaded the shuttle. *Please let me not have made the mistake of my life,* he thought.

The pilot eased the fully loaded shuttle out of the bay. Rather than the standard square, the bays were rounded capsules, shaped like the tanks on the *Pearl.* It made for a more convenient design, attaching them in a ring around the ship's axis.

"What do you like, Nose?" the shuttle pilot asked, when they neared the surface of Triton.

"Slow circle around the crater," Darrin replied. "Then close it in until you cross the center." Darrin sat in the copilot seat and was glued to the display monitor that was tied into the nose cam.

After the pilot completed his tour of the crater, he looked over at the first mate, expecting a decision, but Darrin sat ruminating on what he'd seen. Finally, he muttered, "That's the strangest-looking, impact crater I've ever seen. Okay, we need to get to work. Set us down about two kilometers back from the edge where we started our circle."

The shuttle touched down, and the weightless environment of the ship's axis was gone. "Ugh, gravity," Darrin grunted on open comm.

"Kind of takes the fun out of vac suits," Aurelia commented to Belinda. She thought she was on a private channel to Belinda, which her partner usually set up. But the survey crews' laughter, which came back to her, told her differently.

"Now, that I agree with, Rules," Darrin said, and Aurelia grinned at Belinda.

When the pilot gave the okay, Darrin ordered the shuttle unloaded. The first piece off, which was the last item on, was a huge expandable shelter. The crew wrestled it off the ship and followed that up with several pressurized air tanks. The ground was cleared of small rocks, which might cut into the tough outer layer, and the entrance to the shelter was pinned to the ground. A hose from the air tanks to the shelter was hooked up, and a tech started the air flow.

"Belinda, you and Rules monitor the expansion," Darrin said, bounding off to the shuttle.

"On the other side, Rules," Belinda ordered. "We keep pulling on the back end of the shelter to ensure it expands fully."

Aurelia grunted and heaved on the shelter's tethers, sewn into the outer cover, to keep the rear end walking back. The shelter was constructed of rugged outer and inner liners, sandwiching a thick core of BNNT. It would serve as a temporary shelter for the survey team, who would search for prime excavation targets. When they were located, the miners would core into the rock near the first site and seal the walls to create a permanent shelter to better protect the crew from explosive decompression accidents and long-term solar radiation exposure.

The shelter's face consisted of a long tube that functioned as an airlock, allowing the entire survey team to enter and exit together. After the initial unloading, the crew split up. Half of them began attaching equipment to the exterior of the shelter — generators, hoses that connected the shelter to and from air scrubbers, and heaters. Then, inside the shelter, they set up stations for medical emergencies, suit repairs, tank charging, meals, cots, personal waste, and assaying the samples.

The other half of the team returned to the shuttle, and the pilot lifted for the *Annie*. Once aboard, the crew loaded the equipment necessary to obtain the core samples — a small rover that could carry four crew members, a collection of core sampling tubes, various safety gear, food supplies, and insulated water tanks with heaters.

The crew worked around the clock to complete the setup of the base camp and shelter. Only when Darrin pronounced their preparations complete was the survey team able to rest. Inside the shelter, each member opened a small skeletal frame to hang up their vac suits next to their cots. In the pecking order of rank, the tanks were recharged, three at a time, starting with Darrin, Belinda, and Aurelia.

Darrin and Belinda, standing in skins and deck shoes, were drawing hot drinks and preparing meals for the crew.

"Look at them," Darrin whispered to Belinda. "They've been worked to exhaustion, but you wouldn't know it."

Belinda's eyes roved over the crew. Most sat or lay on their cots in various poses of rest, but contented smiles played on their faces. Immediately, Belinda looked at Aurelia. She sat on her cot, her legs crossed, and her eyes closed. Belinda had rarely seen such a look of pure bliss on the young girl's face.

"And how do you feel, Darrin?" Belinda asked quietly.

"Me? ... I feel good," Darrin replied, frowning slightly at Belinda, before he realized he was enjoying the same effect as the crew, and he searched out Aurelia. "Oh," he muttered when he saw the expression on the girl's face.

Belinda chuckled. "She's ecstatic. So, everyone in her immediate vicinity will be too. She can't help it, not yet, anyway."

"I hope happy doesn't mean unsafe," Darrin replied.

"I've spent weeks training Rules, Darrin. When I got serious, so did she. When she focuses on the work, so will the crew. Trust me on this."

Darrin nodded his acceptance of Belinda's words and kept his reservations to himself. After a meal, he spoke to Yohlin, confirming the completion of the base camp and giving her a start time for their renewed efforts after some rest.

The team slept for nine hours with the shelter's safety equipment monitoring air pressure, air quality, electrical supply, and several other critical factors.

Darrin stirred when his comm unit beeped at him, and he sat up on his cot with a groan. "Ugh, gravity," he heard and glanced over at Aurelia's cot. She sat in her preferred, cross-legged position and was smiling at him.

"Did you sleep, Rules?" Darrin asked, with concern. He couldn't afford to have a sleep-deprived crew member on his team.

"I'm well rested, sir," Aurelia replied cheerfully. "I slept deeply. Perhaps, it's my youth that allows quicker recharging."

"Yeah, youth," Darrin grumbled. He stood and stretched. The popping of a few vertebrae was audible, and Aurelia winced at the sounds. There was much she could do to help the crew with their mental strength, but nothing she could do to spare the spacers the accumulated wear and tear their bodies experienced from a life in space.

After a meal and a rotation at the scarcely private and extremely utilitarian wash basin and toilet, Darrin assigned responsibilities for the day's outing. Many of the crew would remain close to the shelter and complete its functionality. The rest would accompany Darrin to the crater's edge.

Belinda and Aurelia suited up. They were the safety team for Darrin and three crew members, who exited the shelter with them. Outside, an engineer, Tully, climbed into the piloting seat of the rover. Darrin sat up front with him, and two techs climbed into the rear seats.

Aurelia stared at Darrin in confusion when she noticed the seats were taken.

"Youth can walk," Darrin replied on open channel, and Tully started the rover forward.

"Don't you dare, Rules," Belinda warned Aurelia on a private channel. She had implemented the secondary channel after she realized that Aurelia wasn't sufficiently versed in multiple channel communication.

Belinda spotted the flash of Aurelia's evil grin, which she could see through the girl's faceplate.

"It was only a thought, Belinda," Aurelia replied over the private channel.

"Keep it that way, Rules," Belinda reprimanded, but she couldn't help the smile that tweaked a corner of her mouth, and Aurelia's grin broadened.

The two women bounded after the rover, quickly catching up to it in the low gravity. Aurelia couldn't resist sailing about 10 meters past it, expecting the inevitable call from Darrin.

"Stay with the rover, Rules," Darrin sent on the open channel.

"Sorry, sir," Aurelia replied, halting her forward progress. "My youth got carried away."

The crew chuckled, and Tully commented, "Got you on the nose on that one, sir," and laughed at his own joke.

"Fine, Rules," Darrin grumbled, asking, "Truce?"

"Of course, sir, I serve to please," Aurelia replied sweetly.

When everyone around Darrin broke into laughter, he replied, "That will teach me not to jest with teenagers."

Aurelia's pleasure wafted through the crew, but it was interrupted when Belinda sent her a message to focus.

Tully selected his private channel with Darrin. "You ever felt anything like that?"

"No, never have, but it's not the right time for it. I think Belinda is keeping Rules on a short safety line. Did you notice how quickly it switched off?"

"Unfortunately, I did," complained Tully.

Hundreds of meters farther on, Tully brought the rover to a halt. He was able to triangulate his position via signals from the shelter and the *Annie*, which was holding station over the crater, while keeping pace with Triton's orbit around Pyre.

"Everyone stay put," Darrin ordered, climbing out of the rover. A tech handed him what looked like a cumbersome walking stick, but it was a sounding device with a sophisticated microsensor that relayed its findings to Darrin's helmet. He took a few steps forward, activated the device, tapped it on the surface, and repeated the process, as he approached the crater's edge.

Aurelia glanced at Belinda, who told her that Darrin was testing the structure for soundness. "Sometimes craters like this have soft edges, because of the force of the impact from whatever caused it," Belinda explained.

"Yes, I can see that it would be the height of rudeness to have us and the rover perched at the edge of the crater when it crumbles," Aurelia replied.

Belinda picked up the reactions of the two techs, who were silently snorkeling. "You two are eavesdropping," Belinda scolded. "Are both of you looking for reprimands in the log?"

"No, ma'am" chorused the techs.

"Bad techs," Aurelia said. "No feel-good medicine for you two tonight."

The meek apologies that came back from the techs had Belinda shaking her head. A reprimand from a second mate received the expected level of apology, but hearing they would lose Aurelia's empathic administrations produced true disappointment.

"Tully, it's safe to the edge," Darrin called back.

The techs climbed out of the rover, and Belinda prevented Aurelia from walking forward by a hand on her forearm. Tully slowly advanced the rover, checking his equipment for microtremors, which might indicate the ground shifting.

Darrin held his hand up when Tully reached the crater's edge. "Did you record anything?" Darrin asked.

"Nothing," Tully replied. "It's solid. What kind of impact crater is this?"

"Take a look for yourself," Darrin replied. "Come on up, crew," he added.

Aurelia started to launch herself forward, but the hand on her arm held her.

"Hook on, spacer," Belinda ordered, and Aurelia's training kicked in.

"Latched on," Aurelia replied, after spooling off a couple of meters of safety line and linking to an eye on Belinda's belt. Belatedly, she noticed that the techs had already linked their safety lines, and she flashed her chagrin at Belinda.

"You'll learn, spacer, if you live long enough," Belinda replied. It was her incessantly repeated warning during training.

"I was looking at the cam shots from the *Annie* last evening before beddy-bye time," Tully remarked. "Kind of an odd formation for an impact crater. Where's the residue lip around the rim? This one has a rim that meets even with the surface."

"Yeah, I noticed that too," Darrin replied. "And look down at the crater's inner edges. They're jagged, heavily undercut in places."

Tully had linked his safety line with Darrin, and he carefully peered over the edge. "Well, if nothing else, we'll be able to easily obtain core samples."

"I want to look," Aurelia sent on the private channel to Belinda. When she received approval, she edged next to the crater's lip. Her boot struck a small piece of stone, and it flew over the edge. The depth and breadth of the enormous hole sent Aurelia's senses swirling, and she instinctively grabbed for the safety line with one hand, but Belinda was already pulling her away from the edge.

"Stare at the rover, spacer," Belinda ordered.

Despite Aurelia's dubiousness about the strange request, she focused on the parts of the rover, one at a time, and slowly her equilibrium was restored.

"Space can create odd sensations," Belinda said, when she saw Aurelia straighten up and look her way. "You have to know what challenges you and how to combat those sensations before you succumb."

"How's our newbie?" Darrin asked over a private channel with Belinda.

"Had her first experience of space vertigo but came through it quickly," Belinda replied.

"Good to know," Darrin replied. Then on the open channel he directed the crew to ready the rover.

Tully hustled to the vehicle, his safety line playing out. He lowered the telescoping arm that was mounted on the rover's forward structure and released the tethering lines from the rear.

"Time to go to work, newbie," Belinda ordered.

Aurelia followed her to the rover's rear. Belinda picked up what looked like a heavy metal stake with a bulging head and which was connected via cable to the rover. Aurelia picked up the other one and followed Belinda. When the cable came up short, Belinda planted her stake in Triton's surface. She directed Aurelia to step about 3 meters away and do the same. Then Belinda ordered Aurelia to step back, and she sent a signal to the stakes.

The only effect that Aurelia saw was that the heads of the stakes popped off. But the shafts of the stakes had elongated, driving deep into the surface crust.

The techs worked to ease Darrin into a harness sling from the cable end of the rover's arm. Once he was firmly seated, they released his safety line to Tully. The techs loaded a bag on the arm. It hung on the end of a thinner second cable and carried a load of sampling tubes. Darrin checked the snugness of the harness fit and gave Tully a thumbs-up.

Meanwhile, Belinda pointed at the stakes and said, "Rules, your job is to stare at those anchors."

"Stare at them?" Aurelia questioned.

"Yes, if they so much as twitch, you let me know immediately."

"Twitch?" Aurelia asked, holding up gloved hands about 6 centimeters apart.

"Twitch," Belinda repeated, but her gloved hands were flat together.

"Aye, no twitching allowed," Aurelia affirmed.

Tully had joined Darrin at the crater's edge. Belinda took Tully's seat behind the guide console. A tech took the seat beside her to handle the arm and the twin cable winches. The second tech supported Darrin and Tully for the drop.

"Nose, you sure you don't want me to do this?" Tully asked for a final time.

"Tully, I'm not missing out on the opportunity to be the first Pyrean to investigate the mysterious Triton crater," Darrin replied.

"You know the captain's not going to like this."

"And the captain can strip hide off my butt, but it'll be afterwards. Ready to lower," Darrin said, a huge grin on his face. Pyreans had discussed Triton's crater for generations, and Darrin knew he'd always carry the honor of being the first human to descend into the cavernous hole. Slightly above him and to his right dangled the core sampler. To his left and lower rested the bag of sampling tubes.

Guided by Darrin's directions, the tech let out the cables, lowering the first mate over the edge. During the next three hours, Darrin roamed the face of the crater. He'd stop at a mineral deposit that caught his eye, often tapping at it with a small hammer. If it interested him, he'd load a tube into the core sampler and fire the recoilless, pneumatic device. Then place the sample into the bag. Its top end was now red, which differentiated the filled units from the empty, green-ended ones.

Each sampling tube was encoded by Darrin's device with its location within the crater wall, which allowed the assay engineer to build an image of potential, high-value, mineral deposits.

"Time," Tully called over the comm.

Darrin checked the chronometer in his helmet's heads-up display, surprised to find the time had passed so quickly, but then it always did when he was prospecting. His air tank was at 25 percent, and it was right for Tully to call a halt to the day's efforts.

The first mate lived for the emotional high that accompanied incredible strikes, and the coin that followed was always a pleasure too. This time around, Darrin was denied the euphoria he'd hoped to feel. There were definitely some attractive veins, but they were small. Nothing in his thirty-two core samples screamed rich deposit.

The tech handling the winch slowly hauled Darrin and the sampling tubes up, until the first mate dangled above the edge. Then he raised the arm and lowered Darrin onto the moon's surface. Tully hooked his safety line to Darrin before he helped him out of the harness. The second tech collected the bag of core samples and stowed them in the back of the rover.

Belinda climbed out of her seat and hurried back to the stakes. She smacked the top of one unit with a hammer and then the other, triggering the shafts' retractions. When she grabbed one stake to yank it free, Aurelia did the same, but while the second mate was careful to balance herself when the unit pulled free, Aurelia did not.

"Have to be careful of the low gravity, Rules," Belinda sent, when she saw her trainee land on her rear end, holding the stake in front of her. She considered hurrying over to help Aurelia up, but the lesson was too important. If a spacer was on her back in a vac suit, even in low gravity, she had to be able to right herself and get to her feet. She watched Aurelia use the stake to strike the ground to her side, which gave her leverage to roll over. Then she used the stake as a crutch to gain her footing.

"Well done, newbie," Darrin commented, before he climbed into the rover. "Hopefully your youthful energy hasn't entirely been consumed. Back to the shelter, everyone."

Aurelia was tempted to race the rover but felt she'd warranted a little too much attention from the first mate. It seemed more appropriate to show Darrin that she could act responsibly.

The entire survey team was finished for the day and went about their chores. After Darrin charged his vac suit tanks and ate a meal, he took food and drink over to Oscar, the assay engineer, who'd immediately dived into the analysis of the core samples.

"Seeing anything interesting?" Darrin asked.

Oscar squeezed some juice into his mouth from a tube and indicated his small screen. "Definitely some stuff here, but the ratios are pretty low. Most of this is common aggregate."

"I was afraid of that," Darrin said, patting Oscar's shoulder. He sat heavily on his cot and unlocked his comm unit with a thumb and called the ship.

Yohlin took Darrin's call in her cabin and was disappointed to hear her first mate's report.

"Captain, I have this feeling there's coin waiting for us down here. We just haven't found it yet. I can tell you one really odd thing about our exploration today. This isn't an impact crater. It has none of the features we'd expect from two bodies colliding."

"If not an impact, then what do you think happened?" Yohlin asked.

"It's difficult to say, Captain."

"Nose, you're not a shy man and have never withheld your opinion. What's wrong?"

Darrin glanced around at the faces that had focused on him. In a survey shelter, there wasn't any privacy. "Let's say, I was on Pyre, Captain, and, let's say, I was looking at a giant crater and assessing its origin. Under those specific conditions, I'd come to the conclusion that we were looking at a giant hole made by a detonation."

"A detonation on a dead moon?" Yohlin repeated, incredulous.

"Captain, I offered a hypothetical comparison to a crater on a planet. That similar conditions exist on Triton have to be merely a strange and extremely unnerving coincidence." Eyes from those surrounding Darrin stared at him intensely. None of his crew liked the sound of concern they heard in his voice. *Rules will have her work cut out for her tonight,* Darrin thought.

"We need to put the mystery aside, Darrin," Yohlin replied.

"Yeah, I know, Captain. It's grid search time. We'll start tomorrow. Layout a grid slice away from today's test point and see if it can direct me toward larger deposits."

"Don't sound so disappointed, Darrin. With luck, you won't have to search the entire moon." Yohlin chuckled, as she closed her comm unit.

17: Rumors

It was Toby who inadvertently started the rumor that led to the exposure of the governor's secret to Pyrean society. His intentions were innocent, merely one good heart defending a momentary befriending.

Toby had become famous, as the boy who met the notorious downside murderer and lived to speak of it. Leg wrapped in bandages from his BRC surgery and seated in his wheelchair, once again he'd been surrounded by other youths, wishing to hear of his incredible encounter.

"How'd the BRC surgery go?" one boy had asked.

"Real good," Toby enthused. "The medics say it's taking well. Looks like I'm going to be walking again soon."

"You met the murderer, right?" a girl asked. "People say you were lucky to survive. Others say that you played freefall with her. Which is true?"

"Aurelia helped me out to a terminal arm, and I taught her freefall," Toby replied.

"Then it's true. She was a downsider," another boy interjected.

"Oh, no doubt about it," Toby replied. "The girl didn't have a clue what to do in zero gravity. It was kind of funny, at first, but she caught on pretty quickly."

"How come you think security can't find her?" a second girl, Pena, asked.

Toby swallowed. Pena was the girl he liked. She was a year older than him and five inches taller, but, to Toby, none of that mattered. "Been thinking about that," he said, dropping his voice, as if it was a secret. Pena leaned in to listen, and Toby's heart thumped. "What if Aurelia isn't a normal?" he whispered to her.

"How can that be?" Pena objected, swatting Toby's arm.

"Think about it," Toby replied.

The small group hung on Toby's next words. The idea that the girl was a sensitive hadn't occurred to them or their parents.

"Security hasn't reported any breach of the airlocks on the station or the terminal arms, right? So, she didn't step out into vacuum. And how long has any fugitive managed to evade security?"

"There was that guy last year who hid out in the air vents intersecting the maintenance corridors," a boy volunteered.

"But he only lasted five days before security caught him," the first girl argued.

"So how has Aurelia evaded security for weeks?" Toby asked. "I think she's an empath, and she's convinced someone to protect her."

"Whoa," one boy said on an exhale of breath. The others were too stunned to reply.

Toby's comm unit chimed, and he glanced at the message. "Got to go. Mom's got dinner ready."

Two boys and a girl gave quick waves and stepped away to give Toby room to maneuver his chair. Pena leaned in and kissed his cheek. "Hope your BRC replacement continues to take," she whispered.

Toby flew home, ignoring the shouts of irate stationers and imagining Pena kissing his cheek again.

It was a brief conversation, but the ramifications of the teens' conversation were tremendous. The foursome, who were with Toby that day, told their parents and friends about the possibility that Aurelia was an empath. The rumors might have never gained traction, except, with every breath that repeated the idea, Toby's name was mentioned.

Soon the station was abuzz with the idea that the escapee from downside was an empath. It neatly explained how the girl had managed to hide from security longer than anyone else.

"Couldn't be," railed some. "The governor would never break the accord."

"But what if she is a sensitive? What does that mean?" others asked.

"If she is an empath, did she kill with her powers? Is she a danger to us on the JOS?" people asked.

* * * *

Rumors ran rampant aboard the JOS and reached Harbour from several sources. She chose to add fuel to the fire and called people, who regularly visited the station, to her cabin. Danny, some artisans, an engineer, and two techs filled up the seating places in Harbour's cabin and she chose to stand.

"You've heard the rumors circulating about Aurelia. We're going to add our own," Harbour said. "You want to be subtle about this. Ask questions rather than spin your own tales. You heard the girl might be an empath, is that true?"

"How far can we go with the questions?" Danny asked.

"Give me an example?" Harbour asked.

"If we get a bite on the question about Aurelia being a sensitive, can we suggest the accord has been broken?"

"Absolutely, but be careful. Let the other individuals drive the conversation. You can agree with them, if what they're saying suits our agenda, but don't argue with them, if it doesn't."

"Does anyone have an idea how we can work in the suggestion that Aurelia has a mother and a sister downside?" an artisan asked. He used scrap metal to create one-of-a-kind centerpieces.

"We could wonder how she got downside," one of the techs said.

"Yes, then you follow that up after a couple of seconds with something like, 'I wonder if she was born downside,'" the engineer added.

"You could even go a step forward like you're musing out loud," the second tech said, jumping into the conversation. "But then that begs the question of who's her mother. If she's an empath, which is most likely, how did she get downside?"

"Those are excellent techniques," Harbour enthused. "But listen carefully. Once you've been able to have a conversation to the extent that's been suggested here, that's it. Don't do it again. Let human gravity take over."

After the individuals left her cabin, Harbour made herself a cup of green. She'd seen six clients today, and she was drained. Her customers were delighted that she'd increased her appointment schedule and were happy to pay the premium Harbour demanded. Every empath was working hard to grow the general fund.

* * * *

Danny's frustration increased daily. On his first trips to the JOS, he hadn't managed to start a single conversation that realized any substantial traction for the rumor mill. Other *Belle* residents reported moderate success, but each one lamented that they were talking to people who shared the same opinions and, more than likely, possessed limited social circles. It struck them that they were talking to the wrong individuals, which gave Danny his idea.

Finishing his shopping list for the *Belle* one day, Danny made an additional purchase and an extravagant one at that. Then he sought out the favorite haunt of well-to-do stationers, the Starlight, a cantina with a transparent wall and an unobstructed view of the stars.

At the impressive doors of the Starlight, Danny squared his shoulders, lifted his head, and made no attempt to hide his prosthetics, as he hit the door actuator and thumped into the cantina. Walking to the bar, Danny drew the looks of many patrons. His face, hands, neatly shaved head, prosthetics, and demeanor screamed spacer, but his expensive skins said a miner who had hit it big.

Danny picked a spot at the bar between two well-heeled patrons, as evinced by the quality of their skins. "Sirs," Danny acknowledged, taking a seat between them. Both men looked him up and down, but Danny ignored them.

"First time here, friend?" the bartender asked, hurrying over to serve Danny. The contrast between the man and the skins said there was a story to hear.

"Yep," Danny replied expansively. "Struck a load of heavy metal, and I'm out to spend some coin on myself."

"I'd be honored to buy your first drink, spacer," the man to Danny's left said. "It's you people who keep Pyre growing."

"Much appreciate it, friend," Danny replied. It would be the first of a series of free drinks. Inevitably, the men to each side of Danny and the bartender wanted to hear his story. It quickly became apparent to Danny that these people had little to do with spacers. The two groups definitely didn't share social circles.

So, Danny spun a story of a tough life, working the asteroid field, until he could buy into a partnership. Then, he'd had the good fortune to test a small, but dense-looking, asteroid. Miraculously, the entire body was composed of heavy metals, and the miners believed it came from the heart of a star that had gone supernova.

Danny told his story succinctly and quickly. He had a plan in mind and needed time to put it into action. "Well, that's my story. So, what's been happening on the JOS, while I've been out there? I heard some commotion about a girl."

Several other patrons had closed in behind Danny, while he told his story, and, now, each of them was eager to educate him with their favorite takes on the Aurelia story.

"Wow," Danny exclaimed, when one woman finished telling him her idea of what might have happened downside. "What did the Review Board decide at this girl's hearing?" he asked.

That comment evoked laughter and the choking of one patron, who'd been taking a swallow of his drink.

"They haven't caught her yet," a man replied.

"Wait. I thought you said she came up via the El weeks ago," Danny objected. "What do you mean they haven't caught her yet? Is she dead?"

"A body has never been found," a woman said.

"How does a downside teenager hide on the JOS for weeks?" Danny asked. "I presume security has her DNA profile."

"Oh, yes," the man to Danny's right said. "They had sniffers going all over the JOS and up and down the terminal arms. Found she'd slipped onto one of Cinders' ships, slipped back out again, and then disappeared."

Danny had the good sense to look flummoxed. It wasn't too hard, since he was working on his third drink. "How is that possible? A ship is locked and coded if no one is aboard or, if open, is guarded at the gangway, and Captain Cinders insists on a tightly run ship."

"I have a theory," a woman said. She'd been sidling closer to Danny, during the conversation, obviously wanting to be heard. "The story goes that Captain Cinders did have a man on duty at the gangway. The crewman said he'd fallen asleep. I've a friend on security, and she says a disciplinary report was never filed on that spacer for falling asleep on duty, and he's a longtime crew member of Cinders, no newbie."

"Okay, what's your theory?" Danny invited.

"I think Aurelia is an empath, and she put the man to sleep."

Several patrons around Danny groaned, and the woman, who proposed the explanation, bristled.

"Hey, everyone has a right to an opinion," Danny said, displaying the mettle of a spacer. It quelled the grumbling, and the woman was somewhat mollified.

"Let me ask you," Danny said, directing his question at the same woman. "If this girl is an empath, she must have originated on the JOS, which means security has vids of her going downside, right?"

That question sobered more than one patron. The man to Danny's left said, "According to my sources, security vids don't show her ever taking the El downside."

"This is confusing," Danny said, waving a hand in front of him, as if it would dispel the contradictory information. "You say this girl is on the JOS for weeks, but she can't be found. You say she can sneak past a spacer on duty and leave again without being seen, but most of you haven't offered an explanation about how that can happen except for this woman."

Wiping the alcohol-infused expression off his face, Danny eyed each one of his audience, and the patrons found themselves face-to-face with a man who had lived a more dangerous life than they could imagine. "I get it. You're having the cantina's newbie on, spinning a tale for my benefit. Good one," Danny said, breaking into laughter.

"No, friend," the bartender interrupted. "What they're telling you is true, except maybe the part of the girl being an empath," he added, shrugging to the woman, who'd offered the concept. *She's a lousy tipper, anyway,* he thought.

Danny stared around him. Heads were nodding in agreement with the bartender. He didn't know if it was the alcohol or the opportunity to be immersed in Aurelia's story that allowed his brain to connect a critical element of his questioning. If he hadn't been surrounded by the Starlight's patrons, he would have jumped up and called Harbour.

"It seems to me that there's an obvious way to figure some of this out," Danny volunteered. For a moment, he thought he was vacuum and the patrons were air, since he seemed to suck them toward him. "I mean this part about the girl possibly being an empath. They've only been born topside, never to downsiders, right?"

Everyone agreed with Danny, so he plowed on. "If this girl is a sensitive, then her parents are from the JOS or the *Belle*, wouldn't you agree?"

Again, there was agreement. By now, patrons would have found it difficult to get a drink. The three bartenders were leaning over the counter to hear Danny, and most of the clients weren't drinking anyway. They were crowded so deep around Danny that those in the outer circles were constantly whispering to someone in front of them, "What did he say?"

"You said security has the girl's DNA profile. So, my question is what did security discover when they ran that profile against the JOS personnel database?" Danny asked.

The question was asked innocently enough, but Danny, in his excitement, could have pumped a fist in celebration. He looked around him. Patrons were regarding one another, wondering who might have an answer to the question.

"I probably have the most contacts in security," the man to Danny's left said. "And I can't say that security ever ran the girl's profile against the personnel database or, if they did, I never heard about it."

"If she's a downsider, they wouldn't get a hit anyway," one patron argued.

"Agreed," Danny replied. "But there seems to be reasonable suspicion about the girl's capabilities. You've got to admit that hiding from security for weeks and sneaking on and off a crew-monitored mining ship are certainly out of the norm." Danny deliberately chose the word norm. It was close to the way in which empaths referred to nonsensitives, which was as normals. "From security's point of view, I'd think they would want to eliminate the possibility, by checking the girl's profile against the personnel database. No match, she's probably a downsider. However, you have to wonder who this girl truly might be if they do get a hit. That means she's a topsider and possibly an empath."

"That would really pop an airlock," one bartender said, "especially if her parents are topsiders, and security shows no record of her descending downside."

"It makes one think," Danny said, nodding his head in contemplation. "Well, I have business to attend to, people. I want to thank all of you for an enjoyable visit to this wonderful establishment." He stood, checked his balance, which was anything but 100 percent, gave his audience a quick salute, and then ambled toward the exit.

Behind Danny, patrons closed in and began arguing with one another. It would be hours before people left, and the bartenders did a thriving business, as tempers escalated. One thing everyone did agree on is that several individuals were going to ask their security contacts if Aurelia's DNA profile had been checked against the JOS personnel registry. They were tasked with reporting back to the audience in two days' time at 1400 hours.

Danny made his way back to the supply shop where he'd obtained the skins and paid the one-day rental fee he'd negotiated. The owner was an ex-spacer and a friend of his. Then, he searched out a cheap sleepover. There was no way he was flying the *Belle*'s last shuttle in his present condition. Before Danny put his head down, he sent a quick message to Harbour telling her that he would be returning late. His text started with, "I met some new friends for drinks."

18: Exposed

Major Finian headed for the commandant's office. Coincidentally, while on the way there, Liam received an urgent message from the commandant to meet with him. He rapped smartly on Emerson's door when he arrived.

"Come, Major," Emerson said officiously. He stood to pose in his authoritative stance, which placed his knuckles on the desk so that he could lean forward. Unfortunately, his voice's pitch, as usual, ruined the illusion.

"I want you to put a stop to these rumors, Major," Emerson demanded. "And I mean all of them about this girl and her fantastical abilities to hide from us."

"I have no idea how we would do that, sir. It's not like anyone is holding a public meeting or speaking on an open forum. They're talking one on one or in private group conversations. Besides, sir, these rumors might be closer to the truth than we imagined."

"What?" Emerson stammered, sitting down heavily. He'd been ready to push his people to quash the calls coming from the station's prominent citizens who'd been pestering him with their theories about Aurelia. What he didn't expect was to have his immediate subordinate announce the reverse of his intentions.

"I received a request this morning from Harbour for a DNA profile comparison, which I ran."

"Whose profile?" Emerson asked, with rising concern.

"Harbour asked me to use Aurelia's DNA profile and search the station's database for a match."

"She hasn't the authority to make such a request in so sensitive a case," Emerson cried, jumping up from his desk.

"Actually, she does, Commandant. She's the defacto captain of the *Honora Belle*. And with the rumors piling up about how Aurelia might be an empath and that's how she's hiding from us, I thought it prudent to run the search and dispel them."

"That was good thinking, Major," Emerson said, somewhat mollified and settling back into his chair. "So now you can announce your finding and end this foolishness once and for all."

"That's what I'd hoped for, sir, but it didn't work out that way," Liam replied, a small grimace twisting his lips.

"What do you mean, it didn't work out?" Emerson demanded, his voice rising again.

"I got a hit in the personnel database, a familial match."

"Oh, for the love of Pyre, who?" Emerson asked, slumping deep into his chair.

"Do you remember the case of Helena Garmenti, sir?"

"Doesn't ring a bell, Major. Who is she?"

"She was a seventeen-year-old stationer who disappeared from the JOS."

"Accident?" Emerson asked.

"No, Commandant. She was never found."

"Is it possible she skipped downside?"

"I checked security records on the extent of the search for her. The cam files were thoroughly reviewed. She never walked onto the El."

"Why did you say it like that?"

"Just putting things together, sir," Liam said cautiously. "Seventeen years ago, we had a seventeen year old go missing. She was considered one of the young girls who everyone liked."

"What's your point, Major?"

"That expression is often used as a description for late-blooming, weak empaths. Now, what age would you say Aurelia is, judging by the vids of her? Maybe sixteen?"

"This is all conjecture on your part, Major. You're trying to piece together disparate details to make a case that Aurelia is an empath. I think these rumors are influencing your judgment."

"On the contrary, sir, I was thoroughly convinced my search wouldn't discover a match. But the DNA evidence is clear. A young girl disappears from the JOS, and a year later she has a baby, who flees to the JOS from downside, seventeen years after the first girl disappeared. How do you connect the dots?"

Emerson briefly held his head in his hands. Everything was unraveling. If events proceeded like this, his liaison with the families would be exposed. Then, losing his position would be the least of his worries. More than likely, he'd face the Review Board and a stiff sentence.

"There's one more thing you should know, sir. On the three days preceding Helena's disappearance, Markos Andropov was on the JOS for the funerals of his wife and brother-in-law, who were killed in a terminal arm accident. He was accompanied by Giorgio Sestos. The two men traveled downside on the day that Helena was last seen."

Emerson stared at Liam. He wanted to appear fierce, but fear squeezed his lungs. "You're proposing that Markos kidnapped Helena and stowed her in cargo with the help of his security? Do you realize how ridiculous that sounds?"

Liam Finian watched his superior closely. He'd long believed that the commandant favored the families. As far as he was concerned, this was a test of where the man's loyalties lay. While the evidence against Markos Andropov was circumstantial, it was compelling, to say the least, and the facts warranted an investigation.

"I presume your search and the response were recorded in Aurelia's file?" Emerson asked, thinking of ways to handle the major's news.

"Of course, Commandant, you can view the results of the comparison for yourself. How would you like me to proceed?"

"Let me review the data first, Major. We don't want to be too hasty. This case is too important to make a misstep."

"Understood, sir. I'll wait to hear from you," Liam said, executing a quick salute and exiting the commandant's office.

Liam made directly for Lieutenant Higgins office, pleased to catch him in. Closing the door, Liam said, "I want the commandant's private comm unit monitored. Any conversations he has with downsiders, especially the families, are to be recorded. Do it now."

If it wasn't for the fact that Liam and he had discussed the commandant's possible collusion with families, Devon might have hesitated or even objected. Instead, he accessed a waiting file and initiated it. "Done," he said.

"You were well prepared," Liam commented.

"I figured by the time you told me that we needed to do it, things would have reached a critical stage, and we'd have to move fast. What's blown up?"

"Harbour requested a comparison of Aurelia's DNA profile against the JOS personnel database."

"That's smart. Why didn't we do it in the first place?"

"Good question. Anyway, I ran it this morning and got a hit. Her mother is Helena Garmenti, the girl who —"

"Disappeared from the JOS nearly two decades ago," Devon finished. "I presume you reviewed the Garmenti case."

"I did," Liam replied. During the next few minutes, Liam explained what he found and his theories about what the governor and his present security chief might have done.

"What was the commandant's reaction to your research?" Devon asked. Before Liam could reply, Devon imitated the commandant's high-pitched voice and said, "This is all conjecture on your part, Major."

"I'd laugh if it wasn't so sad," Liam said, shaking his head in regret.

"Speak of the enemy," Devon said, holding up a finger and pointing to his monitor. "The commandant has finished a call downside. Interested?"

"Absolutely," Liam replied, leaning on Devon's desk to listen closely.

Devon pulled up and opened the recording.

"Lise, we have a problem," the men heard Emerson say.

"I'm listening," Lise replied.

"My major, the idiot, ran a search on the station's personnel database for comparisons against Aurelia's DNA profile and matched it to a young woman, Helena Garmenti."

"And how is this a problem?"

"The major's theory is that Helena Garmenti was kidnapped by Markos and Giorgio, spirited downside, and Aurelia is her daughter. Is there something that you've forgotten to tell me?"

"Why do you ask?"

"Based on what the major's found, it's going to be impossible to stop an investigation into Governor Andropov's affairs."

"You're saying you don't have control of your men?"

Devon smiled conspiratorially at Liam.

"The major has been suspicious of me for a while, Lise. My point is that Markos will probably be arrested once all this comes out. The question is: Who is going to be the next governor?"

"I would think I would have your support, Emerson. I've sent a great deal of coin your way."

"Then you need to be forthcoming with me, Lise, if you want my support. Is Helena Garmenti Aurelia's mother?"

"Yes."

"Is the woman still alive?"

"Yes."

"In the governor's house?"

"Yes."

"Does Helena have any other children?"

"One more ... a younger daughter named Sasha."

"And why didn't you come forward with this information sooner, Lise? It would have been so much easier to control the situation."

"How did I know that Aurelia would disappear? Markos has his own assets aboard the JOS. What if he'd recovered Aurelia without a fuss? Where would your proof of his crimes have been? Furthermore, how could I have known you had Helena's profile in your records? I say it is what it is, Emerson, and we have to deal with it."

"No telling what my major is going to do if I don't move first. I'll keep you informed."

The conversation ended and Devon closed the file. "Didn't think the commandant would space himself with one call," the lieutenant said.

"Surprising, isn't it?" Liam replied, wondering what to do with the information he held.

"Uh-oh," Devon said, glancing up at the glass walls of his office.

"What?"

"I just saw Harbour pass by, and she didn't look happy. Did you share the search results with her?"

"Yes, after all, it was her request, but I didn't think she'd react so quickly," Liam said, twisting around, but Harbour had already passed.

"She's probably headed for the commandant's office," Devon remarked, which galvanized Liam into action. He jumped up and ran after her, catching Harbour before she made it to Emerson's office.

"Harbour, we need to chat before you go into the commandant's office. I know why you're here, but there's a great deal more you need to hear first."

The emotions Harbour felt from the major told of quiet desperation. His eyes implored her, and she'd never heard disparaging remarks against the man, which attested to his reputation.

"My visit with the commandant can wait a few moments, Major. What do you have to tell me?"

"If you'll come this way, Harbour, we need some privacy," Liam replied, and he led Harbour to Devon's office.

Devon jumped up when Liam escorted Harbour through his door.

"Total privacy, Devon," Liam urged, and the lieutenant used his comm station to signal his glass wall, which faced the corridor, to darken.

During the course of the next half hour, Liam and Devon brought Harbour up to speed on what had been discovered and the call between the commandant and Lise Panoy.

Harbour debated what to tell the two security officers about what she knew. Everything the men had shared pointed to crimes committed by the commandant, the governor, and Lise Panoy. As far as they were concerned, Aurelia would still have to face a Review Board for the murder of Dimitri. However, the one thing that kept her quiet was the fact that it was Jessie Cinders who had shared the information about Aurelia and was protecting the girl, and Harbour was intent on protecting his trust.

"What do you intend to do, Major?" Harbour asked.

"Good question, Harbour. I can't march into the commandant's office and take him into custody. Only the Review Board can order his arrest, and, until the commandant is replaced, I can't take charge of the investigation against Governor Andropov."

"There are two sensitives downside who need our help, Major."

"I know, I know," Liam replied in frustration.

Harbour let the officers' emotions play through her. She could sense the synchronicity between their words and their feelings. Both appeared to her to be honest men — honest men handicapped by dishonest people in power.

"Perhaps, sirs, this is the point at which you need an outside influence, one who owes nothing to your masters," Harbour said, smiling, as she stood. Devon cleared the glass wall and unlocked the door. When she left the office, the two men looked at each other, not knowing whether to smile or frown.

* * * *

First things first, Harbour thought, as she marched to the commandant's office. She could share what she knew about the DNA profile match, but she couldn't share anything else without giving up Liam, Devon, or Jessie. However, she could direct the conversation toward what she desired.

"Harbour, so good to see you," Emerson said, jumping up to greet her. "Such an unexpected pleasure."

"I doubt that, Commandant Strattleford," Harbour replied testily, which halted Emerson's progress around his desk. "I'm sure your subordinates have informed you of the inquiry into the JOS personnel database that I requested and the results."

"Why, yes, they did. I must say it came as quite a shock to me."

"Shock or not, I'm here to learn what you intend to do about it."

"With all due respect, Harbour, while your request generated a unique piece of evidence, I fail to see what this has to do with you or even why you chose to make the request in the first place."

Harbour didn't need her capabilities to perceive the fear rolling off Emerson. Just the same, she attenuated her sensitivities to prevent his emotions from overwhelming her.

"As the acting captain of the *Belle,* the leader of the empaths, and as a woman, I've legitimate concerns to see that justice is pursued." Harbour had heard the captains use this phrase many times at the commandant's monthly meetings. Saying it gave her a particular pleasure.

"Harbour, the information has only recently come to light, as you well know. It will take some time to process."

"Commandant, Aurelia was in the governor's household. He admits it. Her DNA profile says she's the daughter of a woman who disappeared about a year before Aurelia was born. What more do you need to take action?"

"Harbour, it's not that simple. I have —" Emerson's voice cut off, but not by Harbour's vocal interruption. He felt a rush of hot anger sweep through him, blanking out his thoughts. "Harbour," he choked out, and the feeling disappeared.

"My apologies, Commandant, your inaction galls me, and I'm afraid it caused a momentary lapse in my control. Men's arrogance can sometimes do that to me." It wasn't true, but Harbour didn't think Emerson needed to know that. If she chose, she could make her control absolute. However, she did enjoy the return of Emerson's fear, which was now driven by an additional reason.

"Well, I see there's no need to continue this discussion," Harbour said, turning for the door.

"That's it?" Emerson asked, greatly relieved. "You'll leave the investigation's progress in my hands?"

"Assuredly not, Commandant. As acting captain of the *Belle*, I have the authority to call an emergency meeting of the Review Board."

"Wait, Harbour," Emerson called urgently, "what is it you want?"

Harbour regarded Emerson, while she took careful measure of his emotions. She sensed various emotions, dominated by his fear, but it was his earnest desire that accompanied his entreaty that convinced her to reply.

"I want you to send a security team downside to make entry into the governor's house and search it for Helena Garmenti. And, most important, I don't want you giving the governor advance notice of your visit. If Helena is there, I want you to recover her and any children she might have and bring them to the station. Furthermore, the presence of Helena would require you to arrest Governor Andropov and Giorgio Sestos."

The fact that Emerson's mouth was hanging open didn't deter Harbour from continuing. "Also, Commandant, I expect to be notified the moment Helena and any children are recovered. I will interview them first."

"Why should you see them first?" Emerson asked, seeing control of the situation slipping from his grasp.

"It's obvious to me, Commandant, if not to you, that this entire series of events is more than a simple murder. I will determine if Helena is a sensitive. If she and her children are empaths, then the agreement has been broken, and the families need to feel topsiders' wrath for their betrayal."

Harbour waited, while the commandant processed her requests. She might have been irked by his slow response, but, after hearing his conversation with Lise Panoy, she comprehended the enormous pressure he was under, trying to figure out a way to prevent standing before the Review Board.

"It will be as you suggest, Harbour," Emerson relented.

"When?" Harbour asked, not intending to let the commandant off her tether, and she watched him process his answer. The fear she sensed lessened. It was replaced by a bit of despair, probably a sign of capitulation to future events.

Emerson realized that if he led the security team below and Helena was discovered in Markos' home, it warranted the governor's arrest. That might end his political career. The families would never forgive him for invading their domain. "I'll order Major Finian to proceed immediately to the Andropov home."

"See that you do, Commandant," Harbour said, with force. She stared long enough at Emerson to make him fear that he would be the subject of another blast from her. When he shrank back, she whirled and strode from his office. She ducked into the lieutenant's office where Major Finian was waiting. She indicated the glass wall with a nod of her head, and Devon darkened it and locked the door.

"It's done, but let's wait and see if my efforts bear fruit," Harbour said.

"What's done?" Liam asked. At that moment, his comm unit chimed and he answered it. "Yes, sir, I'll be right there." He looked questioningly at Harbour.

"You should be getting orders to take a team to the governor's house and search for Helena and other children she might have. I expect them to be brought to the JOS. You will notify me if you find them, and I will be the first to interview them. Am I understood?"

When Liam nodded to her, Harbour flicked her head at the glass wall. Devon reversed the settings, and Harbour quickly left.

"People should never irritate that woman," Devon commented quietly.

"Agreed," Liam replied. "I have a feeling that the commandant's orders are going to match her words almost verbatim. If she makes us nervous, he's got to be scared out of his skins."

19: Arrested

Major Finian left the commandant with a different attitude than when he walked into the office. Emerson's instructions were exactly as Harbour predicted they would be and entirely opposite from what Liam expected. He'd always admired Harbour for her beauty and feared her for her power, but he'd never considered her to be a political force. *Going to have to rethink that one, old son*, he thought.

On the way to Lieutenant Higgins' office, Liam considered his timetable for action and decided to make all haste before Emerson changed his mind.

"Is the JOS about to stop spinning?" Devon asked, with concern.

"What?" Liam replied, not understanding the reason for the question.

"The look on your face," Devon said, pointing a finger at him.

"Oh, sorry, Devon, I'm still processing what happened. Essentially, we're on. I'm ordered to go downside and search the governor's house. The commandant is procuring the warrant from the Review Board as we speak."

"Well, I'll be," Devon replied in amazement. "I'll assemble a team."

"Devon, I need people I can trust, individuals who'll follow my orders explicitly. Also, ensure we have a mix of men and women."

"Guess you won't want Corporal McKenzie." Devon chuckled when Liam threw him a dirty look. "I'm checking the El schedule. I presume that you want to move on this in a hurry. We can catch the 14:30."

Liam checked the time on his comm unit. "Commandeer seats for us, if enough aren't available, and I don't care whom you have to upset. Also, you're not going, Devon."

"I'm not going?"

"This search is going to create a political mess. If the commandant manages to keep his job, and I'm the one tossed out an airlock, someone with integrity has to remain in place. I'll take Sergeant Rodriguez. Get started, Devon. I'm running to my cabin to change. Have to look officially presentable, if I'm going to arrest a governor."

"Good luck with that. Go straight to the El, Major. I'll have the team meet you there."

Liam chose to duck through maintenance corridors to shorten the trip to his cabin, which didn't do much for the confidence of the crews working there, who watched a security officer race past. He managed to change into his dress uniform and make the El passenger-loading capsule with ten minutes to spare.

As Liam walked toward the front of the queue, he tapped the shoulders of his team, consisting of Sergeant Rodriguez, Corporal Cecilia Lindstrom, and three privates, who waited in line.

"Exigent circumstances," Liam announced, from the front of the line. "These officers and I will take the next capsule. Please stay where you are."

When the cap arrived, Liam and his team loaded quickly and strapped in. Once the door slid closed, Liam began his briefing. "Aurelia's DNA profile is a familial match to that of Helena Garmenti, a girl who went missing seventeen years ago. We're confident that the mother is being kept in the governor's house. We'll search the primary residence and the grounds, if necessary, and take her and any children of hers into protective custody. If Helena is present, we will be arresting Governor Andropov and Giorgio Sestos."

"What if Helena Garmenti is there, and she states that she went willingly to the governor's house?" Miguel asked.

"It'll be the same actions on our part. It's up to the Review Board to sort it out. Whether Helena went willingly or not, taking her downside was against the agreement. And, on that note, surveillance didn't ever show her boarding the El."

Miguel Rodriguez eyed his corporal and three security officers. "We'll be on our best behavior and do it by the book, Major. Won't we, people?" He received a chorus of agreement."

"Major, are you authorizing the use of shock sticks?" the corporal, Cecilia, asked.

"Negative, Corporal, only Sergeant Rodriquez and I are authorized to employ force." Liam wanted to say more, but the cap arrived and the lights signaled release. The security team stuck their deck shoes firmly to the floor and released their shoulder braces and harnesses.

Liam's comm unit buzzed and he glanced at it, as they made their way to the El car. The message was a note from Devon with his boarding passes and the search warrant.

"But my associates and I have business to conduct downside," a man who was being ushered off the El was heard to say to the El manager.

"And my sister and I must get home to our families," a well-dressed downsider complained.

The individuals being shown off the El car ceased their complaints when they spotted security marching onto the El. In recent history, there had never been such a sight. Suddenly, comm units were being accessed, but everyone found the downside link offline.

Liam spotted the disturbed faces of the downsiders, who stared at their comm units in frustration. *Good job, Devon,* he thought.

Once aboard the El, Liam moved a few passengers into other seats, so that his team could sit together in a more secluded spot on the car. "Once we get to the governor's house and I present the warrant, we divide up. Corporal Lindstrom, you will take the three officers and search the house. Stay in pairs. If you find a locked door, request it be opened. If you're unreasonably obstructed or delayed, then break it open. Sergeant, you stand by Giorgio. Be careful with that one. I'll stay with Governor Andropov."

"What if the principals aren't in residence, Major?" Miguel asked.

"Once we serve the warrant I expect them to arrive shortly, Sergeant. You and I'll wait inside the front door for them."

"Do you expect trouble from anyone in the household?" Cecilia asked.

"I can't say, Corporal. That's why I want you to work in pairs. If you're confronted, remain calm, be polite, and comm me with your location. Either Sergeant Rodriguez or I will remove your impediment, one way or the other."

Miguel nodded his understanding of Liam's implied message. They would search every inch of the house, whether the governor or the household liked it or not.

The El car began its descent precisely on time, and Liam leaned back in his seat to think through the possible issues he would encounter. He would have preferred a larger force, but it would have taken longer to organize. At this moment, time was his friend. Hours from now, it might well become his enemy.

When the El car transited the dome's airlock, Liam sent a message to the car manager that his team would exit first. As the El touched its landing pad, the manager announced to the passengers that they should briefly remain seated. It was an unnecessary message. None of the passengers had any intention of getting in front of the security team. However, recognizing that they had comm unit service within the domes, they busily called family, friends, and associates.

Liam gritted his teeth when he realized they had no control over communication within the domes. It reminded him of the manner in which Pyre had developed into separate fiefdoms. It wasn't the way it was supposed to be, but Earth was a long distance away and unable to raise an objection.

At the bottom of the car's landing ramp, Liam paused. It hit him that this was his first trip downside. "Who's been downside before?" he asked quietly. When everyone shook their head in negation, he muttered, "Oh, for the love of Pyre."

"Major, my duty station is the tech department," Cecilia said. "Lieutenant Devon told me to assist. I haven't been downside, but I'm familiar with their tech."

"Thank goodness," Liam replied. "Lead on, Corporal."

Cecilia hurried toward a line of e-trans vehicles, where passengers were unloading to catch the El's next ascent. Liam kept pace beside her. "I would suggest you and two others in this first vehicle, Captain."

"Don't be so polite, Corporal," Liam replied. "Tell us what to do."

"Yes, sir. Sit behind the console. You two," Liam ordered, pointing at two of the privates, "join the captain."

"We've got the next car," Miguel said, indicating to the last officer with a wave of his fingers that she should join him.

"Save the console seat for me, Sergeant," Cecilia called out. She accessed her comm unit for the priority override codes, which would allow their e-trans cars to supersede all other vehicles transiting through the domes' airlocks. She leaned in front of the major and quietly said, "Priority access, tango, kilo, echo, one, seven, three, oscar."

"Priority override accepted," the car's computer replied. "Please state destination."

"Governor's residence in a two-car entourage."

"Please code the second car," the computer requested.

Cecilia eyed the number emblazoned on the front of the e-trans vehicle the sergeant sat in and repeated the number for the computer.

"Ready," the computer replied.

"Initiate," Cecilia replied. She stepped back to allow the major's car to make a sharp turn and proceed at speed toward the dome's airlock. The second car whisked past her and she jumped in, banging her knee.

"Well done, Corporal, except for that part of injuring yourself," Miguel commented drily.

"Thank you, Sergeant," Cecilia replied, rubbing her knee.

"What made you study downsider tech to the point that you could program priority codes?" Miguel asked.

"Lieutenant Higgins' orders, Sergeant. He said that you never knew when things like this might be needed."

"Interesting," Miguel replied. "And how long ago was this?"

"About a year and a half, Sergeant."

Approaching the first airlock, the captain's e-trans computer communicated its priority code and transports on both sides of the airlock were halted. Their cars zipped to the front of the line and through the open gate on their side. As soon as their cars were inside, the gate behind them closed and the opposite gate opened. Then they were quickly on their way. Transport vehicles in front of them slowed and pulled to the side, and they flew past.

"You wouldn't think these little things could move this fast," Miguel said, grasping a safety bar on the side of the vehicle.

"Amazing, aren't they?" Cecilia replied. "I have to admit though, that I never checked into whether they've ever had accidents. I mean accidents that resulted in loss of life." She kept a straight face, but the officer in the back seat snickered.

"Funny, Corporal," Miguel growled, keeping a firm grip on the safety bar.

The e-trans vehicles made excellent time, navigating the domes and airlocks to the governor's residence, and they arrived seconds after Markos and Giorgio exited their vehicle in front of the house.

When Markos spotted the security team, which he expected, having been alerted to their coming, he glanced at Giorgio and tossed his head toward the house. On the way from a meeting, which they had hurriedly abandoned, Markos had told Giorgio to get the women out of the house by the residence's garden entrance and have the household staff straighten up their rooms. What he couldn't understand was how the security team had arrived so quickly. He was sure that Giorgio and he had another fifteen minutes.

"Governor, halt," Liam called, leaping from his car.

"Major Finian, this is quite unusual, isn't it? Descending downside without an invitation or an announcement?" Markos replied, as if Liam was making a social call.

Miguel spotted Giorgio walking toward the house, and he leapt clear of his car and raced after him. "Giorgio Sestos, you're ordered to halt,"

"I'll just be a moment, Sergeant," Giorgio replied over his shoulder, as he kept walking.

Miguel ran to place himself directly in Giorgio's path. "No, you won't, sir. You'll stay where you stand and await the major's pleasure," Miguel said forcefully, placing his hand on the head of his shock stick. He saw Giorgio's eyes travel down his arm and take in the message. Then Miguel watched Giorgio deflate, and he thought, *That's acceptance of guilt.*

"Major, you've no right —" Markos started, but that was as far as he got.

"My warrant," Liam said, holding his comm unit in front of the governor's face. "I have the right to search your residence and the grounds for Helena Garmenti. Corporal, proceed."

Markos took the comm unit and scrolled through the details, recognizing it was properly issued by the Review Board at the request of the commandant. His face screwed up in a grimace. "Might we wait inside, Major?"

"Certainly, Governor," replied Liam, gesturing toward the front door.

Cecilia led the three officers into the house, divided them into pairs, a man and a woman in each pair, and directed their search on the first level. The residence was completely foreign to her and the officers. It didn't resemble the logical, organized, and repetitive layout of the JOS. Nonetheless, they checked behind every door, often finding a closet or a storage room.

When Cecilia and her team circled back to the front of the house, where the major and the sergeant waited with Markos and Giorgio, she shook her head briefly at Liam and accessed the lift to the second floor. They conducted another thorough search of that floor's premises.

One of the household staff, who stood aside as Cecilia passed, cut her eyes to the left. The corporal didn't assign it any significance, but when they passed the woman on the way to the lift, the woman repeated her action, and Cecilia's brow furrowed.

The third floor, the residence's upper level, received the same attention from the team as the first two floors without success.

Standing at the third-floor lift, one of the officers, Bowden, said, "Corporal, does it strike you as strange how quickly the search went on this floor?"

"It does," Cecilia acknowledged. "You two," she said pointing to the other team, "stay here. Bowden, you're with me."

Cecilia took the lift down to the first floor. "Bowden, out the front. I want to know if the third floor extends as far out as the other two floors. Hustle." She jogged down the main hallway, out the back door, and onto an expansive patio. She stepped out and gazed upward. The third floor was even with the first two.

A noise captured Cecilia's attention. A groundskeeper gave her a salute of fingers to his brow, and she hurried back inside. Bowden was waiting for her at the lift. "Same?" she asked.

"Same," Bowden replied.

"Imagine that? Back to the third floor," Cecilia ordered. But, in the lift, she chose the second floor.

"What's up, Corporal," Bowden asked, when he saw the change in destination.

"I just realized the staff has been trying to direct us."

"How so?"

"A woman on the second floor cut her eyes twice toward the rear of the house, and the groundskeeper gave me a weird salute. He tucked his small finger under his thumb and touched three fingers to his brow."

"You're thinking we have to get to the third floor from the second floor, but not via the lift?"

"That's my guess."

Exiting the lift on the second floor, Cecilia walked toward the rear of the house. A window looked out on the beautifully kept grounds. She took a moment to admire the expanse of green, something she'd never seen before. It seemed exotic and unsettling at the same time.

"Look here, Corporal," Bowden requested. He was kneeling to the right of the window, looking at the floor. "There's the hint of a track under this section of the wall.

Cecilia stepped back. The sides of the wall opposite the window were identical. Decorated as they were, it was difficult to ascertain if any section of the wall was designed to move. She accessed her comm unit. "Major, I'm convinced there's a rear part of the third floor, which we can't access. However, on the second floor, there might be a hidden passageway."

"Governor, you can either give us access or we can tear our way through every door, wall, or floor, if necessary, until we've searched the entire house," Liam said.

"Those rooms on the third floor were the private chambers of my wife, Major. They were sealed after her death and haven't been opened since. I'm sure you can respect that."

"My apologies to the memory of your wife, Governor Andropov," Liam replied sincerely, "but there will be no exceptions. What will it be?"

Markos sighed, and, to Liam, it seemed the very life of the man drained out of him in that one breath. "May I?" Markos asked, gesturing toward Liam's device. Once he had the comm unit, Markos said, "Corporal, go to the last doorway on your left, as you face the rear of the building. Rotate the plate of the actuator one hundred and eighty degrees clockwise. Then hit the button."

Cecilia followed the governor's direction, and Bowden and she watched a section of the wall at the rear of the building slide away. The two of them hurried to enter a lit stairwell, and they made their way to the third floor. There was nothing to stop them from entering a short corridor.

Liam reached for his comm unit, but Markos held a finger up to forestall him. "Are you on the third floor, Corporal?" Markos asked.

"Yes."

"Second door on your right, Corporal. Reach above the top frame at its center. You'll feel a small latch. Flick it to the left," Markos said, and then handed the comm unit back.

Cecilia grunted, as she stretched to the top of the door. Throwing the tiny metal protrusion, she found produced the soft snick of a lock unlatching. She stepped through the doorway, and a young girl in the middle of the room froze and stared at her in confusion. "I'm Corporal Lindstrom of JOS Security. We're looking for Helena Garmenti," Cecilia announced.

The girl's face twisted in anger, and Cecilia felt unreasoning dark hatred flood her thoughts. It was anguish, pain, and dread rolled into one, and she staggered backwards from the attack. Bowden caught her, but it was obvious that he was suffering from the same onslaught.

"Sasha, no!" Helena screamed, rushing to embrace her daughter. "They're not here to hurt us. They're here to help."

The ugly sensation disappeared from Cecilia and Bowden's minds, but they were dry retching from the attack. Helena came toward them and reached out her hands, but the security team pulled away.

"Please. Let me help. My daughter couldn't know who you were. These rooms have been her entire life since the day she was born," Helena entreated.

The plea of a mother allowed Cecilia to stand still when Helena reached out and grasped her hands. The corporal felt pleasure and gratefulness. It was soothing, and it erased the lingering dark sensations.

"Better?" Helena asked, and Cecilia nodded and smiled her thanks.

When Helena approached the other officer, he pulled away.

"Trust me, Bowden, you want this," Cecilia said.

Acquiescing to the woman's administrations, Bowden remarked afterwards, "That helped. Thanks."

"I take it you're Helena Garmenti," Cecilia said.

"Yes, Corporal Lindstrom," Helena replied, reading Cecilia's name on her uniform. "And this is my daughter, Sasha," she said, stepping back and throwing a protective arm around her daughter's shoulders.

"Please gather your personal things, Helena. You'll be escorted to the station," Cecilia directed. "I'll have additional officers up here in a moment to help you pack."

"Are we being arrested?" Helena asked.

"No, certainly not," Cecilia replied, holding up her hands to forestall Sasha's reactions. The girl's face started to twist with hostility.

"You and your daughter are being freed, Helena," explained Cecilia. "I'm so sorry it took this long to discover what happened to you."

"What about my sister?" Sasha demanded.

"She's missing," Bowden replied.

Cecilia could have kicked her subordinate. His answer obviously frustrated the young girl, and that was the last thing they needed.

"Let me correct that, Sasha," Cecilia said gently. "Your sister made it to the JOS, the station. We believe she found help and has been in hiding since then."

Sasha stared at the woman for a prolonged moment. She turned to her mother. "That one," she said, pointing to Cecilia, "believes what she's saying."

"Good to know, Sasha," Helena said, kissing her daughter's forehead. "Why don't you go to your room and pack what you wish to keep."

Sasha disappeared into her bedroom and the living space filled behind her with delightful happiness.

Helena approached Cecilia, wringing her hands. "You've seen Sasha's powers. She's a willful, young girl who's been terribly tortured by her imprisonment. Aurelia constantly soothed her, but since she's been gone, Sasha has become almost uncontrollable. You must be careful with what you say."

"We can always trank her," Bowden volunteered.

"Private, step outside and call the other team up here. Meet them in the corridor and stay there." Cecilia ground out.

"Did he mean that?" Helena asked.

"I hope it won't come to that, Helena. If we can get her to the JOS without incident, I understand Harbour is waiting to meet you both."

Helena's hands clapped together and came to her lips. Tears of joy ran rivulets down her face, and Cecilia folded the woman into her arms, while she sobbed.

"Corporal, report," the major said over Cecilia's comm unit, which broke the women apart. Helena hurried to Sasha's room, and Cecilia answered her comm.

"Major, we have Helena Garmenti and her daughter, Sasha, and are preparing them for transport. When you have secured your individuals, we need to speak privately."

"Understood, Corporal," Liam replied, exchanging glances with Miguel.

Cecilia heard voices in the hallway and stepped outside. "Who's a parent?" she asked.

Officer Nunez raised a hand. "I have a little girl. She's nine."

"Perfect," Cecilia replied. "Here's the situation. You've probably already heard from Bowden that we found Helena and her daughter, Sasha. What he might not have told you is that Sasha is a powerful, untrained empath with anger issues. Bowden and I have already had a dose of her displeasure, thanks to his ill-considered response."

Bowden started to object to the corporal's statement, but thought better of it.

"Here's how this is going to work," Cecilia continued. "We're going to help the women pack up their belongings and load out the boxes or what-have-you to the front porch. When Sasha is in earshot of any of us, only Nunez and I will speak. Is that clear?"

Cecilia waited until she had her team's agreement on her directives.

"Nunez, we treat her like any other young girl. No better and no worse. She needs to understand the world of normal adults. I'll ask Helena to stay close to her daughter. Okay, let's go."

Cecilia's team was able to pack, bag, box, or wrap in bed clothing everything the women wanted to take, and carry it down to the porch.

At one point, Sasha picked up a coverlet full of her things and marched to the door. Cecilia was across the room and caught off guard. Nunez stepped in her path. "Could I help you with that?" he asked gently.

"No, I want to carry this one myself," Sasha stated forcefully.

"Okay, you can do that, but you'll have to wait and take it down later," Nunez replied.

"Why?" Sasha asked. She hadn't formed an opinion of this man, whose emotions felt warm to her.

"Because I have a major and a sergeant downstairs right now, and they're very, very busy."

"Doing what?"

Nunez leaned over conspiratorially to Sasha, who tilted her head to listen to what the man had to say.

"They're busy arresting Governor Andropov and Giorgio Sestos for the crimes committed against you and your mother," Nunez whispered.

Sasha smiled and laughed delightedly, although the sound had an edge to it. She dropped her load to the side and skipped back to her room to help with the packing. Those in the living room were struck by a powerful, mental force. It wasn't dark or bright in sensation. It felt more like the onslaught of a strong wind, which had suddenly blown up.

When the team's final transfer of personal items was ready, Sasha asked Nunez, "Now?"

"Now," he agreed, and Sasha wound the ends of the coverlet in her hands and slung the heavy load on her back. She struggled through the doorway, never looking back. Nunez kept pace with her, and the pair followed the other privates to the back stairway.

Sasha paused and looked down the steps' steep pitch.

"Stairs," Nunez said, his heart breaking at the thought that the young girl lived in this house for more than a decade and never got to use them.

"It's okay," Sasha said, setting down her load and taking the man's hand.

Nunez nodded numbly, as warmth filled him. He picked up Sasha's load, transferred it to his left, and gripped Sasha's hand with his right to help her down the stairs to the next level. Sasha never let go of his hand until she saw Markos and Giorgio standing with Liam and Miguel. Then her hand slipped out of his, and she stalked toward the men.

"Sasha, no," Helena called out sternly and ran forward to embrace her daughter. "Remember what I told you. If you hurt these men, you'll affect everyone around you, even those who are helping us."

Sasha paused and looked back at the man, who felt so deeply for her. She tossed off her anger with a quick, "humph," and walked back to take Nunez's hand. When she passed Markos, she said tersely, "We're leaving," and enjoyed the rush of pleasure it gave the people, who had arrived to free her mother and her.

"The two of you," Cecilia said, to Bowden and the other officer, "support Sergeant Rodriguez. Major, a word outside, if I may?"

Liam hid his smile at the manner in which Cecilia was taking charge. Out on the porch, he watched Nunez holding Sasha's hand, as the girl examined the flowering trees and waved happily at the bees. "What's up, Corporal?"

"Major, Sasha is a powerful and untrained empath."

"Okay?" Liam replied, not sure where this was going.

"No, Major, Sasha is a young girl, who is upset at being kept imprisoned for her entire life in a set of rooms, and she has the capability to drop this team on the deck with one outburst of anger. We might even attempt to harm ourselves if we thought it would relieve the terror she unleashes."

Liam watched the girl playing with his officer. She looked like any happy child. "Nunez seems to have formed a quick bond."

"My suggestion, Major, is to get a transport for the women's things. Commandeer three e-trans vehicles. Sasha sits in the front car with her mother, Nunez, and me. It'll be a treat for her."

"You realize that if Sasha acts out, I might have no choice but to shock her. I'd prefer a trank, if needed, but I don't see us getting a chance to use it."

"I understand, Major. I think if Nunez and I can keep her entertained until we get her to Harbour, we'll have been successful. I can tell you one thing, sir. She'll have to be in Harbour's care for years until she learns to manage her emotions and control her power."

"Okay, *Sergeant* Lindstrom, set up the vehicles, and let us know when you're ready."

Cecilia crooked her head at Liam, giving him time to acknowledge what she'd heard.

"We'll make it official tomorrow," Liam said, grinning.

"Yes, sir," Cecilia replied, smiling in return, and took off to arrange the transportation.

Cecilia collected the first e-trans car that passed and directed it to the front of the house. She entered her priority code and requested three more vehicles, two e-trans, and an e-cart. The major returned to the governor's side, which freed her and the privates to load the e-cart with the women's belongings. When all was ready, Cecilia signaled the major.

"Helena, will you and your daughter take the first vehicle, please?" Liam requested.

"Certainly, Major," Helena replied. She paused in front of the governor. "Markos, in case there's no opportunity, in the future, to relay to you my infinite pleasure at my imprisonment, let me say this." Then Helena swung her open hand as hard as she could at Markos face, and it struck with a resounding slap. The governor stumbled against the corridor wall, and Helena shook her stinging hand. She hadn't expected it to hurt that much, but she wouldn't have missed the opportunity for the universe.

As Helena marched out the front door, Markos suffered the added indignity of the major and sergeant's delighted smiles.

20: Rescued

Outside the governor's home, downsiders had gathered to watch. Not knowing how Sasha would react to them, Cecilia ordered them to retreat to the far side of the ped-path. The crowd was reluctant to move until two privates advanced on them with hands on shock sticks. While they were indignant at the threat of force, nonetheless, they hurried to the far side.

Cecilia signaled Nunez, who whispered to Sasha. The girl glanced toward her, and Cecilia encouraged her with a wave of an arm. Sasha took Nunez's hand and strolled her way. The child was in no hurry. She was enjoying every moment of her newfound freedom.

But, as a mother of a young girl, Cecilia wasn't fooled. She'd suffered her child's outbursts and tantrums alongside moments of joy and love. The difference was that her child wasn't capable of turning someone's mental state to mush when she was resentful.

"Would you like to ride up front with me?" Cecilia asked, standing beside the lead e-trans.

"Where do you ride?" Sasha asked Nunez.

"Oh, I like to be chauffeured," Nunez replied, without missing a beat.

"What's chauffeured?" Sasha asked.

"That's where we sit in the back like bigshots and make people drive us around."

"I want to be chauffeured," Sasha exclaimed, and climbed into the rear seat.

Nunez grinned at Cecilia and announced loudly, "The El car, Corporal, and make it snappy."

"Yes, make it snappy," Sasha echoed.

Cecilia sketched her best imitation of a bow. "Yes, your ladyship," she intoned solemnly.

Helena hid her smile behind a hand and ran around the car to climb into the seat next to Cecilia.

Of special interest to the onlookers was the sight of the woman and the child, whom they had never seen before, and comm units recorded every moment. More shocking to them was witnessing the governor and his chief security officer led out of the house and loaded into e-trans vehicles. Conjecture flew among them, and rumors spread by comm calls throughout the domes.

When the two privates finished loading the women's baggage into the e-cart, they split up and climbed into the console seats of the last two e-trans cars. Liam sat in the back of the second vehicle with Markos, and Miguel shared the rear seat of the last car with Giorgio. Unlike the major, who sat relaxed beside the governor, Miguel had pulled his shock stick and activated it. The subtle whine of the charging circuitry was not lost on Giorgio, and Miguel underlined his intent by locking eyes with the security chief.

Liam signaled Cecilia, and they were whisked quickly away from the governor's house. Traffic was stopped in both directions for the priority-driven vehicles. As soon as they were underway, Liam tested his connection to the JOS and was pleased to find that Devon had restored the link. *Good man,* he thought before he placed his call.

"Devon, we have the woman, her daughter, the governor, and his security chief," Liam said.

"Wow," Devon said in a rush. "And I missed out."

"Better safe than sorry, Devon. I'll let you arrest the next governor."

Markos stared at Liam. He attempted to appear belligerent, but it was a desultory expression.

"Do you want me to notify the commandant?" Devon asked.

"Negative, with capital letters, Devon. I need Harbour to meet us as we exit the El. Is she still aboard the JOS?"

"Affirmative, Captain. Is everything all right?"

"What would you consider the level of intelligence of someone who locked up an extremely powerful empath?" Liam asked, and he switched his device to speaker mode so that Markos could hear the answer.

"I'd consider the man an idiot, at best," Devon replied.

Liam switched his comm unit back to private for the remainder of the conversation.

"Is it the mother?" Devon asked.

"No, it's about a ten or eleven year old with little emotional restraint and massive anger issues."

"Oh, for the love of Pyre, are you sure it's safe to bring her topside?"

"Not really, but I'm not leaving her down here with these people. That's why I want Harbour onsite at our exit. I do have good news. Corporal Lindstrom has been invaluable. Good choice there, Devon. Tomorrow she's promoted to sergeant."

"That's good news, Major. She's deserved it for a while."

"The other good news is that Sasha, the daughter, has formed a quick attachment to Officer Nunez."

"Understandable. Have you not met his family?"

"Afraid I haven't."

"His daughter is bright. I mean really smart, and she's a handful. Nunez and his wife are kept on their toes with her, and he's a great dad."

"Good to know, Devon."

"I'll make the arrangements with Harbour. See you topside."

Liam closed his comm. Protocol demanded he inform the commandant of the discovery and arrests, but he was loath to tell Emerson anything that might potentially interfere with his transport of the women and his prisoners. Then it occurred to him the commandant wouldn't bother checking the timeline of events. He could say that the downlink from the JOS to the domes was cut to prevent warning the governor, and he hadn't thought it had been restored. Undoubtedly, Emerson would receive a call from Lise Panoy before they made the JOS. Liam was interested to see if the commandant inadvertently leaked information about what happened downside before Liam informed him.

The train of vehicles moved swiftly through the domes and airlocks, arriving only minutes before the El was scheduled to depart. Cecilia ran ahead to inform the manager that they needed ten seats and needed crew to unload the e-cart baggage into a cargo container for transport.

"Ten seats," the manager squeaked. "But we're full up, and we depart in a few minutes."

"Get your cargo crew moving, sir, or you'll leave even later. I'll take care of the ten seats," Cecilia replied.

The manager called the cargo chief on his comm unit, and Cecilia ran up the ramp to the passenger level. Meanwhile, the security team and their passengers waited in their e-trans vehicles. Passengers, who had disembarked the El, were surprised the vehicles weren't being made available but wisely chose not to ask. Instead the queue moved down the line to take the empty e-trans cars, which had arrived behind the e-cart.

An El cargo member drove a container next to the e-cart and crew crawled over the baggage, transferring the contents in a matter of minutes. Then the container was loaded into the belly of the El car.

"We're going to ride in that?" Sasha asked. She'd begun to fidget, and Nunez exchanged quick glances with Helena.

"Yep, it's going to take us into space, and I need to tell you something important," Nunez said, turning toward Sasha and adopting a serious expression. When Sasha did the same thing, it took great self-control on Nunez's part not to smile.

"When the El car rises, it leaves the gravity of Pyre," Nunez explained.

"I know that."

"And I was sure you did," Nunez allowed. "But, here's the important thing. Many people find becoming weightless, for the first time, to be difficult, and they get sick."

"If they yuck in zero-g, doesn't that stuff go everywhere?" Sasha asked. Her little face screwed up in disgust.

"It could. That's why there are special bags for everyone next to their seats."

"Do you think I'm going to yuck?"

"I don't know. I did the first time I felt weightlessness."

"You did?"

"Yep."

"Okay, if you can, I guess I can."

Nunez glanced up to see a line of disgruntled passengers coming down the ramp, and he glanced back at the major, who stepped out of his e-trans. The team followed, disembarking and assisting various individuals from the cars.

In the El passenger cabin, Cecilia had considered asking for volunteers, but she knew who she would get — hardworking stationers. Instead, she picked out downsiders and wealthy stationers and informed them they would be giving up their seats for a JOS security emergency. She heard all manner of objections and accepted none. The ten passengers were sharing their anger with one another, as they disembarked, until they passed the security team accompanied by the governor, his security chief, and two other downsiders.

When Liam boarded, he found Cecilia had already rearranged the passengers to allow the group to sit together in one of the quieter areas.

"Don't know, Major, maybe you should promote the corporal to lieutenant," Miguel whispered, spotting Cecilia's arrangements.

"I don't want to give her ideas, Sergeant. She might be after my job. Did you notice whom she bumped off?"

"Sure did ... only Pyre's best. Had to work hard from snickering when we passed them by."

The group settled into their seats after Cecilia and Nunez ensured that Helena and Sasha were comfortable and belted. The two officers bracketed Sasha, and Nunez kept up a conversation with Sasha, as the El car rose.

Cecilia belatedly realized that neither the prisoners nor the women were dressed properly for the JOS environment. She sent a quick message to the captain, which read, "Our four individuals are without skins and deck shoes."

Liam's message to Cecilia said, "Thought of that too, Corporal. Devon is scurrying to find proper clothes. We'll have these people change in the El restroom."

When the El reached the JOS, Liam had the manager unload the other passengers first. Soon after, a security officer hurried aboard with a duffel bag full of clothing and deck shoes. The two security women helped Helena and Sasha out of their seats and towed them to the restroom.

Sasha was giggling. "Look, Mommy, we're flying," she shouted.

The clothes were poor fits, more so for Sasha. Cecilia did her best to deal with the oversized skins on the child. Sasha couldn't care less. She was more intent on practicing walking with her slightly big deck shoes, forcing Cecilia to stay close to her. The thought crossed Cecilia's mind that she should have had the major request some safety line and hooks. Markos and Giorgio refused the undecorated, black skins but accepted the deck shoes.

With Cecilia and Nunez accompanying Helena and Sasha and leading the way, the group made their way off the El passenger level to the transit ring. Liam sent one of the privates with the four who were in front and ordered the group to wait for him on the other side. Before their capsule left, he ordered another one.

Inside the cap, Cecilia reached out to grasp Helena's hand. The mother was shedding quiet tears of relief at her return to the station, and she smiled at the security officer's consideration.

* * * *

Harbour was browsing in some stores, killing time, when she received Lieutenant Higgins' urgent call.

"Where are you, Harbour?" Devon asked anxiously.

"I'm here on the JOS, waiting for an update."

"Good, good. The major has found Helena and another daughter, Sasha."

Aurelia was telling the truth, Harbour thought, but what she said was, "Is the major bringing the women to the JOS?"

"The women, the governor, and his security chief."

"Even better news, Lieutenant."

"I agree, but taking the men into custody is only the first step."

"I quite agree," Harbour allowed, but she knew Devon was thinking about the upcoming trial, while Harbour was considering the power vacuum created by toppling the Andropov family and the opportunity it represented for many of the other families.

"Harbour, the major has requested you meet him at the JOS El passenger transition gate. There are indications that the daughter, Sasha, who is probably about ten, is a powerful empath."

"What kind of indications?"

"The major wasn't specific, but I could detect some heavy concern in his voice, and he doesn't frighten easily. He did say that the girl has some anger issues."

"Not surprising, considering she's been locked in a house all her life. Not to worry, Lieutenant, tell the Major I'll meet the women at the exit gate."

"Thank you, Harbour," Devon replied. "With their priority transports downside, they should catch the next El lift. I place them aboard the station in about fifty minutes."

There had been time to get a snack, but despite having missed lunch, Harbour was too unsettled to eat. If anything, she wanted to talk to Jessie. He was the catalyst for the events that were unfolding, whether he wanted to take credit for them or not. She thought, if they could talk, they might devise a plan that would accomplish more for Pyrean society than simply accepting the downfall of the Andropov family only to be replaced by another group of wealthy downsiders.

Harbour perused a few more stores, scarcely registering what she was seeing. Thoughts of the women, Sasha's power, the governor's arrest, and the commandant's treachery tumbled through her mind. The chime of her comm unit interrupted her musings, and she hurried to the El exit gate. The feed over the gate counted down the minutes until the El car docked.

Stepping to the corridor side, Harbour watched as family members, friends, and associates greeted the arriving passengers. Many were abuzz with the news of who was riding the El with them, but the groups, either spotting Harbour or being warned of her presence, hurried on. Soon, she was left alone in the corridor.

After a few minutes delay, the cap doors rolled aside, and Harbour watched a security team unhook and unbelt Helena and Sasha and then lead them onto the station deck.

Sasha was terribly disappointed by the return of gravity, but that quickly shifted when she saw the bustle of the station — people wearing incredibly decorated skins and shops displaying enticing goods.

Harbour's sensitivities were attenuated to prevent being overpowered by the normals, who had surrounded her at the gate. Despite that, she could feel Sasha's broadcast. Not only was it considerable, but it shifted in an instant from dark to bright, unhappy to elated.

"Harbour," Cecilia called out, and directed the group's attention toward her.

Helena hurried forward and threw her arms around Harbour's neck, and she reciprocated with support and strength.

"I've thought about you for seventeen years," Helena said, sniffling and swiping at her tears.

"There are more steps to take," Harbour said, holding Helena's hands, "but this is the beginning of the end. Have courage. You're safe now. I'll see to that."

Harbour stepped to the side and regarded Sasha. The child's broadcast was mercurial, as emotions swung in different directions. She noticed that Sasha's hand had never left that of a tall security officer. The name patch said Nunez. She sensed a balance of concern and intention from him.

"Sasha, say hello to Harbour," Helena invited. "This is the woman who I've told you and your sister about so many times."

Before Sasha could reply, the cap behind them opened, and the group turned around to see the security team exit with Markos and Giorgio in tow.

Harbour sensed the hostility from Sasha ratchet to an incredible level, but it dropped when Nunez bent down to whisper in her ear.

"Everyone, let's head for security administration," Liam announced, but he hesitated when he caught Harbour's minute shake of her head.

"We'll join you soon, Major," Harbour replied. She stepped in front of Markos, smiling warmly. "It's so good to see you governor ... under arrest."

Liam pulled on Markos arm, and the governor was denied an opportunity to retort, but he definitely heard Sasha's giggle. Giorgio lunged and hissed at Sasha, who was caught off guard and jerked back.

However, Harbour wasn't about to let Giorgio get away with a slight against one of her people.

Giorgio gave Harbour a nasty grin as he came abreast of her, but a massive onslaught of panic caused him to shriek and jump. He spun out of Miguel's grip, searching for the danger.

"Some tough security chief," Miguel commented, grasping Giorgio's arm and pulling him forward. He gave Harbour a tiny smile, as he passed her.

"I thought we weren't supposed to do that?" Sasha asked Harbour, as her tormentors were led off.

"Did you feel what I did?" Harbour asked Sasha, noting the girl had let go of Nunez's hand.

"Barely, but Giorgio jumped like he was shocked," Sasha replied. She giggled and added, "He deserved that."

"What I did is called directing. It enables an empath to focus the power on one person instead of everyone around them. Would you like to learn to do that?"

"Okay," Sasha replied. She made it sound as if she didn't care one way or the other, but the small pulse of excitement that Harbour detected gave Sasha away.

"Pretty," Sasha said, tracing the filigree pattern on the side of Harbour's skins.

"Pretty bad," replied Harbour, doing the same to Sasha's skins, eliciting a giggle from the girl, who regarded her skins and then Harbour's. "I think those skins of yours call for some shopping." Before Cecilia could object Harbour added, "Lindstrom and Nunez, I'm sure Sasha would love to have you join us."

"Please," Sasha said excitedly, and clapped her hands when the security team nodded their acceptance.

As the group left the passenger gate side corridor, Cecilia sent the major a message, which said, "We're going shopping." Cecilia glanced at the reply, "Please clarify." She typed quickly, "Harbour's leading, and we're following." There wasn't a reply, and Cecilia sent, "Harbour's helping Sasha adjust to the station. It's better than taking the child from a room in her house to a room in security."

The captain's reply was simply, "Agreed."

* * * *

Major Finian reported in person to the commandant after accompanying Sergeant Miguel and the prisoners to the lockup. He left Devon and Miguel to file the charges against the two men. As Liam expected, the commandant was livid and screeching at the top of his thin voice when he discovered he hadn't been kept in the loop.

"Commandant, I ordered Lieutenant Higgins to shut down the communications link downside before we descended. It gave us the edge we needed. Our team arrived seconds after the governor and security chief exited their vehicles at the house. It was obvious that they had been warned by downsiders on the El once we were inside the dome. There's no telling what they intended to do to hide their crimes."

"You could have called me on the way up, Captain. It's your responsibility to keep me informed."

"That's my fault, Commandant. I assumed Lieutenant Higgins hadn't restored the link. I learned afterwards that he had. Regardless, my attention was focused on ensuring that those in my custody received the proper clothing when they arrived and the daughter was kept entertained."

"Entertained?" Emerson repeated.

"Sasha is a young, bitter girl, who is a powerful empath. Her anger stems from the fact that she's been confined to some third-floor rooms in the governor's house for her entire life."

"How powerful is she?"

"I'm no judge of these things, Commandant, but she was able to mentally cripple some of my people within a few meters of her."

"Well, I think it's best that the girl is isolated for now ... Harbour, so pleased to see you."

Liam took in the commandant's choked expression, before he whirled around. Harbour was standing in the doorway, a stormy expression on her face.

"I thought you'd like to meet Helena and Sasha, Commandant," Harbour said. "I wanted to inform you that I'm formally declaring these women are now under my protection."

"We haven't even sent the charges for the governor and his chief of security to the Review Board, Harbour. It's imperative that we keep them under our protection until events have run their course."

Liam winced. He expected Harbour to retaliate, either mentally or vocally, but she merely smiled and turned to speak to those who waited outside the commandant's office.

"Ladies, come say hello and goodbye to the commandant," Harbour requested.

Helena stepped through the doorway first and nodded politely to Emerson.

When Sasha entered the room, she looked up at Harbour and asked, "What's a commandant?"

"That's a commandant," Harbour replied, pointing at Emerson. "He's the person who is in charge of station security."

Emerson was puffing up with pride, when Harbour added, "He's the person who would be responsible for rescuing lost people, like your mother."

A scowl crossed Sasha's face, and Emerson deflated.

Harbour placed a hand on Sasha's shoulder, which curtailed the rising storm. Instead, Sasha glared at the commandant and announced, "He's not very good at his job, is he?"

The security team, who had accompanied Harbour, Helena, and Sasha, crushed their snickers, but Harbour laughed. "No, he's not," she agreed. "Come, ladies, we've taken up enough of the man's time. Call me, Commandant, when you need their testimony for the Review Board's initial interviews to confirm your charges. We'll remain on station for the next two days.

"Sasha," Liam called out, "nice skins."

The little girl wore a pair of deep silver skins with delicate, bright blue filigree worked around the shoulders and arms. Her long hair was pulled into a ponytail, like Harbour's, and was captured by a rainbow-colored clip.

Sasha flashed a brilliant smile and preened. She nearly rose off the deck from the compliment.

As Harbour ushered the women out the door, she winked at Liam and sent a small amount of warmth his way. In the hallway, she said, "Sasha, you have to say goodbye to Cecilia and Nunez. They have to go back to work."

"No, they can stay with us," Sasha loudly objected.

Nunez interrupted the brewing storm, dropping down on his knees in front of Sasha. "You know the governor and Giorgio were bad men, right?" When he received a stubborn nod of agreement, he plowed on, "Well, that's what the corporal and I do for a living. We catch bad people."

Sasha looked at Cecilia for affirmation.

"There could be other little girls out there who need our help," Cecilia said.

"Okay," Sasha agreed grudgingly. She threw her slender arms around Nunez's neck, and the entire group was treated to a blast from her.

The commandant watched Harbour lead the women away. "I can't believe what I just felt," he said, smiling and placing a hand on his heart.

"It was meant for Nunez," Liam replied. He wasn't happy that Emerson received something precious, which he didn't deserve. "The girl hasn't any control. She can just as easily devastate a group of people, while meaning to hurt one person."

The thought quickly sobered Emerson, thinking he could be the girl's target for his failure to rescue her mother and her.

"With your permission, Commandant, I'll see to expediting the charges and calling an emergency session of the Review Board. I'm sure that you have your own calls to make," Liam said, with a tip of his fingers to his cap.

Emerson's eyes narrowed at Liam, wondering if there was an underlying meaning in his last sentence, but the man wore the blandest of expressions.

"Get to it, Major. Dismissed."

21: Jessie

The *Spryte* was docked at the YIPS, unloading a pile of ingots that the crew of the *Annie* had produced before leaving for Triton. The three bay loads of valuable metals added a substantial amount of coin to the company's coffers, and, because the individuals who signed with Jessie received a stipend plus a share of the company's annual gains, it made for happy crews.

It had been a risky decision on Jessie's part to chance exploring Emperion. Captain Rose was the first to sail to Minist, the closest moon, while he possessed a single mining ship, the *Annie*. The other miners plied their trade in the belt. Although farther away, the massive collection of diverse asteroids guaranteed a haul of one cargo type or another.

But, on Minist, Rose found nothing but common aggregate. If his ship had carried the proper smelting equipment, so that he could have set up production on the moon, he might have carved out a decent profit. But he lacked both the equipment and the auto-controlled sleds that Jessie later produced for the company. Minist became known as Rose's Reward and was used in the negative when a captain described an unsuccessful trip to the belt and back.

After unloading at the YIPS, Jessie intended to return to Emperion and help the *Pearl*'s crew with the shoveling of the massive fields of frozen gases. Two ship crews could work the moon's rich surface twice as fast. Jessie knew word about the increased frequency of the *Pearl*'s visits to the YIPS with full tanks was spreading quickly. It wouldn't be long before other mining captains decided to cease prospecting the belt, add tanks to their ship's axis, and come for loads from Emperion.

It was the growth of Pyre's society that had increased the demand for the frozen gases. The YIPS produced methane and other products for the construction of the JOS terminal arms, hydrogen for engine mass, oxygen for ships and stations, and, to a limited extent, water, which everyone needed. The *Annie's* original survey of Emperion indicated that the moon was completely covered in frozen gases to a minimum depth of 60 to 80 meters.

While at the YIPS, Jessie heard from sources of the arrests of Markos Andropov and Giorgio Sestos. *Couldn't have happened to better people,* Jessie thought when he heard the news for the first time. But the part of the announcement that Jessie paid close attention to were the recoveries of Helena Garmenti and her young daughter. In his gut, he'd trusted the story Aurelia had told him. Now, he had proof that he was right to protect her.

"Captain, you have a call from Harbour," Ituau announced, over his comm unit.

"Transfer it, Ituau, and you can stop your grinning before I find some scutwork for you to do," Jessie replied.

"Absolutely, Captain," Ituau deadpanned, before she made the connection. She thought it was a good thing the captain, who was in his cabin, couldn't see the broad grin she had on her face, which she was unable to erase.

Rather than take a seat at his desk station, Jessie took his hand unit and eased into his comfortable reading chair. "You've had a busy day, Harbour," Jessie said, without preamble.

"To say the least," Harbour replied. "By the way, this call is secure. It's my back channel through the JOS."

"You still aboard the station?"

"Yes. Helena needs to testify before the Review Board to substantiate the charges so that security can hold Markos and Giorgio over for trial."

"How're the women doing?"

"Helena is happy to be rescued, but I think she's a little lost. She's come home after seventeen years and the birth of two daughters. The station isn't the familiar place she left behind."

"I can't imagine the life she's led downside. It's a wonder the woman never did in the governor."

"Helena is a soft-spoken woman. Not the type to strike out ... more the quiet, desperate type."

"What's the daughter like?"

"Sasha is another thing entirely," Harbour said, laughing. "Willful, temperamental, and angry, and, on top of that, a powerful and untrained empath."

"Yikes," Jessie replied.

"You can say that again. But, I believe I have Sasha following my lead."

"So quickly, what did you do to her?"

"I met a resentful, young girl dressed in a secondhand pair of oversized skins, and I did the one thing that would appease any female, young or old. I took her shopping."

Harbour heard Jessie laugh, and she curled her legs under her on the chair. It was the first time she'd heard his laughter.

"Tell me, does security have them, or do you?" Jessie asked.

"The women are under my protection. I've stated that formally to the commandant."

"And how is our dear commandant doing?"

"Funny you should ask. I've listened to a recorded conversation between Emerson and Lise Panoy. It's evidence that he's colluding with Lise to help her gain the governor's position."

Jessie sat up in his chair. "And how did you learn this?"

"This is shared under the blanket of conversations that we've been having, agreed?"

"That goes without saying, Harbour."

"Major Finian and Lieutenant Higgins are onto the commandant and have been for a while. When the commandant was stalling about taking action from my search results, the major's suspicions were confirmed."

"I'm not tracking here, Harbour. What search are you talking about?"

"Sorry, Jessie, things have been happening so fast. I'd shared the information you relayed to me with my spacers, empaths, and a few select residents. We spread rumors about Aurelia and the possibilities of how she must be evading security. That led Danny, my pilot, to develop an idea, which led me to request that Major Finian search the JOS personnel database against Aurelia's DNA profile."

"And that led to the match of Helena Garmenti," Jessie finished for Harbour, "which gave the major an excuse to request a warrant from the commandant. Harbour, you're a clever woman."

"Thank you, Jessie." What Harbour really wanted to know was whether Jessie liked clever women or preferred the silent type.

"When does the Review Board interview Helena?"

"Tomorrow afternoon. The commandant was forced to call an emergency session to gain permission to holdover Markos and Giorgio for trial."

"I say throw the pair of them out an airlock and be done with it," Jessie said.

Harbour heard the vehement undertone in Jessie's voice, and she sought to understand the reason for it. "What happened to a spacer's demand for justice?" she asked.

"Under the circumstances, I think expediency would be better."

Then it clicked for Harbour. Jessie's support for his crew members extended throughout their lives. It didn't matter whether they were active, retired, or broken, in which case they needed Harbour's support. Once he adopted them as crew, so to speak, he took on the responsibility. In this case, he'd done the same for Aurelia. She might have been a trainee who he was hiding from security, but, as far as Jessie was concerned, she was now his to protect.

"Jessie, where are you now?"

"The *Spryte* is docked at the YIPS. We've finished unloading, and I'm giving the crew some rest before we sail back to Emperion and support the *Pearl*'s crew."

"Are you planning to stop in at the JOS?"

"I wasn't planning to, Harbour. Did you need to speak to me face-to-face?"

It was a loaded question for Harbour. The answer was yes, but for more than one reason.

"I wanted an opportunity to discuss in detail your trainee's future, the future of the governorship, and the possibility of a change in the way we run our society."

"Are you planning to have me over for an evening or a year?" Jessie replied, laughing. "That's one enormous subject list you have there."

"Why don't we start with dinner, Jessie? I'll be free once the Review Board has completed Helena's interview. Can we say eighteen hundred hours?"

"It's a date. See you then, Harbour," Jessie said, closing his comm unit.

* * * *

The next afternoon, Harbour and Sasha sat in the waiting room outside the Review Board's meeting. The grizzled mining captain, Henry Stamerson, who had retired years ago and now headed the Board, had come out personally to collect Helena. It was an indication of the Board's intent to take seriously the charges against the governor.

Sasha sat still for all of four minutes after her mother was led away, before she started fidgeting. "When can I see my sister?" she suddenly asked.

That didn't take long, Harbour thought, and she tried desperately to figure a way to explain the complexities of the issues to a young girl who couldn't understand why she couldn't see her big sister.

Harbour was still thinking, when Sasha asked, "Do you know where Aurelia is hiding?"

Harbour glanced around to ensure no one was within earshot, before she replied. "Not specifically, but I have a good idea."

"Where?" Sasha demanded.

"I can't tell you. It would jeopardize your sister's safety and those who are protecting her."

"Why?"

"What the governor did to your family is separate from what Aurelia did. She's wanted for the murder of Dimitri Belosov."

"Dimitri was effluent," Sasha said in disgust.

"I've heard that. Still, Aurelia must stand before the Review Board, which will determine her innocence or guilt."

"I could make those people like her," Sasha stated, with determination, and Harbour could sense the child's power spinning up.

"I bet you could," Harbour replied, which placated Sasha, diminishing her dark anger. "Forcing people is not how we do things aboard the JOS," Harbour explained.

"Why not?" Sasha retorted. "The governor did. Giorgio did."

"And look where they are now ... locked up and awaiting trial," Harbour replied.

Sasha must have accepted the explanation, because her body and emotions lay quiet for a few minutes before she started to fidget again. It gave Harbour an indication of the time and attention it would take to train the child. Suddenly, it occurred to her who would be the perfect individual to teach Sasha — her best friend, Yasmin. But after Yasmin spent some time with the girl, she might not be her friend anymore.

"Tonight, I'm seeing someone important to your sister," Harbour said, to capture Sasha's attention.

"Who?"

"I could tell you, if I knew you could keep a secret."

"My mother made us swear to never tell Markos or Giorgio about her secret place, and we never did. I can keep a secret really good."

"Her secret place?" Harbour asked.

"Mother was saving up little stuff for years to help us escape topside. When Aurelia had to run, she gave her all sorts of things to help her make it up here, and she did too."

"Yes, she did. Your sister's a clever girl."

"Yeah, she's the smart one."

"And which one are you?" Harbour asked, trying to understand how the girl saw herself.

"I'm the sneaky one," Sasha replied, with a grin.

Perfect, Harbour thought wryly. The aspects of the child's personality seemed to be forming a dangerous storm.

"Who are you seeing tonight?" Sasha asked.

"I'm meeting a man for dinner who knows Aurelia," Harbour replied. She checked the time on her comm unit. The Review Board interview with

Helena was running long. More than likely, the Board members were checking data in security's files to confirm Helena's answers, which was understandable. A downside governor had never been charged with criminal offenses and brought to trial. With a twinge of regret, Harbour saw that it was 18:12 hours.

"Is he security?" Sasha asked, pointing over Harbour's shoulder. She turned her head to discover Jessie walking toward them.

Harbour clamped down hard on the momentary thrill that ran through her. Despite her efforts, she was sure a minute amount of her emotions leaked to Sasha, but the girl gave no indication of it. "Hello, Jessie, I see you found us," Harbour said, as evenly as she could. "Sasha, I'd like you to meet Captain Jessie Cinders. Jessie, this is Sasha, Helena Garmenti's daughter."

"Is this the man you're seeing tonight?" Sasha asked, instead of responding to the introduction, catching both adults off guard.

"Yes, it is." Harbour replied.

"He likes you," Sasha said simply, as if stating a fact.

During the uncomfortable silence that followed, Sasha added, "And you like him."

"Much more powerful than you indicated," Jessie murmured.

"Do you know my sister, mister?" Sasha asked.

"We address him as Captain Cinders," Harbour said.

"Strangers call me that," Jessie explained, squatting down to meet Sasha at eye level, "but I wonder if we can be friends."

"Okay," Sasha replied noncommittally.

"It's not as simple as that," Jessie warned, gaining Sasha's attention. "Friends have a duty to look out for one another. It's not something to take on lightly."

Sasha stared at Cinders, and Harbour could feel the girl's power growing and knew she was sampling the captain's emotions. "I like you," Sasha announced. "We can be friends."

"That's good, Sasha, because here's my secret," Jessie said, and then he leaned over to whisper in the girl's ear. "Aurelia and I are friends."

"You are?" Sasha exclaimed.

"Shhh," Jessie replied, a finger over his lips.

"You are?" Sasha repeated, whispering, and Jessie slowly nodded twice.

Sasha leaned over to whisper again. "That's good. Then you're protecting her, right?"

Jessie leaned back and glanced up at Harbour, who said, "I'm probably guilty of whatever it is you two are discussing."

Jessie turned to Sasha and replied enigmatically, "Maybe," but he gave Sasha a conspiratorial wink. She returned his wink, but it looked more like she had something painful in her eye.

The door to the Review Board meeting room opened, and Helena walked through. She appeared tired, as if she'd relived the last seventeen years in real time, and both Harbour and Sasha lent their support. The difference was that Harbour's efforts were directed, and Sasha broadcast to the room.

"Wow," Jessie murmured, when the wave of affection hit him.

"Mother, this is Harbour's friend, Jessie. He's my friend now," Sasha said, after taking her mother's hand and pulling her over to Jessie.

"I'm pleased to meet you, Captain Cinders," Helena said, reading the name tag on Jessie's dress overalls.

"The pleasure is mine, Helena. While I'm pleased to learn of your release from the governor's house, I lament the time you lost downside."

"Thank you for your sentiments, Captain."

Sasha crooked her finger at Jessie, who leaned down to hear her whisper, "Can I tell mother that you're Aurelia's friend."

Jessie cupped his hand to hide his whisper. "Later, when the two of you are alone, and you must explain to your mother that it's a secret."

Sasha's face was a study in seriousness. "Okay," she whispered.

"Ladies, allow me to accompany you to your cabins," Jessie said.

"That's kind of you, Captain, but it's really not necessary," Helena replied.

"Oh, but it is, mother. Harbour and Jessie are going out afterwards. They like each other," she pronounced, and pranced off toward the JOS main corridor.

"Apologies, Captain, she can be a little direct," Helena said, slipping past to catch up with her daughter.

Watching Helena and Sasha, Jessie murmured, "Spacers call that blunt."

Harbour smiled at Jessie and strode after the women.

At Helena's cabin, Jessie took note of the female security officer who welcomed the women. "Around the clock?" he asked Harbour. When she confirmed it, he asked, "Whose coin?"

"Security," Harbour replied.

"Are you ready to go, or do you need some personal time?" Jessie asked, after the three other women disappeared into the cabin.

Harbour smiled to herself. It appeared Jessie wasn't accomplished at the subtleties of male-female relationship building. "No personal time needed, Jessie. I'm ready to go."

"Where to?" Jessie asked.

"I thought we'd celebrate the recovery of Aurelia's mother and sister and try the Starlight. I've never been there."

"Actually, I haven't either."

"Really? Then this should be an interesting experiment for the two of us."

Strolling through the station's main promenade, walking side by side, Jessie and Harbour drew stationers' attention. Each individual alone would have garnered a passerby's second look, but, seen together, shoulder to shoulder, the station's rumor mills were set churning.

At the Starlight's entrance, Jessie tapped the actuator and motioned Harbour through the door.

"Why thank you, kind sir," Harbour replied.

That was to be their last moment of pleasure until they left the posh cantina. What should have been an opportunity to relax and celebrate became an exercise in ignoring the stares and frowns of the patrons, who surrounded them.

When a server failed to materialize at their table, Harbour asked, "Was this a mistake?"

In reply, Jessie stood and offered his hand, which Harbour accepted. Jessie placed her hand in the crook of his arm, and the two sailed out of the expensive cantina, laughing at the pomposity of the patrons.

"Well, my idea for an evening dinner blew up. Your turn to pick, Jessie," Harbour said, when they reached the corridor.

"I know a place where we'll be appreciated," Jessie replied.

"I'm latched on, Captain," Harbour replied, with a grin and glanced toward her hand in Jessie's arm.

"You *have* been spending time with spacers," Jessie replied, laughing.

Harbour got lost as Jessie navigated twists and turns in the corridors, but he ended at a familiar door. "The Miners' Pit?" she asked, but she gave the actuator a good smack.

"Harbour," Maggie called out with enthusiasm. She gave Harbour a brief hug and touched a couple of fingers to her brow when she greeted Jessie. Then she led them to a table situated away from the bar and against the wall where they would have a little more privacy.

They were no sooner seated than several spacers, led by Ituau, strolled over, wearing their downtime finery over their skins. Each one passed the table, touching their forehead with fingertips, saying, "Captain, ma'am," and returned to their table or bar.

"They're your crew, aren't they?" Harbour asked

"All of them," Jessie allowed.

"Do they always greet you that way?"

"That wasn't for me. They were honoring you or, more specifically, they were paying respects to what you are."

"You're going to have to explain that one."

Jessie was interrupted by Maggie, who asked, "What can I start you two with?"

"We need to start with celebration drinks," Harbour said, lightly slapping the table with both hands.

"Oh, of course. Are you celebrating the recovery of Helena Garmenti or the downfall of the governor?" Maggie asked, with a wicked smile.

"Why can't we celebrate both?" Jessie asked.

"That's the spirit, Captain. Special celebratory drinks coming up," she declared, and made for the front desk, while tapping the order into her comm unit.

"You were going to tell me about your crew's procession," Harbour reminded Jessie.

"The third mate, Belinda Kilmer, serving on the *Pearl*, was developing space dementia. She didn't have far to go before she would have to be put off on the station. Captain Hastings ordered his first mate, Angie Mendoza, to assign Belinda to Rules for spacer training. When the *Pearl* rendezvoused with the *Annie*, a transfer was worked out and the pair was kept together. As of the last report from Captain Erring of the *Annie*, Belinda shows no sign of her dementia."

"Fascinating," Harbour breathed out slowly. She faded into private thoughts, and Jessie sat quietly, studying the planes of her face. The arrival of their drinks interrupted Harbour. She nodded politely to the server and took a sip. "Oh, for the love of Pyre," she exclaimed. "It's good, but it's potent."

"Delicious but deadly," Jessie agreed, after taking a swallow.

"I think I need to wait on some food before I finish more of this," Harbour said, setting the drink on the table.

"Not much alcohol in the diet?"

"Rarely had the occasion, and you, Captain?"

Jessie's eyebrows rose, recalling many of his exploits during downtime, especially when he was young. "On more than one occasion, I must admit."

Harbour sensed a subtle shift in Jessie's emotions. It began with a twinge of regret, which faded, to be replaced by his usual calm.

"You're doing it," Jessie said.

"Pardon?"

"You're reading me."

"Are you guessing or are you stating what you believe to be factual?" Harbour was slightly miffed that Jessie had guessed what she was doing. Reading people she was speaking to was an old habit, but she wanted to refrain from reading Jessie this evening. Yet, she'd already done it several times. Harbour watched Jessie lean back in his chair and lock eyes with her. *Probably a technique you use on your captains and crew,* Harbour thought, noting that it was extremely effective.

"I give ... guilty," Harbour admitted, throwing her hands in the air. "Now, I need to know how you knew."

"Your eyes," Jessie replied.

"You saw the tiny color shift?" Harbour asked, shocked, and Jessie tipped his head in agreement. "Only empaths know that sign, and we'd greatly appreciate it if you would keep our secret," she added.

"Not a problem. We seem to have a growing list of secrets to keep for each other."

"On a positive note, Jessie, I take it as a compliment that you were staring so closely at my eyes," Harbour replied, taking a heavy swallow of her drink to keep her hands busy. Unfortunately, the strong alcohol hit her throat, and she choked. She raised her hand, as Dingles had done, to wave off the cantina's concerned patrons. "Keep this thing on your side of the table until the food comes," Harbour said, pushing the drink across the table and taking a deep swallow from her water glass.

"Jessie, I want to be sure I understand what the crews' gestures meant when we first sat down. They were paying their respects to me, even though I didn't do anything. It was Rules who helped Belinda."

"My crew members see you as the leader of the empaths ... the queen, if you will."

That comment set Harbour to laughing loud and hard, and spacers around the pair were grinning for several reasons. Not the least of which was that no one could recall Captain Cinders bringing a dinner date to the Pit.

"A queen?" Harbour questioned, when she stopped laughing. "I hardly think so."

"You two ready to order?" Maggie asked. When she received their choices, she communicated them to the kitchen and left.

"I want to ask about your trainee, Jessie," Harbour said, taking on a serious expression.

"She's doing well, exceptionally well. If you're asking about her future, I can tell you that whatever happens with the governor, it will not affect security's desire to apprehend her."

"That's what I thought. So, what does that mean for her?"

"Too early to tell. If nothing else, she'll make a great spacer."

"What do you think the Review Board will decide about Markos and Giorgio?"

"Those two are cooked. The DNA evidence you discovered, and security finding the women in a secret location, with no means of exiting from the inside of the suite, destroys any defense they might mount. They'll be the first downsiders to receive long sentences."

"I wish we could take advantage of the governor's absence to change the politics downside."

"No hope of that, Harbour. Lise Panoy has that position virtually tied up. And, unfortunately, you don't have a shot at the commandant, not with the major having authorized an illegal comm tap."

"I expect a more supportive conversation from my dinner dates," Harbour pouted. The alcohol in her drink seemed to be loosening her inhibitions. Thankfully, the food arrived, and she reached across the table to recover her drink.

"Have many of those ... cooperative dinner dates, I mean?" Jessie asked.

"Haven't had many dinner dates," Harbour replied, shrugging and taking a sip of her drink. It didn't seem so strong now.

Jessie started to speak, but he chose not to ask his question.

"Jessie," Harbour said, after digging into her meal, "if you could design our government, what would you create?"

Jessie rested his fork on his plate and took a sip of his drink. "I always liked what I read about the arrangements of some of Earth's democracies. They used checks and balances to ensure that no one structure had total power over the others."

"And what it would it take to move toward that type of arrangement?"

"Well, first we'd have to get the entire Pyrean population to agree to the election of a single leader. Don't see the downsiders agreeing to that."

"What could force them to the table?"

"Historically, as Captain Rose used to tell me, it would be something elemental — food production, access to clean water, war, or something extraordinary that was entirely unforeseen."

"Are any of those available to us?"

"You're serious about this, aren't you?"

Harbour took another deep swallow of her drink. It tasted better and better. "I am. I'm concerned for the future of the *Belle*. I think the downsiders would love to offer the empaths free room and board downside, but they wouldn't spend a single coin for the rest of the residents. In my estimation, it's time to halt, if not reverse, the downsiders' power expansion."

Jessie finished his meal and set his fork down. It was a spacer's bad habit to quickly clean a plate, while the opportunity presented itself. "Harbour, I understand your concerns. Spacers are the minority here too. The stationers are the only ones with the numbers to outvote the downsiders, if it came to that, but they're absorbed in their daily lives. It would take something mighty momentous to shake them out of their complacency and force the downsiders to the bargaining table. If it came to that, each side would be soliciting the *Belle*'s residents and the spacers, trying to win them to their side."

Harbour finished most of her meal but had to quit. It was more than she usually consumed in a sitting. She did manage to finish her drink. A quick check of her comm unit revealed the late hour.

"Well, Jessie, as much as I have enjoyed the company, I've got to get some rest. My days are sorely tested by Sasha."

Jessie stood first, and Harbour said, "We haven't paid. Oh, that's right, owner's privileges." When she rose, she was a little unsteady and found Jessie's hand under her arm. At the door, Harbour gave Maggie a hug and sent the pleasure she felt.

"Oh, that's nice," Maggie gushed, when the emotion passed through her mind.

On the way to her cabin, Harbour wrapped her hands around Jessie's arm. It helped to steady her, but the truth was she enjoyed it. At the cabin's door, Harbour asked. "Sailing tomorrow?"

"First thing in the morning," Jessie replied.

"I enjoyed the evening, Jessie."

"I did too. Be careful, Harbour," Jessie replied and left.

Wow, Harbour thought, leaning against the wall. *No offer of a second date. Not even a kiss.* Disappointed, she touched the actuator of her cabin door with her card key.

On the way to the *Spryte*, Jessie examined the turmoil he felt. He believed in keeping life simple. It made it easier to manage the company and take care of his people. Since meeting Harbour, life had gotten ever more complicated. *No, that's not right,* he thought. *It began with Aurelia ... another empath.* Yet, Jessie no longer saw Aurelia in that category. She'd become crew to him, falling neatly into an existing slot. Harbour didn't fit into any slot.

Worse, Jessie knew he couldn't treat Harbour as spacers did one another, hooking up for some downtime and amicably calling it quits when ships sailed. Besides, Jessie wasn't sure he could stop if he started something with her. He'd deliberately kept his eyes off her face at her cabin, afraid of what might have happened if he had kissed her.

Jessie's musings brought him up short. His imagination was suddenly overwhelmed by the possible complications that might arise during an affair with a powerful empath, not to mention the potential risks of a bad breakup. He tried to put the events of the evening out of his mind and walked with purpose toward his ship. Despite turning into his bunk early and being aided by a strong drink and a full meal, he didn't get a good night's sleep.

22: Exploring

Darrin and his prospecting team explored an ever-expanding semicircle out from Triton's crater where they first descended. It required them to relocate the shelter several times. The assays were tempting for the quality of ore found, but further tests indicated the team was only discovering small deposits. There was nothing that made the expenses of the trip to Triton and the exploration worth the coin.

"Nose, it looks like I might have to recommend to Jessie that we abandon Triton, unless he's prepared to spend the coin to set up a processing operation here to refine the aggregate," Yohlin said. She was talking to Darrin after receiving another report of an unsatisfactory day's core samples.

"I can't argue with you, Captain. It's too far to the YIPS, and it offers too little return to make the investment in more sleds worthwhile," Darrin replied. "Thing is, Captain, I know there's quality stuff here. I can feel it."

"Okay, Nose, but we can't keep going the way we've been doing, searching on a grid pattern. I'm going to have the crew drop the search rover. I want you to double your grid spacing to cover more ground. I'll send Tully and Hamoi out wide in the rover to take some samples."

"Are you going to track them?" Darrin asked. Without comm repeaters above the moon, the *Annie* was limited by its ability to cover the survey team and the rover if it ranged past the horizon.

"Negative, Nose. I'll keep the ship over the shelter. That's where the majority of our crew is positioned."

"Understood, Captain. In that case, I recommend Belinda and Rules take seats in the search rover."

"You want the newbie aboard on an extended mission? Jessie might consider that an unnecessary risk of the girl."

"I don't disagree with that last part, Captain. But it gets ugly crammed inside that rover with a crew of four aboard. Rules can keep everyone happy."

"That's unless she goes boggy herself," Yohlin retorted.

"I doubt that will happen, Captain. If it's a new technique or a new experience for Rules, she's all over it. Darnedest thing I've ever seen ... a natural-born spacer, if there ever was one."

"Okay, Nose, give the orders. I'll have the rover downside tomorrow morning. Let's hope Rules can be a talisman too. We need some luck."

Soon after Darrin finished his conversation with Captain Erring, the remainder of the crew cycled into the shelter, and he took the four individuals aside to give them their marching orders. The group felt a flash of enthusiasm from Rules, and there were smiles all around.

"Don't get too excited, Rules," Darrin warned. "An extended mission stuck inside a search rover except to exit for samples and short breaks can be grueling." He'd no more delivered his message than the group felt another pulse of excitement. "Okay, Rules, have it your way," he said, laughing. "The rover will drop early tomorrow. After we check it over, you'll launch on a search wedge that I'll outline."

* * * *

Belinda woke in the morning and experienced a brief moment of trepidation. During the days aboard the *Annie* and downside on Triton, she'd felt like her old self and her confidence had returned. But spending days and nights enclosed in the limited space of a search rover would test her. The problem was that if her space dementia went full-blown aboard ship, the captain could order her sedated until they made station, but, with a small team depending on her as the senior crew person, the thought of risking their lives on an extended foray frightened her.

Warm support flooded through Belinda's mind. It flushed away her concerns, and she took a deep breath, exhaling slowly. She expected it to cease quickly, but Aurelia kept sending to her until even those around her wore goofy smiles.

"Okay, Rules, we've all had our happy dose. Save some for the expedition," Darrin announced. But his words did nothing to curb the crews' appreciation. They clapped and whistled, which gained them a grin and another shot from Aurelia.

After the checkout of the delivered search rover and the completion of its loading, Belinda assigned Tully, the engineer, the driver's seat. He had the most experience with the vehicle. She took on the role of navigator and would guide their course with the rover's system, which was loaded with Darrin's search wedge and would track its position via the shelter and the *Annie*. This would work until they got beyond the horizon. Then tracking beacons would be planted to guide them on their return to the shelter.

Aurelia and Hamoi, the assay tech, were assigned the second pair of seats. Entry into the rover was through a small airlock system built in a cylindrical shape, allowing the twin hatches to rotate within a tight radius. It was large enough to accommodate one good-sized spacer in a vac suit.

Tully boarded first, Belinda followed, Aurelia went next, and Hamoi climbed aboard the rover last. All systems had been checked out by three techs. Nonetheless, Belinda had Tully run his own tests. When she ran a comm check with the *Annie* and the shelter in a twin link, she had Yohlin and Darrin feeling comfortable with her as team leader.

"Vac suits stay active and sealed," Belinda ordered, when they got underway. "We stay sealed up for an hour until we're assured the vehicle is tight while we navigate terrain."

When Belinda's allotted time passed, the team took turns helping one another out of their vac suits. There was sufficient room at the rear of the vehicle next to the airlock to hang them up.

Following Darrin's requests, which weren't geographically specific, but a wish list of formations that he wanted tested, the rover crew made for a distant mountain range. It took the rover most of the day to reach it.

Aurelia began the trip by crossing her legs under her and immersing herself in the wonderful memories she'd accumulated since making it to the El car. She saw the faces of JD, the cargo crewman; Toby, whose face always made her smile; and, of course, Captain Cinders, her rescuer. The faces of many supportive spacers marched through her mind.

Hamoi, who fell into a state of bliss from Aurelia's unblocked emanation, began whistling softly. He whistled tune after tune, the crew discovering he was marvelous at it.

"Sorry to break up the party," Belinda said, a few hours later, "but it's meal time. Rules, Hamoi, break out some tasty prepackaged whatevers for us.

By the time they reached the base of the mountains, the crew was anxious to stretch their muscles. Belinda paired Aurelia with Tully, and she took Hamoi. Only Tully and Hamoi were experienced at recognizing what might be good sampling sites.

Tully and Aurelia were outside for three hours, collecting an armload of cores before they returned to the rover. Hamoi ran the assay tests, while Belinda prepared meals. Unfortunately, the assays were consistent with what the shelter-based survey team had found — aggregate with hints of tempting heavy and rare minerals.

Belinda reported the first day's failure to Darrin.

"How's the crew holding up, Belinda?" Darrin asked.

"We're doing fine, Darrin. Rules is keeping us in good spirits."

"Funny thing about that, Belinda, I've noticed a marked downturn in the shelter crew's attitude. I guess I forgot how hard these long-term stays in a shelter can wear on you. Crew members are already asking me how long Rules is going to be away."

Belinda wanted to laugh at the turnabout of the crew from their original opinion of Rules, but she refrained. Her nagging worry of what would happen to her when Rules was no longer around kept her sensitive to what the shelter crew was experiencing. *Empath withdrawal,* Belinda thought, *what spacer would have considered it possible?*

"Darrin, Tully and Hamoi think we're going about this wrong."

"Do tell?"

"Don't get your nose bent out of shape," Belinda replied, wishing she hadn't said that.

"I see the Rules effect is pretty heavy in that rover."

"Sorry, about the pun, Darrin. The problem is that I've crewed on the *Spryte* and the *Pearl*. I've never worked the expedition side of this company, which means that I don't have the experience to understand if what they want to do makes sense or not."

"I'll tell you one thing, Belinda. So much about this business relies on technology, which you can't dismiss, but a small part relies on intuition. You're in charge of the mission. It's your decision. You can't do any worse than the base camp. We haven't found anything either."

"Understood, Darrin, thank you for the advice."

The team darkened the windows and tilted the seats to nearly horizontal positions to get some rest. A few hours later, Belinda woke them, and after a quick use of the tiny facilities closet and a small meal, she called a meeting.

"I want to hear from you two," Belinda said, pointing to Tully and Hamoi, "what you would do if you were out here without orders. You have three days to gather samples before you must turn around. Nobody is giving you directions. Where would you go?"

Tully and Hamoi grinned at each other. Spacers referred to Belinda's request as an officer offering to let them slip their leashes. Belinda was encouraged by their reactions, but, after a half hour of arguing, there was no consensus. Worse, each of them had more than one proposal.

"Enough," Belinda said, interrupting the latest argument. "We could sit here for the next four days, and I think you two would still be arguing. No wonder Captain Hastings said Captain Erring's job was the toughest one. Discovering an ore strike, if you don't find piles of frozen slush, seems more like gambling than science."

"I have an idea," Aurelia volunteered.

It would have been rude to let their jaws drop on hearing a newbie suggest she had an idea on how to find heavy metal, so they merely stared at Aurelia in confusion.

"Well, if no one else has a good idea, I want to go toward the buzzing."

"Buzzing? What buzzing?" Tully asked.

"You don't hear any buzzing?" Aurelia asked, looking from face to face. "I admit it's really high-pitched, and, if I'm wearing my helmet, it's attenuated."

Belinda searched the faces of Tully and Hamoi. It was obvious they had no idea what Rules was talking about. She didn't either, but her mental health was a direct result of Rules' ministration, which made her a believer in the extraordinary capabilities of empaths.

Tully started to ask a question, but Belinda held a hand up to halt the discussion and think. The *Annie*'s mission was the discovery of new opportunities for the company, which depended on the historical success of Captain Erring and Darrin Fitzgibbon. A lot was riding on them finding something of value on Triton, and, so far, that had amounted to a huge mound of aggregate that had to be processed onsite, which meant capital expenditures for more sleds and processing equipment. But the simple matter was that it was more expedient and profitable to put all the crews to work harvesting Emperion's frozen gases and outfit either the *Annie* or *Spryte* with tanks like the *Pearl*.

"Have you ever heard this buzzing before, Rules?" Belinda asked.

"At base camp," Aurelia admitted, "but I thought it was something that happened to everyone."

"And was it as strong as it is now?" Tully asked, warming to the subject.

"Oh, no, Tully, it was very faint at base camp, but it has grown stronger the farther we moved the shelter in this general direction."

"Why didn't you say anything, Rules?" Belinda asked. "You could have been developing a medical problem."

"I considered that, Belinda, but when I focused my power on the buzzing, it went away."

"Could that have been just you ignoring it?" Tully asked.

"I'm sure it wasn't. I've spent a few hours throughout the weeks playing with the noise. I can eliminate it, if I want."

"Let's get back to this direction thing," Belinda said. "You felt it increase as we moved the shelter. How about during the trip out here?"

"It has been increasing in strength, up until we turned toward the base of this mountain. Then it fell off a little."

"Then you can sense this buzzing's direction?" Hamoi asked.

"Not really. I don't sense really well where emotions come from. I have to look at people and match what I'm feeling with an expression or apparent attitude to figure out who might be broadcasting."

"Okay, but like a magnetometer, you can sense the increase in intensity. What I mean is, can you direct us toward the source of this buzzing?" Tully asked.

"Probably," Aurelia volunteered.

"Wait. Everybody, wait a minute," Belinda said. "We don't know what Rules is sensing. It could be anything."

"Normally, I'd agree with you, Belinda," Tully said, leaning against the rover's steering column to consider his words. "But, here's the way I see it. None of us doubt Rules' capabilities. They're extraordinary."

For the compliment, the crew felt a wave of appreciation.

"Just focus on my reasoning, newbie," Tully cautioned, and the sensation ceased. "Better. So, it's a given that we have a powerful empath in our midst, and none of us know how she can do what she does. We think of her talent as sensing and affecting our emotions. But maybe that's a simplistic concept. Does anyone know of another empath who is a spacer?"

When he received negative responses, Tully continued. "What if it's because Rules is the first empath out here, that we're discovering unknown capabilities about sensitives?"

"Where are you going with this, Tully?" Belinda asked.

"It's this, Belinda. Energy, as you know, comes in many forms, one of which is magnetism. What if Triton has a huge deposit of magnetite? The iron content of this mineral is usually above seventy percent, and, if the magnetite is loadstone, then its mass could be producing a weak magnetic field. What if that's what Rules is picking up? And, if that's what it is, the iron in that concentration would make ingots easily, and we'd probably find a lot of other metals in the mix."

Belinda stared at Tully, as if the engineer had lost his mind. "Tully, even if I believed what you were saying, how am I going to explain this to Darrin?"

"Didn't he say that part of exploration is using your instinct? What have we found out here? Nothing that's going to make us rich. I know what I'm saying sounds like chasing air, but what have we got to lose?"

"Fine," Belinda said, throwing her hands up in capitulation.

"Are you going to tell Darrin?" Tully asked.

"Despite any rumors to the contrary, Tully, you don't have a fool for a second mate. Of course, I'm not going to tell him. I'll report the day's findings to him, but I'm not saying that we're chasing a whimsy. Okay, Rules, which way?"

Aurelia grinned at her friend and pointed a finger. Tully kicked the rover in gear, tossing aggregate behind the wheels, and he squinted apologetically at Belinda.

"Trade places with me, Rules," Belinda said, climbing into the aisle and stepping rearward of Aurelia's seat.

"Is this a promotion?" Aurelia asked, plopping into the front seat.

"Let's hope this isn't the end of our contracts," Belinda grumped.

"Who has a contract?" Aurelia quipped.

Aurelia's comment produced a round of chuckles, and Belinda stared at the rover's ceiling. "For the love of Pyre," she whispered.

Tully navigated the rover based on Aurelia's feelings of the signal's direction. He chose to weave the vehicle on a long, slow S-curve. That allowed Aurelia to judge whether the buzzing, as she called it, was increasing or decreasing in strength. Many times, there were detours and backtracks to avoid crevices and uplifts.

At one point, Hamoi commented, "For a moon composed of common aggregate, there seems to be a great deal of surface deflection."

"I was thinking the same thing, Hamoi," Tully said. "This surface is reminiscent of a planet's topology, which was shaped over time by geological forces."

"If that were the case, why haven't we found the types of mineral deposits that would give rise to such mechanisms?" Hamoi asked.

"The logical answer," Tully replied, "is that we're making false assumptions because we possess too little data."

"If I'm following this discussion," Belinda interrupted, "you two think these surface formations are irregular for this type of moon. Even more confusing, nothing we've found in our sampling is offering us a credible, alternative explanation."

"That's about it," Tully replied.

"Wonderful," Belinda sulked. "Which makes us treating Rules like some sort of signal detector we're supposed to be following even more bizarre."

"I'm good with bizarre," Aurelia added from the front seat, holding up a hand for Tully and indicating he should bear a little left.

"You would be, newbie," Belinda replied acerbically, but she moderated its sting with a pat on Aurelia's shoulder.

At the end of the day, Belinda reported to Darrin that nothing extraordinary had been found. They had taken a few samples when the rover was stopped a couple of times so that they could stretch their muscles. She didn't tell him that other than those two stops they had been driving continuously, searching for a mysterious signal, which only Rules could detect.

After a few hours of rest, some packaged meals, hot drinks, and facilities visits, they were underway again. The light of Crimsa was available to them for another few hundred kilometers, but they were losing comm signal strength with the *Annie*. They lost line of sight with the shelter a day ago, and calls were routed through the ship after that.

"Tully, stop on that upcoming ridge," Belinda ordered. "I want Rules and you to plant a comm repeater and pull a few samples before we travel any farther."

After suiting up and exiting the rover, Aurelia tapped Tully on the shoulder and held three fingers up, and he switched to a discrete comm channel.

"What do you think, Tully, about chasing this signal?"

"Are you asking me whether I think it really exists, or if I think you're nuts and I'm trying to placate you so that you don't turn our brains to mush?"

Aurelia giggled. "Yeah, I guess that's what I mean."

"You believe you hear it, don't you?"

"It's not so much hearing, as it is sensing it, like I do people's emotions."

"Here," Tully said, indicating where Aurelia should plant the comm device. The shaft fired its charge into the ground to anchor the device, and she activated it per Tully's directions. Then she followed him to a small outcrop he wanted to sample.

"Rules, I think if this was all inside your head ... sorry, you know what I mean ... if you were imagining it, I don't think that you could direct us toward it. I've been tracking our overall route. We've had to make numerous detours, and I've been weaving like I closed the cantina after a long night of drinking. Do you know you've unerringly kept us on the original direction we first headed before I started weaving?"

"No."

"Of course, you wouldn't. My point is that if you were imagining what you believe you sense, it wouldn't have directionality. I don't know where we're going, but it's something real to you that I can tell you."

"Stupid vac suits," Aurelia said.

"Problem?" Tully asked. He was worried Aurelia was experiencing a suit malfunction.

"No, not that. I wanted to give you a hug for what you've said."

"Oh. Well, I'll tell you what you do. Save it for me after we discover what we're chasing. Okay?"

"Okay."

When the pair climbed into the rover, they shucked their suits and charged their tanks. Tully took up the driver's position, kicked the rover into gear, and took his cue from Aurelia.

"Well, you two must have had a good chat," Belinda remarked.

"I'd say," Hamoi echoed. "It's a particularly nice glow you're sending out, Rules." He was holding out his hands toward her and rubbing them together, basking in the warmth.

Aurelia smiled at him and winked.

Two days later, before they rested, Belinda contacted Darrin. She gave her report of no change.

"Time to turn around, Belinda," Darrin said.

Belinda looked at the faces of the other three in the rover. The crew had become obsessed with finding the source of Rules signal, and, today, she'd said it was close. When asked how she knew it was close, she'd said, "The direction has changed slightly."

"In what way?" Tully had asked. "With this type of terrain, my heading hasn't changed in the three hours ever since we skirted that crevice and you gave me the new course direction."

Aurelia had straightened her fingers and pointed directly forward. Then she sucked her lower lip between her teeth, winced, and tilted them slightly down.

"But that's excellent," Hamoi had replied, smacking the back of Tully's seat. "If it's a significant deposit, it would be in the ground. We must be near it."

Now, in the face of Darrin's directive, Belinda saw her crew silently beseeching her to plead for more time, and she made a snap decision. Rules had saved her life. She'd never wanted to be anything else but a spacer, and the prospect of losing that when dementia reared its ugly head had devastated her. She owed Rules, and spacers paid their debts.

"If it's all the same to you, Darrin, an interesting formation has been spotted that Tully and Hamoi are anxious to check out, and I have to rely on their expertise. Systems onboard the rover are functioning perfectly. I would advise letting the techie-types get their samples and satisfy their urges," Belinda said, chuckling over her characterizations.

"Time estimate?" Darrin asked.

"Three hours rest, travel time of four hours, sampling and testing for two more hours ... we should be headed back in nine hours."

"Within nine hours, I get a call that you're headed back, Belinda. Am I clear?"

"Aye, Darrin."

"Good hunting, Belinda," Darrin said, closing the comm.

"Well, you heard the man. Anyone want to get some rest?"

In response, Tully looked at Aurelia, who said, "Straight ahead."

"My turn to make meals," Hamoi said, heading to the rear of the rover.

"I'll help," Belinda added.

23: Discovery

"You're going to have to call Darrin now," Tully remarked.

The four crew members broke protocol to exit the rover together. They were poised on a small ridge looking down at a large, cleared space. Possibly centuries of accumulated space dust lay over the remains of some sort of structure. The men had started to investigate it, when Belinda called a halt to their actions. She placed a call to Captain Erring, bouncing the signal through the rover and the string of comm beacons. After connecting to the *Annie*, Belinda requested a downlink to add Darrin.

"We're online, Belinda," Yohlin said.

"Well, let me say, Darrin, that we found your high-grade metal deposit. The bad news is that it looks like someone has already processed the ore for you, but don't ask me what they made."

Yohlin's first thought was that Belinda's dementia had returned and was now full-blown. "Who else is on this call, Belinda?" she requested.

"The entire rover crew, Captain," Tully replied.

"I need a more detailed report than the cryptic one I heard," Yohlin ordered, her voice stern.

"I'm not sure I know where to begin, Captain," Tully replied. "But I can tell you, we're not the first to land on Triton. Well, maybe we're the first humans, but not the first individuals."

"It's my fault, Captain," Aurelia said. "I picked up on some sort of signal, and we tracked it here. Tully thought it might be lodestone."

"Back up, Rules," Darrin said, jumping in. "A signal? Something the rover could detect?"

"Negative, Darrin," Belinda interjected. "We detected nothing on the rover's instrumentation. This was something only Rules could sense. It was Tully's interpretation that perhaps it was a weak magnetic field, which would have represented a tremendous, high-grade, ore discovery."

"Captain, I'm uploading a visual to the *Annie*," Hamoi said. "I apologize that it's a single image. Our repeaters won't handle continuous vid on top of our comm link."

"We have it," Yohlin replied. She was staring at her bridge monitor with a couple of other crew members and had ordered the image sent to Darrin.

"The light's not great, people," Darrin commented.

"The structure's in the shadow of this ridge we're standing on," Belinda replied. "Do you see the faint ridge in the foreground?"

"Affirmative," Darrin replied, and highlighted his image, which was relayed to the *Annie*'s bridge display.

"That appears to be the base of the structure. It extends in a complete circle that's perhaps one hundred meters across," Belinda said.

"You keep saying structure, Belinda. We don't see a structure in your image," Yohlin said.

"Captain, look at the center of the shot and to its left," Hamoi replied.

"Looks like rock formations," Darrin said.

"I can tell you positively, Darrin, that they're not natural," Tully said. "I know the image is small and poorly lit, but, from our vantage point, I would say the center item is a platform and the structure to the left of it is control equipment."

"Control equipment in a vacuum? That doesn't make much sense, no matter who put it there," Yohlin commented.

"Captain, there's the possibility that this location was originally protected from vacuum," Belinda replied.

"Do you see any indications of dome material near you?" Yohlin asked.

"Negative, Captain," Belinda replied. "But what if they didn't use our traditional building methods?"

"You're suggesting that advanced individuals ... skip that ... I'll use the word that no one is saying. You're suggesting this edifice is the remains of advanced aliens."

"Yeah, Captain, pretty much," Tully replied.

"Pack it up, Belinda," Yohlin ordered. "I don't want anyone to touch this thing. Get in your rover and get your butts back to base camp."

Tully and Hamoi looked at each other. In the shadows, they could see the other's chagrin clearly through the helmet's faceplate.

"Uh, Captain, about not touching the alien thing," Tully started.

"I did it, Captain," Hamoi admitted. "I didn't ask permission either."

"You did what, crewman?" Yohlin demanded.

"I wanted to sample the base that circles this place. Test it for the substances that were used to make it, you know."

Darrin, who was surrounded by his survey crew in the shelter, stood quickly from his small comm station, and the crew paused to listen to the exchange. "What did you find, Hamoi, specifically?" he asked.

"Nothing," Hamoi replied.

"What our eloquent tech is trying to say is that he was unable to take a sample of the ring," Tully explained. "He brushed away the layer of dust and found pristine metal underneath. The base has a slender groove along the top that appears to run right around the circle."

"Surely, you ran a mass spectrometer test on the surface," Darrin said impatiently.

"That he did, Nose," Tully added. "The analysis said the metal was an unknown substance."

"Guess the notion that this is an advanced alien construction is pretty much dead on," Belinda said drily.

"In the rover now, Belinda, and get back to the shelter. Am I clear?" Yohlin ordered, her voice rising

Before Belinda could respond, Darrin jumped in. "Captain, I've some questions before they leave the site, if I may?"

"Fine, Darrin, but I don't want you asking for anything that requires them to approach or test it," Yohlin replied.

"Understood, Captain. Rules, you said you could sense this edifice, right?"

"No, sir, I felt something like a buzzing or high-pitched frequency, and we chose to follow it. It led us here."

"How far were you out from the shelter before you detected it?"

"Darrin, we discovered that Rules picked up on this thing while she was at the shelter," Belinda interjected. "She didn't mention it because she thought everyone heard it."

"Darrin, she directed us unerringly to this place," Tully added. "We drove around crevices, across ridges, and around outcrops, but she always put us back on course."

"Okay, here's what's not making sense," Darrin replied. "I get that Rules has been your direction finder and led you to this place. And, I get that you found some kind of evidence of an ancient alien civilization. But what you're not explaining is the source of the signal that Rules followed if this place is defunct."

"That's just it, Darrin," Belinda replied. "We didn't say this place was dead."

"What?" Yohlin said, leaping from her bridge chair. "What're you saying, Belinda?"

"Captain, Rules is still picking up the humming, buzzing, or whatever it is," Belinda replied.

"From where?" Darrin blurted.

"Under the circle, sir," Aurelia replied. "It's strong and soothing, in a strange way."

"That's it. No more questions; no more discussions. About face it, people, and march ... now!" Yohlin ordered. There was no mistaking the urgency and commanding tone in the captain's voice.

"Aye, aye, Captain," Belinda replied. "Move it, people, into the rover. We're out of here, Captain."

* * * *

"This will make a great call to Jessie," Yohlin lamented to Darrin after the link to the rover crew was cut.

"Not great news," Darrin agreed, and he launched into his imitation of her call. "Well, Captain Cinders, it's like this. Our trip isn't an entire bust. No, Captain, we haven't found any high-quality ore strikes or quantities of slush, but we did discover an alien structure, and, according to the team, our empath is sensing that it might still be active."

"Not bad, Darrin. I think I'll have you make the call."

"I'd rather pop a helmet out here on Triton's surface before I volunteered for that."

"Who said anything about volunteering?"

"With respect, Captain, I believe you carry the stripes of ultimate responsibility."

"Don't remind me."

"What do you want us to do, Captain?"

"Hold where you are, Darrin. You can take samples, but you're not to move the shelter. The rover will take a few days to return. When it arrives, I want you to run analysis on every centimeter of the rover, the equipment, and our people, before anyone exposes themselves to the vehicle or its contents."

"They were in vac suits, Captain, and Triton is an airless environment."

"Suddenly, you're an expert on aliens?"

"That's kind of my point, Captain. I'm definitely not even a newbie on the subject, which means I wouldn't know what to look for on the rover. Based on what Hamoi said, our equipment will probably be useless, which means something could be there and we wouldn't detect it."

"Do it anyway, Darrin. Make your captain happy."

Yohlin closed the downlink, and Darrin mumbled, "I aim to please, Captain."

Yohlin sat in her command chair. A crew member replaced her cold drink with a fresh, hot one, and that one went cold. In the end, she admitted that the entire issue was over her head, and she hadn't a single, intelligent suggestion for Jessie. She cleared the bridge. It wasn't to isolate the discovery of the alien place. She could bet that the entire crew of the *Annie*, topside and downside, already knew everything there was to know about it. What she wanted to keep private was her conversation with Jessie.

"*Spryte*, this is Captain Erring requesting a private comm call with Captain Cinders," Yohlin sent.

"One moment, Captain, connecting you," Nate, the second mate, replied.

"Hello, Yohlin," Jessie replied. He finished drying his hair, wrapped the towel around his waist, and sought a chair in his cabin to take the call.

"Hello, Jessie, what's your position?"

"I'm two days out from Emperion, why?"

"I think you should divert to Triton."

"Care to give me a reason, Yohlin? After all, I am the company's owner," Jessie said, enjoying teasing Yohlin. She could be as serious, if not more so, than even him, which is why he liked her style.

"We've found an alien artifact, Jessie."

"Interesting. What did you do with it?"

"Maybe artifact is the wrong term. It's big, maybe one hundred meters across."

"That's certainly scary. What's its condition?"

"It's covered in centuries of accumulated space dust."

"Can we reclaim the metal ... maybe learn something from a compositional analysis?"

"Jessie, I don't think you're listening to me, and maybe I'm not laying this out properly. The metal under the dust is clean, like it was laid yesterday. According to the crew, who discovered it, they can't sample it, and they didn't get a compound identity with a spectrometer."

"Sounds like some advanced entity was on Triton before us, but they're gone now, and what they left behind is of no commercial use to us. Is that about right?"

Yohlin stared at her comm unit, as if it had come alive in her hand. She couldn't understand Jessie's reaction.

"Okay, Yohlin, enough fooling around. You have to be in a great mood to try to spin this yarn. Sounds like Nose made a rich strike. I'm looking forward to studying the assay report when he completes it. By the way, you have my congratulations!"

"Jessie, this is no joke. We haven't made a strike. We've found nothing on Triton, except an alien structure. And, to make this story stranger, Rules believes the place is active."

There was dead silence on the comm. Then Yohlin heard Jessie ask, "Are any of our people hurt or in danger?" She breathed a sigh of relief. This was the Jessie she knew. He could cut to the heart of a problem faster than anyone. "We're all safe. I've recalled the crew from the site. Four of them were out in the search rover."

"Hold, Yohlin," Jessie ordered. He called Ituau, who was off shift and asleep. "My cabin, on the double," Jessie said tersely when Ituau answered his comm in a groggy voice. Then Jessie switched back to the original call. "Yohlin, who was in the rover?"

"Tully, an engineer; Hamoi, a tech; Belinda, my new second mate; and —"

"Rules," Jessie finished for her.

"Affirmative."

"And she found the place, didn't she?"

"Yes, how did you guess that?"

"Let's say that I've had a crash course in the capabilities of empaths, and there's a lot that we normals don't understand about them. Hold again, Yohlin."

"Come in," Jessie shouted, in response to the tap on his door.

"Captain?" Ituau queried. She'd jumped into a pair of skins and deck shoes, but it was obvious she wasn't fully awake.

"Wake Jeremy, have him plot a course to Triton, execute it immediately, and burn some mass. I want to be there soonest. Dismissed."

"Aye, aye, Captain," Ituau replied. She stepped out of the cabin, closed the door, stood in the corridor, and ran through a quick series of breathing exercises to clear her head. Then she dashed for Jeremy's cabin.

"I'm back, Yohlin. Is there any reason to suspect that there might be other alien sites on Triton?"

"We've explored maybe six percent of the surface, Jessie. I've kept the ship stationed over top of the shelter for safety reasons."

"Understood, and I concur with your protocols. What precautions are you taking?"

"I've got Darrin checking out the rover, equipment, and people, before there's any transfer or open contact with the crew. But, Jessie, based on the report from Tully and Hamoi, who were at the site, Darrin's worried that if there is a potential of contamination, he won't be able to detect it."

"They were in vac suits during the entire time, correct?"

"Affirmative."

"Did they take any samples into the rover, alien items or ore samples from the site?"

"I forgot to ask," Yohlin replied, swearing at her failure to question the crew more thoroughly. "I'll contact the crew and determine that."

"If they did, I want those items or samples dropped far away from our people and the location marked. Then I want the crew, then and there, to open the rover to vacuum for a half hour. Clear?"

"Understood, Jessie."

Jessie felt the ship's slight acceleration. "Hold, Yohlin." Switching channels, he asked the bridge for status.

"Nate here, Captain. Ituau and Jeremy have returned to their cabins to freshen up. A new course is locked in and we're on a three-point-five percent increase in burn. Estimated arrival at Triton is eight-point-four days, Captain."

"Thanks, Nate," Jessie replied and picked up Yohlin's call.

"We're eight to nine days out, Yohlin."

"In the meantime, what do you want me to do with our people and equipment downside?"

"Put the shelter in extended leave status. Shut down the equipment; it will stay downside. Recover our people, as soon as you can. Then I want you to orbit the moon from pole to pole. I want to know if there are other alien sites on Triton."

"It'll be done, Jessie."

"Be careful, Yohlin. Over and out."

After the call with Yohlin, Jessie called Nate. "Have Ituau meet me on the bridge when she's ready. I want to talk to the two of you." Then he hung up and hurried to dress.

When the three of them, Jessie, Ituau, and Nate, were alone on the bridge, Jessie regarded his officers, for a moment, and then asked, "Have you two ever seen protocols for handling alien artifacts?"

Nate laughed and said, "What, Captain? Did Nose find some little green men?" He looked at Ituau, expecting to find her sharing his humor, but her face was a stern mask. Ituau had witnessed the worry evidenced by Jessie during the call to Captain Erring.

"No, no little green men, Nate. So far, it's only a large, alien installation made of a material that doesn't register on a mass spectrometer test."

"Sorry, Captain," Nate replied. He dipped his head in apology.

"Anyone hurt or ... contaminated?" Ituau asked.

"No one hurt. As to contamination, we don't know and maybe won't be able to tell."

"Captain, is it smart to expose this crew to the *Annie*'s people, if we don't know what we're dealing with on Triton?" Nate asked.

"I understand your concern, Nate. I'll work to limit the exposure of this crew to any potential infection. But those are our crewmates on Triton, and I'm headed there to help them. So, what's the answer to my question?"

"Sorry, Captain, I've never seen or heard of anything like that," Nate volunteered.

"Ituau?" Jessie asked, when his first mate failed to answer.

"I haven't either, Captain, but I have a thought where we might find it."

24: Trial

Most Review Board hearings were attended by a small collection of individuals — the defendant, his counsel, witnesses, and security. The Review Board collected the evidence and witness statements prior to the actual trial, which was the opportunity for the defense to review the evidence. In addition, it had to be remembered that much of the station was covered in cams, and there were often an ample number of witnesses. That meant that the opportunity for defendants to argue against the evidence was minimal, if not nonexistent.

However, there was no chance that the governor's trial was to remain unobserved. Stationers hounded the Board members and commandant to make the event public, and the family heads lobbied the commandant for a viewing. The requests were so numerous that Captain Henry Stamerson, the head of the Review Board, agreed to have vid cams in the meeting room, for the first time.

As the trial date neared, Toby became ecstatic. The rumor he'd inadvertently planted about Aurelia being an empath, which explained how she was able to hide from security, had been proven to be true. For someone who had been a bit of a loner, he suddenly had a lot of friends. Then there was the BRC operation. The bone replacement had taken, and he was walking with the aid of crutches until the healing completed.

But, best of all for Toby, Pena had taken notice of him. She'd visited him in his cabin, while the BRC was taking hold. Sometimes, she'd push him and his chair around the station, while the two of them talked. To Toby's delight, Pena was a fan of freefall. The moment Toby was off crutches, the two of them headed for terminal arm 2 for their first venture together into weightless playtime.

In the Starlight, several patrons asked if anyone had seen the miner who struck it rich. They vividly recalled his idea that Aurelia might be an empath.

While no one could recall exactly how he'd arrived at that conclusion or whether they had been led to it in response to his musings, they clearly remembered, although mistakenly so, that he was the first to voice the concept. Now that the miner's theory had been proven to be true, the patrons, who remembered him, were anxious to buy him drinks. A person like that, who fortune followed, was an individual to befriend and keep close.

For Markos Andropov's trial, the Board required the attendance of Helena Garmenti, Major Finian, and Sergeant Lindstrom to rebut any defense testimony. Sasha was not called by the Review Board to attend the trial, and when she learned that, she argued vociferously and continuously with Harbour. She was adamant that she be there.

Harbour tried reasoning with Sasha, but found she was unable to dissuade her. Worse, she couldn't override the child's emotional focus. *You're willful, Sasha*, she thought in lament, *and, worse, you're stronger than terminal arm metal.* Harbour placated Sasha by saying that she would request permission for her to attend, and she broached the subject with Captain Stamerson.

"Harbour, we're talking about an undisciplined child with incredible power, who holds enormous animus toward the defendant. I hardly see that as a recipe for a fair and balanced trial, and, let's not forget, this will be broadcast across Pyre."

"Ask yourself this, Captain Stamerson: If Sasha were a normal child of ten, who demanded her right to face her tormentor, would you refuse her?"

"Probably not, Harbour. However, she isn't a normal. What if she tries to influence the Board members, the defendant, or a witness?"

"That's why I'll be there, Captain, to ensure that doesn't happen. It will be a promise I extract from Sasha before I'll permit her to attend. If she breaks her word, I'll exit the proceedings with her, even if it takes the assistance of security. In fact, I have the perfect officer to sit beside her with me."

"Very well, Harbour, she may attend," Stamerson relented. "But hear me well. She's your responsibility. I'm depending on you to see that she doesn't influence this trial. This one is too important."

On the day of the trial and after all parties were assembled, Stamerson called the Review Board to order. He opened the trial by addressing the defendant. "Governor Markos Andropov, you're appearing before this Review Board accused of crimes against Helena Garmenti, Aurelia Garmenti, and Sasha Garmenti," Stamerson announced in a sonorous voice. "The Board has noted that you've not retained counsel. Is this correct?"

"I haven't, Captain," Markos replied, "and I don't intend to."

Pyrean citizens everywhere were riveted to their chairs, cantina stools, and monitors. For many who resided topside, the first view of the mighty downside governor was a significant disappointment. The audiences expected to see a proud, defiant man, ready to take on the JOS Review Board. Instead, the governor appeared deflated, as if he had shrunk in his chair.

"Then, we will proceed," Stamerson said. "Mr. Bondi, please read the charges."

Bondi, the newest member of the Board, rose and read the lengthy list of charges. Throughout the stations, ships, and domes, audiences heard the first complete version of what had transpired at the JOS, seventeen years ago, and then at the governor's house. That a stationer was kidnapped, kept imprisoned downside, and forced to father two children by the governor, no less, incensed nearly everyone. It was an example of what was wrong with Pyrean society that there wasn't a single, cohesive government, which controlled a security force that had a purview over all locations, including the domes.

Bondi finished reading the charges and took his seat.

"Markos Andropov, you've heard the charges preferred against you. How do you plead?" Stamerson asked.

Markos said nothing. His hands were clasped together on the table in front of him, and he was staring at them.

Stamerson repeated his question to Markos, who let loose a long, shuddering breath and announced, "I'm guilty, of course."

Audiences everywhere were shocked. A short utterance of guilt from Markos Andropov had cut the trial short. In an instant, it was over.

"Governor Andropov," Stamerson said, "you have the right to defend yourself against any or all charges. The Review Board is prepared to give you all the time necessary for you to prove your innocence."

Markos turned in his chair to the small gallery seated behind him. His sad eyes took in Helena and Sasha. "I'm so sorry for what I did to the three of you," he said.

Harbour felt the anger drain from Sasha. She smoldered, while the charges were read, each one reminding her of what she had endured. But, to her credit, the emotions were kept bottled inside. She sat next to Officer Nunez, her hand entwined in his.

Helena shook her head slowly at Markos. To her, his apology didn't make up for the theft of half her lifespan, although she had produced two daughters, whom she dearly loved.

Markos turned around and faced the Review Board. "I stand by my guilty plea, Captain. I offer no defense. The charges are true, every one of them."

"The Review Board will adjourn to deliberate and pass sentence on the defendant at a future date," Stamerson said and tapped the table with a piece of meteorite shaped into a semi-sphere with a small knob extending from the flat side for a handgrip.

Sooner than anyone expected, which was the following day, Giorgio Sestos was on trial. He did retain counsel, a well-known downsider, who was known for defending heads of families accused of financial indiscretions against stationers.

Stamerson opened the trial and Bondi read the charges. Except for an occasional change of noun, verb, or phrase, the indictments were the same as that of Markos.

"How do you plead, Giorgio Sestos?" Stamerson asked, when Bondi sat down.

"Not guilty to all charges," Giorgio replied.

"You will address me as captain or chairman, Mr. Sestos," Stamerson said, his voice cutting through the room, as the captain he once was.

Giorgio grudgingly nodded, but said nothing more.

"I find a simple movement of your head in response to my request to be insufficient, Mr. Sestos," Stamerson added, his voice hardening.

Giorgio's counsel whispered in his ear, and the security chief locked eyes with Stamerson and said, "Understood, Captain."

Stamerson refused to back down from Giorgio's stare, and the meeting room witnessed an eerie moment of silence before Giorgio looked away.

Topside audiences cheered, as the captain faced down the downsider. More than one drink in a cantina was spilt during the momentary celebration.

"The defendant having pled not guilty may present his rebuttal arguments and evidence," Stamerson announced.

To Giorgio's detriment, he had no evidence to contradict the charges. His presentation consisted of an argument that he was in the employ of Governor Andropov, at the time of the kidnapping, and was unaware that Helena Garmenti was sedated and locked in a shipping crate in the hold of the El car. He'd transported the crate to the house on the governor's orders. Afterwards, household members had taken the woman from the crate and locked her in the dead wife's suite on the third floor.

"The Board must remember that I was nothing more than a security officer when Helena was kidnapped. I didn't obtain the position of security chief until many years later," Giorgio argued.

Harbour felt Sasha's anger grow, and her power leaked out. She grasped the child's hand and gently squeezed. Sasha glanced up at her, and she frowned in reply. The broadcast ended, but Harbour suspected Sasha's enmity smoldered beneath the surface.

"Mr. Sestos, we have statements from Helena and Sasha Garmenti that they interfaced with you nearly daily over the lifetime of their incarcerations. Furthermore, Helena Garmenti contradicts your statement that you weren't involved in the kidnapping. She testified to the Board that she was talking to Governor Andropov when she was grabbed from behind and a trank gun pressed against her neck. Prior to that moment, she contends, that there were only the three of you in the room. How do you respond to those statements?" Bondi asked, reviewing Helena's testimony on his comm unit.

Giorgio listened to the whispers of his counsel before he said, "The kidnapping happened seventeen years ago to a young girl. That's a long time to keep memories straight after such a traumatic event. As for my supposed interactions with the woman and her child, I'm sure they have a great deal of loathing for the governor. Under the circumstances, that's extremely understandable. I believe they're lashing out at me, simply because I was in the employ of the governor. Nothing more."

To every question put to Giorgio, he offered the same points that he had no knowledge of the kidnapping and the women's incarcerations. It was becoming a question of Giorgio's word against that of the women. Proof to substantiate Helena and Sasha's claims of his involvement wasn't in evidence, although the Review Board found it difficult to believe that a security chief wouldn't be aware of the presence of three women, who were locked in rooms on the third floor of a house that he held responsibility for safeguarding.

Major Finian had traveled downside to procure testimony from the governor's household, as to Giorgio's interaction with the women, but they were too frightened to speak on the record. They were downsiders, and future employment depended on whether they kept silent about another downsider, even one as distasteful as Giorgio Sestos.

At one point, Harbour whispered in Sasha's ear. "You have to stop. You can't let it out."

"I can't help it," Sasha replied. Tears threatened to spill down her face. She was trying desperately to control her power, but her anger at Giorgio's testimony was overwhelming her woefully inadequate skills.

"Nunez, we're leaving," Harbour said earnestly, and indicated Sasha with a tip of her head.

Nunez swept Sasha into his arms, and she clung to him, her arms around his neck and her face buried against his throat. Harbour hurried right behind them. Their leaving caused a moment's stir in the room, but Stamerson quickly returned to the questioning.

But the audiences didn't miss the threesome's exit, and conjectures bloomed like new algae in an environment tank. A young, but strong, sensitive had to be removed from the room. Everyone assumed that she was disgusted by Giorgio's lies and couldn't control her emotions. It did much to convince the audience of Giorgio's guilt, despite the lack of evidence.

Finian leaned over to Sergeant Lindstrom and whispered, "Giorgio's going to get off, if we don't do something quick."

Cecilia racked her brain, reviewing the day they released the women from the governor's house. As the Review Board's questions continued, she walked through each step she had taken. Suddenly, she grabbed Finian's arm and hissed, "We need a continuation, Major ... a few hours at most."

"You sure you have something?" Finian asked.

"I don't have anything, sir, but I believe I know where we might find something," Cecilia said. Her eyes implored Liam to trust her.

"You have additional evidence to present, Major Finian?" asked Stamerson, having spotted Liam's signal of a partially raised hand.

"If it pleases the Review Board, Mr. Chairman, it's come to my attention that we might have evidence that contradicts the testimony of Mr. Sestos. We'll need a few hours to review our records."

"Might have evidence, Captain? That's mighty thin. We're in the middle of the trial." Stamerson glanced left and right to the other four board members. Their expressions urged him to allow the interruption. None of them were convinced of Giorgio's innocence, but, short of any proof, he was going to walk free and return downside.

Stamerson tapped his meteorite gavel and announced an adjournment for three hours.

Giorgio's counsel looked concerned, but Giorgio wore a smug expression. He'd spent the days reviewing every aspect of his actions, during the kidnapping and at the house. He'd paid to have the crate that housed Helena delivered to the El car. In addition, there were no vid cameras on the third floor or the back stairs, nothing to prove he'd visited the women's rooms. No matter how he viewed it, he couldn't find a hole in his plan to simply deny any knowledge of the women's predicament.

Cecilia exited the room, as speedily, but as decorously, as was respectful, and Liam followed behind her.

Emerson sought to catch his subordinates' attentions, but they were moving too quickly to notice his hand signal. He wasn't sure what he felt about the possible outcome of Giorgio's trial. In a moment of honesty, he admitted that he had no opinion. It was a matter of what Lise Panoy wanted, but he chose not to contact her until the Review Board delivered its decisions for both men.

"Where are we going, Sergeant?" Liam asked. When they'd hit the initial corridor, she'd taken off running, and he was forced to sprint to catch up to her. There was little pedestrian traffic to weave through. The station's corridors were completely deserted, but people turned from their monitors to witness the security officers race past. The major and sergeant heard encouragements from the onlookers. As a group, stationers wanted to see Giorgio convicted.

Cecilia ignored the major's question. She was attempting to dial on her comm unit, while she ran. "Sergeant Rodriguez, where are you?" Cecilia asked, when she was finally successful.

"Sitting at my desk, waiting for the major and you," Miguel replied. He'd watched the trial on his desk monitor, frustrated by the turn in the proceedings. In his heart, he knew Giorgio was guilty, but it didn't occur to him that there was the possibility of the charges being dismissed. A governor's security chief would know every inch of the house and its grounds without fail, or he wasn't worth the coin he was paid.

"Tell me that we have my DAD records on file for that day," Cecilia asked breathlessly.

"Did you upload them?" Miguel asked.

"I can't recall. I usually do, but that day was a little disconcerting," Cecilia replied.

"One moment, I'm checking," Miguel replied.

Liam wanted to ask, but he was running short of breath. For a short woman, Cecilia was keeping up a blistering pace. *Twenty years makes a big difference,* Liam admitted to himself.

"Found them," Miguel yelled.

"Yes," Cecilia shouted, skipping into the air, without slowing her pace.

Maybe more than twenty years, Liam thought.

When the pair reached security administration, Cecilia raced to Miguel's desk, and he jumped out of his seat. He glanced with concern at his major, who was bent over with his hands on his knees and gasping for breath. Seconds later, Devon raced up to the desk.

"You okay, Major?" asked Devon, mirroring Miguel's worried face.

"I will be, if someone, who doesn't want to be demoted back to corporal, will explain themselves to me," Liam said between ragged breaths.

"Sorry, Major, if I had erased the contents of my sniffer instead of uploading them, there wasn't going to be anything to say."

"Okay, you have your files, now what?" Liam asked, standing upright but still taking deep breaths.

"It occurred to me that Giorgio's defense is hinging on his word against those of the women, and there's no vid evidence to contradict him. However, there might be DNA evidence."

"Explain," Devon said.

"I was running my DAD when I entered the house. I expected to pick up a match to Helena's profile, which I'd loaded before we went downside."

"Smart," Miguel allowed.

"I checked it several times, but I never got a hit, while we were searching the floors. By the time, we discovered the secret passageway, I was paying attention to the governor's directions and never checked the sniffer again," Cecilia explained. "Ready. Miguel, I need a DAD."

Miguel unlocked a lower drawer in his desk and handed his device over to Cecilia. She hooked it to his system and reloaded the data records from the governor's house. The sniffer stored the DNA profiles that were detected.

"Now that we have the five profiles in our databases for the people involved in these trials, we can run a broader comparison," Cecilia explained.

"Five?" Devon queried.

"She's including Aurelia, aren't you, Sergeant?" Liam replied.

"Yes, sir," Cecilia said, glancing up at Liam and grinning. She completed the upload of the five profiles, refreshing the one the DAD held on Helena, and then requested matches. The DAD output was nearly instantaneous. "And there you have it. Five matches," Cecilia announced with deep satisfaction.

"We need locations," Liam said, coming around the desk to peer over Cecilia's shoulder, Miguel making room for him.

"Agreed," Cecelia replied, with a little frustration. Every match the DAD recorded was related to its physical surroundings at the time. However, the security team was downside when the records were made, which meant the data couldn't be compared to a known structure such as the JOS.

"I have an idea," Devon said.

Cecilia jumped out of the chair, as Liam and Miguel made way for him at the desk.

Devon stripped off the entire stream of data locators with the matching profiles from the sniffer. The device's first matches were those of Markos and Giorgio at the entrance of the house. He gave those points to an architectural program, as the starting positions. Then he fed the remainder of the match positions into the program, which plotted each new point in relationship to the previous position.

Within several minutes, the team was viewing a 3D, skeletal outline of the governor's house, as Cecilia had searched through it. Clearly evident was Cecilia's progression from the first floor to the third floor, down to the first floor, out to the patio, up to the second floor, and finally to the third floor via the back stairway.

Devon pointed to a location on his monitor and then slid his chair back from the desk to make room for the others. He was beaming.

Liam, Miguel, and Cecilia crowded close to the monitor for a better look. On the third floor, in the area that corresponded to the private corridor, were five matches — Markos, Giorgio, Aurelia, Helena, and Sasha.

"Our escapee," Liam commented, pointing to a spot on the screen, and then added, "Look at the areas inside the suite."

"Five matches," Miguel said quietly.

A moment of silence was followed by an explosion of celebration, before Liam cut it short. "Devon, you're in charge of putting the data together in a meaningful way for the Board. Remember, this is the first time they would have seen this form of evidence. Miguel, you're responsible for getting the equipment we will need to present the evidence. Cecilia, you're with me. We have to organize your statement for the Board to validate how and why you collected the data. Let's move, everyone. We have a guilty man to bring to justice."

The Board reconvened promptly three hours after Stamerson's dismissal. "I presume you're ready to present your evidence, Major," Stamerson said. There was an element of hope in the chairman's voice.

"We are, Mr. Chairman," Liam replied. He carefully walked the Review Board through the presentation. They were familiar with DADs and how they managed their DNA profile comparisons, although using a stream of data to describe an officer's movement in an unmapped location was new to them.

Liam fielded a series of questions from the Board, which sought to ensure they understood what they were viewing. It was the fact that a DAD was built to keep the DNA data and matches secure that gave them confidence in the evidence.

Giorgio's counsel tried his best to punch holes in the evidence's validity, but the major's presentation had been thorough.

After the presentation's conclusion and the end of questions, Stamerson asked, "What have you to say, Mr. Sestos, in response to this new information?"

Giorgio Sestos lifted his hands in surrender and smiled at Stamerson.

"I take it that you have no response to the evidence, Mr. Sestos," Stamerson replied. "Are there other comments or evidence that you or your counsel wish to present in your defense?" he asked. When there was none, he adjourned the trial for the Board to deliberate.

Two days later, in quick succession, the Review Board reconvened and announced the conviction of both men. Each was given a seventeen-year sentence, a year of incarceration for each year that Helena Garmenti had been held prisoner.

"It is the decree of this Board that these sentences aren't to be reduced under any circumstances and that includes a commandant's pardon," Stamerson announced, eyeing Emerson.

The raucous celebration of thousands of the audience near the meeting room penetrated its walls, and Stamerson paused to let it subside.

"Furthermore, it is the opinion of this Board, although not its purview, that a review of security procedures to enable downsiders to report crimes and security to conduct criminal investigations be undertaken by the commandant. It's been proven to the satisfaction of the members of this Board that the domes are incapable of self-policing their people. Whether it is willful or merely uncaring on the part of the families to ensure that every Pyrean is protected is unknown. The result is the same."

* * * *

A series of critical exchanges between individuals took place immediately after the sentencing of Markos and Giorgio, who were led out of the Review Board chambers by security.

Emerson left the meeting room in a hurry to return to his office. He needed privacy for his downside call.

"I presume you watched the trials," Emerson said to Lise. He'd reached her immediately. Obviously, she'd been waiting for his call.

"Every moment of it," Lise replied.

"Now that the way is clear for you to take over the governorship, we have things to discuss, you and I," Emerson pronounced. He was feeling a renewed sense of confidence, now that he'd dodged an investigation into his own affairs and Lise had more need of him now than ever.

"I presume I can inform the other family heads that I have your support, Emerson. That would ensure that I receive the governorship."

"You'll have it, Lise, although there are conditions."

"I'm listening."

"Your monthly payments have been paltry, compared to the enormity of recent events. Now that you're about to become governor, I think you can do better ... much better."

"I'll see that you're adequately compensated, Commandant," Lise replied. "Is there anything else?"

"You heard the Board's statements concerning the undertaking of a review by my office of the domes' security procedures."

"Yes, and you and I know it's not binding."

"It isn't, but I feel it's in the interest of all concerned to initiate such a review and implement the findings."

"You're overreaching, Emerson. Be careful."

"On the contrary, Lise; you and the other family heads are the ones who have exceeded your authority. Sentiment is running very high on the station against downsiders. If I fail to take action to ensure the likes of what happened to Helena Garmenti and her daughters can't be repeated, I will be out of a job. Then it's likely that the next person who sits at this desk might not be so amenable to your charms."

"I presume that you can undertake your review at your leisure, Commandant," Lise said, adopting a more considerate tone.

"Reviews of this sort take time, Lise. There are so many steps to the process before we achieve an implementation stage."

"Then we understand each other, Emerson," Lise said sweetly, and ended the call. "Not fit to be called discharge," she muttered, and called for her personal assistant. She had an important meeting to arrange.

* * * *

Devon finished listening to the recording of Emerson and Lise. The captain hadn't ordered him to cease monitoring the commandant's private comm calls, and he saw no reason to stop. Devon reasoned that the recordings could be potential evidence for future prosecutions, even though they were illegally obtained. The thought occurred to him to release the recordings to the Review Board and take the hit for the unauthorized monitoring. What stopped that line of reasoning was that it occurred to him the Board would probably be forced to dismiss them because of their unwarranted procurement. Instead, Devon sent a link to Liam with a message that said, "Listen to this one."

Liam had no sooner reviewed the recording than he looked up to find Harbour standing in his doorway. He was thankful for his habit of listening to audio portions of his monitor or comm station via his earpiece.

When Harbour saw Liam crane his neck to look behind her, she said, "Sasha is with her mother, Major. You're safe for now." Without invitation, Harbour stepped in and closed the door. "You still recording the commandant? After the Review Board's pronouncements, I'd be interested if Emerson reached out to Lise."

"Harbour, we've done some good work, recovering Helena Garmenti and her daughter. The perpetrators have been arrested, tried, and convicted."

"Interesting that you answer my query with an events summary, Major, and, if I were to extend your misguided attempt at deflection, I would ask you: What about Aurelia?"

"What about her? She's still a fugitive and still wanted for the murder of Dimitri Belosov. When she's caught, she'll stand trial before the Review Board."

"Even though we know her to have been a prisoner for her entire life, who was merely fighting back against a tormentor."

"That's for the Review Board to decide, Harbour, and you know that."

Harbour kept a rein on her power. Liam's displeasure at what he was saying was distinct, but she felt that she'd lost an ally in the fight against the commandant and the families. Something had changed, and she wasn't sure what it was. "What about the next time there's a transgression against a sensitive?"

"That's for us to handle when it happens. At this moment, it's time to stand down."

"That path might be your choice, Major, but some of us don't give up that easily."

"I caution you, Harbour —" Liam started to say, but he halted when he felt a quick spike of anger.

"Don't be presumptuous, Major," Harbour said, glowering at Liam. "I'm not one of your subordinates, and I don't wish to be an adversary of station security, unless you choose to make me one."

Liam never got the opportunity to respond. Harbour was gone before he drew breath. He picked up a water bottle and took a deep drink, reminding himself that it was a foolish man who irritated a powerful empath.

Harbour stalked through the offices of security administration, intent on clearing the area as quickly as possible. Halfway to the exit, Sergeant Miguel Rodriguez asked for a moment of her time. Her first thought was to ignore him, but she cautioned herself not to let rancor get the best of her.

"What can I do for you, Sergeant?" Harbour stated tersely. She felt Miguel's small spike of fear, and she regretted her harsh tone. "Forgive me, Sergeant, I've had an unsettling conversation."

"A lot of those happening around here lately," Miguel acknowledged. "I wanted to give you a heads-up, Harbour. It's been reported to me that Corporal McKenzie, in his downtime, has been reviewing vids of Cinders' crew and the man himself when they're on station."

"Still after Aurelia, is he?"

"It's an obsession with him. What I wanted you to know is that I've reviewed the logs of the segments he's already viewed. In those cams covering Cinders, Corporal McKenzie has seen you. So, you've become a person of interest to him."

"I'm surprised such a base individual is still employed by security."

"He enjoys the commandant's support, which means it's long been suspected that he has a downside patron."

"Now, who do you think that could be, or should I say was?"

"More than likely the patron has changed but the support hasn't, Harbour. All I'm trying to say to you is be careful. Don't give Corporal McKenzie any excuse to confront you."

"I thank you for your concern and your warning, Sergeant," Harbour replied, and sent him soothing sensations.

"Thank you, ma'am," Miguel replied, as the delicious feelings flooded his mind.

Harbour smiled at him and continued toward the exit.

25: *Spryte*

"We're standing off the *Annie*," Nate announced to Jessie, when the captain arrived on the bridge. "We arrived about two hours ago."

"Good work, Nate. Get some food and rest," Jessie replied. "You're relieved."

"Aye, Captain, you have the bridge."

"This is the *Spryte* calling the *Annie*," Jessie called over the bridge comm system.

"Yohlin here, Jessie. I don't think I've ever been happier to see the *Spryte*."

"And here I thought it was me you missed," Jessie teased, but a response from Yohlin wasn't forthcoming. It gave him an indication of the pressure she was under.

"I'll be taking a shuttle over to you, Yohlin. We've a lot to discuss."

"Do you think that's wise, Jessie? Right now, you're completely isolated aboard the *Spryte*. If you come here and return, you'll share the possibility of exposure with your people."

"Is your crew displaying any maladies or unexplainable symptoms, Yohlin?"

"No, none as yet."

"Putting aside the fact that Rules detected a power source beneath the site, has there been any indication of activity there?"

"Belinda had the good sense to leave a cam, overlooking the site, which has been feeding back visuals. To increase the definition, we've resorted to having it send a still every few seconds. So far, we've seen no change in the site."

"Then it sounds safe enough to me, Yohlin. I'm coming over."

"Aye, aye, Jessie," Yohlin replied, and Jessie heard a faint amount of relief in her voice.

"Captain, ready to relieve you when you're ready," Ituau said from the hatch. "The pilot's in a vac suit, has the shuttle prepped, and is waiting aboard."

"Then you have the bridge, Ituau," Jessie said, clearing out of the command chair and ready to leave.

"Captain," Ituau said.

Jessie watched his first mate hesitate. It wasn't her style. He often couldn't prevent her from expressing her opinions.

"What's on your mind, Ituau?"

"What are we supposed to do if something happens to you, Captain?" Ituau asked in a rush.

"You do what you've always done."

"Which is what, Captain?"

"The best you can Ituau, which is what you've always given me."

"Aye, Captain, good luck!"

Jessie hustled around the wheel to a spoke, which led to the equipment room, and climbed into his vac suit.

"Spryte, systems check," Jessie requested. As with all suit checks, the wearer was required to visually toggle the heads-up display to ensure the vac suit wasn't triggered by the use of its name in a comm call.

"All systems at one hundred percent functionality," Spryte replied.

"Let's get this done," Jessie muttered to himself. A small part of him wanted to run back to his cabin and lock the door, but it wasn't the way he'd lived his life, and he wasn't about to change now.

Jessie exited the gravity wheel and his mag-boots clicked on the surface of the axis corridor, as he made his way to the *Spryte*'s single shuttle bay. He transited the airlock, climbed aboard, sealed the hatch, belted into a seat, and called the pilot to launch.

During the flight, Jessie considered his options again, concerning the discovery. It was the same line of thought he'd run through his mind a thousand times since he'd first heard of the find from Yohlin. The primary question was whether to warn Pyre's leaders. He saw the answer to that question was fraught with problems, no matter which way he chose to go. The second question was whether to investigate the site. There was an opportunity for tremendous technical discoveries and, quite possibility, incredible harm. After these two questions, the remainder of them lined up like spacers at a cantina, demanding another drink and refusing to take no for an answer.

The bump of the shuttle against the *Annie*'s hull shook Jessie out of his reverie, and he called the pilot. "You clear on the routine, Claudia?"

"Aye, Captain, I maintain vacuum in the main cabin. After you exit the craft, I detach and perform a blow out before I return to the *Spryte*. Then the shuttle is to be maintained in vacuum within the bay."

"No deviation from this routine, Claudia."

"Understood, Captain ... and Captain, good luck."

"Thank you, Claudia. Sail safe," Jessie replied. He accessed the deck hatch after the telltale confirmed vacuum in the airlock. He slipped through the double hatches, locking first the shuttle and then the airlock's hatch. He signaled Claudia that she could detach after he was safely inside the airlock.

When the airlock was pressurized, Jessie dropped into the *Annie*'s axis corridor. He paused. The corridor resembled each of his ships. While he'd returned many times, since leaving the *Annie* to serve on the *Pearl*, it always felt like coming home. He expected to see Rose clumping down the corridor toward him. Shaking his head to clear the thoughts, he made his way to the *Annie*'s gravity wheel.

Once in the wheel, Jessie shucked his vac suit. A spacer was standing by to hang it up and charge his tanks, while Yohlin waited for him. Behind her, Jessie spied Aurelia. The teenager was bouncing impatiently from foot to foot.

"Jessie, it's good to see you," Yohlin said, shaking Jessie's hand.

"You've kind of outdone yourself this time, Captain. I send you for metal and slush, and you bring me an alien site instead." Jessie kept trying to lift Yohlin's spirits, but it didn't seem to be working. Worry lines furrowed her brow.

When Jessie stepped aside, Aurelia took it as her cue, and she rushed forward, slamming into Jessie, and threw her arms around his neck. "Thank you, thank you, for my mother and sister," she gushed.

"Decorum, spacer," Yohlin admonished.

Aurelia immediately released Jessie, but her broad grin said she was unrepentant. "I believe, Captain Erring, that my status is that of a trainee without contract or coin. Until that's changed, I prefer to treat Captain Cinders as a friend ... a really good friend."

"I take it, Captain, you and the crew followed the trial," Jessie said.

"Courtesy of the *Belle*'s transmissions. We probably have Harbour to thank for that."

"You do," Jessie agreed.

"It was tough to get regular maintenance shifts conducted, while the trials were on," Yohlin said. "The entertainment really started with the arrest of the governor and his chief of security. That's when the crew discovered our Rules was the missing Aurelia."

"Your secret is out?" Jessie asked, eyeing the girl.

"Sorry, Captain Cinders," Aurelia replied. "I couldn't help myself. I was so happy to see my mother and my sister rescued that I blurted out who they were to me. Besides, later on, they showed my picture and identified me."

"I think some of the crew had their suspicions before then, but since we haven't made the YIPS or the JOS in more than a month, no one saw the commandant's alert about the hunt for Aurelia," Yohlin added.

"To be fair, Aurelia, I can't take credit for their rescue. You'll have to thank Harbour when you see her. She instigated it."

"Understood, Captain, but it would never have happened, if you hadn't bought time for those events to unfold by hiding me."

"I have to agree with that assessment, Captain," Yohlin said.

"I take it everyone knows about the convictions of Markos and Sestos?" Jessie asked.

"Do they ever, Captain!" Aurelia exclaimed. "We celebrated when Markos pled guilty and again when the Board convicted Giorgio.

"And, as if the crew wasn't happy enough about the governor's downfall, Rules added her version of celebration."

Aurelia ducked her head in embarrassment, when Jessie's penetrating gaze held her. "It gets away from me sometimes," she admitted.

Jessie chuckled at Aurelia's characterization that her power was similar to a child's pet escaping from its enclosure. "Before you return to duties,

Aurelia, let me adjust your understanding of your circumstances aboard this ship. Your no-contract status ended when you first set foot on Triton. That day, you became a working member of this crew. I couldn't set up a private account for you, but I have a subaccount under the company account where your weekly coin is deposited."

"I'm earning coin?" Aurelia asked, even more excited than before. "Okay, last hug," she said. This time she whispered, "Thank you for everything, Jessie," and kissed his cheek before she released him and hurried off.

Jessie and Yohlin walked around half of the giant gravity wheel to reach the captain's cabin. He passed spacer after spacer, who smiled and warmly greeted him. Most were jovial in their mannerisms.

In Yohlin's cabin, Jessie said, "I expected to find your crew scared out of their wits, having found an alien construction, and my concern doubled when I noticed the worry on your face, Yohlin. What's up with the crew?"

"That's Rules' doing, Jessie. I wish I could partake of her empath largesse, but I'm wondering where all this will lead. I can tell you one thing. If we ... when we make dock again at the JOS, security will have their hands full when they come to arrest Rules. For this crew, there'll be no polite stepping aside at security's request."

"Is it because she's that strong?" Jessie asked.

"I don't know how to judge her power, Jessie. She's the first empath who I've been close to for any length of time. But, it's her personality. Despite all that she's been through, she's a beam of starlight to this crew ... always up. Even now, though they know her real name is Aurelia, the crew continues to call her Rules. To them, it's a sort of private name by which they know her."

Jessie absorbed the implication of what Yohlin was saying, blinking a couple of times at the incredible discovery. "Maybe I should hire an empath for each ship," he finally said. "Think of all the trained spacers we've lost through the years to dementia or personal conflicts."

"Well, you'd have to find a pair of sensitives who take to space like Rules and who come with her positive personality, if you want it to work."

"Of course, I could always rotate Aurelia among the ships."

Yohlin laughed. It was the first time Jessie had heard that from her since he came aboard. "You could do that, Jessie, and I guarantee that you'd have riots, if not mutinies, faster than you could believe."

"You're really serious about the crew's adoption of Aurelia?" Jessie asked.

"I'd tell you to hang around this crew for a few days and you'd see for yourself, but, on the other hand, I'm saddened that you chose to come aboard."

"Speaking of what's bothering you, Yohlin, I want to see the images of the site."

Jessie and Yohlin moved to her desk to view the large monitor. Jessie scanned the images quickly and discovered that Yohlin had directed the cam to be occasionally turned and zoomed in on details at the site.

"No one crossed the ring, right?" Jessie asked, when he finished his perusal.

"No. However, a tech did test the ring with a mass spectrometer when he couldn't obtain a sample."

"Did he scratch it?"

"Negative."

"What we couldn't do with the knowledge to make that type of material," Jessie said, staring wistfully at the image.

"All this doesn't frighten you, Jessie?" asked Yohlin, with incredulity.

"A little ... I think I'm more curious than scared. What are the lumps scattered inside the ring?"

"Probably rock outcroppings."

"Hardly," Jessie replied. He flipped through the images again. "There aren't any closer views of these supposed rocks?"

"What are you thinking, Jessie?"

"Inside the ring, the floor, or deck, whatever it is, is perfectly flat, except for the platform and the instrumentation. So, why would these little rock formations be left there for the aliens to trip over. That makes no sense."

"Well, your guesses couldn't be any further afield than some of the ones I've heard."

"Such as?"

"You don't want to hear."

"Oh, but I do," Jessie replied with a grin.

"The best one is that aliens came out here to perform for their audiences in low gravity. The platform was their stage, and the instrumentation was used in some way to aid the show."

"A performance stage?" Jessie asked incredulously. "For the love of Pyre, Yohlin, you're giving me images of naked aliens dancing under the stars."

"You wanted to know, Jessie, and I did warn you," Yohlin chuckled.

"Okay, what about any serious ideas?"

"One engineer believes that because Rules is able to detect the power below the surface, it must be substantial. He thinks it could be some sort of beam weapon that could be directed into space against adversaries."

"The platform looks solid. How would they direct the beam, if they couldn't rotate the platform? Not to mention that a weapon anchored to a moon can only be deployed, at best, in a hemisphere. What about defending the other one hundred eighty degrees of arc?"

"A couple of engineers agree that the platform is able to transmit a beam. The other concepts are that the beam could have been used to power an exploratory vehicle via microwaves or that it was an experiment that was never fulfilled and was terminated."

Jessie left a wide image of the site on the monitor and stared at it.

Yohlin let Jessie absorb the impact of what he'd seen. It had taken her days to come to grips with the thought that they'd discovered alien technology ... an intelligent, nonhuman species existed. But what struck her hardest was the possibility of contamination by virus, parasite, or some unknown thing that could infect and wipe out humans.

"Well, whatever this site is or was, I've come to the decision that I've got to notify Pyre's leaders," Jessie announced. He opened his comm unit and said, "Bridge, get me the *Belle*."

"The *Belle*, Captain?" came a questioning voice.

"Never mind. Patch me through to Ituau aboard the *Spryte*."

"Aye, aye, Captain."

"Ituau here, Captain."

"Ituau, I need the *Belle*."

"Aye, Captain. One moment."

"You speak regularly with the *Belle*, Jessie?" asked Yohlin, one eyebrow lifted in query.

"Often enough," Jessie replied.

"Dingles here, Captain Cinders."

Jessie grinned, and Yohlin's mouth dropped open.

"How are you faring, Dingles?" Jessie asked.

"Tight as a new hatch, Captain. Couldn't be better."

"Taking a turn on comms, I see."

"Yeah, Captain, it's been hectic lately with all the ..."

"You can say it, Dingles. Only Captain Erring is with me."

"Good to hear your voice, Dingles," Yohlin said.

"Thank you, ma'am. As I was saying, Captain Cinders, it's been busy what with the ship's preparations. All systems are checking out. Some have needed work, but we're bringing them up to ready, ready."

"By the sound of your voice, Dingles, it must be good to be a spacer again," Jessie said.

"And I never suspected I'd crew on a ship this big, Captain."

"Congratulations, Dingles," Jessie said, and laughed at the thought of his retired navigator crewing again on an even greater ship.

Seated next to Jessie, Yohlin mouthed the word "crew" to him, a frown on her forehead, but Jessie waved off her question with one hand.

"Dingles, I need Harbour. Is she aboard?"

"Negative, Captain. She's on the JOS with Sasha. She has that one with her at all times. It's best to keep the little one occupied. We found out the hard way that if Sasha doesn't sleep so good ... nightmares, you know ... then those sleeping near her don't either. Harbour has commented several times about the incredible power that Sasha possesses."

"Does she make you nervous, Dingles?" Yohlin asked.

"That's a big negative, Captain. She's a child who's had it tough, and she's angry about it. But, I think if we give her some time and attention, she should be fine. Hold, Captain Cinders, I'll connect you to Harbour."

"Jessie, how are you?" asked Harbour.

The warmth in the empath's voice had Yohlin lifting both eyebrows at Jessie, the hint of a smile forming on her lips.

"Harbour, Captain Yohlin Erring of the *Annie* is on speaker with me. I need a favor."

"Whatever you need, Jessie," Harbour replied.

"This is to be a conference call with Commandant Strattleford, Captain Stamerson, Major Finian, Governor Panoy, and yourself. I need it to happen now, if not sooner."

Silence followed Jessie's request, and he asked, "Did you copy, Harbour?"

"I did, Jessie, sorry. Your request sounded so ominous that it took me aback."

"Can you make it happen, Harbour?"

"Most assuredly, Jessie. I'm not far from security administration. I'll start there."

"Once you have the group together, Harbour, add Dingles to the mix, and he'll connect me to the conference link."

"Be back to you soon, Jessie," Harbour said, ending the call.

Yohlin eyed Jessie, who tried to ignore her. Not to be denied, she said, "That was the all-powerful, intoxicatingly beautiful Harbour, who just said, 'whatever you need, Jessie,' wasn't it?"

"It's a turn of a phrase, is all," Jessie replied.

"Uh-huh," Yohlin commented.

Jessie spent the intervening minutes reviewing the photos again. None of the ideas that Yohlin had relayed from the crew seemed to fit. "Do you have a theory on what your people have found?" Jessie asked.

"Jessie, I'm a spacer and a miner in that order. I was never an engineer. I haven't a clue what that site is all about. Right now, I wish we'd never come to Triton. Sorry, Jessie, I didn't mean it as a comment on your orders," Yohlin quickly added, when she saw the wince at the corner of Jessie's eyes. "I was as anxious as you, make that more anxious than you, to come out here."

"Captain Erring, call patched from the *Belle* through the *Spryte*, ma'am," said a bridge voice over Yohlin's comm unit.

"Transfer the call to Captain Cinders' comm unit," Yohlin ordered.

"Aye, aye, Captain."

"Jessie, everyone you requested is on the call," Harbour said.

"What's this about, Captain Cinders? I was made to understand this was a critical call, and I abandoned an important meeting for it," Lise Panoy complained.

"Governor Panoy," Stamerson said evenly, "I believe if you let Captain Cinders speak, this might proceed a little faster."

"Per the Captain's Articles, I'm informing you of a find at Triton," Jessie said. He was referring to an agreement a captain signed before he took command of a ship. In addition to stating that the captain must act in a responsible manner, which did not endanger the crew, other ships, or the stations, it required the captain to promptly report any situation to Pyre's leaders that might be considered a danger. "We've discovered an alien installation."

Jessie waited, but not a word was said in reply. Yohlin and he exchanged looks of commiseration.

"You're serious, Captain?" Emerson asked. "This isn't your idea of a joke, is it?"

"I wish it was. On the surface is a shallow ring of metal one hundred meters around. In the center is a low, round platform, and nearby is some sort of instrumentation. The entire complex is covered in centuries of space dust."

"You're saying it's a long-abandoned site. In other words, it's neutralized," Stamerson asked, wishing to confirm its status.

"Afraid not, Captain. We've detected the hum of a significant power source belowground."

"Have you investigated the structure, Jessie?" Lise Panoy asked, an idea taking shape in her mind.

"Captain Erring's crew of the *Annie* discovered the site. Their investigation was minimal. A tech tried to sample the metal, but couldn't. Then he ran a mass spectrometer test, and it came back as unknown substance. It didn't even identify the elements in the material."

"Then your people were exposed to the alien site," Lise said.

"As I said, Governor, briefly, but they were in vac suits during the entire time. What's your point?"

"And where's your ship, Captain?" Lise pressed on.

"The *Spryte* is also at Triton."

"And have any of your people set foot on Triton?" asked Lise.

"Negative, Governor."

"But have your crew, Captain, had contact with any of the *Annie*'s crew?" Lise persisted.

Jessie and Yohlin glanced at each other.

You could tell them no, but you won't, will you, Jessie? Yohlin thought.

"I'm aboard the *Annie*, Governor, but no other member of my crew boarded with me."

"But your shuttle had to make contact with the *Annie*. Is it still attached, or did it return to the *Spryte*?" Emerson asked. He was beginning to understand where Lise was headed with her line of inquiry.

"It returned," Jessie admitted.

"Then it seems obvious to me that we have to order the *Annie* and *Spryte* to remain isolated at Triton to prevent any chance of contamination," Lise summarized.

"For how long?" Harbour asked.

"I would think indefinitely," Lise replied. "This site was part of an alien civilization. We have no idea what sort of contagions we could be dealing with. Are we willing to risk the life of every Pyrean citizen to rescue a few spacers, who've been unfortunate enough to be exposed to an alien construct?"

Dingles, who was monitoring the call, could feel his jaw grinding. He ached to tear into the governor and denounce her for the handful of effluent that she was, but he kept his mouth shut. This conversation was above his pay grade.

"I deem permanent isolation unnecessary," Stamerson stated. "I would ask this group to consider a reasonable period of time for the Captain's ships to be quarantined to give us some assurance that there has been no contamination."

"Captain Stamerson, how would you define some assurance?" Lise demanded. "As governor of the domes, I think it is proper to ask for zero risk. What if the contagion isn't biological? What if it's mechanical in nature, a tiny piece of tech waiting to propagate in the right environment?"

"In my opinion —" Liam Finian started to say, before the commandant cut him off.

"Major, I have no idea why you've been asked to be part of this conference, but it would be best, at this point, if you remained silent," Emerson stated forcefully.

"That's where you're wrong, Emerson," Jessie said. "Major Finian, Captain Stamerson, and Harbour are here at my request, because I respect their opinions, as opposed to how little I value that of Lise and yours. So, do be a good boy and be quiet, while I hear what Major Finian has to say, or I'll sail my ships back to the JOS. And you can deal with the consequences."

Yohlin glanced at Jessie. She'd never heard him so angry that he disregarded the use of titles and surnames.

"I was going to say, Captain Cinders, that we should rely on the opinion of others, who've had time to consider the implications of these types of discoveries," Liam said.

"You're speaking of Earth's scientists and any files they stored on the colony ship," Jessie said.

"When I get back to the *Belle*, Captain Cinders, I'll comb through the libraries. There's bound to be a reasonable period of time for quarantine," Harbour said.

"No need, Harbour, I'm looking at the protocols now," Lise said coolly. She couldn't believe her luck. First the governorship falls into her hands, and now she was presented with the perfect opportunity to isolate one of the spacers' most influential captains.

"How is it, Governor, that you have a copy of the *Belle's* files?" Harbour asked.

"I don't think it's a copy, Harbour. If I'm not mistaken, the coding on this file indicates it's an original," Lise replied.

"And how did you come by it, Governor?" Stamerson asked, seeing the possibility of the Review Board intervening in this matter.

"Your argument isn't with me, Captain Stamerson. The Andropov family had these files and many others from the *Belle* in their private library, which I've only just discovered," Lise replied. It wasn't true. Each of the family heads had copies of the Andropov files, which were taken from the *Belle* soon after the establishment of the second dome.

"What do Earth's scientists recommend?" Jessie asked, breaking into the argument.

"Six months," Lise said. She felt like standing up and cheering, but settled for a broad grin in the privacy of her salon.

"We can't last that long out here, and you know it," Jessie ground out.

"I regret, Captain Cinders, it's not a matter of you and your people lasting. It's a matter of protecting Pyrean lives."

"Governor, I'll require the return of all original files to security administration," Emerson said. "You may keep copies, but those original files were not the Andropovs to take."

"Certainly, Commandant, if Major Finian will tell me where to deposit them, I'll send them this evening."

"Captain Cinders, providing I verify the authenticity of this particular data file, I think we must follow these protocols," Emerson stated officiously. "Earth's scientists surely had more time and resources than we do to determine the steps to take in an eventuality such as this."

"I'm afraid I must agree, Captain," Stamerson added. "Without any other credible guidelines, we must follow these protocols."

"In addition," Lise said, hurrying on. "Triton and the space around it must be quarantined. This is alien technology. By Captain Cinders' own account, it exists beyond our normal understanding. Its power source has persisted in a hostile environment throughout the centuries, while the site has been abandoned. Who knows what capabilities it possesses to destroy our people? Furthermore, the protocols state that if any alien technology or samples are collected, the containment facilities must be permanently isolated from the population."

"You're condemning two ships full of spacers to death over a threat that hasn't even been realized, Governor," Harbour argued. "We could wait two to three weeks and see if anything develops among the crew. Surely that would be more sensible. In the meantime, we find a way to get them additional supplies."

"The protocols state otherwise, Harbour," Lise replied. She loved it when things went her way. "Anyone who aids Captain Cinders' ships will join the quarantine, forcing the clock to reset to zero and await the passing of another six months, and that's providing that none of the technology or samples were brought aboard Cinders' ships."

Lise was confident that no mining captain could afford the trip to ferry supplies to Triton and wait out a six-month period. Furthermore, the attempt might bring about a crew's mutiny, all of which would serve her end goal, that of fomenting enough divisiveness among the people to create and take the position of Pyre's first president.

"Lise Panoy, you had better stay downside, while I live," Harbour ground out. "If we ever cross paths, you'll regret your stance against these people."

"There's no need for threats, Harbour," Emerson said.

"Save your breath, Harbour," Jessie said. "Lise and Emerson have found the perfect opportunity for a power grab, and my people have handed it to them. And, unfortunately, the problem has enough credibility that Captain Stamerson must concur. Well, in the time we do have, we will be investigating the alien site. Maybe there's something we can learn about alien technology that might be of value to us all."

"Captain, I would advise —" Emerson began, only to see the link to Jessie drop off.

"I believe, Commandant, that Captain Cinders considers your advice unnecessary," Stamerson said. He was developing a bad taste in his mouth and wondering if he'd made the mistake of his life by agreeing with Lise and Emerson's proposal.

"Harbour, you need to tell us if you can dispassionately take part in this discussion. Otherwise, it might be better to excuse yourself," Lise said, targeting the next individual she wanted to remove from the call. She was pleased to see the commandant had dropped the links to the *Belle* and Major Finian.

"You're absolutely right, Lise. As a woman, who lacks any compassion, you're well-suited to take advantage of these spacers' misfortune. I'll leave it to the commandant and you to decide how to cut up the spoils and share the pieces among your cabal. Captain Stamerson, I wish you good day," Harbour replied, and closed her comm unit.

"Well, sirs," Lise said, with equanimity, "it appears to us to safeguard the Pyrean populace."

Harbour stalked out of Major Finian's office. She was challenged to squelch her anger, so as not to broadcast it throughout security, as she made her way out. Passing by Sasha, who was waiting in security's outer lobby, Harbour said, "Come, Sasha, we have work to do."

Sasha observed the tension in Harbour's face and fell quickly into line.

26: Alien Site

"That didn't go so well," Yohlin commented drily.

"Kind of what I expected," Jessie replied. "I've found out from Harbour that Emerson is in bed with Lise. Harbour has reviewed recorded conversations between the two and heard them colluding on power politics. Plus, Lise is paying for Emerson's support."

"Why that little excuse for a human being!"

"I think Lise Panoy has been planning Markos Andropov's downfall for a long time. The death of Dimitri and Aurelia's escape played right into her hands."

"And now we've done the same."

"Yeah, but we're going to be a lot harder to take down than a tawdry excuse for a governor."

"If you say so, Jessie."

"I say so."

"Okay, what's the first order of business?"

"I have to tell our crew what's happening."

Jessie had the *Annie*'s bridge link to the *Spryte*, and his address was sent throughout both ships. He explained in detail the conversation between Pyre's leaders and himself, leaving out the part about Emerson and Lise taking advantage of the situation.

"I'm aware that the thought on everyone's minds right now is that we don't have six months' worth of supplies. Well, if you're wondering if I'm going to sit out here until they run out, then you've signed on with the wrong captain. We might have a little slack in our skins by the time we make our move, but then I notice a few of you could do with the loss of a few kilos here and there. Bottom line is this: If we sit out here for two or three months and see no ill effects from the site, we're running for supplies, and I've a good idea where to get them."

From inside Yohlin's quarters, Jessie and she could hear the crew yelling and clapping.

"Rousing speech," Yohlin commented. "You think you can make it happen."

"I know I can, Yohlin. There's things I can't share with you, yet, but we have more supporters than you think."

"Okay, Jessie, what's next?"

Jessie picked up his comm unit again and called his first mate. "Ituau, I want you to work with Captain Erring. Inventory the food supplies onboard the *Spryte*. The captain will do the same for the *Annie*. Both crews are now on rations, to be doled out at seventy-five percent of the usual volume."

"Any exceptions, Captain?"

"Yes, anyone downside gets a full ration."

"I thought the *Annie*'s crew was back aboard, Captain. By any chance, are you intending to do some sightseeing?"

"I want a closeup view of the alien site, Ituau. I'll be taking a small team downside tomorrow."

"Be careful, Captain. You'd look even funnier than you do now if you started growing a second head."

Jessie laughed and closed his comm unit.

"Are you serious about investigating the site, Jessie?" Yohlin asked.

"Absolutely."

"What's your grand plan for us after we wait out the two or three months you mentioned? Emperion has slush and the *Pearl* has basic processing gear. We could extend the time there."

"We'd add a month, maybe two, but we still wouldn't reach six months, and our crews would have been on reduced rations the entire time."

"Then what do you intend to do?"

"Me? I'm going to check out the site."

Yohlin shook her head in exasperation. "Fine, Jessie. Keep me in suspense. Okay, if you're adamant about going downside, I suggest you take the original discovery team, plus Darrin, my first mate, if they're willing. I'll have my people prep the large search rover. It's equipped to handle the six of you."

* * * *

Five crew members sat around the captain's table: Darrin, Belinda, Aurelia, Tully, and Hamoi.

"I'm headed downside to take a close look at the alien site. It'll be a cursory exploratory expedition. This is volunteers only," Jessie said.

"I'm in," Aurelia announced excitedly.

"It's polite, Rules, to wait until Captain Cinders finishes," Belinda said.

"Sorry, Captain."

"As I was saying, accompanying me is strictly voluntary. If you wish to opt out, I'll completely understand. Questions?"

"What's your opinion about the possibility of alien contamination, Captain?" Hamoi asked.

"I have no idea, son," Jessie replied to the young assay tech. "I do know the six months of quarantine seems overly cautious. If anything were to develop, it should have done so by now."

"But if we investigate deeper, that could change," Belinda said.

"I can't argue with that, Belinda," Jessie replied. "That's why I am asking for volunteers."

"But what does it matter, who goes downside, Captain, if those people return to the ship? We'll all share in their exposure," Darrin said.

"True. That's why the shelter will be moved close to the site and be attended by a couple of volunteers. Once I'm satisfied with our research on the site, we'll stay in the shelter for two weeks before we return to the ship. If the contaminant is biological, it should develop by then. If it's some form of mechanical nanotechnology, then it's probably already aboard this ship, but continuous inspections have revealed nothing. Any more questions?"

When no one replied, Jessie said, "Raise your hand if you're volunteering." Five hands went up.

"Thank you," Jessie said, and everyone felt Aurelia's pulse of pleasure. "We launch tomorrow morning. Darrin, you're in charge of our drop and the relocation of the shelter to a point within five kilometers of the site. Belinda and Tully, you'll review the prep of the rover. Hamoi, work with the two crew members who'll be stationed at the shelter. Captain Erring is gathering the pair. Check with her. Dismissed."

As the five stood, Jessie said, "Aurelia, please stay." Once the door closed, Jessie said, "I want to understand how you led the team to the site, what you felt, initially, and what you felt at the site."

Aurelia walked Jessie through her perception of the site's power, starting from the shelter's original position and how the signal increased and shifted as they moved closer.

"I think what was probably oddest to me, Captain," Aurelia said, applying Jessie's title to sound more like a spacer, "was that the signal was more of an irritant, until we got within a few hundred meters. Then it smoothed out and felt, I don't know, relaxing."

"Why do you think that is?" Jessie asked.

Aurelia blinked twice at Jessie. The question surprised her. Since she joined the crew of the *Annie*, she had followed one order after another. Only the rover crew had asked her opinion about anything. She relaxed, breathing slowly, and closed her eyes. It was how she calmed herself when she became frustrated with her imprisonment in the governor's house. She replayed the sensations from the initial detection through the days until they reached the site.

Jessie watched Aurelia relax. The baseline warmth he felt in her presence disappeared, as her breathing slowed. *Always on*, he thought of her power. Suddenly, Aurelia's eyes popped open.

"What?" Jessie asked.

"That power resonation is tuned to soothe the aliens who built it," Aurelia said, energized by the realization. "I don't know if they were sensitives, but they must have been able to feel it somehow. Once you get away from the site, Triton's surface must disturb the resonance. Hamoi continually talked about the way sound waves penetrate various substrata differently."

"You're learning about geology from Hamoi?" Jessie asked.

"I'm learning from everyone, Captain. People like to teach me."

"And you reciprocate."

"It's only polite. It's not like it costs me anything to make my power," Aurelia replied, shrugging her shoulders.

You're right, Yohlin. An exceptionally generous young girl, Jessie thought. "Interesting theory about the power source's resonance. When we return, I want you to pay close attention to when the power shifts to a pleasant sensation. I want it marked where and when it happens. Copy?"

"Understood, Captain."

"Dismissed, spacer."

Aurelia jumped up, flashed a bright smile, and Jessie was flooded with a delicious combination of sensations, as the teenager exited. On the one hand, he was disturbed by its unrequested distribution, as he saw it; and, on the other hand, he had to admit it was a heady experience.

* * * *

"We're down, Captain," the *Annie*'s shuttle pilot called to Jessie. The captain and crew were wearing vac suits. They donned their helmets, activated systems, and waited for the suits' responses.

Jessie looked around and everyone gave him a thumbs-up. "Let's unload," he ordered.

Darrin hit the ramp actuator, and the shuttle's main cabin was cycled to vacuum. When complete, the ramp lowered and Tully backed the six-seat search rover off the shuttle onto Triton's surface.

They'd landed near the shelter, and crew set about breaking it down. Within two hours, the shuttle's cabin was completely filled with the shelter and its equipment, and the pilot was lifting and heading for a site about 5 kilometers from the alien construction. Jessie and the exploration team climbed into the rover and headed for the same destination.

By the time the rover made the new base camp site, the crew was completing the setup operation. Jessie's team pitched in to help, and, soon after, the shuttle was lifting, taking the excess crew members to the *Annie*.

Jessie didn't waste any time. His crew swapped out their tanks and left them behind to be charged. Then, loaded with fresh tanks, they engaged the rover and headed for the site.

"Here, Captain," Aurelia called out from the rear seat, when they were near the site, and Jessie ordered Tully to stop.

"What's up, Captain?" Darrin asked.

"Tully, mark this exact position in the nav."

"Got it, sir."

"How far to the small overlook where you planted the cam?"

"It's about two hundred eighty-five meters, Captain."

Jessie glanced back at Aurelia, and she grinned, as if she'd won an award.

"To answer your question, Darrin, Aurelia has a theory about the shift in the perceived resonance of the power source. She's just pinpointed the location where the ground geology ceases to disturb the signal and it smooths out."

Hamoi eyed Aurelia, held out a hand, and she smacked it.

"Why is this important, Captain?" Belinda asked.

"I have no idea, Belinda," Jessie replied. "I'm treating the discovery of this site like it's a giant puzzle. Every piece of information we collect adds to the final picture."

"And what do you hope that image will be?" Darrin asked.

"Let me ask all of you a rhetorical question. In another ninety to one hundred years, how do you envision Pyrean society ... scraping along or sailing to the stars? The technology embedded in this site might possess the keys that will make possible the latter path."

Tully glanced over at Jessie, who was seated next to him, and Jessie hand-signaled forward.

Jessie noticed that the previous tracks out and back that Tully had been unerringly following led directly toward a cut in a tall outcrop.

"Straight at it, Captain, like she was tuned into a homing beacon," Tully commented, when he saw Jessie look back at their tracks and compare them to the forward view.

Tully stopped the rover just below the cut. "Do you want me to take it through, Captain?"

Footprints marked the trek up and through the cut, but the rover hadn't gone that way. "No, we'll leave it here," Jessie replied.

Everyone was ready for the word to get started, but Jessie sat quietly in the front seat.

"Anything wrong, Captain?" Darrin asked.

"No, Darrin, thinking is all. I was wondering how the aliens entered and left this place."

"We've only examined the site from the one side, the overlook, Captain," Belinda replied. "For all we know, there's an exit on the other side that leads to a landing pad or some other alien construction."

"Hmm," Jessie mused.

"Something else, Captain?" Tully asked.

"Darrin, Tully, you two are engineers. If you were told to build an incredible power system below the ground that was to last for centuries or more, and you had your choice of Pyre's three moons, which would you choose?"

"Definitely not Emperion, Captain," Darrin replied quickly.

"Definitely not that slush ball, as profitable as it is for us," Tully echoed.

"And probably not Minist," Darrin said.

"Agreed, Captain. Too much tidal action, due to its proximity to Pyre," Tully added.

"Which leaves Triton," Jessie said.

"I wouldn't phrase it that way, Captain," Darrin said. "Triton is an excellent build site. Based on the survey work we've conducted, this is a solid aggregate world. It's dense and stable."

"Okay, that answers why here for their underground power installation. Let's go see if we can discover any more pieces of our puzzle," Jessie replied. "Move out."

The team exited the rover and trudged up the cut. They stood in the same footprints, as when the group first saw the site.

"Listen carefully, everyone," Jessie said, drawing his team's attention. "I know we're anxious to check out something that's caught our eye. Feel free to examine whatever catches your attention. Record it visually. But do not touch anything. Do I make myself clear?"

The acknowledgments were audibly clear.

"Have at it, team. Be careful," Jessie said.

The crew walked down to the outer ring. The two engineers and tech stepped over it and made straight for the instrument package, the long console, while Hamoi was interested in the platform.

Jessie stood outside the ring. It was his first time at the site, and he was interested in taking in the entire structure, trying to grasp the big picture, asking himself: Why did they build it here? What did they do with it? Why was it open to vacuum?

Of all the possible things to examine, Belinda walked toward one of the small rocky outcrops. They were the oddities that Jessie had asked Yohlin about. Jessie noted with satisfaction that Aurelia followed at Belinda's shoulder.

"We could use something to fan the dust off this panel, Captain, if you'll allow it," Darrin called over the suit comm.

"Not now," Jessie replied. "We don't disturb anything."

"I think it's going to disturb us, Captain," Belinda said, her voice shaky. She was on her hands and knees at the far side of the nearest, small outcropping, her helmet close to the structure. "You need to come here, Captain."

There was urgency in Belinda's voice that galvanized everyone to move quickly to her location. Jessie picked up Aurelia's wide-eyed stare through her faceplate, as he came close. Belinda's side of the small pile of rocks was in shadow, and Jessie ordered his suit lights on, as he knelt.

What Jessie saw was the last thing he expected to find. A small figure in a vac suit was tightly curled and covered in a thick layer of dust. The team could make out a head and portions of an arm and hand. It appeared as if the figure was trying to emerge from the ground.

"Well, this moon finally makes sense," Darrin said. "Not necessarily finding that," he added, pointing at the figure. "It's that big crater that's been bothering me ever since we first investigated it. I told Captain Erring it was strange. Then we find this place. On top of that, we find a body. You might ask how come the aliens didn't recover their comrade."

"Okay, I'm asking," Jessie said.

"This moon was the site of some sort of conflict," Darrin replied.

"The crater's edges," Hamoi remarked. "They were cut, jagged, torn from the inside."

"Exactly," Darrin said. "That crater was exploded outward. Either it was drilled and the charge planted or something extremely powerful was down there, and it detonated."

"Why does that explain this?" Jessie asked, swinging an arm across the width of the site.

"There's too much soft dust over this moon," Darrin replied. "The aggregate is compact ... the stuff that formed this satellite. The core samples have this odd layer of top dust and then heavy rock. The lines are pretty distinct, and it's been consistent across this moon."

Jessie's forehead furrowed in a frown. "Let me get this straight. Your theory is that during this supposed conflict, a huge crater was blown and, over time, most of the debris was pulled down by Triton's gravity to cover the surface in a heavy layer of dust and rubble."

"That makes sense," Hamoi added, while Tully was nodding his head in agreement.

"That leaves the nasty question of who was this guy fighting with ... his own people?"

"Don't think so, Captain," Aurelia replied. She was kneeling in front of another shallow outcropping.

The team hurried to her side, and Aurelia made room for Jessie. The faceplate of a suited figure was broken and the helmet was partially filled with dust, but Jessie could make out the faint outline of formidable teeth. He stood and stepped back, so others could get a look. The first thing that Jessie noted was the second figure was considerably longer and heavier than the first one.

"Okay, we have two alien types," Belinda said, "but does that mean they were fighting? Couldn't it have been an accident? Maybe, it was a sort of power unit that blew, taking out that crater?"

"I've been thinking about what Darrin proposed," Hamoi said. "Our samples from the crater face were thorough. There was nothing from the assay tests or the mass spectrometer readings, which returned a report of an unknown substance like this ring tested out, and nothing came back as unexpected. I don't think a structure blew up from the bottom of that crater, and I don't think it was drilled to plant a weapon deep belowground."

"Which leaves what?" Jessie asked.

"Well, we're obviously looking at aliens, who could build this odd thing out here on a moon and put a power plant in the ground that hums invitingly when close," Hamoi replied, nodding toward Aurelia. "I think that we have to stop thinking about this place from the normal human frame of mind."

Hamoi found himself the center of everyone's quizzical expressions, the lights in their helmets highlighting their quirked eyebrows and odd twists of lips. "I'm just saying that these aliens can do stuff we can't," Hamoi persisted. "Who says that during this skirmish, someone couldn't have fired a weapon from a ship that blew out the crater, a weapon based on a laser or a beam of some type?"

"Point taken, Hamoi," Jessie acknowledged. "Before this gets any weirder, I want a body count. Everyone spread out from this one. It's number one of the large version."

"What if we find a third or fourth type, Captain?" Aurelia asked.

"Record what you see, and we'll change the count, as we go," Jessie replied.

The team fanned out and bent down to study every small rocky ledge. Each was the body of an alien. After some puzzling and a little consultation among team members, it was determined that there were only two types of aliens. The count was six small bodies and thirteen large bodies.

"Now what, Captain?" Darrin asked.

"Back to the rover and the shelter," Jessie replied. "The tanks are approaching the safety limits, and it's been a long day. Plus, I need time to think."

The team climbed up through the cut to the rover parked beyond. Not a word was exchanged. The desiccated remains of the aliens were foremost in everyone's minds. The thought that there had been a fight between species was even more unnerving, considering that these were technologically advanced creatures, which begged the question as to how humans could compete with them.

The silence continued through the trip to the shelter. The *Annie*'s crew was excited to see the rover return and was anxious for news. But, as they regarded the faces of the search team, once helmets were removed, they kept their questions to themselves and hurried to help the team strip out of their vac suits.

"Hamoi, collect the images and upload them to the *Annie* and the *Spryte*. Mark them private for Captain Erring and Ituau."

"Aye, aye, Captain," Hamoi replied. He grabbed his comm unit, which he plugged into the suits to offload their stored images.

"The ships are on second watch, Captain," Darrin said, indicating that Captain Erring and Ituau would be in bed.

"Those two are probably wondering why in the name of Pyre I haven't called and updated them. Watch," Jessie replied.

"Captain Cinders calling the *Annie* for Captain Erring," Jessie said into his comm unit. He left it on speaker. There wasn't much to keep secret from the downside crew.

"Captain Erring here," replied Yohlin, and Darrin received a quirk of Jessie's lips.

"Please link this call with Ituau, Captain," Jessie requested. A moment later, Ituau's voice acknowledged that she was on the call.

"The two of you are on speaker with the entire downside team," Jessie said. When Hamoi signaled the images had been uploaded, Jessie added, "You're receiving imagery marked for your attention. Please start reviewing them."

After a few minutes, Ituau asked. "Captain, are we looking at bodies?"

"Two types of bodies," Yohlin quickly added.

"That's what we've found," Jessie replied. "Now, here's the good part. It's the engineering team's consideration that the crater was formed by some type of weapon or device that exploded and left no residual matter behind. It threw a huge amount of dust and debris into the space around Triton, which eventually was pulled down to the surface and covered these bodies, after some sort of fight that destroyed the site we're investigating."

Jessie looked at the faces of the two shelter techs, who had been examining the photos on Hamoi's comm unit. They were staring at him in astonishment with slack mouths.

"Did you touch or move the bodies, Captain?" Yohlin asked.

"Negative," Jessie replied. "But I don't think it matters."

"I don't follow," Yohlin replied.

"We've been quarantined for six months, Captain. What's going to happen, if and when I report we've found alien bodies?"

"The powers-that-be will probably make our quarantine permanent," replied Ituau, the disgust evident in her voice.

"I'm not sure that wouldn't be a wise decision on their part," Yohlin said.

"Unfortunately, I can't disagree with you, Captain," Jessie replied. "This has gotten way too complicated for a bunch of miners. But, I know one thing, if I know anything, and that's this bunch of miners is not going to end up like those aliens because some people are afraid of contamination."

"Even if the threat is real?" Yohlin asked.

"I didn't say we'd risk transferring our exposure to the population, Captain," Jessie replied, an edge in his voice. "One way or the other, I'm going to get us help, while we wait out our quarantine time."

"What's next, Captain?" Ituau asked.

"Food and sleep," Jessie replied.

"And tomorrow?" Yohlin asked.

"Don't know about tomorrow yet, Captain. I need to think on it. Cinders out," Jessie said, thumbing off his comm unit. He stretched out on his cot, and the two shelter techs hurried to make hot meals for the search team, delivering juice containers and meal packets to each of them. One of the techs caught Darrin's eye and nodded at Jessie, who rested with a forearm over his eyes, and Darrin shook his head.

"So, who was here and who came here?" Jessie said quietly, without uncovering his face.

"You're supposing one of these species was resident on Pyre," Belinda replied. "Could they have lived on a planet that was more volcanically active than it is now? It's taken almost three hundred years for the air quality to improve by forty percent. What would it have been like before that time, when they would have been downside?"

"Think about it, Belinda," said Darrin. "We have an incredible alien site with a power system still active, a crater that appears to have been exploded by an unknown weapon type, and a planet in a state of eruption that's slowly subsidizing."

"A fight," Jessie said.

"More important, Captain, a massive fight with weapons the like of which we can't imagine," Hamoi added.

"Sirs, you're implying weapons disrupted the planet," Jessie replied, sitting up, and a tech hurried to heat some food for him.

"That's my guess," Darrin replied, and both Tully and Darrin nodded enthusiastically.

"Darrin, you couldn't have found us a nice deposit of high-grade metal?" Jessie asked.

"But, I did, Captain," Darrin replied with a smile. "It's already refined. Of course, I've no idea of its properties. And, better news, the deposit came with its own power supply."

Jessie swung his head toward Aurelia. She was sitting cross-legged on her cot, her empty meal packets beside her. Ever since they had reached the shelter, he was aware of a constant intrusion into his mind. At first, he thought to object, but his mind was troubled by what they had found and its implications. So, he ignored it, or he thought he had. While he lay on the cot, he relaxed into its soothing presence. As it eased his mind, it allowed him to think clearer. Staring now at Aurelia, who had her eyes closed, the value of her presence aboard the *Annie*, with Belinda, and with the downside team, struck him. He understood Yohlin's message on how her crew would react to anyone offering an affront to their empath, much less attempting to arrest her.

27: Challenge

"Dingles, I need the spacers in a meeting, now," Harbour ordered, while she was en route to the *Belle*. "I'll be aboard in about fifteen minutes."

"Aye, ma'am. We'll be ready," Dingles replied. He saw his comm link icon blink off before he'd finished his reply. *Trouble at the JOS. Imagine that,* he thought with a quirk of his lips.

Harbour marched to the usual meeting room for the spacers. She could sense the tension in the room and chose to do nothing about it.

"Captain Cinders and his people are in trouble," Harbour announced, without fanfare. That brought the emotional level of the room to a peak, and she let it simmer. "Of course, that's not to say that the captain's people might have something to do with the commotion," Harbour continued, adding a bit of humor to her delivery. "It started when the *Annie*'s crew discovered an alien site on Triton."

It was one of those rare times for an empath when she could stand in a group of strong-willed people, who were broadcasting little to no emotion. The only time an empath might find the same condition was if the people were fast asleep. These spacers were wide awake, but blinking eyes and open mouths indicated that their brains were working to catch up with Harbour's words.

Harbour laid out the discovery of the site, summarized the conversation with Pyre's leaders, and ended with the decision of the three key individuals that a quarantine of six months must be imposed. The spacers were on their feet, angry and yelling, and Harbour let their heated reactions sweep through her. She wanted it, needed it, to bolster her decision, which she'd yet to share with anyone.

Dingles restored order, after the spacers had an opportunity to vent, and signaled Harbour to continue.

"I need a report of the *Belle*'s worthiness to move," Harbour said.

Each team leader updated Harbour on everything from comm systems to engines and environmental systems to hydroponics.

"If I understand you right," Harbour said, when the reports were completed, "the *Belle* is ready to move, but you're not confident that we can push the engines past about fifty percent and several systems aren't ready to go for the year that I requested without additional parts, which haven't been purchased."

"Aye, ma'am, that's correct," Dingles replied.

"Do we have the necessary crew number to make the upgrades and maintain the systems if we don't have access to the JOS soon?" Harbour asked.

"No, ma'am," Dingles replied. "We're short about eighteen crew members, at a minimum, to accelerate the readiness process and make the repairs. Can we afford to hire? If so, there are retirees, who might wish to help us sail this old lady.

"Give me a list, Dingles, with the coin it would take to hire the personnel for a year," Harbour replied. "Add to your list any supplies that are necessities. I need everything sourced now ... the crew aboard and the goods onboard, as soon as possible."

"We going somewhere, Captain?" Dingles asked.

"I thought that was obvious, First Mate Mitch Bassiter. We're going to Triton," Harbour replied, grinning.

There was a stunned moment before the spacers erupted in cheers. The nearest spacers to Dingles pounded him on the back, and the others chanted "captain," over and over, to Harbour.

Harbour raised a hand, and the spacers quieted immediately. It occurred to her that the title of captain had been fully awarded her by men and women who'd served under those individuals. "We've work to do," Harbour said quietly. "Keep this announcement to yourself. We don't want anyone interfering with our plans, and you know who I mean."

"Aye, aye, Captain," Dingles replied, touching two fingers to the brim of his cap.

"Finish up here. There'll be a general meeting soon, which you'll need to join," Harbour said. As she turned to leave, the spacers jumped to their feet.

I guess if I'm the captain, then they must be my crew, Harbour thought, and she experienced a moment of trepidation at the extent of her inexperience to successfully manage the job.

* * * *

Harbour called a general meeting of the *Belle's* residents. The only place that could hold the nearly 3,000 individuals was a central staging hold for freight. Gravity was light in the massive area, and, while there was air, it was far from warm. People showed up swathed in combinations of skins, leggings, trousers, heavy work boots, and coats. Many had taken to wrapping their heads in scarves or shirts.

"I'll make this short," Harbour said, opening the meeting, while stragglers were still arriving. "Earlier, I let it be known that this ship might be moved for a period of time, and some of you told me you would need to relocate to the station to accommodate your patrons. It looks like everyone has to rethink that announcement."

Harbour shared with the contingent the same story she related to the spacers. When she was finished, the empaths felt a mix of emotions — concern, fear, anger, and excitement.

"Why you?" Arlene asked. She was one of the more outspoken artisans, always requesting better accommodations, more heat in her cabin, and access to more coin from the general fund.

"Why me what, Arlene?" Harbour asked. She could sense the animosity from Arlene, who sat near her.

"Why are you able to dictate where we go? There are three thousand of us. Who said you should be in charge?" Arlene jumped off her crate and walked to the middle of the assembled residents. "I say that we of the *Belle* have a right to elect our leader. Harbour protects the empaths, but she shouldn't speak for all of us, especially when she intends to put us at risk for maybe thirty spacers." Arlene rounded to face Harbour and stared defiantly at her.

Dingles stepped into the center and eyed Arlene, who gave way so that he could have the deck. "I'm new here. So, maybe I don't understand everything that's going on aboard the *Belle*. Then again, maybe I understand a great deal more that's going on out there in the JOS and downside. If you think the governor and commandant's quarantine makes sense, think again. They're targeting one of the most successful captains of the spacers, and if he and his people are left out there to die, they'll use the event as an excuse to tighten the controls on all spacers. After that, who do you think will be next?"

"Is Dingles right, Harbour?" asked Makana, the artisan who decorated Harbour's skins.

"I can tell you two things, Makana," Harbour replied. "The first ship on Triton was the *Annie*. She's been there for weeks. According to Captain Cinders, the crew isn't suffering any maladies or showing any odd symptoms. And, second, I have heard proof that Commander Strattleford is colluding with Governor Panoy and was doing so before the arrest of Markos Andropov."

Arlene strode to the center again. "How do we know Captain Cinders is telling the truth? He would say anything to have the quarantine dropped or to be delivered supplies."

That comment caused such an uproar from the spacers that Arlene backed away. The crew was irate at her impugning Captain Cinder's honor. Dingles' whistle cut through the chilled air, and the spacers quieted.

"Arlene, you don't know how far you are from the truth," Harbour replied, laughing at the thought that Jessie could be characterized as a liar. "I can say that I know Captain Cinders well enough to tell you that he's blunt, hardheaded, and utterly faithful to his people, but he's not dishonest. In fact, I would say that if I were to call him and offer assistance that he would refuse it."

"Well, Harbour, what about the general fund?" Arlene shot back. "Your empaths generate the majority of monthly coin. How are you going to get clients if we move this ship to Triton? For that matter, how are the artisans supposed to get supplies to deliver on our consignments?"

"Our income," Harbour replied, indicating the empaths, who surrounded her, "will probably be curtailed, in the near future, especially after I threatened Lise Panoy."

Heads whipped toward Harbour. She was known as a level-headed and even-tempered woman. As one of the strongest empaths, it was a prerequisite for leading the empaths. Hearing that she threatened the governor shocked some, but brought chuckles from others, who felt no love for the downsiders.

"It's already begun to happen," Yasmin announced. "Downsiders have been canceling for the past few hours."

"Residents of the *Belle*," Harbour said, raising her voice, "I've not taken this decision lightly. With the help of our spacers and tech teams, we've worked to ready the ship. We've made upgrades to many of the systems, stocked up on equipment and parts, and we'll be hiring additional spacers to maintain the ship. As for the general fund, the empaths and I have been working diligently to build it up. And, not to put too fine a point on it, I don't think Captain Cinders will appreciate being in our debt for his rescue."

"Got that in one, ma'am," Dingles said loudly, and the spacers heartily agreed.

"I imagine Captain Cinders will do whatever it takes to reimburse us for our investment," Harbour finished. "What you need to know is that this ship is ready to move. I believe it's critical we save the spacers at Triton. We can't let them be sacrificed to the governor's power play."

"I say it's too risky, Harbour," Arlene yelled. "We have a right to elect a leader who has the general population's interest at heart."

The assembled were too great and diverse to allow Harbour to sense the mood of the crowd. For the moment, she was taken aback. It hadn't occurred to her that she might face a general uprising from the residents.

Yasmin had worked her way over to a crate at the far left of the assembly, while Arlene spoke, and a young tech was happy to boost her on top of it when she pointed. "I agree with Arlene," Yasmin called out from her perch. "An election is fair, and I propose we decide the question now. Those who wish to elect Harbour as the *Belle*'s captain come to this side. Those who wish to hold a general election walk to the other side."

Yasmin's proposal froze the residents. This was happening too fast for them to process. Nadine ended the standstill when she announced clearly, "I stand with Harbour," and the residents watched the empaths follow her, as Nadine made her way through the residents to stand beneath Yasmin's crate.

"The spacers stand with Harbour," Dingles announced, and he and the crew took up places next to the empaths.

When Bryan Forshaw, the propulsion engineer, made his vote known, the engineers and techs followed in his wake to side with Harbour.

The empaths, spacers, and technical people were a small minority of the residents, but they were critical to the *Belle*'s operations.

"Time to decide," Yasmin announced.

"Okay, let's vote," Arlene called out, galvanizing others. She walked to the right side and crossed her arms in defiance. Some residents, mostly artisans, came to her side. Their number equaled those opposing them.

Harbour wanted to plead her case, but something made her stay quiet. Conversations were taking place in small groups. People kept mixing and reforming, sharing their opinions. The first residents to move made for Arlene's side, and Arlene smiled in victory at Harbour. The number of dissenters slowly increased to nearly twice those who faced them across the deck.

After the initial mixing of the residents, they formed larger and larger groups. People could be heard arguing their cases, but the number of voices didn't allow the words to be understood by Harbour.

A group of more than two hundred residents, who were close to Harbour, stopped talking and turned to regard her. Harbour kept her face neutral and said clearly to them, "Vote your conscience." The residents turned and worked their way over to join those supporting her.

One by one, the larger groups made up their minds. A few individuals left to side with Arlene, but most took up a place with Yasmin. The center of the deck was cleared, except for a blind artisan, Yardley, who worked in metalcraft. He was quite renowned for his work.

"Yardley, you have to make a choice," an artisan, standing next to Arlene, yelled out.

"I believe I'm making my choice known by standing here," Yardley replied.

"Let it be known that Yardley abstains," Yasmin called out, which drew laughter from most of the residents.

When Yardley came to the *Belle*, he was a shell of a man, who bitterly resented the infirmity that had been inflicted on him in an accident. It became Yasmin's choice to focus on helping him, and it was her idea that Yardley pick up with what he knew best, metalworking. Instead of thinking of it as building material, Yasmin convinced Yardley to consider metal from a creative aspect.

Yardley's initial works were crude, but interesting. Throughout the years, his work refined and Harbour gained space in a gallery for a few pieces. Those creations sold quickly and demand soared for his often-whimsical designs.

"It's been decided by a clear majority of our residents," Yasmin called out. "We've elected Harbour as the *Belle*'s captain to command this ship." She emphasized the term command for Arlene and her compatriots' benefit.

"Those of you who chose to hold an election have had an opportunity to voice your opinions. You might not be happy with the outcome, but I want you to know that I hold no ill will toward you," Harbour said. "You have a choice to make ... stay aboard the *Belle* or leave. I regret that if you choose to leave, you'll have to wait until the day of our departure. Those who wish to depart, please submit your name and baggage loads to my first mate, Dingles. He'll work out a schedule of transfers with Danny."

In the silence that followed Harbour's announcement, Dingles, who thought it best to end the meeting on that note, called out, "Captain, is there any other business to transact?"

"No, Dingles," Harbour replied, and Dingles said loudly, "The residents are dismissed." It was a reminder from a spacer of the change the ship's status had undergone in the last several minutes. Stunned, many stayed in place, but the empaths, spacers, and technical people promptly cleared out.

* * * *

"How did I not see that coming?" Harbour said to Dingles, when she closed her cabin door for a private conversation with her first mate.

"Command is not an easy thing, Captain," Dingles replied.

"Maybe I'm not the right person for the job," Harbour replied quietly, leaning against her food prep surface.

"I've seen all types make captain ... engineers, rock prospectors, and regular spacers. The individuals who were successful shared common traits. They cared deeply for the safety of the crew and the ship, treated their people fairly, and led, despite the problems thrown at them. You have all those traits, Captain."

"I don't feel like a captain, Dingles. I feel overwhelmed."

"Yet, the majority of the residents voted you as their leader, as the *Belle's* captain. One of the things you have to grasp, Captain, is that you have crew to count on. They'll have your back if you have theirs. Lip service doesn't count."

"Okay, Dingles, enough of my wallowing in self-pity. You wanted to talk to me too."

"This doesn't seem like the time to mention it, Captain."

"Out with it, Dingles. I laid myself bare to you."

"Well, Captain, I'm grateful for my position, but I wouldn't take it poorly if you replaced me as first mate. There are two engineers who are better qualified than me."

Harbour broke into laughter. "Aren't we a pair?" she managed to choke out. She adopted a serious expression and asked, "Are those engineers from Captain Cinders' ships?"

"No, ma'am."

"Then I want you aboard."

"Aye, Captain, latched on," Dingles replied, touching two fingers to his cap.

"Okay, Dingles, first thing, I need help. Somewhere in this ship's extensive library has to be the rules and regs for the captain of a colony ship. Where would I find them?"

"We call them the Articles, Captain. May I?" Dingles asked, gesturing toward her desk. "I'll need your comm unit, ma'am. You have the required access level."

Harbour unlocked her comm unit, plugged it in to the monitor, and proceeded to make them hot drinks. She set Dingles' drink next to him and curled up in her reading chair to enjoy hers. She nodded off, while Dingles worked, but woke to his vehemence, which shot through her.

"Sorry, Captain," Dingles said, when he realized the mistake he'd made. *Behave yourself, old man, in her presence,* he thought, recrimination rushing through him.

"Easy, Dingles," cautioned Harbour, sensing the man's emotional swings. "We're new to each other, but we'll learn. What did you find?"

"It's what I didn't find, ma'am. I couldn't find the Articles, but I found a log laying out the database organization and the files contained in the various directories within the library. There are a good number of files missing."

"The Andropov family," Harbour said, with disgust.

"Aye, ma'am, and now that piece of female effluent has them," Dingles replied.

"Dingles, you old rascal, were you listening to the conference call?"

"For most of it, Captain, until I was disconnected soon after you cut your connection. I thought it was important to maintain the comm connections," Dingles said. His expression was as neutral as he could make it.

"Nice try, Dingles. I like the sincere face, but you forgot to control your spike of nervousness at being uncovered."

"That's not fair, Captain. How am I supposed to play my role as first mate?"

"You'll have to become more inventive, Dingles. Doesn't age bestow wisdom?"

"Supposedly, ma'am. I'll have to go looking for some. Maybe Nadine can give me some pointers," Dingles replied with a grin.

"You be careful there, Dingles. That might be more woman than you can handle."

"Understood, ma'am, but spacers like challenges."

"Enough banter, Dingles. I need those files. Any chance that there are copies somewhere on this ship?"

"As I heard the story, ma'am, the last captain didn't make Pyre's orbit. It was the first mate who brought the *Belle* into this system. Why they didn't wake an alternate captain, I don't know. I can check the captain's cabin for a secondary file storage system, and there's a slim chance that the first mate pulled the Articles to study up on them. I doubt either of the two men will have the full number of files missing from the library, but they might have the Articles."

"Find those Articles for me, Dingles, if you can. I think they're going to prove very informative, if the Andropov family removed them."

"Aye, aye, Captain. Will there be anything else?"

"Two things, Dingles. Who runs the Miners' Pit, specifically, who is responsible for its management?"

"Why that's Maggie, Captain."

"Set me up a meeting, Dingles. Something in the early morning before she opens. I need a private conversation, and you're attending."

"Understood, Captain, and the second thing?"

"Can we call the *Spryte* from my cabin?"

"Aye, Captain. When do you want to do that?"

"Now, Dingles."

"Aye, aye, Captain." Dingles disconnected Harbour's comm unit and plugged his into the monitor. It carried a set of apps that could control the *Belle*'s comm system remotely. "This is the *Belle* calling the *Spryte*," Dingles announced over his comm unit when he was ready.

"Ituau of the *Spryte* here. Is that you, Dingles?"

"One and the same. Been resurrected from the refuse pile."

"What are you doing now, you old space dog?"

"That's First Mate Space Dog to you, you undersized excuse for an officer."

Ituau's deep belly laughter echoed over the comm. Harbour, who stood beside Dingles, smiled at the affectionate conversation.

"Wait, Dingles. If you're first mate, are you saying the *Belle* has been reorganized?"

"Yep. I'm calling you to connect our duly elected Captain Harbour with Captain Cinders."

"Congratulations, Captain," Ituau replied, straightening up from a slouch in the bridge's command chair.

"Thank you, Ituau," Harbour said. "Is your captain still awake?"

"He's not aboard, Captain."

"I would hope he's aboard the *Annie*, but I've this unsettling feeling that you're going to tell me he's downside."

"You guessed it, ma'am. He's been investigating the alien site. Right about now, the team is tucked into their cots for the night. We'll be speaking with them before they return to site." Ituau itched to tell Harbour about the alien bodies, but that would be Jessie's decision, not hers.

Harbour swore under her breath, and Dingles hid his grin.

"Can't disagree with you, ma'am," Ituau added, whose keen ears had picked up Harbour's expletives.

"Maybe it's just as well that I give you my message to relay to him, Ituau," Harbour said.

"I can connect you to Captain Erring, if you prefer," Ituau replied.

"No, Ituau, come to think of it, you're the perfect messenger."

"Why do I think I'm about to be hit by a shock stick?" Ituau grumbled.

"We have a few weeks of preparation, and, after that, we'll be moving the *Belle*."

"Where to, Captain?" Ituau asked.

"See, Captain," Dingles commented. "I told you we needed to speak to someone who doesn't have vacuum between her ears. Where do you think, you excuse for a first mate?"

"You're moving the *Belle* here?" Ituau asked, with incredulity.

"You got something against being rescued?" Dingles growled.

Harbour thought to tone down Dingles' side of the conversation, but she could sense the warm pride in his emotions. He was a spacer, who was of critical use, once again.

"No, no ... I love the thought that I won't become a piece of space trash orbiting Triton. But, I don't think Captain Cinders is going to like this."

"Which is why I'm not asking his permission," Harbour said tartly.

"Oh, I get it. Instead of you talking to him, I get to deliver the message. Let me, at least, get some details, Captain. When do you expect to arrive?"

"Dingles?" Harbour asked.

"Three weeks of prep and then four weeks to reach Triton," Dingles replied.

"Four weeks?" Harbour asked in surprise.

"You have a huge ship there, Captain," Ituau said. "It takes time to get her moving, and then you'll begin deceleration at the halfway point, unless you plan to orbit Triton."

"Negative, Ituau," Dingles replied. "The captain wants a stationary position relative to Captain Cinders' ships."

"Understood. What about food and supplies for your people and ours?" Ituau asked.

"We'll be provisioned for a year to cover us all," Harbour replied.

There was a moment of comm silence. When Ituau resumed, her voice was husky with emotion. "Hopefully, you won't mind, Captain, if I forget decorum when you arrive and give you a big hug."

Harbour laughed, wishing she could send some comfort Ituau's way, but then it occurred to her that she already had done that exact thing. "You'll remember that I've met you, Ituau. As long as you don't break anything vital, your hug will be welcome."

"You sure about this, Captain? I mean what with all the talk about alien contamination."

"You heard of any issues, Ituau?" Harbour asked.

"No, ma'am, everything is boringly quiet, except for worrying about the downside crew."

"Understood, Ituau. We're coming. You tell that to your hardheaded boss."

"Will do, Captain. I can't say how Captain Cinders will take this message, but I know another captain and two crews, who will remember you fondly forever, Captain Harbour."

Dingles glanced at Harbour, and she signaled to end the call. "*Belle* out," Dingles said. He disconnected his comm unit from the monitor and sat staring at the device in his hands.

Harbour could feel wave after wave of poignant pleasure from the old spacer and, oddly, some deep frustration.

When Dingles looked at Harbour, tears glistened in his eyes. "Best call I ever made, Captain," he said, touching his cap, and he left the cabin.

"Me too," Harbour whispered, after the door closed.

28: Oops

Jessie woke in the morning with a stiff back and a crick in his neck, which he worked on releasing.

"Long time since you worked a full day in a vac suit, Captain?" Belinda asked.

Jessie looked around and discovered everyone was either eating or finishing a morning meal, and he'd slept through the noise. He glanced at Aurelia, who wore a pained expression. "Problem, spacer?" Jessie asked. It came out much harder than he intended.

"What is it you find objectionable, Captain?" Aurelia asked bluntly. "Me, my powers, or both?"

"Neither, Rules," Jessie replied. He stood and popped his neck. The crack of the vertebrae was audible in the confined space. "I prefer to make my own way under my own power."

"You're saying you can help others, but others can't help you?"

In various ways, the team members tried to catch Aurelia's attention and wave her off. She was treading on dangerous ground with the captain.

Jessie stopped stretching and eyed Aurelia. If he thought his stern expression would intimidate her, he was wrong. *Guess sixteen years in confinement, ending in molestation and a death hardens a teenager,* he thought, which eased his growing anger. He glanced at the faces of his team. Eyes were downcast; mouths twisted in displeasure. Yohlin's words came back to Jessie. The *Annie*'s crew had adopted Rules. She was more than a crew member to them, and he'd roughly rebuffed her help. It was rare to feel like an outsider in the company of his own people, but Jessie had to admit that's right where he stood.

"Okay, Rules, but let's not make a habit of this," Jessie said.

"Yes, Captain," Aurelia replied. She meant it to sound mature, but her excitement was evident. She hurried to Jessie's cot, sat down, and patted the space next to her.

Jessie reluctantly sat down and placed his hand in the one Aurelia offered him.

"Close your eyes, Captain," Aurelia requested. It wasn't necessary, but Aurelia had picked up on the emotional swing of the team when Jessie grew angry at her. She needed him to isolate himself from them. It was something she requested Sasha do so that she wouldn't stare at the walls, which would feed her resentment.

Aurelia started slowly. She could sense Jessie's discomfort caused by the aches and pain. He was a proud man, but the years in space had taken their toll on his body. She soothed his mind. The body's troubles would still be there, but he would be less aware of them, for now. When she felt his mind quiet, she projected a sense of excitement, imagining her own hopes for the day's adventure.

Jessie felt when Aurelia withdrew her hand from his. For a brief second, he regretted it, but it was immediately overtaken by the demands of command.

"Some food, Captain?" one of the shelter techs called out.

"Actually, yes, I'm starved," Jessie replied. He admitted to himself that Aurelia's ministrations had brought him a marvelous sense of peace, which she turned into expectation for the day's outing to the site. Against his better judgment, he leaned over and kissed the top of Aurelia's head. It was the only apology she would get.

"I never got kissed, Captain, even when I discovered that huge layer of slush on Emperion," Darrin objected.

"Would you like yours now, spacer?" Jessie challenged.

Darrin's tease had been turned back on him, and he sat frozen on his cot, unsure how to reply to Jessie, which broke the team into laughter.

Jessie grinned and walked over to the food prep area. He was starved and grabbed a couple of extra food packets. In no time at all, he polished off his breakfast and picked up his comm unit to update Nate, since Yohlin and Ituau would be in their bunks, catching up on some much-needed sleep.

"Morning, Captain," Nate said. "Ituau said to wake her when you called. She has an important message for you."

"Probably best to let her sleep, Nate," Jessie replied.

"Captain, Ituau told me if you said that and I listened to you, she would beat me black and blue, and we both know she can do it."

Jessie chuckled. "Okay, Nate, wake her up."

A couple of minutes later, a sleepy Ituau picked up her comm unit. "Morning, Captain," she said.

"Morning, Ituau. What's so important it can't wait until you're on duty?"

"I was wondering, Captain, if you'd like to be rescued?"

Jessie looked around the shelter. He thought that perhaps either Ituau or he was sleep deprived and failing to communicate. The shelter team wore astonished expressions.

"I'm certainly not opposed to being rescued, Ituau. Did Pyre's leaders come to their senses and shorten the quarantine, or is someone foolish enough to make a supply run?"

"That would be the latter, Captain."

"Okay, Ituau, it's a little too early in the morning to be playing games with people's heads. You and I both know that no captain is crazy enough to risk ship and crew to make the passage out to Triton to save a bunch of competitors."

Jessie regretted starting the call on speaker, and he was writing Ituau's disciplinary report in his head, while he waited for her reply.

"I don't think you could consider Captain Harbour and her ship as a competitor, Captain, but maybe you can ask her about that when she gets here, in about seven weeks."

The shelter's crew members were reaching hands out to one another in excitement and hanging on every word of the conversation.

When Ituau heard nothing from Jessie, she couldn't resist a final word. "Did you have a message for Captain Harbour, sir? Something that you'd like me to relate to her?"

"Ituau, if you're —"

Ituau jumped in to cut Jessie off. It occurred to her that she might have gone too far. "Seriously, Captain, it was Dingles who made the call. That old space dog was deadly serious about coming out here. Harbour was elected to the captaincy by the ship's residents, and she's determined to move the *Belle* to Triton ... says she has the equipment, spacers, and supplies to hold out for a year."

"Ituau, relay that message to Captain Erring when she wakes. She can announce it to the crews of both ships. We'll be leaving the shelter within a half hour. Downside out."

"Let's get moving, team," Jessie ordered. He donned his vac suit quickly and cycled out of the shelter before anyone else was ready.

"What just happened?" Darrin asked. "I was ready to celebrate."

A sign of the times was that the team looked to Aurelia, who replied, "The captain is uneasy, anxiety bordering on trepidation."

"Don't forget there are nearly three thousand people on the *Belle*," Belinda added. "That's a lot of residents to put at risk. We don't know for certain that there's no risk of some sort of alien contamination."

"And Harbour's there," Aurelia added, which garnered her quizzical expressions. "The captain's distress spiked when Ituau mentioned her name."

"You're talking about Jessie Cinders, Rules," Darrin objected. "You might have read that one wrong, but enough jabbering. Let's get a move on. The captain's waiting."

The team donned their vac suits in a hurry and made their way out to the rover. Seat backs were reset to accommodate the vac suits, which were left on. The ride would be a short one.

Tully drove, as usual, and Jessie sat beside him. Occasionally, a crew member would glance at Aurelia, and she would subtly shake her head. Jessie's mood wasn't improving, and his silence confirmed it.

When the rover stopped, Jessie was shaken out of his brooding. He was having trouble compartmentalizing his feelings, which had always enabled him to exercise tight control. Like his crew, he wanted to rejoice at the quick answer to the quarantine's dilemma. He told himself he was worried for the *Belle*'s residents, but it was Harbour's face that he kept seeing.

"Team, don't touch the bodies today," Jessie said. "The discovery of the aliens meant we didn't get to investigate the instrumentation, platform, or ring. We need to come away with something valuable that makes this entire fiasco of a trip to Triton worthwhile. The composition of the alien materials, the type of power generated, its resonance frequency, and anything like that would be extremely useful."

Helmets were locked, systems checked, and portable equipment grabbed before the crew exited the rover. Rather than lead the team to the site, Jessie followed at their rear. When the site was reached, everyone fanned out to explore it. The technical team concentrated on the console and platform, and Belinda worked to identify the parameters of the signal that Aurelia was receiving.

Jessie stood on the cut, but his mind wandered time and again to Ituau's message. Finally, to break his reverie, Jessie walked down to the ring where Hamoi had first brushed off the layer of dust. Jessie scrubbed a hand over the metal, revealing the carvings in the ring. He removed a meter of fine debris and discovered the entire surface was decorated in the elaborate symbols.

Fascinated by the alien markings, Jessie climbed back to the lookout position and picked up some instruments and tools the team had deposited. When he returned to the ring, he hopped over it to examine the inner portion. He scrubbed away another section. The writing was on both sides of the ring, and Jessie collected recordings of the markings.

Leaning over the ring, Jessie examined the slot that ran along the top of the ring. Above all things, this mystified him. If they had found debris in and out of the ring that signified a dome, he could have imagined that the slot was where the panels fitted, although it was extremely narrow. He sat his mass spectrometer on top of the ring and sorted through a tool bag. He was intent on removing some of the dust and discovering how deep the slot ran.

While Tully inspected the console, brushing away the dust and collecting imagery of the controls and markings, Hamoi was intrigued by the possibility of learning how the instruments received power. Examining the console's rear panel, the tech noticed a 6-centimeter, circular fitting that projected low from the console's rear panel. He got down on his knees to study it and was disappointed to find it was empty.

It was Hamoi's habit to scratch the back of his head when he was mystified, and his hand automatically went there only to be reminded for the hundredth time, as he touched his helmet, that he was wearing a vac suit. He reached down to push himself erect, and his left hand hit something buried in the dust. He brushed away a length of it. To his amazement, it was a length of tubing of the same material that projected from the console's back.

Hamoi examined the end of the hose he pulled from the dust and compared it the stubbing of the console's tube. It appeared to be similar. He freed a length of the tubing from Triton's surface. It ended at a small section of polished metal set into the surface. Hamoi sought to pull at the base, thinking that it had been torn from its fitting, but it was solid. Looking at the hose in his hand, Hamoi brought it close to the console's tube to confirm his thought that the piping might have been cut.

Hamoi's mistake was to touch the two ends of the tubing together and was stunned to watch the cut seal. Suddenly, exclamations and yelps echoed in Hamoi's helmet, and he hurried to the front of the console. The panel's controls were glowing, as was the platform base. Overhead, a shimmering dome of blue light enclosed the site.

"Captain," Aurelia shouted, having detected Jessie's spike of panic.

The team rushed to Jessie's side. He was flat on his back and stretching an arm out to facilitate turning over. Aurelia bent to help Jessie, but Belinda's hand caught her shoulder. The second mate's face, shaking in the negative, was clear through her helmet's faceplate.

"Are you all right, Captain?" asked Darrin, alarmed.

"Fine, fine," Jessie replied. "I was spooked. That's all."

"Oh, for the love of Pyre," Hamoi lamented. "Look at the instrument on the ring base."

The shimmering light that formed the dome was exiting the ring base through the slot. Jessie's spectrometer lay in two pieces, neatly cleaved in half with one part inside the dome and the other outside.

"I was peering into that slot and leaned away to get another tool when that light flashed in front of my eyes," Jessie explained.

"I'm so sorry, Captain, it's my fault," Hamoi blurted out. "The tubing was empty. I had no idea it would self-repair."

"Self-repair?" Tully asked.

"What part of alien-constructed site didn't you understand, spacer?" said Darrin, heat coloring his face. That Hamoi had triggered the activation of the instrumentation was worrying, but that his actions had nearly decapitated Captain Cinders had him quaking in fright.

Jessie regained his feet and was about to address his team, when his eyes went to the platform. One by one, the crew members turned to see what had caught the captain's eye. The dust on the platform was swirling in a small eddy. As the crew watched, it grew larger and larger, engulfing the entire platform and soon the complete site. The team covered their faceplates with their hands to prevent surface scratching, which would obscure their vision.

Tully switched on his helmet's audio pickup and listened to the muffled sound of the dust beating against it. Several minutes later, the sound disappeared, and Tully slowly removed his hands from his faceplate. "It stopped," he sent over the suit comm to his team members.

Jessie and the others stared in awe at the site. Every speck of dust was gone. Where it went, no one knew, having protected their faceplates from the abrasive mineral dust. The site was immaculate. The base was made entirely of gleaming metal and divided into wedges, like a dessert might be cut for serving. The alien symbols covered the entire deck, and the bodies stood out in stark relief.

"Captain, look there, in the alien's hand," said Belinda, pointing to the nearest body of the smaller species.

The body was near the console, and Jessie slowly approached it and knelt. The team craned over his shoulder and around him to see.

"A weapon maybe," Jessie said. "Odd-looking though."

"It's not a weapon, Captain." Hamoi said, and he ignored the glare Darrin sent his way. "It's a cutting tool. I found a hose at the back of the console that looked separated from the rear panel. I meant to compare the two ends. Unfortunately, when I touched them together, they joined. I mean the material sealed itself. That's when the power came on."

"Hamoi, you didn't hook up any cable or wires or something like that?" Tully asked.

"The tubing was empty ... both ends of it. I thought the guts of the tube had been stripped out. Now that I see this alien with the strange tool in his hand, I get it," Hamoi explained.

"You get what?" Darrin demanded.

"Earlier, the captain wondered which bodies represented the interlopers and which bodies were the Pyre-based creatures. Of course, both species could have been fighting on this moon for possession of the system. But, then, you'd have to ask why —"

"Spacer, get to the point about the tool," Darrin requested, interrupting Hamoi's running commentary.

"Sorry, so much is going through my head," Hamoi replied. "That thing the little alien is carrying is some sort of beam-cutting tool."

"Interesting, Hamoi. How did you arrive at that conclusion?" Jessie asked.

"That body is the closest to the back panel," Hamoi replied. "If that tubing is self-sealing, a sawing instrument might not have gotten through the entire diameter before the cut would start sealing behind it. It had to be a beam tool that could slice through it quicker than it could repair itself."

"I have only one problem with that theory, Hamoi," Jessie replied. "You're suggesting immediate separation of the power supply, which, if we interpret what just happened, should have immediately shut down the dome."

"Yikes, explosive decompression," Tully said.

"Which means the bodies would have been blown into space instead of lying around here," Belinda added.

"Captain, come look," Aurelia said. She was crouched on the metal deck, her helmet close to the feet of one of the alien figures.

"Please, nobody touch anything," Jessie called out sternly.

"I'm not," Aurelia objected. "I'm taking a close look at this alien's boots."

When Jessie knelt beside Aurelia, she leaned back. "Look at the soles, Captain."

Jessie felt like he was examining a mirror image of the metal deck that was reflected in the soles of the alien's boots. "It's the same material," he said. "These boots are especially made to adhere to this decking."

"An explosive decompression event, and the aliens stay attached to the deck. I want that," Tully said wistfully.

"Captain, take a look at the front of the body," Belinda said. She moved aside as Jessie crabbed over.

"A burn hole," Jessie remarked, examining the clean hole punched through the center of the alien's chest.

"And look at what it went through, Captain," Belinda added.

"Some sort of control panel, I would bet," Jessie replied.

"The hole comes out the back, Captain," Aurelia said.

Jessie stood and looked at the bodies, the glowing platform, and the dome, organizing his thoughts. "These little guys didn't want these big guys operating this base for some reason, and they came here to destroy it. A fight breaks out, and the little aliens cut the power. The dome disappears. Instant vacuum, but they stay adhered to the deck and continue to fight, employing beam weapons to kill one another. When their suits are damaged, the boots no longer adhere to the deck and they fall over."

"Good summary, Captain," Darrin acknowledged. "If the big ones are local, why didn't they repair the station?"

"Maybe there was a greater fight with ships, and this was a small element of the conflict," Belinda volunteered.

"Let's not forget the crater," Hamoi said.

"There's time for conjecture, later," Jessie said, cutting off the questioning. He gazed around. The brightly glowing dome formed a complete hemisphere. There was no exit or airlock in sight. Jessie bounded over to the tool bag, he'd been using. One thin blade, which he had used to clean debris out of the slot, lay next to the ring's base. He picked it up and said, "Step back," to his team. When everyone was a good 4 meters from the base, Jessie tossed the tool at the dome. He expected some sort of reaction, a spark or something, but the tool bounced off the shimmering light and fell to the metal deck.

"Great," Darrin grumped. "An impenetrable alien shield."

"Captain, what about cutting the power cable that the aliens cut the first time?" Hamoi volunteered.

The team hurried over to the little alien and examined his tool without disturbing the body.

"The tool has a cable that's plugged into the suit," Belinda noted.

"Probably the tool's power source," Tully surmised.

"If that's the case," Darrin reasoned, "then the beam was electronically controlled by the alien's suit, and, with the controller damaged, if that's what that central panel is, then there goes the opportunity to use this thing to cut the power cable."

"Then we cut it ourselves," Jessie said. "What do we have?"

To the crew's disappointment, no one came up with any sort of saw or edged tool. Hamoi smartly kept his mouth shut about the cutting tool in the rover.

"Okay, we divide into two teams," Jessie said, putting strength behind his words to give his crew members confidence. "Darrin, Tully, and Hamoi, you examine the panel. See if you can figure out a shutdown switch. Don't touch anything, yet. The other three of us will walk every centimeter of this deck. We're looking for any sort of exit panel or outline in the metal that might indicate an exit is present. Let's get to it."

While Jessie walked a circle around the ring's base, he attempted to contact the rover to relay his signal to the shelter, but he couldn't raise the vehicle. He said nothing to his team, hoping no one else had tried. He needed to keep their hopes up. Ironically, everyone else had tried and chosen not to say anything too.

Hours later, the team had found no exit, and the technical crew was absolutely confused as to what constituted the console's controls.

"Captain," Darrin said, "these displays don't even look like readouts to me, and there certainly isn't anything resembling an on-off switch. My thought is that once the aliens powered up this device, it was meant to stay up."

"Captain," Belinda sent on a private channel, "my suit is reading five percent air in my tanks, and the carbon-dioxide scrubber is nearly used up."

"I've got three percent," Jessie replied, switching back to the team's comm channel. "Check the other bodies. No time for subtleties. We're looking for an operating weapon to fire at the panel or the dome."

The team spread out, rolled bodies over, and searched for alien weapons.

"What is it with these characters?" Tully complained. "Didn't any of them like to carry a simple hand weapon?"

"Every weapon I've found is attached to the suit too," Belinda added.

"And mine are shot through the chest, directly through the central panel," Aurelia said.

"The weapons were probably aimed and controlled by the vac suit. Perfect kill shot every time," Darrin reasoned.

The team reformed in front of the panel. Jessie was the first individual to hear his suit's final tank alarm. He'd been hearing Spryte warn him of his suit's low air level since it dropped below 5 percent. This was his last warning. His tanks were empty.

Aurelia felt Jessie's horror cut through her like a knife. She screamed Jessie's name, as he grabbed his helmet, gasping for breath, and pulled it free of his vac suit's collar ring.

* * * *

"Triton base calling the *Annie*," Orson said.

"Captain Erring here," Yohlin answered.

"Captain, this is Orson. The investigating team hasn't returned to the shelter, and we can't raise Captain Cinders."

"I presume you've tried to contact the others," Yohlin replied.

"Affirmative, Captain, but no contact with them either. And the link to the rover is solid. We show it parked at the base of the cut where it was parked yesterday."

"What can you see on the cam at the site, Orson?"

"Nothing, Captain, we lost that signal hours ago."

"You what?"

"We thought Captain Cinders might have moved it or shut it off."

"Did he inform you that he was going to do such a thing?"

"Well, no, ma'am, but it didn't seem important to call the captain and ask him why he stopped the imagery feed."

"And it didn't occur to you, Orson, that the cut off might have been an indication of trouble."

"But the site is inoperable, Captain. It didn't seem possible they'd have a problem."

"Except for that power supply operating in the ground, spacer," Yohlin replied, her voice hard. "I'll be back to you, Orson," she added and cut the comm. "*Annie* calling the *Spryte,*" Yohlin sent.

"Ituau here, Captain,"

"Problem downside, Ituau. We've lost communications with the rover team."

"Can the shelter reach the rover, Captain?"

"Affirmative, Ituau, and no response. They see it at the site. And before you ask, the cam feed went dead hours ago."

Ituau swore under her breath, and Yohlin let the first mate vent. "Captain," Ituau said, pulling it together, "if the team can't reach the rover for some reason, we can't effect a rescue before their air runs out."

"Nonetheless, Ituau, I want a fast prep on your search rover. Get it downside in a hurry with Nate and one other inside. Get it done, Ituau."

"Aye, aye, Captain," Ituau replied. She cut the call and grabbed her comm unit. "Nate, emergency ... vac suit in the rover bay, now."

Ituau's call popped Nate awake. Adrenaline flooded his body, as he slipped on deck shoes, grabbed the comm unit, and hurried from the cabin. He bumped into a spacer, by the name of Kasey, who was running in the same direction.

"Ituau, report," Nate called.

"Erring's order, Nate," Ituau replied. "I'm getting into my suit now. We're prepping a landing shuttle and the search rover for a rescue. We've lost contact with the team at the site."

Nate would have replied, but he caught up with Ituau at the vac suit room.

"Nate, Kasey and you have the rover. Climb aboard and drive it into the shuttle. When the ship lands, get to the site immediately."

Nate opened his mouth, and Ituau cut him off. "Don't say it, Nate. We're all thinking it. Just don't say it."

"Understood," Nate replied and finished closing his vac suit.

From the shelter's call to Yohlin and the landing of the shuttle near the site, it was two and a half hours. By Nate's estimation of when the shelter lost the cam signal, which he guessed was the clue as to when trouble began, the team would have had nearly five hours of air, if their tanks were full when they started out from their rover. As Nate drove off the rear-loading ramp of the shuttle, his thought was that the team was dead and had been dead for hours. He banged his fist on the rover's console in frustration.

29: Get Them Out

Nate parked the *Spryte*'s search rover next to that of the *Annie*'s and exited the vehicle with Kasey, the tech. He experienced a feeling of dread, walking toward the cut, and prepared himself for what they would find — the investigation team dead.

"Approaching the cut now, Captain," Nate said. Yohlin and Ituau were online, hanging on every word the second mate transmitted.

"We're losing your visuals, Nate," Ituau said, watching interference build on the image transmission.

"How are you receiving Kasey's transmission?" Nate asked, thinking the problem might be with his suit.

"His imagery is fading too," Ituau replied.

"But you're reading me okay, Ituau?" Kasey asked.

"Voice signals aren't great, but we can read you," Ituau replied.

The officers could hear the labored breathing of the rescue team, as they hurried to climb the rocky cut. The minutes dragged by, and the anxiety of both officers ratcheted up.

"Approaching the top of the cut, Captain," Nate relayed. "We can see some blue light." The next part of the transmission was garbled, when Nate and Kasey shouted something simultaneously.

"Captain, the dome's on," Nate said in the clear.

"What dome, Nate?" Ituau demanded.

"Sorry, Ituau, the rim that we saw in the imagery is projecting a dome of energy over the entire site."

"Understood, Nate, but what about our people?" Yohlin asked.

"Heading closer now, Captain."

"Don't touch the dome, Nate," Ituau cautioned.

"I hear that." A couple of minutes of labored breathing occupied the transmission until Nate spoke again. "What the ... the team is outside their vac suits."

"Say again, Nate," Yohlin ordered.

"All the dust in the dome is gone, Captain. The base inside the dome is a shiny metal deck with carvings, and our people are lying on it without their vac suits. This is as weird as it gets."

"Are they asleep or dead, Nate?" Yohlin demanded.

"Hang on a minute, Captain. I'm zooming in with my helmet cam on one of our team. He's lying on his side and facing me. Captain, your first mate, Darrin, does he snore?" Nate asked.

"Oh, for the love of Pyre, Nate," Yohlin replied, ready to lose her temper, but she paused and thought. "Yes, yes, he does. He snores up a racket."

"That explains it, Captain. I'm watching the man's lips vibrate. I wanted to be sure it wasn't from some source within the dome or something. I'm checking other details. Belinda is kind of a big girl, and her skins are definitely rising up and down."

"If it wasn't for the fact that I'm relieved to hear our people are alive, Nate, I'd smack you for your observations," Ituau said.

"Let's not get ahead of ourselves," Yohlin said. "Are our people asleep, or have they been put to sleep? How come we can't communicate with them, and how come they're in there and not outside the site?"

"Captain, do you mind Nate tossing a small stone against the dome?" Ituau asked.

"We'll need to test it sooner or later. Go ahead, Nate, but use a small stone."

Nate picked up a thumbnail-sized rock and pitched it at the dome. "It bounced off the dome, Captain. No spark from the energy field or a launching of the rock back at me. It hit and dropped to the surface, like it hit a monolith."

"Nate, look to the far right," Kasey called out excitedly. "Someone's rolling over. It's Rules. Hey, it's Rules." Kasey was bouncing up and down a meter off the surface and waving his arms to get Rules' attention.

"Rules has seen us, Captain," Nate reported. "It looks like our people were asleep, waiting for us. Rules is crawling over to someone ... it's the captain. She's waking the captain. Cinders is fine. He's sitting up, and Rules is waking the others. Our people are fine, Captain! They're fine!"

The two officers breathed enormous sighs of relief.

"Strange ... the captain is waving his fingers at me, but it's real odd-like," Nate said.

Kasey started laughing. "He's not talking to you, Nate. He's talking to me. I was born deaf, and I had to wait until I was fifteen when my head was adult size before I could apply for aural implants. My Mom and I communicated by sign language and text on my comm unit. The captain wanted to learn how, so I taught him. Who knew we'd need it?"

"What's he saying, Kasey?" Yohlin asked.

"Captain wants to know if we have communications with the ships. I told him yes," Kasey reported.

"Ask him what happened," Yohlin requested.

"Sorry, Captain, hold a minute," Kasey replied.

Two minutes later, Yohlin repeated her question.

"Captain, we've a problem," Nate sent. "We're trying to communicate with two masters, and one of them is spelling out his commands and questions in sign language."

"Understood, Nate. Captain Cinders has command. We'll expect a running update from Kasey and you," Yohlin said, relinquishing her place as the primary officer.

"The captain is asking how long we've been here," Kasey said, beginning a running report of his observations and communication with Jessie. "Rules is speaking to him. He's signing that Rules detected our excitement when we arrived, and that's what woke her."

"Wow, we can transmit our emotions through vacuum," Nate commented.

"The captain is signing that he discovered Rules' ability to do that when he hid her in the hold of the *Spryte*. Said he packed her into a vac suit in his cabin and stowed her in an equipment locker. She detected him, when he came to retrieve her."

"Aha, that's how he fooled the sniffers," Ituau exclaimed.

"The captain is walking over to the ... yikes —"

"This is where I translate for our young spacer," Nate said. "The captain is pointing to a set of bodies on the metal deck. He's indicating that there are small and large bodies."

"What bodies, Nate?" Yohlin asked.

"Sorry, Captain, they're alien bodies. One type is too small and oddly proportioned to be human, and the other type is much larger and more elongated."

"How did they get there?" Yohlin asked.

"Hold a minute, Captain Erring. Captain Cinders is explaining that," Kasey said.

"My apologies, men," Yohlin said.

Ituau knew how Captain Erring felt. Questions were popping into her mind as fast as she could think, and it was frustrating to have communication reduced to the speed of sign language.

"The captain said the bodies were here. They were the rocky outcroppings we saw on the earlier imagery," Kasey reported. "What?" he suddenly said.

"What do you mean, what?" Nate asked.

"I'm asking for more details. Hang a minute," Kasey said.

"Okay, the captain says when power was restored to the dome, everything lit up, and the space dust and rock was sucked out of the inside of the structure. He says it was like a whirlwind. That exposed the bodies, which they had already discovered."

"Kasey, ask if the captain knows how the dome got activated," Ituau requested.

"Okay," Kasey replied. A couple of minutes later, he said, "The captain says they did it ... it was an oops!" Kasey chuckled, Nate frowned, and Yohlin swore.

"That's my captain," Ituau said laughing. "His people discover an alien site, and his team manages to activate it."

"Can they shut it down, Kasey?" Yohlin asked.

"Captain Cinders beat you to it, Captain," Kasey reported. "He says they tried to shut it down and don't have the tools. He's signing more. Hold on."

The next delay was extensive, as Jessie and Kasey went back and forth. The trapped team, originally excited by the discovery by their comrades, had sat back down. A couple of them stretched out and used the vac suit legs as pillows to await orders.

"Wow," Kasey finally said. "Captain tells me that the small aliens are the attackers. One of them possesses a cutting tool of some type, probably beam, but it's powered by its suit. Only problem is that a beam hole through the suit was centered on the control panel located on the chest. The strikes on each body are through the chest to take out the vac suit controls. Hold, please, more coming."

"Um, captain says they discovered there was air by accident when his tanks ran dry. Says he snapped off his helmet and discovered he could breathe." Kasey halted his conversation with an utterance too low to be intelligible, and those on the call were sympathetic. It was the worst nightmare of spacers to run their vac suit tanks dry in vacuum. It was nearly impossible to resist the temptation to pop the helmet to breathe. Jessie was describing the moment when he expected to die. Shivers ran through every one of those on the comm.

"Give us a few minutes, Captain," Nate said. "Captain Cinders is directing us to come close and indicating some sort of effort on our part."

The officers heard a constant stream of short questions and answers between Nate and Kasey that Yohlin and Ituau had difficulty following, but both remained silent.

"Okay, Captain," Nate reported. "Captain Cinders indicated that if the small aliens are the attackers, it makes sense that the bigger aliens are the defenders. Furthermore, he surmises that the installation was never meant to be shut down. His final thought is that there must be some form of ingress-egress that the larger aliens used to enter the dome, and he wants us to search the outside of the dome for the entrance."

"Hold," Kasey said, interrupting Nate's report. "The captain says that the entrance is probably covered in a layer of dust and rock from the explosion that created the crater. Says the crater was probably blown out by an alien weapon. Says we'll need some cavity detection equipment to locate it. And, um ... of course, they have no food, but they have water in their suits that will last maybe another day or two."

"Kasey, please relay the following to Captain Cinders," Yohlin said. "I'm ordering Nate and you to walk the perimeter and check for an entrance. We might get lucky and locate it quickly. While you two do that, I'll be sending support. Ituau, recall your shuttle. Get it loaded with engineering crew and tools. Land it at the site and leave it there. I'll contact the shelter and drop our shuttle with people to relocate it to the site and support the efforts at the dome. Once everything is reestablished, we can recover the shuttles."

"Aye, aye, Captain," Ituau replied. She transferred the bridge call to her comm unit, switched to a new channel on her hand unit, and contacted the people she required, while keeping Captain's Erring's channel in the listen mode. While she was ordering the recall of the shuttle and preparing engineers and techs for loading, the question shot through her mind: What type of tools did you need to free people from an alien installation with an unknown energy dome?

* * * *

"That was pretty fancy, Captain," Belinda said. "Some sort of communication that only Kasey understands?"

"Sign language, Belinda. Kasey was born deaf, and that's how he communicated with his mother until he received his implants before his sixteenth birthday," Jessie explained.

"And you learned it because ...?" Belinda asked.

"Just curious," Jessie replied laconically. "Speaking of curious, did anyone notice the discrepancy between our tech inside and outside the dome?"

"Not sure what you mean, Captain," Darrin said.

"I zoomed in on the cam on the crest after this place lit up. Its power light was out."

"That unit should have been good for two more days," Tully objected.

"On the other hand, our suit comms worked for us after the site powered up," Jessie commented. "But we can't communicate through the dome."

"That makes Rules the only one who got a signal through that energy wall," Belinda said.

"Guess the aliens didn't think about filtering empaths," Jessie said, shaking his head at the absurdity of the realization.

"What did you get across to Kasey, Captain?" Darrin asked.

"You can see them searching," Jessie replied, indicating Nate and Kasey, who were walking in opposite directions around the dome, scraping at the surface with their boots. "Captain Erring is moving the shelter to this site, and Ituau is loading the *Spryte*'s shuttle with engineers, techs, and tools. I relayed our belief that the small aliens were the attackers and the big ones were the defenders. The dome appears to be impermeable, which means the larger aliens required a means of ingress and egress. I think it will be a deck section that moves on a signal from the console."

Jessie's words sent Hamoi hurrying over to the console to scan the icons.

"You, Hamoi, are forbidden to do anything but look," Darrin said forcefully. "You keep your hands at your side, and, if you have a stroke or something, you make sure you fall backwards. Do you read me?"

"Aye, sir," Hamoi replied meekly, cowed by the reprimand.

"Let's make ourselves useful," Jessie said. "Each of us is going to walk around this dome's deck. I realize it's covered with symbols that don't mean anything to us, but I want you to think about an exit or entrance, as you look. Maybe you'll find something helpful to our efforts to get out of here."

The trapped team spent hours searching the deck, checking it section by section, often walking from one to another to compare a line of symbols. Jessie called for a rest and a few sips of water when he saw his people's attention flagging.

Belinda was sipping on her suit's water tube, when she said, "If I close my eyes, I can see bright alien symbols swirling in the dark."

"I'm wondering how long it will take to forget my images," Tully grumped.

While Jessie's team was taking their break, the engineers and techs from the *Spryte* and *Annie* arrived, carrying portable equipment. Jessie worked through Kasey to tell Tobias Samuels, the lead excavation engineer from the *Annie*, to survey the ground around the dome.

"Ask the captain what he hopes we'll find," Tobias asked Kasey.

"You mean besides a way out?" Kasey quipped. "Okay, okay, just joshing," exclaimed Kasey, when Tobias turned hard eyes on him. After a short conversation, Kasey reported, "Captain believes you'll locate a tunnel that extends from under the dome to an entrance point beyond the dome."

"What if these aliens never came aboveground except to enjoy the view of the stars?" Tobias asked.

Kasey translated the question to Jessie. "Captain says if that's the case, the team is probably screwed."

"Best get to it then," Tobias commented. He sent the *Spryte* team to the left, and he took the *Annie*'s team to the right. They swept the ground, looking for anything besides aggregate.

Jessie let his people rest, while he followed the rescue crews with his eyes. Progress was slow. No one knew how deep a tunnel might be located beneath the surface, and they didn't want to miss it. Jessie broke from his observations to look at his team. They appeared calm, relaxing against their suits. It wasn't until he turned around and saw Aurelia in her cross-legged pose, eyes closed, and the corners of her lips turned up in a tiny smile that he understood how his people's attitudes were possible. He examined his own feelings, surprised to find he wasn't anxious, as if he was sure they would get free of the place. His lips tweaked in a smile. *You were right, Yohlin, and I think I need an empath for each ship,* Jessie thought.

Tobias' team reached the halfway point around the dome when the lead engineer, who had been carrying a portable monitor, touched a tech's arm, who was swinging a ground sensor on a wand. Tobias indicated several areas around the tech's feet.

Jessie got up, signaled Kasey to walk around the dome, and hurried over to watch the proceedings. He could see Tobias speaking to him before the engineer realized his mistake.

Tobias looked around and spotted Kasey bouncing toward him. They spoke for a few seconds, and then Tobias directed his tech on a line away from the dome and followed him. The *Annie*'s crew planted small markers in the ground to indicate what they found, and the *Spryte*'s team hurried to join them.

Kasey communicated to Jessie, indicating the growing line of markers that led away from the dome. His smile was evident through his faceplate. Jessie turned to call to his people but found them standing behind him, waiting for a translation.

"The engineers have found a metal casement the width of what you can see by those markers," said Jessie, pointing to the rocky ground beyond the dome. "The good news is that it's not too deep, which means we can probably expect an entrance nearby."

The wait dragged on for the trapped team, as the engineers tracked the metal structure that they had detected below, and they returned to their vac suits to wait. Kasey signaled that he needed fresh tanks, and he headed off to the shelter.

To expedite the detection process, Tobias' team tracked the right-hand edge of the underground object, and Nate's team stayed with the left side. Within 60 meters, the crews came to a ledge. It was a 7-meter drop to a flat plain, visible for kilometers.

"The depth of the metal has barely changed since the dome," Tobias said to Nate. "The opening has to be under this ledge. I think we should contact the shelter for the survey rover. We'll need its tools and hoist arm to lower us. We certainly can't take a chance on someone jumping down there, only to discover that there's a thin crust over some cavern."

"That small rover can't make it through the cut or around the dome without us clearing a bunch of rock," Nate replied. "And that will take too long."

"You have a better plan?" Tobias asked.

"Maybe," Nate replied. "I say we get back to base, load the survey rover on your shuttle, and have it transport us to that plain. Then we drive the rover to whatever is under this ledge."

"I like that plan," Tobias said, smiling through his faceplate, and tapping Nate's vac-suited shoulder with a gloved hand. He called to a tech to plant a beacon at the edge of the ledge, centered between the markers.

"Everyone back to the shelter," Nate sent over the general channel. "Kasey, when you get back here, I want you to explain what's happening to the captain and then get back to base for some food and rest."

"Going to be dark soon," Nate commented, as the group hustled to the shuttle.

"And our portable lights won't last the night, unless they're hooked to a generator, shuttle, or rover," Tobias replied.

Nate grunted in reply, and Tobias gave Yohlin and Ituau an update.

"I like your idea, Nate," Yohlin replied. "Good thinking!"

"Thank you, Captain."

"How are our people looking?" Ituau asked, with concern.

"Jessie talks to Kasey with his fingers for a bit," Tobias said. "Then he relays the message to the crew, and everyone lies back down. I'm thinking Captain Cinders is having them conserve their energy to reduce water consumption. And, of course, you see Rules sitting in her favorite position."

When Tobias and Yohlin laughed softly, Ituau asked, "What's the position?"

Nate jumped into the conversation, saying, "I've seen her sitting cross-legged with her eyes closed. Is that what you mean?"

"Yes, Nate," Yohlin replied. "When Rules is sitting like that, it seems to calm her and allow her to maximize her broadcast. She's soothing the crew."

"Why is it that Rules possesses the only means of sending and receiving through the dome?" Ituau asked.

"You'll have to ask the aliens," Nate replied. "Oh, you can't. They're dead."

"As captain," Yohlin replied, "I have privileges, Ituau. I get to smack him first, and then you can have a go at him."

"You're in trouble now, spacer," Tobias commented, chuckling through his breathing exertions, as the teams bounced their way quickly toward the shuttle."

It was dark when the shuttle, carrying the crew and the survey rover, with its hoist arm, lifted for the flat plain. It wasn't so dark for the trapped crew members. They lay down and did their best to cover their eyes with their arms or the sleeves of vac suits to shut out the dome's persistent glow.

At one point, Belinda tried to find a more comfortable position and a better means of covering her eyes. She quipped, "Whoever was the last one up, turn off the lights." The chuckles she received were halfhearted. Time was ticking down for the crew, and it was measured by their limited supply of water.

The rescue shuttle set down on the flat plain, and the crew offloaded the survey rover in record time. They didn't need the beacon to guide them. The blue energy field of the dome shone brightly in the distance. The rover was limited in speed by the rocks and boulders that were strewn across the plains. Progress was slow enough that the crew members, forced to walk, reached the ledge face far in advance of those riding.

"We've got a pair of doors," Nate sent over the general comm to Tobias, who was riding. "They're metal and covered in symbols like the deck under the dome." Nate started laughing.

"What?" Tobias asked.

"There's a convenient plate to the right of the doors that's set in the rock. It's begging to be pushed."

"Maybe I should wait out here," Tobias replied on a private channel. "You know ... just in case."

Nate turned around. He could see the rover's lights continuing to make progress across the plains. "Thought you were going to play it safe, Tobias."

"Don't you dare touch that plate until I get there, you poor excuse for a spacer," Tobias replied.

When the rover finally reached the ledge face, Tobias checked the doors closely. "Did you see the thin slots along the four sides of the doors?" he asked Nate.

"Yes, they look like the same slots in the ring. You don't think they emit an energy field, do you?"

"That wouldn't make sense, but, then again, we're talking about an alien site. Just the same, I'd touch that plate with a tool of some sort, sir."

"You finally give me credit for my officer position," Nate said, laughing. He searched through the rear of the rover and came up with a long rod used to plant a beacon. Returning to the doors, he ordered everyone back, extended the rod, and touched the plate.

The crew watched Nate disappear in a cloud of dust. In the low gravity, it took several minutes for their view of him to clear. He was standing in the same spot, the tool at his side, and he was covered in a coat of gray. The twin doors were open.

Nate heard the cheers of his people, as he wiped the faceplate of his helmet, before he could see and understand why they were celebrating.

"Well, now we know what the slots were for. Great design," Tobias said, patting Nate on the shoulder, as he peered into the tunnel. "Clean the doors before you open them to prevent dust grinding up the works. I approve."

Nate assigned half the team to stay outside. "If these doors close, you'll need to keep your hands on them so you'll feel me pounding with this," he said, hoisting up his tool. "Shall we go, Tobias?"

"Senior crew members first," Tobias replied.

"I'll remember that," Nate said, ordering his vac suit to turn on the shoulder-mounted light. It would only give him a few hours, but he hoped that would be enough.

Nate and Tobias led two crew members into the metal tunnel. It was perfectly rectangular, the creases of its four edges sharply defined. The symbols were present on every surface.

Ten meters in, the team ran into another set of doors. Inset to the right was another plate, which Nate touched with his tool. Twin beams of light lanced out, scanned him before he could move, and shut off. The crew stood expectantly, but nothing happened. Nate reached out a gloved hand to touch the plate. The beam scan repeated, but that was the only thing that moved.

"This is disappointing," Tobias commented.

"Any ideas?" Nate asked.

"Not a one. We already know this alien metal is impervious to everything we brought. That means we're not getting through these doors or digging around them."

"It's late, Tobias. We need to get back to the shuttle. I suggest some food, rest, and a rethink. We start again at daylight."

30: Double Helix

At first light, Kasey wolfed down breakfast, used the facilities, donned his vac suit, and hurried out of the shelter, making the climb through the cut. Jessie's crew was still asleep when he arrived, their heads covered to keep the dome's light out of their eyes. He recalled what woke Rules before, and he tried to project anxiousness, but it didn't work. Then he hit on the idea of imagining a break in his air delivery mechanism. The thought of air flooding out of his suit, panicked him and sharply brought Rules' head up.

Aurelia glanced at her people, trying to determine who might be suffering through a nightmare. They were all lying peacefully. She was still receiving the feeling of anxiousness, although it was segueing to excitement. *Kasey*, she thought, looking around for him. As before, he was bouncing up and down, waving his arms, and she waved back. Crawling over to Jessie, she gently shook his shoulder, and he awoke with a start.

"Your translator is back," Aurelia said, indicating Kasey with a finger over her shoulder. "By the tone of his emotions, he has something important to relate to you."

"Okay," Jessie mumbled.

Aurelia watched Jessie get to his hands and knees and gather himself before struggling to his feet. Then she hurried to wake the others. None of them exhibited Jessie's grogginess.

"Something's wrong with the captain," Aurelia whispered to Belinda.

"Explain," Belinda replied.

"I woke him, and he seemed disoriented. It took him a while to stand."

Belinda checked to ensure Jessie had his back to her before she crawled over to his suit and checked his water supply. Then she motioned the others to her side. "Time for a mutiny," she whispered. "Captain's not drinking his water. He's saving it for us."

"Easy enough to correct," Darrin replied. "He doesn't drink; we don't drink."

"We'll have to check his water supply each time to make sure he participates with us," Tully added, and more than one crew member blanched.

"I'll do it. Newbie, remember," Aurelia replied. "Besides, what can he do ... exile me to some alien installation?" She grinned, but the crew failed to join her. They were tired, had eaten no food for nearly two days, and were dangerously low on water.

"Here he comes," whispered Hamoi.

"Kasey says that the underground structure they were tracing turned out to be a tunnel. It has a pair of outer doors with a plate that they pressed, which opened the doors," Jessie reported. "But they ran into a second set of doors and another access plate. When they pressed on that one, beams scanned them but nothing happened. That's when they retreated for the night."

"What are they going to try this morning?" Darrin asked.

"Kasey doesn't know," Jessie said, sitting down heavily. "It's time for our water rations. Everybody get a couple of sips." Jessie crawled to his suit, and Aurelia met him there. "And what are you doing, spacer?" Jessie growled, but it came out with little force.

"I'm your newly appointed water monitor, sir," Aurelia replied. "I'm to check your water level before and after you drink. For this morning, you're required to take three portions of your allowance."

"Cute, Rules. Now crawl back to your suit before I put you on report." Jessie watched his crew leave their suits, stand, and gather around him. "You're treading on dangerous ground, spacers."

"If we die in this place, Captain, we die together," Belinda said. "You don't get to go first because you saved your water for us."

"I could declare this a mutiny," Jessie said. He sought to stand and demonstrate his defiance, but his legs wouldn't support him, his thoughts swam, and dark spots danced in front of his eyes, despite the dome's glow. Suddenly, arms cradled him, and he was lowered to the ground. Jessie felt a vac suit dragged beside him, and the water tube placed against his mouth. He tried to shove it away, but hands restrained him.

Through Jessie's confused thoughts came a craving for water. He felt his body was in danger of drying up, and he would blow away like dust. The desire grew until he was desperate to drink, and he did, long drags on his water tube. The cool water energized him, and he took more than he knew he should, but he couldn't help himself.

It took some time for Jessie to swim back to consciousness. He was lying on his back, his head cradled in Aurelia's lap. "This is a rather an undignified position for a captain," Jessie said, pushing up into a sitting position with Aurelia's help.

"The indignity is having your captain deprive himself of water for our benefit. None us would want that on our conscience," Aurelia fired back, tears in her eyes.

"Good, Captain, you're awake," Darrin called out. He was standing beside the console with everyone else. "Come check this out."

Jessie rolled onto his knees and stopped. "I believe you took unfair advantage of me," he said to Aurelia.

"You needed persuading. I helped you with that."

"Yes, you did," Jessie replied quietly. He stood and gently patted Aurelia's head. "Yes, you did," he repeated softly.

"Okay, go ahead Hamoi, this is your crazy idea," Darrin said when Jessie joined them.

"Take it slow, Hamoi," Belinda said, tipping her head toward Jessie.

"Captain, you gave me the idea when you explained that our crew found doors, with plates that they used to open them, and, at the second set of doors, a beam scanned them," Hamoi said. He waited until Jessie nodded. "Well, look here."

Jessie leaned over the console. Hamoi was pointing to a rectangular plate. On either side of the plate, cut into the console's metal, were two symbols. On the left was a circle with two lines that formed a wedge. The lines extended from inside the circle's arc to its center. On the right was a second circle, but its wedge was outside the circle. Coincidentally, the open side of the two wedges faced each other across the plate.

"At first, Captain," Hamoi rushed on. "I thought these wedges were describing the deck sections, and I couldn't figure out their meaning. But, what if they aren't deck sections? What if they're beams?"

"And, if they are, Hamoi, what do you think that means?" Jessie asked. He knew his thoughts were still a little muddled, which prevented him from making any intuitive leaps.

"I'm not sure, Captain, but my guess is that this left icon represents egress from the dome, and the right one represents ingress, using the tunnel that was discovered."

"I'm following you, Hamoi, what I'm not seeing are lit icons. Look at the various symbols on this console. Half are lit; half are dark. If this pair is supposed to allow movement through the tunnel, how do we get this section operable?"

"We've been talking about that, Captain," Tully replied. "We think the plate is the answer. Touching it will activate the icons and get us access to the tunnel."

Jessie regarded the bodies of the aliens on the deck. "You do notice that the aliens are all wearing vac suits. What if there is no airlock mechanism?"

"We discussed that too," Darrin said. "This place is beautifully constructed. It's an engineering marvel, alien or not. It's our best guess that an airlock system is provided."

"We think the two alien groups were fighting for an extended period of time," Belinda added. "Destroying this place was one fight, and both sides would have been in vac suits as a matter of safety."

"Well-thought-out," Jessie commented. "I take it the plan is to trust to alien intelligence and push the plate?" When everyone nodded or murmured their agreement. "You started this, Hamoi. It's your honor," Jessie said.

Hamoi grinned and dug into a belt pouch for a small tool. He regarded his companions for a second, and then touched the plate. Nothing happened. The icons remained dim.

"I was sure I had this figured out, Captain. Stupid alien works," Hamoi said, angrily striking the plate with the ball of his fist. "Ow, that tingled," he remarked, shaking his hand.

"Look at that," said Tully, pointing to the console.

"It's a double helix, like our DNA," Darrin exclaimed.

Twin beams erupted from the top edge of the console and scanned the group. Most of the crew jerked nervously but could do no more than that in the time it took the beams to start and stop.

"The icons are lit," Hamoi said excitedly.

The team turned around in expectation of seeing a wedge open up and grant them an exit from the dome. Nothing moved, and disgruntled comments filled the air.

"Quiet, all of you," Jessie said. He stepped a couple of meters away from the group, as if the distance would allow his thoughts to clarify. He looked back at the console, and Tully flicked Hamoi's arm, indicating he should step out of the captain's view of the plate and its icons.

Then Jessie turned to start in the direction of the identified tunnel. In his head, he replayed the news Kasey had shared about the rescue team's efforts in the tunnel. One more time, he regarded the double helix projected above the plate. It spun slowly in the air, a gossamer image of blue light.

Jessie started to hurry toward where Kasey stood, but his legs cramped from the lack of water, and he was forced to hobble the remaining distance. In a flurry of sign language, Jessie explained what they'd done on the console and his idea.

When Kasey understood Jessie's directives, he contacted the team waiting aboard the shuttle on the plains. In frustration, he realized he couldn't raise the ship, due to his suit's insufficient comm power and interference from the dome. Rather than bounce a comm call through the ships, Kasey took off around the dome, bounding dangerously over boulders and rocky outcrops. Reaching the demarked path of the underground tunnel, Kasey made for the ledge, signaling the entire way until he reached the shuttle.

"Nate, here. Kasey, go ahead."

"Captain has an idea. He requests you get your butts over to the tunnel entrance."

"On our way, Kasey, explain the plan to Tobias and me as we go."

"They did what?" Tobias exclaimed, when Kasey reported the activation of the icons on the console.

"Sirs, it's not my place to say, but you haven't witnessed what I have this morning. The captain was struggling, and he passed out. The crew fed him water. I think they're about dry, and the captain was saving his for them."

Both Nate and Tobias swore over the comm.

"While the captain was out, the crew, except for Rules, was huddled over the console. They're desperate to find a way out. When the captain woke, that's when they tried the console, and the double helix popped up."

"And you say beams scanned them," Nate asked.

"Two beams, really quick."

Nate and Tobias regarded each other. They were both riding today, tired from the long day yesterday and the short night's sleep.

"Sounds like the beams above the second pair of doors," Tobias commented.

Nate grunted in reply and stayed focused on their path, driving the rover at its top speed and slewing around rocks and small craters.

At the tunnel's entrance, Nate and Tobias joined the crew, who had jogged ahead. The rear of the rover was loaded with spare tanks for the trapped crew.

"You two, with us," Nate said, picking out some crew members. "The other two of you stay outside. One of you keeps a hand on these doors if they shut. You'll hear me banging," Nate added, hefting his tool. "The other one stands near the rover. I want you to be able to communicate with Kasey, in case this tunnel's metal cuts out our comm."

Nate looked at Tobias, who nodded and touched the plate. The clean metal doors slid aside.

Tobias bowed and swept his arm toward the tunnel, indicating Nate should again precede him.

"About time you recognized that beauty should go first," Nate retorted.

At the second pair of doors, Tobias tapped the plate without hesitation. Instantly, the beams scanned them, and they heard a shout over the comm before glowing symbols on the walls, floor, and ceiling lit the tunnel.

"We've got air pumping into this section," Tobias commented, examining a portable environment tester.

"Okay, looks like we'll be able to experiment with egress," Nate said. "We've obviously entered an airlock and have been granted access by virtue of what they did on the dome's console, but we're not carrying any of the tanks they need."

"Oh, for the love of Pyre," Tobias lamented.

"Follow me," Nate said, and reversed course. At the first set of doors, which were now closed, Nate tapped the inner plate. "And now," he asked Tobias, who was watching his instrument.

"Pressure's dropping back to zero."

Soon after, the outer doors slid aside.

"Everybody grabs spare tanks and water bottles," Nate ordered. "I think we have the access we need."

When the team was ready, Tobias tapped the first plate and then, later, the second plate. Once again, the beams scanned them.

"Knock, knock, humans at the gate," Nate said wryly over the comm, but he didn't generate any laughter.

"Full atmospheric pressure," Tobias reported. Immediately after he spoke, the second set of doors opened. The long tunnel shaft was lit by the blue light of the symbols.

"I would love to know what these markings mean," Tobias asked, as they trekked the length of the tunnel.

"Probably virtuous sayings about giving to one's fellow aliens," Nate remarked.

The tunnel ended in a set of steps, which led upward to a flat ceiling.

"Okay, this is disappointing," Tobias said.

"Look around, everyone, we need another plate," Nate said. The crew examined every centimeter of walls and ceiling without finding a plate.

"Well, if there isn't one where you assume it to be, it must be where you don't," Tobias commented, dropping to his knees to search the floor, and the crew imitated him.

Moments later, a crew member called out, "I found it."

Nate and Tobias hurried to her side. The plate was set into the face of the first step and was nearly indistinguishable from the step itself.

"Huh, a kick plate," Nate quipped, tapping it with his toe. A wedge of the ceiling dropped a half meter toward them and rotated aside. Nate ordered his suit to activate his exterior audio system and helmet mic. Climbing the steps, he announced in a loud voice, "Delivery." On spotting Jessie, he added "Spare tanks and water, as ordered, Captain. Sorry it took so long. We knocked yesterday, but no one answered the door."

"I'll forgive the asinine remarks, Nate. It's good to see you," Jessie remarked, clapping his hands on Nate's shoulders.

The rescuing team dropped the spare tanks and cracked the seal on their helmets, intending to save their air. Then they handed out the spare water bottles.

Jessie's people consumed much of the water, spilling a great deal of it down the front of their skins.

"Who knew water could taste so good," Tully commented.

"My team, change out these people's tanks and pick up the empties," Nate ordered. "Captain, you ready to leave, or do you have more investigating to do?"

"We're leaving, Nate. I'm looking forward to getting some sleep in an entirely dark room."

Jessie's people climbed back into their vac suits.

"These are going to need a good cleaning," Aurelia commented, wrinkling her nose. The crew had visited their suits' facilities to eliminate body waste, and the containment limits had been reached.

When everyone was ready, Jessie and his team paused at the opening of the tunnel for a last look around. Jessie's eyes roved over the alien bodies, strewn across the deck. He felt a surge of sympathy that the aliens hadn't received a final dignity, but, then again, he had no idea what the services would be for either species. The one item he was extremely hopeful about was that the aliens, who'd built the site, were as advanced in air filtration as they were in metal working. Forced to remove their helmets and breathe the installation's air meant Jessie's people were now exposed to whatever alien microorganisms had managed to survive the intervening centuries.

"I get that the console plate sampled my skin," Hamoi said. "That's no big deal, and I can understand that it could project our DNA, seconds later.

That seems like elemental alien stuff. But what's got me flummoxed is how did this place know to give us air we could breathe and how did it know to grant us access based on our DNA?"

"We might never know the answer to those questions, Hamoi," Tully said, laying a comforting hand on his young tech's shoulder.

"I'm not sure we, as a species, are ready to know the answer," Jessie commented.

"By the way, Hamoi, that was some great deductive reasoning on the console," Belinda said.

But before Hamoi could reply, Darrin said, "Good thing too, since he was the same crew member who hooked up the console and powered this place."

"Enough chatter. Let's exit this place before it decides we should all stay," Jessie said, while Nate led the way out.

At the bottom of the steps, Tobias waited until everyone passed by him before he tapped the toe plate. Jessie paused to watch the wedge slide into place and shivers ran up and down his spine. Immediately, he felt a soothing presence in his mind, and he glanced toward Aurelia. She had rarely left his side, since he had passed out from lack of water.

"I'm fine," Jessie said to Aurelia over a private channel, but the pleasant sensation continued.

"I'm so tired of blue," Belinda said, watching the glowing icons pass by.

"I like the color," Aurelia replied.

"Empaths," Belinda quipped, "there's no accounting for their tastes."

"Would you rather have had pulsing red?" Aurelia asked sweetly.

"Rules, can you sense the power down here, and is it any different?" Jessie asked.

'Oh, it's stronger down here, Captain, and it increased after Hamoi activated the icons with his DNA. The signal is more pleasant, if anything. I'll miss it. It's been very soothing, and I feel as if it gave me more power, if that makes any sense."

Several of Aurelia's compatriots confirmed that it had.

"I think we're all saying that we felt your ministrations to be much stronger in the dome, Rules, especially at the moment we were rescued," Belinda explained.

"Interesting," was Jessie's only comment.

"Helmets on, Captain," Nate said. "We're about to enter an airlock."

When everybody signaled their readiness, Nate tapped the doorplate. The team entered the short tunnel segment before cycling to the outside. Once clear of the tunnel, Jessie's team watched the final set of doors close and relief flooded through them. They might have been standing in vacuum, but it was an environment that spacers understood. It wasn't alien.

Jessie tested his relay to the shuttle, found the signal strong, and reached out to his ships. "Cinders calling the *Spryte* and the *Annie*."

Ituau jerked out of her sleep and slapped the comm button. "Captain," she yelled.

"Captain Cinders, this is the *Annie*'s navigator. It's great to hear your voice. Captain Erring dropped into her cabin for a few hours' sleep. She's been on duty since she heard you were offline."

"Let her sleep then. I'll update her later," Jessie replied, and the navigator dropped off the call.

"Captain, you're free," Ituau exclaimed. "Is everyone okay?"

"We're all fine, Ituau, and it's good to hear your voice too."

Jessie asked after the status of his people, and Ituau updated him on the disposition of the shuttles, the shelter, the rovers, and the crew.

"Ituau, we'll take the *Annie*'s shuttle, disperse the crew, return the rover, and let the pilot drop us back at the *Spryte*. I have a job for the shelter team, and then those rovers and the shelter can be collected too."

"Understood, Captain."

"Any news from our friends at home, Ituau?"

"Just an update from your girlfriend, Captain."

"I don't have a girlfriend," Jessie ground out.

"Well, I don't think Captain Harbour would risk the residents of the *Belle* to come out to Triton to rescue my ample butt, sir."

"Oh, for the love of Pyre," Jessie sighed. "What's the update?"

"She said they're on target to launch in about seventeen days. Dingles confirmed that the travel time for the *Belle* would be slightly less than four weeks."

"Understood, Ituau. Cinders out."

"Ready for you, Captain," Nate said, indicating the empty seat next to Tobias. "Captain rides."

Jessie was too tired to object, residual weakness from the water deprivation still plaguing him, and he climbed into the rover beside Tobias. Immediately, the crew took off in bounding steps headed for the distant shuttle. Tobias adopted a more leisurely speed than the one Nate had exercised on approach to the tunnel. An engineer respected his equipment.

"Tobias, I need you to communicate to the shelter and set up something for me. If they don't have the gear, get it."

"Aye, Captain, what do you need?"

"The original cam at the site, is it functioning?"

"It's not sending, Captain, I think it might have been fried when the dome was formed."

"I need a long-range cam with a solar power supply and a heavy-duty relay."

"How far are we transmitting, Captain?"

"Can we reach the *Spryte,* even if the ship is anywhere between here and Pyre?"

"We don't have a transmitter with enough strength."

"Okay, Tobias, have the shelter set up the cam and the power supply. Set the cam to record its visuals to memory."

"The cam memory would be full in a matter of a month or so, Captain."

"And set the cam's sensing mode to monitor motion."

Tobias swiveled his head to stare at Jessie. "Motion sensor, Captain? Are we expecting visitors?"

"You never know, Tobias, you never know," Jessie replied, and settled back in his seat.

31: Cantina

Harbour boarded the *Belle*'s shuttle, nodding at the collection of passengers, and took a seat next to Dingles. It took her a moment to recognize what had caught her attention. She'd passed two spacers, who were wearing skins. Aboard the *Belle* and over time, the spacers who she'd rescued or hired had taken to wearing the typical thermal layers of the residents. Lately, she'd seen spacers, engineers, and techs wearing new skins.

After docking at the JOS, the passengers prepared to exit, collecting personal items, but waited in their seats. Harbour, who was seated forward in the main cabin, waited for Danny to pass and secure the gangway connection before the hatch was released.

"Captain," Dingles said, gesturing down the aisle after Danny thumped by. "Privileges of rank."

Harbour gritted her teeth, rose, and walked down the aisle. In the gangway, she mumbled to Dingles, "That was embarrassing."

"Captain, aboard a ship that's underway, there are hundreds of things that can go wrong. On a ship, as big as the *Belle*, that's probably thousands. People will not jump to and do what's necessary, unless they believe in those who command. Someday, that might be a spacer sacrificing his or her life to prevent a tragedy that could cost the lives of many others. And they'll willingly do it for those people they trust and respect."

Harbour considered Dingles' words. She thought that the demeanor of the ship captains she had met, including Jessie, seemed standoffish, cold. Now, it appeared to her as the isolation of command, and she wondered if she could make the transition. She knew she was partway there, but the remaining distance looked daunting.

It was while traversing the terminal arm that Harbour noticed Danny had caught up to them and was walking next to her on the opposite side from Dingles. Danny had also shucked his resident-style clothing and adopted the spacers' skins.

At the line for the cap, Dingles and Danny marched to the front, turned, and faced the waiting people. When the next capsule arrived, no one moved. Instead, those at the front turned to look down the line, eyes focused on Harbour.

"Captain, your capsule is waiting," Harbour heard in her ear. She glanced behind her. The two skin-wearing spacers, whom she had noticed aboard the shuttle, were standing behind her. One of them was indicating the front of the line. Harbour squared her shoulders and took what seemed to be a long journey, the twenty steps from the back of the line to the capsule. She expected to feel resentment and suspicion from those she passed. Amazingly, she sensed little emotion, except for some of the usual jealousy her looks engendered.

Once Harbour and the four spacers were aboard the capsule and locked in with shoulder restraints and harnesses, she expected another person to join them. Harbour glanced at the first person in line, a woman, who wore a bored expression. Apparently, she was content to wait for the next cap.

"What's going on?" Harbour asked, after the doors of the terminal arm and the capsule closed.

"It's a captain's introduction, ma'am," Dingles said.

When Harbour frowned, Danny added, "It's done to demonstrate to the stationers that the crew has the captain's back."

"Then this is meant to be some form of intimidation," Harbour replied, not happy with the concept.

"It's a reminder, ma'am, that when stationers see our captain, they should envision the crew standing behind her," one of the spacers said.

When the five of them completed the transit to the JOS, they exited into a short corridor and turned right at its end onto the main promenade. Dingles and Danny walked beside her and the two tall spacers walked behind and slightly off her shoulders. Stationers, who might have brushed past Harbour before, were forced to make way for the group. At no time did Dingles and Danny attempt to evade individuals. They walked with purpose, proudly, and Harbour sought to adopt their pose.

Winding their way inward and to another level, they arrived at the Miners' Pit, and Dingles tapped the door actuator. This time, the hatch stayed closed. Harbour glanced up at the door cam, about the time the hatch finally slid open.

"Captain Harbour," Maggie said, with relish, tipping two fingers to her brow.

"Word travels fast," Harbour remarked.

Maggie laughed and said, "Captain, if one spacer knows it, rest assured every spacer knows it well before you think it's humanly or technically feasible."

"Captain or not, where's my hug?" Harbour replied.

"Ah, I see rank hasn't gone to your head, yet," Maggie said, hugging Harbour, who basked in the sensation, physically and emotionally. "And the station has been introduced to a new captain, has it?" Maggie said, stepping back and eyeing the four spacers.

"You mean my self-appointed escort," Harbour said, with a small grimace.

"It's a captain's duty to command respect for herself, the ship, and the crew," Maggie replied sternly.

"That's what I've been hearing," Harbour said, glancing at Dingles.

"Guiding a new captain in her duties is all," Dingles replied modestly.

"I bet you are," Maggie said, laughing. She hooked an arm into Harbour's and guided her to a table. "You boys can belly up to the bar. I laid out some food for you."

Danny and the two spacers made for the bar.

"You're not hungry, Dingles?" Maggie asked.

"I require my first mate to attend our meeting," Harbour replied, smiling.

"First mate! Why you old space dog," Maggie said, slapping Dingles on the shoulder. "When you have downtime, the first drink is on the house."

"Only the first drink?"

"Yes, only one. Okay, let's sit and hear why you came, Captain."

"I need a cantina, for lack of a better word," Harbour said.

"You thinking of going into business, Captain? Maybe becoming my competition?" Maggie asked, and Harbour detected a cooling of the woman's usually pleasant aura.

"Hook on, spacer," Dingles growled. "The captain doesn't have time to be your competitor. She has somewhere to be," Maggie was taken aback by her friend's tone, but she had always considered herself a fairly bright person. She quickly parsed Dingles words, and her eyes popped open wide in realization. "Apologies, Captain. I've been too long aboard the JOS. I'm latched on now."

Harbour felt a flood of excitement and endearing warmth from Maggie.

"Let me think. You have what, thirty, or so, spacers now?" Maggie asked.

"Make it fifty," Dingles replied.

"And another sixty tech staff," Harbour added.

"Okay and you've got another fifty to sixty out, you know where," Maggie said, dropping her voice to a conspiratorially level, and Harbour found it difficult to keep a smile off her face. "Let's call it two hundred crew even. How long, Captain? Six months?"

"I want provisions for a year," Harbour replied.

"Smart, Captain, who knows what else they've uncovered out there or what that piece of effluent, called a governor, might try next. So, are we talking drink, food, or both?"

"Both, Maggie. In addition, I'll be ordering supplies for my three thousand residents."

"Aye, Captain. When, where, and how?"

"I need the processes of purchase and installation to go through you, and that includes any secondary vendors whose services you need to secure, Maggie."

"Right, you don't want to signal your intentions. And how long do I have?"

"Three weeks. Sooner, if you can manage it. Dingles tells me the trip will take four weeks. So, that's all the time I can afford."

"Understood, we'll get it done, one way or the other, Captain. Do you know where you want the cantina installed, and what services are available there now?"

"Work through Dingles, Maggie. He'll connect you with the engineers aboard the *Belle*, who will define the space for you and answer any questions. Message me the amount of coin you'll need in advance or as you pay out, either way."

"Which reminds me, Captain, what's my budget?"

Harbour realized that she had no idea of what the cantina and the provisions might cost. She did know that her general fund was more robust than it'd ever been, and, if the spacers had to spend six months or more at Triton, they'd need a friendly place to unwind. "Tell you what, Maggie. Give me a second Miners' Pit with maybe a new face. What do you say?"

"I say can do, Captain," Maggie said, extending her hand to seal the deal.

"Spacers," Dingles called out, "swallow those mouthfuls. We're making for the exit."

Maggie gave Harbour a long, sincere hug at the door, whispering, "Go take care of our people, Captain."

* * * *

"You heard?" Liana Belosov asked Lise Panoy.

"Are you speaking about Harbour, Liana?" Lise asked. The two women were sitting in Lise's front parlor, enjoying cool fruit drinks.

"Captain Harbour! Can you believe the woman's presumption?" Liana said hotly.

"Stranger things have happened, Liana. How can I help you?"

"I see. Not much chatting, anymore. Is that it, Lise? Or should I start calling you governor?" When Liana didn't receive a reply, she colored with resentment and embarrassment. *The Andropov family has been displaced; long rule the Panoys,* she thought with disgust. "Regardless of what has befallen my brother, who I believe the Review Board has been overly harsh in condemning, the murderer of my son is still free. I want to know what you're going to do about it."

"Nothing," Lise replied.

"Nothing?" Liana echoed, in a screeching voice.

"Calm down, Liana, and I'll explain," Lise replied. She'd been waiting decades for this moment and was intent on drawing out the pleasure. She'd hated Liana since they were children, and those feelings only deepened when the two women reached adulthood. "We know who killed your son. Everyone knows who did it, and yet no one can find her. She might be a powerful empath, but someone should have noticed the odd habits of those protecting her. Certainly, the reward would have drawn people out to report what they've seen, but it hasn't."

"What's that mean, Governor?" Liana asked, near choking on Lise's title, but, if she was to have justice, she had to accept that she no longer possessed the cachet she once had as the governor's sister.

A thrill raced up Lise's spine. Liana's bow to her position was a validation of the patience and cunning she had exercised to depose the Andropov family, and revenge tasted wonderfully sweet.

"We have an idea where the girl is hiding, Liana," Lise replied, choosing to draw out the conversation. She intended to give Liana enough information to whet her appetite, but not enough to satisfy it. It would force the woman to return to her, time and again, to hear the latest news, deferring to Lise's position of power each time. Secretly, Lise hoped Aurelia Garmenti would never be brought to justice. She couldn't care less about the murder of Dimitri Belosov. As far as she was concerned, the little piece of effluent was better dead. "We don't know exactly, Liana, but all evidence points to Aurelia secreted aboard a mining ship."

"You mean she's off station?"

"That's what the evidence indicates, Liana. We've engaged some security officers to make inquiries offline to investigate this aspect of the case, and we'll continue to apply pressure. After all, we can't have anyone, downsider or topsider, thinking they can get away with murdering one of our own." Lise managed to add a sincere smile for Liana's benefit.

"Thank you, Lise," Liana said, rising and offering her hand.

"I'll keep you informed if I hear of any progress we make, Liana. My maid will show you out," Lise said, accepting Liana's hand and indicating the woman who'd appeared in the salon's doorway.

Lise was enjoying the afterglow of interaction with Liana when a tapping at the door indicated that Idrian Tuttle and Rufus Stewart, who had seen Liana leave, were ready to resume their conversation.

"That must have felt good," Rufus chuckled.

"You have no idea. I could bask in that sensation for a year and never get tired of it, but enough about Liana's downfall. Where were we?"

"Discussing the recent events concerning the *Belle*," Idrian reminded Lise.

"Yes, this bit of news about retired spacers communicating with ... what was the name of that one aboard the *Belle*?"

"Dingles?" Rufus replied, laughing.

"Where, for the love of Pyre, do these people get these absurd names?" Lise said, shaking her head.

"To the spacers, Lise, they're a sign of respect from the crews, who endow their veterans with these nicknames. We need to be careful not to adopt a dismissive attitude about them. If anything, these should be a warning sign to us that we're speaking about someone who has influence within the spacer community."

"Whatever," Lise said, waving off Idrian. She was annoyed that she couldn't enjoy thinking of the spacers as individuals she needn't consider in her grand strategies. "How certain are we of this information that this Dingles is intending to hire spacers for the *Belle*?"

"It's solid, Lise," Rufus replied. "We learned from Emerson who it was that Giorgio Sestos was communicating with aboard the JOS for station intelligence. It was a Corporal McKenzie. Apparently, he's one nasty piece of work. With the arrest of Markos and Giorgio, the corporal lost his patron, and we conveniently offered him a new opportunity, which he was eager to take. The corporal has a heavy and costly taste for coin-kitties and kats. Seems he's constantly penalized for medical services afterwards."

"Ugh," Lise commented. "Well, whatever works for station trash."

"This has to be adding up to something, Lise," Idrian speculated. "The *Belle* holds a snap election, and Harbour emerges as the captain. Now, one of her senior spacers is hiring retired spacers. If I didn't know better, I'm thinking Harbour is intending to move the colony ship."

Rufus laughed uproariously at Idrian, who frowned in resentment. But, it was Idrian who had the last laugh, when Lise pointed a manicured finger at Idrian and nodded her head, while she considered the idea.

"That makes sense, Idrian," Lise said. "But the real question is: Where would she move the *Belle*? Maybe far enough out that shuttles couldn't reach her, but what good would that do her and her people? No, if she moves that ship, it has to be for something greater."

Rufus was about to voice a suggestion, but his eye caught the drumming of Lise's nails on the arm of her chair, a sure sign that she preferred not to be interrupted, while she ruminated on a subject.

"No, Harbour's no idiot. She has something unique in mind. I've always thought her capable of so much more, but she's preferred to remain passive when it came to politics. Maybe that's changed," Lise posited.

"My thought, Lise," Idrian volunteered. "It's about the spacers at Triton."

This time Rufus kept his laughter to himself. Instead, he eyed Lise, waiting for her reaction.

"Idrian, sometimes genius flows out of that mouth of yours," Lise commented, rising from her chair. "That's it. Captain Harbour is sailing the *Belle* to Triton," she exclaimed. A knuckle of her fist was held between her exquisite teeth to prevent her from emoting any further in front of the two men, who she now considered subordinates, although they wouldn't have agreed with her.

"We can't let those spacers be rescued. We have to stop her," Rufus demanded.

Lise pulled her hand away from her mouth and eyed Rufus coldly. "Think, before you attempt to give me orders, Rufus," she said, her voice biting. "This couldn't be better if we planned it. If, and I say if, Harbour is planning to take the *Belle* to Triton, she'll fall under the same quarantine restrictions, and it'll restart the clock again for Cinders' people."

"But the *Belle* can easily haul the supplies that the spacers need," Rufus commented. He was smarting from Lise's rebuke and was determined to regain some favor.

"True," Lise replied. "It would have been more useful to remove Cinders and two of his ships, but that was never my primary intention."

"No?" Rufus queried.

"No, Rufus. Stranding Cinders and two of his ships at Triton for six months would have crippled his company, even if he found a way to survive the quarantine. Essentially, the quarantine was supposed to ruin him and his reputation. The beauty of Harbour taking the colony ship to Triton is that she would be out of our hair for six months."

"And it would be better for your governorship, Lise, if the quarantine, which was imposed for the safety of the citizens, didn't lead to the death of the spacers," Idrian added.

"Yes, it would, wouldn't it?" Lise mused. Finally, it was her turn to laugh.

"What?" Rufus asked.

"I was just thinking of calling Harbour and asking her how I can help her prepare for her journey to Triton," Lise replied, laughing and clapping her hands.

* * * *

"How's the work proceeding on the cantina, Dingles?" Harbour asked.

"Better than expected, Captain," Dingles replied. "Maggie will have it completed within the timeline we requested."

"I've been stocking the shuttle with the cantina's supplies on return trips," Danny added. "Maggie told me on my last trip that it was the final load."

"Good thing too, Captain," Dingles said. "The coolers and shelves are filled to the brim."

"What's left?" Harbour asked.

"Furniture and bar installation," Dingles replied. "We're expecting a shuttle delivery tomorrow. The foreman said he could have it done in two days."

"And our extra spacers, Dingles?"

"Ready to go, Captain, just waiting for the word."

"Anything else holding us up?"

"Nope, Captain. When the work crew and the delivery shuttle leaves in a few days, we're ready to begin the final transfers of our people and the new crew," Dingles replied.

"Speaking of which, what's the final count of the departing?"

"Everyone who voted against you, Captain ... two hundred and ninety-eight people. Arlene made sure of that," Dingles replied.

"The sooner that woman is off the ship, the happier this place will be," Danny grumped.

"What's that number mean for you, Danny?" Harbour asked.

"These people are carting a lot of baggage, Captain. I estimate it'll take ten or eleven shuttle trips. The trouble is that loading and unloading all that gear will triple the usual roundtrip time. I'll need two days to transfer everybody off the *Belle*.

Dingles tipped his cap back on his head to scratch an itch on his forehead. "My concern is that security and stationers will notice the stream of people from Danny's shuttle, Captain, and they'll be doubly curious when they get a look at the loaded carts arriving at the cargo landing platforms of the JOS. There's always the possibility that the commandant will object to what you're intending. He might not have a right to do so, but that won't stop him from interfering with our launch, if he gets enough pressure from topside or downside."

"I don't intend to give the commandant the opportunity, Dingles," Harbour replied. "We'll get the *Belle* underway after Danny completes his fifth run. Didn't you say, Dingles, that one of the spacers you're hiring is a shuttle pilot?"

"Yes, ma'am."

"Good, Dingles. Get him over here now. He'll work with Danny on the transfers. We're going to shorten this process from two days to thirty hours. And once we're underway, security's shuttles won't be able to block us. A ship underway and all that," Harbour said, winking at the men.

"Captain, you've been studying!" Dingles exclaimed.

"We have a great deal of missing documents from the library, but the ones on basic navigation, ships' right-of-way, and so much more are still there. It's made for some educational evenings."

"Whatever the plan, Captain, don't you dare leave me behind," Danny said, with mock seriousness.

"It would never happen, Danny," Harbour replied, laughing, and she sent him a token of her appreciation, as she left.

"I'll never get tired of that," Danny commented.

"It's like a thirsty man getting a drink of water," Dingles added, having benefited from standing next to Danny.

Danny regarded Dingles, and he started chuckling.

"What?" Dingles asked.

"I had a vision of the future. I saw a bunch of us spacers working to please Harbour for a touch of her power. When one of the crew was successful, the rest of us would close up on him to share in the reward."

"We would look mighty silly," Dingles agreed. "Makes you wonder what those around Aurelia are experiencing."

"Guess that would depend on the girl's personality. Is she like Harbour or Arlene?"

Dingles shivered at the prospect of a strong empath with a nasty personality. Danny saw the reaction and grimaced in agreement.

32: Sasha

Helena and Sasha shared a cabin aboard the *Belle*, but it wasn't the most convivial arrangement. Helena was content to be free of her imprisonment and to live safe and secure under Harbour's protection, but Sasha wasn't content with much of anything. At least when Sasha was downside, she had a view. She could look out a window and see trees, blooming flowers, and a gardener or household member. In the *Belle*'s cabin, she felt she was transported back to her downside bedroom and stuck staring at four walls.

Sasha had taken to the habit of waiting until her mother fell asleep and then slipping on some thermal clothing to wander the giant colony ship. The first night she'd become lost for nearly a quarter of an hour before she ran into a young tech, who guided her back to the cabin. After that, she was careful to memorize the twists and turns of the corridors during her investigations, so that she could find her own way back.

Tonight, Sasha was venturing into a new area of the ship, a direction she'd seen taken only by older empaths, and her curiosity drove her to explore. A heavy hatch confronted her at the end of a corridor. No door actuator was present, but a manual, wheel-locking mechanism was well worn. The wheel turned easily in her hand and with some effort, Sasha was able to push through the hatch, locking it in the open position.

The short corridor was lined with cabins, which had well-appointed doors. It was a superior area of the ship, which intrigued Sasha. Pausing to regard the first cabin door, a voice called out to Sasha, "Child, cease your ranting."

Sasha triggered the cabin door open and peeked into the salon. A grandmotherly woman sat in a comfortable chair with her comm unit in her hand. "I didn't say anything," Sasha says quietly.

"Who said you spoke, child? Your mind screams anger. Who's been teaching you?"

"Who's been teaching me what?"

"Are your faculties not working, child? I'm asking about your training to control your power, of course."

"Nobody, yet. I only arrived here from downside."

"Ah, you would be the rescued child, Sasha."

"Uh-huh, who are you?"

"I'm the previous Harbour. Now I'm called by my original name, Lindsey Jabrook. You weren't warned this was a restricted section of the ship?"

"Uh-uh, why's that?"

"Because people like me can't stand loud children."

Sasha laughed, thinking Lindsey was teasing her.

Regardless, Lindsey was relieved to sense a lessening of the bombardment of the young girl's ever-present animus.

"Seriously, why can't people come here?" Sasha asked, taking a seat on Lindsey's couch.

"If you're going to invite yourself to visit, child, the least you can do is close the door behind you."

"Sorry," Sasha replied, popping up to close the cabin door and regaining her seat. She adopted the same position favored by her sister.

Lindsey was aware that the more she engaged Sasha, the quicker the youngster gained control of her power, which was considerable, if Lindsey could detect Sasha's broadcast through the cabin door.

Lindsey educated Sasha on the empaths' ugly end-of-life sentence. She explained that, at some point, the elderly empaths lost the ability to prevent the emotions of others from reaching their minds. The only answer appeared to be isolation and to be visited by only the most mature empaths, who had firm control over their powers.

Sasha listened intently to the story, and Lindsey expected an outburst of tears or a bitter denial that she would end that way. Instead, Sasha regarded Lindsey with a child's sad eyes. "Then you're in your own prison."

"I would say that's true."

"I'm sorry for you. Prison sucks."

Lindsey broke out in laughter. It felt good. She couldn't remember the last time she was entertained by a guest and by a child, at that. "Yes, my dear, it does."

"Can't you fix what's wrong with you?"

"No, Sasha. We' haven't found any means of protecting the older empaths from the feelings of others, especially angry, young children."

Sasha grinned at the jab. Much of Lindsey's style reminded her of Aurelia, when her sister would redirect her attention away from Sasha's resentment of their imprisonment.

"Maybe I can help," Sasha said. "I'm really strong. I know that, because I scare people."

"Your offer is appreciated, Sasha, but I'm unsure how you could do that."

Before Sasha could reply, the cabin door opened. "Lindsey, I found the hatch blocked open, and I was checking to make sure everyone was okay," Nadine said, before she noticed Sasha seated on the couch.

Nadine was about to reprimand Sasha when Lindsey quickly intervened. "Nadine, please join us. Sasha and I are having a lovely conversation."

Caught off guard, Nadine took a seat next to Sasha, as the girl slid over, flashing a bright smile. So much of the rancor Nadine had sensed from the child was gone. How that had happened in the presence of the retired Harbour was the first question in her mind.

"Nadine, I was explaining to Sasha the predicament of elderly empaths, and she kindly offered to help me."

"Did she?" Nadine replied. "That's generous of you, Sasha." Nadine was uncertain how the child could help, but she kept the thought to herself, but, unfortunately, not her emotions, although she thought she had.

Sasha eyed Nadine. "You don't think I can do it," Sasha accused, her power spinning up.

Alarmed, Nadine was about to object, even though she knew Sasha had perceived the truth.

"I can show you. My sister, Aurelia, and I played this game all the time." Sasha bounced off the couch, kneeled beside Lindsey's chair, and took her hand. "Now, Nadine, send us your strongest emotions, light or dark, it doesn't matter."

"Sasha, please, I don't want to hurt my friend. Lindsey's sensitivity is wide open," Nadine pleaded.

"You won't hurt us," Sasha declared, jutting her chin out. As insurance, she cupped Lindsey's hand with both of hers.

"I'm interested in this experiment, Nadine. You have my permission to proceed as Sasha directs," Lindsey said. She hadn't had this much entertainment in years and was prepared to accept a hefty dose of pain to encourage it to continue. "Ready, Sasha?"

Sasha nodded firmly, closed her eyes, and projected her power with all her might.

Nadine chose to project her love for her long-time friend and sent it with a significant amount of power, hoping the warm feelings would mitigate the discomfort.

Lindsey felt enveloped in a child's sense of humor. It was a giddy sensation, and it was all-encompassing. She couldn't help but laugh, and she heard Sasha's giggles. Her mind was flooded with colors that accompanied the sensations, and she chose to embrace them, feeling as if she could strip off her clothes and dive into them. But, the wonderful input soon faded.

Nadine stared in awe at the two, one elderly and one young. They were grinning at each other like idiots. "Didn't you feel what I sent?" Nadine asked.

"Not a thing, Nadine," Lindsey replied, and she held out her arms to Sasha, who crawled into her lap. Lindsey hugged her and kissed the top of her hair.

"How did you do that?" Nadine asked.

"You didn't think I could," Sasha challenged.

"You're right. I was wrong, and I apologize."

Sasha leaned into Lindsey's embrace, feeling some of the comfort that Aurelia had always offered her. "It's a game my sister and I played. I would protect mother, while Aurelia tried to get through to her with an emotion. Aurelia always won, but lately it took her longer and longer to do it, and she said she had to use more of her power each time. One of these days, I'll be as strong as her."

"How long can you protect someone?" Nadine asked.

"Depends," Sasha answered simply. "If it was against you, maybe I could last a half hour. Against weaker sensitives, I could protect Lindsey all day."

"Sasha, how would you compare my power to Aurelia's?" Nadine asked.

"Are you asking about just now or about your whole power?"

"Sasha, you could tell that Nadine wasn't using her entire capability?" Lindsey asked.

"Sure, can't we all do that?" Sasha asked, looking up at Lindsey.

"No, we can't," Lindsey replied, chuckling. She glanced across at Nadine, who was working hard to control her reactions. "Sasha, if Nadine had used everything she had, how would it compare to Aurelia?"

"She's much weaker," Sasha replied. "Sorry," she added, tweaking her mouth in apology at Nadine, who waved a hand in dismissal. "But that's not all."

"What's not all?" Lindsey prodded gently.

"There's no ... I don't know ... there's no twisting in her sending?"

"What's a twisting, Sasha?" Nadine asked.

"Aurelia's projections can be sneaky, getting behind my shields before I know it. Her power has these funny twists in them, and she can vary them, depending on what she wants to do."

"Does Aurelia tell you that you can do this?"

"No," Sasha replied, giggling. "My sister tells me I'm a rock. I smash through everything. Pure power she says." At the mention of her sister's name, this time, she thought about her and grew sad. "I miss her," she said, and then yawned deeply.

"I think its bedtime for one young lady," Lindsey said.

"Okay," Sasha replied, too comfortable to move.

"Come, Sasha, I'll walk you back to your cabin," Nadine said, offering her a hand up.

Sasha nodded sleepily, accepted the hand, and followed Nadine to the door, where she stopped. "Can I come again? I promise not to be an angry child."

"Anytime you wish," Lindsey replied, waving.

* * * *

"Am I interrupting anything?" Nadine asked. The door to Harbour's cabin was open, and she heard Harbour and Yasmin chatting.

"Nothing critical, Nadine. Join us," Harbour replied.

"I wanted to update you two on an interesting conversation I had with Sasha in the early hours of this morning," Nadine said.

"Early hours?" Yasmin asked.

"Yes, I've felt our disgruntled child passing by my cabin more than once in the midnight hours," Harbour explained.

"This morning I found Sasha in conversation with Lindsey," Nadine replied.

"Oh, for the love —" Yasmin started to say, but Nadine interrupted her. "No, no, the two of them were having a nice chat, and Sasha was calm, believe it or not."

"What were they discussing?" Harbour asked, leaning forward in her chair, suddenly curious about the meeting.

"Apparently, Sasha wanted to help Lindsey, after learning of her disability."

Yasmin wanted to laugh at the absurdity of the idea, but one look at Nadine's face told her more had transpired than was yet told.

"And?" Harbour asked, prompting Nadine to continue.

Nadine briefly explained what had happened during Sasha's demonstration.

"And this was a game she and her sister played?" Yasmin asked.

"Repeatedly, but wait, this gets better," Nadine replied. "Lindsey asked Sasha to compare the amount of power I used, against what Aurelia applied, and Sasha responded with a question about the power I used or the power I was capable of using."

"The child can sense empath depth," Harbour said softly, leaning back in her chair to think.

"What did Sasha say?" Yasmin asked.

Nadine's face reflected her unhappiness having to relay this next point. "Apparently, I fall short of her sister's power, even at my full capability, plus I'm not twisty."

"You're not what?" Yasmin asked.

"By the way, you're not either," Nadine replied, with a little satisfaction.

"I don't know if that's a good or bad thing," Yasmin said. "Did she explain that?"

"Not in a way I could understand," Nadine said.

"Did she compare Harbour and me to Aurelia?" Yasmin asked Nadine.

"Oh, yes, she's a regular chatterbox, once you get her going. You're similar to me and, as I said, you're not twisty."

"And Harbour?"

"This I found curious. Sasha said she couldn't tell. She said that Harbour's protection was too strong, and that she couldn't get a full read on her power."

"How did the meeting end with Lindsay?" Harbour asked, with concern.

"Sasha nicely asked if she could return, and Lindsey was all too happy to say yes. You should have seen Lindsey's face when Sasha protected her. It was euphoric, and the two of them were giddy afterwards."

When Nadine's audience appeared lost in their thoughts, she excused herself, citing that she had work to do, and quietly left, closing the cabin door behind her.

* * * *

The time to launch the *Belle* was down to the final two days. Danny, working with a crew of spacers, started transferring the residents who wished to leave to the JOS. As predicted, the going was slow. The passengers, mostly artisans, had significant amounts of baggage and equipment. The spacers helped the work to go smoothly, as they fetched carts at the JOS, offloaded the gear, and wrestled the loaded carts through the transition capsules of the lower ring.

Harbour kept busy aboard the *Belle*, but she decided to collect Sasha and accompany Danny on one of his trips and make a final journey to the JOS to fulfill a list of personal items requested by the empaths and the spacers. Once aboard the space station, Harbour hustled Sasha from vendor to vendor, ordering supplies and requesting they be promptly delivered to the *Belle*'s shuttle. When she finished with her list, she decided to check on how the artisans, whom Danny had delivered that morning, were settling into their cabins, despite knowing she probably wouldn't be welcomed.

Following the guide directions on her comm unit, Harbour took a series of corridors to reach the lower-rent cabins, far off the main promenade, unaware that Sasha had stopped to peer into a shop display.

"Well, well, well, just the person I wanted to see," Corporal McKenzie said, stepping around a corner and confronting Harbour.

"Somehow, I doubt this is a chance meeting, Corporal. What do you want?"

"Some of your time, Harbour. I have questions for you that you're required to answer."

"I don't have the time today, Corporal. Have your superiors call me and make an appointment."

"I'm afraid that won't work. This is a formal security request for you to immediately accompany me to security administration."

"You're overstepping your authority, Corporal. I'm the lawfully elected captain of the *Belle*, as you undoubtedly know."

"Actually, you're not. I checked you out, Celia O'Riley, and you haven't been registered in the commandant's records as captain of anything."

"Out of my way, Corporal, I haven't time for your nonsense," Harbour said, stepping past him. She thought she'd left sufficient room to clear him, but, before she knew it, his shoulder was there, and she bumped into it.

Terrell grinned savagely, having created his provocation. He slammed Harbour against the corridor wall and shoved his shock stick tightly against her throat, cutting off her air.

"Celia O'Riley, a supposed captain, resisting a security officer's lawful order. That's bad form," Terrell hissed, spittle spraying Harbour's chin. "I'm arresting you for interfering with a security officer's duty."

There was nothing Harbour could say. The shock stick was depressing her windpipe, and she was becoming dizzy from lack of air.

"And don't try any mind tricks either. If I feel anything, you'll get the business end of this stick, and I'll be happy to drag you to security confinement."

As was his style, Corporal McKenzie in his zealousness went too far. Harbour's eyes turned up in her head, and she slid to the floor. He reached for his comm unit to call for backup, but he never got that far.

Slowly, Harbour returned to consciousness, feeling taps on her cheeks and a flood of anxieties. As quickly as she could, she closed off her sensitivity. She focused on Danny's anxious face. "What happened?" she attempted to ask, but she only managed to cough, and Danny offered her a water flask. She sipped at it, and the pain of swallowing had her gingerly touching her throat.

"You need to be careful, Captain," Danny said. "You've got an awful bruise on your neck. Shock stick I take it."

"Terror's work," Harbour managed to choke out. "Thanks for chasing him away."

"About that, Captain, Terror's still here."

Danny, who had been kneeling in front of Harbour, crabbed to the side. He'd been deliberately blocking her view of Terrell. The man was on his rear end, wedged against a corner, his shock stick extended in front of him. He was furtively waving it at Sasha, his eyes wild with fear.

Sasha faced Terrell, arms extended to her sides, and her small fists balled in fury.

Harbour eased her mental blocks, and a massive wall of loathing and fear struck her. She clamped the blocks down to an absolute minimum. Danny was experiencing the onslaught and was having difficulty coping. Fortunately, Sasha had focused her attentions toward the corporal, as best she could.

"Sasha, enough," Harbour coughed out. "Come here." She felt Sasha's anger dissipate, replaced by a burst of relief.

Sasha ran to Harbour, knelt, and clung to her, sobbing. "I didn't mean to hit him that hard, Harbour," She cried out. "Honest I didn't, but I got scared when I saw you drop to the floor. I thought he killed you, and I was mad."

"He's been like that since I arrived a few minutes ago, Captain," Danny said. "It's fortunate that I was on my way to the artisans' quarters too. I noticed your comm location was fixed in this corridor and decided to come this way, in case you needed any help. Do you want to get Terror some assistance before we go?"

"I'd rather kick him in his private parts."

"Maybe we should just leave, Captain."

"Agreed, help me up, Danny," Harbour said, untangling Sasha, and struggling to stand. She tried to take a deep breath, but her throat tightened in rebellion. She leaned against the wall, waiting for her airway to ease. Danny offered her more water, and she sipped slowly.

"I think no talking is best until we get you to medical, Captain."

"No medical," Harbour whispered. "To the shuttle ... that's an order."

"Aye, aye, Captain."

Harbour threw an arm over Danny's shoulder to steady her steps, and Sasha ducked under the other arm, offering what assistance she could. The three of them made their way to the main concourse, but, before entering, Harbour halted. She released their support and straightened her posture.

"Um, Captain," Danny said, gesturing toward Harbour's head.

"Men," Sasha said, with disgust, as if she was a mature woman. She stepped behind Harbour, removed the hair clip, smoothed Harbour's luxurious ponytail, and reattached it.

 Harbour nodded her approval to Sasha and stepped out into the main corridor, as steadily as she could manage. Danny and Sasha fell in beside her. Harbour made it the entire way to the shuttle without aid. But her progress was punctuated by stationers who stared at her throat. Harbour could imagine the bruise that must be forming. In that respect, she was wrong. A glance in a mirror, once aboard the shuttle, showed the damage to be more extensive than she had thought.

"He could have killed you, Captain," Danny commented, when he saw Harbour checking her throat in the hand mirror.

"Everyone aboard, Danny?"

"The crew is accounted for, Captain. All passengers and their freight have been offloaded. A few things on your list haven't arrived yet. Here's your comm unit that you dropped."

"Launch the shuttle, Danny. We've got to get back to the *Belle*."

Harbour waited until she felt the shuttle detach from the JOS terminal arm, before she picked up her comm unit and called Major Finian.

"Captain Harbour, you have to speak up. I can't understand you. Are you in trouble?"

Dingles, who'd been keeping a worried eye on Harbour, released his seat belt and smoothly floated over the top of his seat to sit beside her. He reached out his hand for the comm unit, which Harbour gratefully handed over.

"Major Finian, this is First Mate Mitch Bassiter. The captain's been injured. A shock stick from Corporal McKenzie nearly crushed her throat."

"What actions on the captain's part instigated the corporal's reaction?" Liam asked. He hated asking the question, especially of Harbour, but he knew that was the first thing Emerson would demand of him.

Dingles saw Harbour's eyes blaze, and he gently blocked her hand from reaching for the comm unit. "For the record, Major Finian, I'll be advising the captain to register a complaint with the Review Board against Corporal McKenzie for violating the Captain's Articles."

Liam smiled to himself. The commandant's darling might have crossed a line, for once, that he couldn't defend. "That would be the captain's right. However, I must have the captain file a report with me. Where are you now?"

"We're aboard our shuttle en route to the *Belle*. The captain is in no shape to speak with anyone now, Major. She's listening and indicating that when she can talk, she'll give you her report. One moment, Major."

Dingles leaned his ear close to Harbour's mouth. The bruising was swelling her throat, and he could barely hear her whisper.

"Major Finian, I'm informing you that you need to send a medical team to collect Corporal McKenzie. I've just sent you the coordinates from Harbour's comm unit where the attack took place."

"How badly is he injured?"

"Physically, not at all, but his mental condition will need some help."

"Oh ... ohhh," Liam exclaimed, understanding how Harbour had defended herself.

"Shuttle out, Captain," Dingles said, cutting the call.

Harbour reached for the comm unit, but Dingles frowned at her and kept it. He did make one more call from her device.

In the hiring process, Dingles had sought out two retired spacers, who had received emergency medical training. They were considered too old to compete with the younger personnel aboard the JOS, who were required to traverse the station, the terminal arms, and docked ships, offering their emergency services. However, the thought of serving again, as spacers aboard the colony ship, tickled the two of them pink, and they signed on.

33: Launch

By the time the *Belle*'s shuttle set down in the colony ship's bay, the swelling in Harbour's throat had reached a critical stage, cutting off her airway.

Herbert McKinley and Stacey Young, the two, newly hired, medical spacers, were alerted by Dingles and standing by. The moment the bay was equalized, they dashed from the airlock and raced to board the shuttle.

Harbour's seat was reclined in preparation for the medical team, and, immediately, Stacey sedated Harbour so that they could work on her without Harbour reacting to their services and transmitting her fears. Then Stacey gently tilted Harbour's head back, and Herbert performed a tracheal intubation.

Placing the medical device between Harbour's teeth, he activated the mechanism, which extruded a slender tube that wound its way down the restricted airway. When the tube reached the end of its extension, Herbert increased the pressure in the tiny cavity, which existed between the device's dual walls. In response, the tube unwound, expanding its diameter. He slowly dialed up the tube's size, monitoring the resistance it encountered, until Harbour was breathing easier.

When the medical team was ready, the spacers transported Harbour to the newly updated medical facilities.

Dingles waited outside medical with Nadine, Yasmin, Sasha, and Helena for several hours. Eventually, the two spacers came out and updated them on Harbour's condition.

"Dingles, I don't mean to be critical, but you should have taken the captain to JOS medical. They're better prepared to deal with this type of trauma," Herbert said.

"Captain's orders ... transport her to the *Belle*."

"Still, Dingles, an accident like this ..."

"It wasn't an accident," Sasha declared, cutting Herbert off. Her anger flared and shot through every mind nearby.

"Sasha, control," Helena said immediately, directing her daughter to curtail her transmission.

"Sorry, there wasn't time to update you," Dingles explained. "The captain was attacked by Corporal McKenzie. That was his shock stick that did the damage."

"The corporal's up to his neck in it now," Stacey declared. "I hope you registered a complaint with Major Finian."

"I'll advise the captain to report the corporal to the Review Board for transgressing against the Captain's Articles.

"Even better," Herbert said approvingly.

"But was he arrested?" Stacey asked.

"No need for that. According to Danny, the corporal is in no state to do anything. Sasha saw to that."

While everyone stared at Sasha with expressions ranging from awe to concern, Sasha lifted her chin defiantly. She didn't regret her actions.

Dingles walked away from the facilities with Harbour's comm unit. The medical team, following spacer procedures for an incapacitated captain, had used Harbour's thumb to unlock the device and changed its settings to remain open.

When Harbour's device chimed, Dingles glanced at the caller ID. It was Commandant Strattleford. With a sigh, Dingles accepted the call.

"First Mate Mitch Bassiter, here, Commandant."

"I'm calling for Harbour," Emerson said hotly. Major Finian was in his office, and Emerson was intent on demonstrating to his subordinate how the incident against Corporal McKenzie should have been handled.

"Are you speaking of my captain, Commandant? If so, I respectfully request that you refer to her as such."

"Fine. Let me speak to your captain."

"I can't, Commandant. The captain is under sedation. She was nearly asphyxiated from the damage done to her throat from Terror's shock stick."

"I'll thank you to refer to the corporal properly."

"I've already had the pleasure of being on the nasty end of the corporal's brand of justice, Commandant, if you'll recall. I believe I can speak from experience about that little sociopath. And, because you've done nothing but protect him, despite the numerous complaints, I'll be advising the captain to have the Review Board prosecute Corporal McKenzie under the Captain's Articles. I'm sure that the Board will take a different view than you of security officers who attack standing captains. Now, is there anything I can help you with, Commandant?"

"No, Mr. Bassiter."

"Well, Commandant, I'll be sure to let Captain Harbour know that you called and didn't ask about her condition after your officer's vicious and unprovoked assault. Good day, sir." Dingles retracted the comm screen. He heard a throat·clear, and turned his head. The four empaths stood behind him. "Did you ladies need something?" he asked, still in a huff over the commandant's call.

"No, no," Nadine replied.

The adults walked past him, and Sasha threw him a huge grin. He was inundated by waves of appreciation, as they passed, and Sasha's ministrations painted a smile on his face that lasted for the next half hour.

Dingles' first call to the crew announced the captain's condition and that he was assuming command. "Make no mistake, spacers, we'll be launching this big lady as scheduled, if not before. Lend support to Danny to expedite the remaining residents who must still leave the ship."

Throughout the rest of the day and into the night, crews loaded and unloaded passengers and their belongings. Word spread about Harbour's attack and about Sasha's retaliation on a security officer. It left many residents, those leaving and those staying, uncertain as to the better place to be, aboard the *Belle* or the JOS, when the authorities got involved.

At 06:30 hours the following morning, Dingles ordered engineering to provide thrust to the primary engines and nodded to the newly hired pilot seated next to him, who activated the plot Dingles had locked into the navigation computer. For an hour, everyone held their collective breath, as the ship got underway. Soon afterward, the empaths perceived a collective sigh from the individuals aboard.

Dingles stayed in touch with Danny, during the shuttle's every trip. The two were counting down the number of passengers still to haul and the time to accomplish the process. For Danny, the trips after the *Belle*'s launch got shorter and shorter. At its closest point, the colony ship would pass within 30 kilometers of the JOS, far closer than its usual station at 125 kilometers.

As Dingles expected, Harbour's comm unit chimed about the time the *Belle* had moved far enough to be noticed by JOS Control.

"Are you experiencing engine problems, Captain Harbour?" a voice said, when Dingles accepted the call.

"Negative, JOS Control. This is Acting Captain Mitch Bassiter. We're moving the *Honora Belle*, letting the old lady stretch her legs, as it were."

"You're kidding," the voice replied. "I mean, where are you going?"

"It's a big universe out there. We haven't made up our minds yet, but there's time to figure that out. Have a good day, Control," Dingles replied, and shut down the call. He shared grins and chuckles with the crew on the *Belle*'s bridge. Retired spacers all, they were once again doing what they loved, getting their ship underway, and heading into the unknown.

Hours after the primary engines' initial thrust, the colony ship approached its shortest distance to the JOS. Dingles would have laughed if he knew the patrons of the Starlight halted the enjoyment of their breakfasts, stunned to watch the *Belle* pass their immense plate windows.

"Dingles, Danny here."

Dingles swapped Harbour's comm unit for his. "Go, Danny."

"I'm on my way back to you, but I've one more run to make. Arlene had some special last-minute requests, and I thought it better to satisfy them rather than have her make a fuss."

"Good thinking on that point."

"It'll take me about two and a half hours to move the last twelve residents, longer if I take time to refuel. I need a vector and intercept point for the *Belle* to determine if I can get by without taking the time to top off my tanks."

"One minute, Danny, let me get to a monitor and run some calculations." Dingles accessed the monitor in his cabin. It was closest. He linked his comm unit into the display, pulled up the *Belle*'s navigation plot, marked her present position, and projected a series of points along the path at two, two and a half, and three hours. "I sent the plot and three time marks to your comm unit, Danny."

"I've got them. Oh, I forgot how slowly that ship accelerates. I'll have no trouble catching you, unless I get another odd request."

"Negative on that, Danny. Don't accept any unusual requests. They go as they signed up or they don't go. It's not like I can hit the brakes on this ship, and I have my reasons for not bringing the *Belle* to rest. Understood?"

"Aye, Captain," Danny replied.

Dingles closed the comm unit. "Hmm, imagine that ... Captain Dingles," he whispered, in the privacy of his cabin.

Dingles' final incoming call on Harbour's comm unit, before the *Belle* passed the station, originated from the commandant again. Dingles sighed and accepted the call.

"Acting Captain Bassiter here, Commandant."

"I'm sending Major Finian in a shuttle to collect Harbour, if she's able to travel, and, if not, he's ordered to collect her statement before he leaves the ship."

"Captain Harbour," Dingles said forcefully, "is still in medical and unable to communicate."

"Major Finian will need to confirm that for himself."

"If you're intent on having the captain land aboard this ship and wait until Captain Harbour is able to speak, does he intend to ride along with us for the duration?"

"I'm ordering you to halt your ship, while we settle this matter."

"One moment, Commandant," Dingles replied. He made a second call, connecting with Henry Stamerson, head of the Review Board. "Captain Stamerson, you're joining a conversation with Commandant Strattleford and me. I'm Mitch Bassiter, acting captain of the *Belle*, while Captain Harbour is indisposed."

"I heard of Captain Harbour's attack. Bad business that. Please give her my wishes for a speedy recovery."

"I'll do that, Captain Stamerson," Dingles replied, and patched the two calls together.

"Thank you for your time, Captain Stamerson," Dingles said. "There seems to be a point that needs clarifying, and because you're knowledgeable about the Captain's Articles, I'm seeking your opinion."

"Pleased to help, Captain, if I can."

"Captain Stamerson, the commandant is ordering the *Belle*, which is underway, to halt so that he can have Major Finian board the ship and speak with Captain Harbour once she recovers her voice."

"Commandant, is Captain Harbour considered a fugitive from justice? In other words, have you issued a warrant for her arrest?"

"Not at this time, Captain. We're simply trying to ascertain the details of the event that transpired aboard the JOS."

"I see, Commandant. Well, the Articles are clear. The *Belle* is not docked at the JOS and is underway, and you have no lawful means of directing the acting captain to defer to your requests. He's free to do as he chooses."

"Thank you for your advice, Captain Stamerson," Dingles said.

"Glad to be of service," Henry said, closing the call. "Spacers," he murmured, "I do love them."

"I believe you have your answer, Commandant. Although, I could have told you the same thing, I thought it better that you hear it from an experienced captain. I think you should study up on the Articles. I have a feeling that you'll need to know them by heart in the future. A good day to you, sir," Dingles said, closing the call.

* * * *

Sergeant Cecilia Lindstrom received a message from the acting captain of the *Belle* minutes before she was due to take a lunch break. But, after reading the request, Cecilia decided to enter the lengthy information immediately, chuckling as she did.

Since the arrest and conviction of Markos and Giorgio, in which she played a significant role, Cecilia had detected a slowly growing undercurrent of dissatisfaction against the status quo. The *Belle,* suddenly underway, seemed to herald a new level of revolt, and Cecilia experienced a thrill, as she posted the message, feeling she was breathing life into a rebellion.

The Miners' Pit was packed full for lunch, which was the usual case. On the wall opposite the bar, hung the Pit's largest monitor, which displayed something as seemingly mundane as the Ships List. That was, of course, if you weren't a spacer. Knowing a ship's disposition and haul kept the spacers connected, especially for the retirees.

"Look," yelled a patron, pointing to the Ships List.

As the data scrolled up on the monitor, the Ships List displayed a new entry. As a new addition to the roll, the *Honora Belle* received premier status by an enumeration of its stats. The first line after the ship's name listed Captain Harbour, and the spacers cheered loudly, but the cantina quieted when Mitch Bassiter was named first mate.

"It's Dingles, you fools!" Maggie yelled, and the crowd broke out into raucous applause and whistles.

Line after line detailed the ship's capacities, engine types, count of crew and passengers, and a never-seen-before line totaling the number of empaths aboard.

The monitor continued to scroll data, revealing information about the colony ship, and the room quieted. The spacers waited for the last piece of information. It would inform them of the ship's destination. Finally, it rolled into view. There was one word: Triton.

The stunned silence lasted for about three seconds. Then the entire room erupted in celebration. Drinks were spilt and food plates hit the floor, as spacers thumped one another's backs and hugged. For once, Maggie didn't care about the mess, and she kissed more than one craggy face.

* * * *

The *Belle* left the JOS behind and headed on an interception course for Triton. All departments reported to Dingles that performance was within specifications, and Danny had landed aboard the ship, catching it about 260 kilometers out from the JOS. Dingles felt he'd cleared every obstacle. He checked in on Harbour, only to receive the same message he'd received the hour before and the hour before that.

In his cabin, Dingles placed his last call before he grabbed a meal break with many of the department heads.

"Dingles calling the *Spryte* for Captain Cinders."

"Ituau here, Dingles. The captain's not available. He's on some downtime. Seems to need more sleep lately after having been rescued from the alien installation."

"What did you bunch of retread spacers do? Leave him downside when you launched the shuttle?" Dingles asked, laughing.

"It started when a tech activated the site and trapped the captain and some crew inside an alien dome. Those aliens know how to make a really pretty field. Impenetrable too! Wish we could do something like that."

"I'm waiting for the part where you tell me you're joking, Ituau."

"I wish I were, Dingles. The whole thing scared me to death. I thought we'd lost the captain and some good friends. We took half a day getting rescue resources to them. And, you won't believe this. The rescue team finds our people asleep on this pristine metal deck, all the dust blown away. Their vac suits were off, Dingles. They were breathing air inside this blue energy field."

Ituau waited for a comment from Dingles. When she heard nothing, she added, "Yeah, that's about how I felt when I got the word."

"Why and how would the alien installation provide a mixture of gases that suited humans?"

"Oh, trust me, Dingles, the story gets much weirder than that. But, before we get too far off track, why isn't Captain Harbour making this call?"

"The captain has been injured, and she's sedated in medical, while she recovers."

"Is she going to be okay?"

"She has a badly bruised throat, courtesy of Terror."

Ituau swore and said, "I should have killed that little piece of effluent when ..."

"When you gave him his comeuppance for beating on me?"

"I'm not admitting to anything," Ituau said coolly.

"You don't have to, Ituau, but thanks anyway."

"I hate to hear that Terror has added another spacer's beating to his harness."

"I think Terror's reign is over, if you'll pardon my pun."

Ituau laughed. "Dingles, you've been hanging out with the smart ones so long, you're starting to talk like them. So why is Terror done for?"

"The corporal put the captain on the deck, but he didn't know little Sasha was coming behind the captain. She's one powerful empath. Sasha got scared, thinking Terror killed the captain."

"Why does this sound familiar, especially since we're talking about sisters?"

"Right, I know. Maybe it's time for normals to be a lot nicer to empaths. They're getting to the point where they can protect themselves. In the corporal's case, word is that he's locked in a medical cell. Seems he prefers it that way. They gave him a soft rod, shaped like his shock stick, and he points it at anyone who enters his cell, and he doesn't speak intelligently anymore, just gibbers."

"Does this mean you're frightened of Sasha?"

"Are you frightened of Aurelia?"

"No, are you kidding?"

"There you go, Ituau. Except for their exceptional capabilities, they're people, just like us. They want to be treated well, like we all do. Just don't make the mistake of abusing them. They don't like that."

"Copy that, Dingles. What's the message for the captain?"

"We've launched the *Belle* and cleared the JOS. We'll be taking up station beside your ships in twenty-six days."

"You do remember how to navigate, Dingles? I wouldn't want you missing Triton and heading for the outer planets."

"Sure, Ituau, I point the ship at something like the *Spryte*, and we drive our ship until we hit what we're aiming at. It's simple."

Ituau broke up. "Looking forward to seeing you again, you old space dog."

"Me too, Ituau, the first drink's on me. I can't wait to hear what happened at the alien site."

"First drink's on you? Yeah, right, like we have alcohol on the captain's ships."

"You don't, Ituau, but we do. You aren't the only one with stories to tell. See you in less than a month. The *Belle* out."

34: Recovery

Sasha's initial days aboard the *Belle,* after Harbour entered medical, were tough for the eleven year old. She blamed herself for dawdling at the storefront to admire the decorative items. *Stupid girl,* she often thought. She found temporary comfort in the arms of her mother, but that soon proved inadequate for her searching mind.

Days after Sasha found emotional equilibrium, she had a conversation with Helena that her mother recognized marked the transition of her daughter from a girl to an independent-minded young woman.

"We're going to see Aurelia," Sasha said, while making the green that Harbour taught her. Helena occasionally consumed one during the day to enjoy Sasha's company, while her daughter drank one, but she didn't care for the mixture, and Sasha could read her mother's distaste. However, Sasha craved the drink, which revitalized her, leading her to make three or four greens for herself every day.

"How do you know that?" Helena asked.

"I can read Harbour when we talk about Aurelia. She's good at protecting her emotions, but, when we talk about Captain Cinders, her control slips. Then when I mention Aurelia, I get more impressions. I think Aurelia is with Captain Cinders, which means she's on Triton."

"Does Harbour know that you can pick up on her emotions when she relaxes with you?"

"We've never talked about it, but I think she knows and doesn't care. I think we both realize that one day I'll be as strong as her, maybe stronger."

Helena did her best to hide her worry from her daughter, but Sasha's next statement showed that she'd failed.

"Don't worry, mother. Aurelia and I will be okay. I met Captain Cinders, who I believe is protecting Aurelia, and Harbour is protecting us. No one is ever going to hurt us again."

When Sasha finished her drink, she rinsed her glass, kissed her mother on the forehead, and left the cabin. She was headed for Lindsey's cabin. Before Sasha approached the hatch, she stopped, relaxed, and calmed herself. The object of the exercise was to curtail every ounce of emotional leakage. When Sasha thought she had control, she walked slowly to Lindsey's cabin door and raised her small fist to tap on the door.

"Come in, Sasha," came Lindsey's voice from inside.

"Again?" Sasha asked, as she entered. She acted annoyed, but she was glowing with love for the woman she'd adopted as her grandmother, and Lindsey basked in the feeling.

"You did well, child. I didn't pick you up until you were at the door."

"And what did you receive?"

"Excitement."

"And why would I be excited to visit an old woman."

"I have no idea. Why would you?"

Sasha didn't respond. Instead, she walked into the tiny kitchen, wrapped her arms around Lindsey's waist, and held her tight. Lindsey laid her chin on top of Sasha's luxuriant head of hair. The two held each other and communed as only empaths could.

Days earlier, a breakthrough came in Sasha and Lindsey's relationship. It was a tumultuous day for Sasha, who was upset about her failure to take action earlier to help Harbour, but Lindsey, who was struggling with Sasha's emotional power, suspected there was a different reason for the girl's unhappiness.

"I can imagine it's a great weight to carry, knowing that you hurt someone," Lindsey said. She knew her words had struck at the heart of Sasha's problem when the girl's face and emotional broadcast went flat.

"I never said that. The corporal deserved what he got."

"I didn't say it wasn't right to protect Captain Harbour. I said that hurting someone can weigh on our conscience."

Once again, Sasha's emotional signals died out. She was seated on the couch with her legs folded under her. Time passed for the two, while Sasha ruminated on what Lindsey had said. Minutes later, tears blurred Sasha's eyes, brimmed over the lower lids, and streaked down her face.

Lindsey hurried to the couch and folded the child in her arms. Sasha cried her heart out to Lindsey that day.

A tapping at the door, interrupted Lindsey and Sasha's hug in the kitchen. "Yasmin and Nadine today," Sasha said, grinning.

"Come in, you two," Lindsey called out.

"Well done, scamp," Yasmin said, entering the door first and acknowledging that it was Sasha who had identified them, despite their efforts to shut all emotional transmissions down.

"Yeah, well, Lindsey caught me today," Sasha admitted ruefully.

"It'll come with practice, child," Nadine cautioned. "You'll get there one day, probably very soon."

"Do you two think that if you gang up on me you can get through to Lindsey?" Sasha asked defiantly.

"We thought it would be an interesting experiment," Yasmin replied, "if everyone agrees."

Sasha looked expectantly at Lindsey, who could feel the girl's power coiling.

"We accept the challenge," Lindsey said.

"Yes!" Sasha exclaimed, rubbing her hands together.

Yasmin and Nadine sat on the couch and held hands. The touch allowed the two empaths to integrate the emotions they wanted to transmit. Lindsey took her seat in her reading chair, and Sasha sat at her feet and tucked her legs crosswise. Lindsey placed her hands on Sasha's shoulders, and, in turn, Sasha reached up and covered Lindsey's with hers.

"Ready?" Yasmin asked.

Lindsey responded for both of them. Sasha had dropped into a deep state of concentration, providing a strong emotional connection with Lindsey.

＊ ＊ ＊ ＊

Herbert and Stacey consulted with Nadine and Yasmin, concerning Harbour's progress.

"It's been eight days," Herbert said. "We removed the intubating tube two days ago. The swelling is greatly reduced, and the airway is recovering."

"What's the question, Herbert?" Nadine asked. "Is she well enough to be woken?"

"The issue is: What will Captain Harbour do once she's awake?" Stacey asked.

"What do you mean? She'll resume her duties, of course," Yasmin replied.

"See, that's the problem," said Herbert. "We can wake her now, if she'll refrain from using her voice for another six or seven days, including no whispering."

The two empaths laughed, as if they shared a secret. "Keep her under, until she's well enough to use her voice," Nadine replied.

"We'll inform Captain Bassiter of what we've recommended to you," Yasmin added, as the two empaths exited the medical facilities continuing to laugh.

It was another six days before Herbert and Stacey considered Harbour's throat sufficiently healed to wake her. However, they informed Dingles and Nadine first.

Harbour swam up from a murky dream, involving aliens, Jessie, and Sasha. In her dream, she was desperate to don a vac suit and had no idea how to do it. Time was running out, and she was failing to make it to safety. Worse, without a vac suit, she was unable to help the others, who desperately needed her.

"Ugh," Harbour muttered, commenting on her dream, as she achieved full consciousness.

"Sip slowly, Captain," Stacey said, placing a water bottle tube at Harbour's lips.

Harbour sucked on the tube until the aching dryness in her throat passed. Her eyes focused on Dingles, hovering over Stacey's shoulder. She opened her mouth to speak, but Dingles held a hand up in protest.

"Please, Captain, the medics want you to take it easy with the use of your throat for a couple of days. I can anticipate many of your questions. How about you let me report, and when I run out of words, if I haven't covered everything to your satisfaction, you can ask your questions, okay?"

Harbour nodded gratefully. Nadine slipped out of the facilities, and Dingles settled into a comfortable chair that Herbert had provided. The first mate started with the events immediately after their departure from the JOS and Terror's attack and Harbour's emergency medical condition. He detailed the *Belle*'s successful launch, and the attempted interventions of the commandant, which were effectively repulsed with Captain Stamerson's help. Harbour smiled at that one.

Dingles ensured his report contained minutiae, which lengthened the time it took him to give it. He deliberately droned on for nearly an hour before Harbour fell back asleep.

Stacey peeked over at Harbour and winked at Dingles. The old spacer rose, tiptoed out of the facilities, and returned to work, a smile on his face. He'd get a call from one of the medics when Harbour woke. They would feed her, and he'd continue his report. Dingles figured he could draw the process out for the rest of the day, which meant Harbour wouldn't begin questioning him until tomorrow, by which time she'd probably want to leave the medical facilities.

Dingles was right. The next morning, Harbour was anxious to return to her cabin and work, but she found the enforced sleep had weakened her sufficiently that she was too shaky to walk. Having first refused the chair, Harbour experienced the indignity of requesting it, after she had sat heavily back down on her bed.

"Delivery service, ma'am," Dingles said, tipping his cap to Harbour, and grabbing the handles of the chair.

Harbour smiled. "My cabin, sir."

"Yes, ma'am. Right away, ma'am. Would you prefer the direct route or a scenic tour?"

"Dingles ... push."

"Aye, aye, Captain," Dingles replied, but he only made it as far as exiting medical's doors.

Harbour had a waiting committee. Sasha bolted free of Helena's arms and wrapped herself around Harbour.

"Easy, Sasha," Helena cautioned, but said no more when she saw the blissful expression on Harbour's face. Sasha was sending with all her strength, and Harbour was the recipient.

Sasha stood slowly and backed away, sniffling. That was when Harbour spied Lindsey, standing between Yasmin and Nadine.

"How —" Harbour started to ask, but Yasmin shushed her.

"Let me explain, Captain," Lindsey said, smiling. "Sasha and I have been playing a game that she used to enjoy with Helena and Aurelia. For lack of a better name, it's called protect Lindsey. Sasha provides an emotional shield for the two of us, and Nadine and Yasmin attempt to penetrate it."

"Sound dangerous," Harbour whispered.

The five empaths chuckled. "You've never had Sasha defend you," Yasmin said.

"Yes, I have," Harbour replied, holding out her hand to Sasha, who took it and held on to it.

"Yes, you're right, in that respect. Sorry. What I meant was that it was quickly evident to us that neither Nadine nor I could individually get through Sasha's shield to Lindsey. So, we decided to try the both of us."

"And they failed," Sasha added impishly.

"True," Nadine agreed.

"The point of this story, Captain," Lindsey continued, "is that somehow the game is awakening my protective capabilities. They've not fully recovered, but I would estimate I'm, at least, fifty percent. The idea is to keep at the game for another two weeks and see where I'm at, before we try this on another retired empath."

Harbour released Sasha's hand, cupped her neck, and pulled her face to hers. She rubbed noses, whispering, "Well done. I'm proud of you."

Sasha didn't need the words. She could feel Harbour's power flooding through her mind. When Harbour eased the pressure on her neck, Sasha stood. Feeling energized, she announced, "We should try the game with Harbour." But the responding denials from the four women quickly ended that idea.

"I could do it," Sasha replied defiantly.

"Perhaps, child," Lindsey said gently. "But the captain would never try her best in the game. It's her job to protect everyone aboard this ship."

"Oh," Sasha replied. Her child's eyes examined Harbour, but it was a burgeoning, young woman who saw Harbour in a different light.

The group separated, and Dingles pushed Harbour to her cabin. He then helped her into a reading chair.

"You can take that chair back to the med bay, Dingles."

"Pardon me, Captain, but I think I've forgotten the way. I'll find a spacer or resident who might be able to help me with that later," Dingles replied.

"Okay, First Mate Bassiter, have it your way. Make yourself useful then, and make me a cup of green."

"Yuck, I don't know how you women can drink that stuff."

"Stop griping and heed your captain's request," Harbour said, before she coughed.

Dingles hurried to bring Harbour a water bottle, silently cursing himself for engaging Harbour in conversation. Harbour was silent, sipping on the water, while Dingles made her drink. When he delivered it, he sat on the couch.

"I have some more news for you, Captain, that I was saving, but I'm only going to tell it to you if you promise me that you'll send your questions to me via your comm unit."

Harbour thought to argue, but the short coughing spell reminded her of her throat's tenderness, and she nodded.

"Thank you, Captain," Dingles replied, as conciliatory as he could sound. "On this first subject, I don't have much detail, but it's important for you to know. The alien site was activated. Wait, Captain," Dingles said, holding a hand up. "You have to let me tell you what I know before you start with your questions." He held his comm unit up, to indicate the agreed-on method since Harbour had started to speak.

"The site was activated accidentally by a tech, while a team was investigating the site. Whatever the tech did, it created some sort of energy field, a dome of some kind, trapping the team. It took a while, but they got everyone out safely. The lucky thing was that after the energy field came on, air, the kind humans need, was pumped into the dome, enabling the team to survive when their tanks ran dry."

Harbour's eyes beseeched Dingles, and he knew what she wanted to know. "Yes, Captain Cinders was leading the team. I spoke to Ituau, and she says that everyone is okay. That's all I know, Captain, on that subject."

Harbour sat thinking. She was full of questions, but Dingles had already said he didn't have any more information. She rolled her finger in a circle, indicating he was to continue.

"The next bit of news is really exciting. Sorry, I know that last news was too, but this pertains to this ship and you. I found a set of files, copies of critical documents pertaining to the colonists' agreement, the Captain's Articles, and a bunch more. I was right that the first mate took a set to study, after he became the acting captain. Whoever cleaned out the *Belle*'s library made certain to wipe the captain's desk monitor, but they forgot to check on the first mate's private unit."

Harbour pointed two fingers at her eyes and then at Dingles.

"Yes, Captain, I've read some of the pertinent ones, but there are hundreds of files."

When Harbour pointed a finger at her comm unit and furrowed her brows, Dingles replied, "Sorry, Captain. I was following protocol, as the acting captain. We thumbed your comm unit open and locked it that way. I took the liberty of transferring copies of the *Belle* files to your monitor, but I left the original copies where I found them. I figured if no one had discovered them after almost three hundred years, they should be safe there."

Harbour pointed to her temple and then cocked a finger at Dingles, winking.

"Thank you, ma'am," Dingles replied. "I copied some key sections out of a few documents and stitched them together in one, noting the original location of each section. When you feel better, I recommend you start with that."

Harbour nodded in appreciation. Then a wide yawn escaped her mouth, before she could cover it.

"I'll be leaving you to get some rest, Captain. The medical team is on rotation. They'll be standing by to help you with anything you need." Dingles touched his cap and left.

Immediately, Harbour eyed her monitor where it would be easier to peruse documents, but, for the moment, crossing the small cabin seemed a risky maneuver. Instead, she pulled a throw over her lap and thumbed open her comm unit. Sipping on her green, she started with the summary document Dingles had prepared. Each section brought to mind several questions. So, as she finished each section, she jumped to the original document and read it in its entirety.

Two hours later, her green and water bottle long drained, Harbour had finished with the key documents that Dingles set aside for her. Her bladder full, she decided to attempt to use the facilities herself. Standing up produced a lightheadedness that didn't fade. She gave in to the ignominy of crawling on her hands and knees to relieve herself and then crawled back to her chair.

Tucking her legs up on the chair and pulling the throw up to her chin, Harbour fell asleep, thinking of the incredible ramifications of the files Dingles discovered. It was no wonder the Andropov family and others had removed the original documents from the *Belle*'s library, working to eliminate copies.

Topsiders had long believed that what developed as a Pyrean leadership organization was contrary to the original intentions of the colonists, but there had never been any proof. Harbour had read that proof tonight. What the families had started downside directly contravened the colonists' original agreements, signed before they boarded the ship.

Essentially, the *Belle*'s captain was responsible for directing the creation of a civilian government based on North American Confederation (NAC) standards and holding general elections to fill the various starting entities of president, court justices, and representatives. The families had usurped that authority, because the *Belle* had no captain at that time and a replacement was neither awakened nor promoted. The commandant and the Review Board were other anomalies, although Harbour wasn't sure how those positions came about.

Harbour awoke to the sound of light tapping at her door. A quick glance at her comm unit revealed she'd been asleep for about three hours. Whoever was on the other side of the door was evincing some concern.

"Come in," Harbour said, trying not to stress her throat.

The door eased open, and Stacey slipped through with a tray in her hands. "I took the liberty of preparing a meal for you, Captain. Some light things that will go down easy on your throat."

Harbour set her throw aside and braced her hands on the arms.

"No, Captain, you sit there. The tray will rest fine on your lap," Stacey said, and bustled about lifting covers and exposing food and juice.

Harbour's stomach rumbled from the smells. Many of the dishes were her favorites, although she hadn't seen them prepared quite this way. Most were purees.

Stacey plopped down on the couch and began reading on her comm unit.

"You don't have to wait, Stacey. You may return to your duties."

"That's quite all right, ma'am. Don't mind me."

"Stacey, do you require an order from me?" Harbour asked, becoming a little annoyed.

"Begging your pardon, ma'am, but you can order all you want. It won't do you any good. See, under the Captain's Articles, medical might have released you so that you could return to your cabin, but we didn't clear you for active duty. Until we do, Herbert and I are technically your superiors. Now, you go ahead and eat. Then, I'll help you get ready for bed."

Stacey went back to reading, as if they never had the tit-for-tat conversation. Harbour swallowed her annoyance and dug into her food, vowing to do whatever needed to be done to regain her health and be released from the clutches of the medical team.

35: Reunion

Harbour had two more weeks to recover the full use of her voice before the *Belle* closed on Jessie's ships over Triton. It was more than sufficient.

To everyone aboard the colony ship, it was evident that their captain was undergoing subtle changes that, taken in their entirety, marked a profound departure from the Harbour they had known months ago. The captain's conversations with others were more direct, tending toward one-sided communication. She was adopting spacers' terminology and their style of speaking.

Quite telling of the change was Harbour's choice of dress the day she emerged from her cabin, having been released from medical's care. She was wearing the skins that the artisan, Makana, had decorated. When Makana saw Harbour wearing them, she slipped out the two, plain, black skins in Harbour's wardrobe and set about decorating those with new designs. Intentionally, she chose to give the skins more formidable appearances, paying less attention to Harbour's female attributes.

Harbour wasn't completely unaware of the changes in her demeanor. What she did feel was a sense of purpose that she'd never had before. It might have started with the desire to go to the rescue of the spacers trapped at Triton by the quarantine. Certainly, she was still rankled by the proposals of Emerson and Lise that the spacers should remain permanently isolated. But the more Harbour thought about it, the more she realized that a deeper anger drove her. The documents that Dingles had found indicated that the hopes of the original colonists for their future society had been usurped by a few, powerful families, who chose to build a life separate from the majority and proceeded to take for themselves the only foothold on the planet.

Harbour was standing behind Dingles' position on the *Belle*'s bridge, as the colony ship drew close to the final stage of its flight to Triton. Dingles had the navigator position, with Danny seated next to him as pilot. The approach the spacers took to the massive moon could be characterized as slow and careful. It was one thing to boost the colony ship into open space; it was another thing to bring it to a halt short of a moon and two ships. On top of that, the spacers, who were Harbour's crew, had never operated a ship remotely the size of the *Belle.*

"Dingles, recommendation for final position," Harbour said.

"Captain, this is the *Spryte,* and the ship to its left is the *Annie,*" Dingles replied, pointing out two dots displayed on his monitor.

"I want the *Belle* placed equidistant from the two ships. Call it showing equal opportunity for Captain Cinders' spacers."

"Aye, Captain, we don't play favorites. Danny, what's your recommendation on distance."

"The *Spryte* and *Annie* are close ... less than thirty kilometers apart, Dingles. I wouldn't want to bring this big girl any closer than fifty kilometers to those two ships."

"Place us at sixty kilometers from both ships, Dingles ... same orbital height," Harbour ordered.

"Aye, aye, Captain. Danny, let's take the declination position, and let's crawl into place. No sense striking fear into those spacers' hearts, while they watch us hurtle at them."

"Decelerating to thirty kilometers per hour, Dingles. We'll tiptoe into position."

Harbour carefully watched the spacers who occupied positions left and right of Dingles and Danny. Before she was elected captain, she had never visited the *Belle*'s bridge and had no inclination to do so. Afterwards, she'd spent more and more time here. Often, before they launched, only one or two spacers would be present, but she would ply them with questions about their operational procedures and the panels, which controlled those operations.

One subject that those conversations uncovered had nearly scared Harbour to death. Several times, spacers had spoken about decompression drills and vac suit protocols. A conversation with Dingles revealed that there were fewer than sixty vac suits on the colony ship. Most of them were owned by the engineering team and some by the spacers, who made occasional trips outside the ship, supported by small repair vehicles.

* * * *

Jessie, Ituau, and Jeremy Kinsman, the ship's navigator, were observing the approach of the *Belle* from the *Spryte*'s bridge.

"Well, the quarantine clock has just been reset to zero ... six more months," Jeremy remarked.

"But this time, we'll have enough food to go the distance," Ituau riposted. She glanced at Jessie, who was wearing a slight scowl.

"She's changing course, Captain, and coming in dead slow," Jeremy reported. He was on duty at Jessie's request. "Looks like they're being careful, Captain. You can appreciate Dingles' oversight of the crew."

"Let me correct your assumptions, my young spacer," Ituau replied, taking on the lecturing tone she used to correct wayward thinking. "I've had several conversations with Dingles, while Captain Harbour was recovering her voice. According to Dingles, after the captain could return to her cabin and before medical even released her for active duty, she was making the decisions. For instance, look at this," Ituau said, approaching Jeremy's navigation screen and pointing to his plotting vectors.

"According to your navigation summary, Jeremy, you project the *Belle*, which is dropping velocity and on this new vector, will end up about here. Now, ask yourself where would Dingles take up station, if he were in charge of the crew? Would it be equidistant from our ships?"

Jeremy obviously didn't have enough knowledge about the man he replaced, so he glanced at Jessie for help.

"It's about loyalties, Jeremy," Jessie explained. "The *Spryte* was Dingles' last ship. He'd have parked the *Belle* as close to our ship as he could safely manage. But, because of the colony ship's size, it would have required him to take up station on the side of the *Spryte* opposite the *Annie*."

"Okay, I get that Captain Harbour, not Dingles, is making the decisions," Jeremy replied. "Then what does it mean that she's choosing to place the *Belle* equidistant from our two ships? I mean, both of them belong to you, Captain."

"And now you're beginning to think like an officer, Jeremy," Jessie said. "What you've asked requires us to consider how this captain thinks. She might be coming to rescue us, and, then again, she might have something else on her mind, who knows?"

"I like the way you're thinking, Captain ... paranoid as usual," Ituau commented.

"It's called being careful, Ituau, not paranoid," Jessie replied, grinning, and he slapped Ituau's broad back. "Let me know when the *Belle* achieves zero velocity," Jessie added, as he exited the bridge.

"Aye, Captain."

* * * *

"Captain, a word, please," Dingles said, and vacated his seat on the bridge. The *Belle* was in the hands of Danny, and he was minutes from bringing the ship to zero velocity.

Danny might have looked calm, cool, and collected, but Harbour could sense his anxiety and could commiserate. Moving the *Belle* was proving to be an enormous challenge for every one of her crew and more so for her.

Harbour paused behind Danny before joining Dingles. She laid a hand on his shoulder and whispered, "You're doing a great job, pilot," and alleviated his angst with a gentle sending.

"It's a small point, Captain," Dingles said, when Harbour joined him. He had finished explaining the issue when Danny called out, "The big girl is stationary," and was rewarded with a round of applause from the crew.

"Comms, the *Spryte*, please. I need Captain Cinders," Harbour requested.

"Aye, aye, Captain. This is the *Belle* calling the *Spryte*," Birdie said. Beatrice "Birdie" Andrews might be the oldest retired spacer aboard the *Belle,* if she would ever admit her age. When she heard Dingles was hiring, she begged him for the chance to sail again, and he found he couldn't refuse the level of experience and superlative ratings she'd held.

"Ituau here," the first mate of the *Spryte* replied.

Harbour tipped her head at the bridge speakers, and Birdie transferred the call. "Captain Harbour here, Ituau. Is Captain Cinders available?"

"Certainly, Captain. Before I transfer your call, may I say we're more than happy to see you reach us out here at our lovely resort moon, complete with a historic alien structure."

"We aim to please, Ituau," Harbour replied, chuckling. She was feeling completely redeemed for her intention to launch the *Belle* and rescue Jessie and his people.

"Captain Harbour, I must say I have mixed feelings about your arrival," Jessie said, when he took up the call.

"How's that, Captain?"

"While I'm grateful for your rescue, I'm concerned for the safety of you and your people."

"By my estimate, it's been several weeks since you've been released from the dome. What symptoms are your people showing?"

"None."

"Anything eating your ship ... you know, dissolving the seals on vac suits or some such things?"

"Nothing like that," Jessie replied. He picked up the snickers of several people over the comm. "It's polite, Captain, to notify someone if they're on speaker."

"True, Captain, my apologies. My mind has been occupied with a few too many things lately. If it's any consolation, I'm on the bridge with my crew."

"Hello, Captain," Dingles called out, hoping to mollify Jessie.

"Dingles, how are you feeling?" Jessie replied. The joy in the spacer's voice was obvious.

"Except for some aging bones, Captain, I'm one hundred percent."

"That's good to hear, Dingles."

"Captain Cinders, Dingles informs me that our shuttle is too large to land in your bay, and it has no bottom docking collar to accommodate entry via your ship's axis. Would you be so kind as to visit us, Captain?"

Dingles smiled to himself. He'd told Harbour about their shuttle's incompatibility with Jessie's ships to boost the impression of her as a knowledgeable captain. Instead, she opted to give credit where credit was due. He'd thought his life was over, when he was put on station because of his dementia. When he was rescued by Harbour from the creeping darkness of security confinement, he thought he'd received the best life a retired spacer had a right to be offered. That he was wrong in both cases delighted him. He was first mate of the largest ship the Pyreans had, and his new captain was proving to be pure metal.

"I'd be happy to oblige, Captain." Jessie replied. "Expect us within the hour."

"And please bring Aurelia, Captain. Helena and Sasha are anxious to see her."

There was a slight hesitation before Jessie agreed.

"The *Belle* out," Harbour said, ending the call.

The crew turned from their panels at the sound of Harbour's soft clapping. They smiled their appreciation, but it was the generous emotion that Harbour shared with them that was equally rewarding.

* * * *

Harbour, Dingles, Danny, and other crew members approached the colony ship's bay airlock. She was anxious to enter it and greet Jessie, Aurelia, and his crew the moment they exited the *Spryte*'s shuttle, but Dingles, clearing his throat, gave her pause.

"Captain, spacer protocol. Captain Cinders and his people will be wearing vac suits. They'll keep airtight until they cycle through the airlock and reach this corridor."

"Why, Dingles. Surely they know the *Belle* has the capacity to pressurize its bays."

"Spacers don't change their habits, Captain, just because of different circumstances, and a mining ship hasn't the luxuries of a colony ship. There's been more than one accident with a docking collar on a ship's axis. I've been involved in three. Each time the ship was protected by the airlock, and we were protected by our vac suits."

Harbour's cool gray eyes regarded Dingles. "You must have been terrified when you first boarded the *Belle*'s shuttle without a vac suit and every time since then."

"Truth be told, Captain, I was so relieved to get out of security confinement that I didn't care. I did study your shuttle's build, the bay's pressurization procedures, and its maintenance history before I boarded it a second time. Earth built some fine shuttles with excellent safety protocols, and Danny here has kept everything in excellent working order, considering the budget constraints."

"What about now?" Harbour asked, with concern.

"Well, Captain, you might say that when you told me to ensure the *Belle* was ready to move, Danny received some additional coin and put it to good use."

"I knew there was a reason I made you first mate," Harbour replied, sending Dingles her appreciation.

"This is Captain Cinders aboard the *Spryte* shuttle calling the *Belle*," Jessie said. He was sitting in the copilot seat, not wanting to miss a closeup view of the colony ship, which, he was sad to admit, he'd never taken the time to observe. "Comms, please relay to the captain our appreciation for the bay signal lights. The view of this huge ship from out here is enough to confuse even an experienced *Belle* shuttle pilot."

"I'll relay your message, Captain Cinders," Birdie replied. "Please signal when you're ready to dock, and we'll open for you."

Per Harbour's orders, Birdie was relaying any communications with the shuttle to her comm unit, but Harbour kept her end muted.

The bay door opened, and the *Spryte*'s shuttle eased inside. It was two-thirds the size of the *Belle*'s shuttle. Dingles cycled the bay via his comm unit, and, when the pilot found atmospheric pressure surrounding his shuttle, the hatch popped open.

Jessie came down the steps first, his vac suit displaying his rank. Three more people followed him.

Harbour's people stepped away from the airlock to give the group room when they exited into the corridor. Helmet seals were cracked, and the *Belle*'s crew went into action, helping the visitors strip out of their vac suits. All of them were wearing undecorated skins, except Jessie, who had a subtle black-on-black pattern over the shoulders and upper arms.

Sasha, who had been waiting impatiently for her sister to climb out of her suit, cried out in joy, and slammed into her, wrapping her arms tightly around Aurelia's neck. Helena joined her daughters, embracing both of them.

Those surrounding the family were engulfed in waves of happiness and relief. Some crew wore giddy expressions, and a few had tears in their eyes.

"You have to love the right kind of family reunion," Belinda whispered to Claudia, the *Spryte*'s shuttle pilot.

"This is incredible," Claudia whispered in return "I feel like a kid after my first freefall game."

Jessie stepped forward, greeted Harbour, and introduced his first crew member. "Captain Harbour, this is Belinda Kilmer, who's been training our newbie."

"And receiving the better part of the arrangement," Belinda added. "It's a real pleasure to meet you, Captain."

Harbour sensed that the woman wasn't pretending to be polite. Her gratefulness was deep and genuine, and Harbour wondered what she'd so desperately needed from Aurelia. The thought came to mind that her condition might have been similar to Dingles.

"And this is Claudia Manning, my pilot," Jessie said.

"Ma'am," Claudia said simply, shaking the captain's hand.

Harbour ignored the smile on Claudia's face. Every crew member was wearing one. The woman's manner of speaking and handshake said she was an uncomplicated, no-nonsense, spacer. What you saw is what you got.

Jessie glanced at the family still entwined in one another, with the two sisters engaging in a rapid-fire conversation, and Helena smiling in relief. "I think you might have guessed the other member of my crew," Jessie said, tipping his head toward the family.

The attention of the captains caused Aurelia to disentangle from her family. She approached Harbour and ignored her spacer training, instead, holding out her hands, which Harbour took. The two empaths communed, while the remaining individuals waited. In one way or another, every member of the group had been greatly impacted by the empaths.

"Thank you, Captain, for your help in freeing my mother and my sister," Aurelia said, when she released Harbour's hands.

"It was entirely my pleasure, and your sister has repaid any debt," Harbour replied.

When Aurelia turned her head to regard Sasha, her younger sister puffed up with pride. "Funny, she rarely repaid me," Aurelia quipped.

Rather than react with annoyance, Sasha smiled at her sister. It was a sign of the changes that Sasha was undergoing, being surrounded by people who cared about her well-being.

Aurelia was led off by Helena and Sasha to visit their cabin. The *Belle*'s crew tended to the cleaning of their guests' vac suits, as a courtesy, and Belinda and Claudia followed them. Dingles stayed beside Harbour.

"Well, Captain Cinders, if you haven't been aboard before, I'd offer you a tour of the ship, but I don't think you have the two or three days to spare right now."

Jessie laughed and said, "She's a huge ship."

Dingles, who'd been in Harbour's company for many weeks, detected the subtle emanations from her. He realized Yasmin was right when she said Harbour was different when she spoke of Jessie. Here was proof, and he looked from one to other. Outwardly, they were cool, calm, and collected.

"Perhaps, a look at the *Belle*'s bridge, before we sit down and talk about what comes next," Harbour offered.

"I'd appreciate that," Jessie replied.

"Dingles, lead the way, please," Harbour said. She walked side by side with Jessie and wanted to link her arm in his, but it didn't seem appropriate, which mildly annoyed her.

"For the love of Pyre, only the holds of my ship are bigger than this space," Jessie said, marveling at the bridge after he stepped through the access hatch.

"Does take your breath away, doesn't it, Captain?" Dingles asked. His chest was bursting with pride.

"I can't tell you how happy I am to hear you made first mate, Dingles, and that you're doing well," Jessie said, clapping the spacer on the shoulder.

"Thanks to my captain," Dingles replied.

"Yes, it seems that all of us are falling into Captain Harbour's debt."

Harbour detected conflicting emotions behind Jessie's statement, but, before she could respond, Birdie called out, "Captain, you have a call from their majesties, the commandant and the governor."

"Give me one minute, Birdie, and then patch it through to my comm unit," Harbour said, holding up her device. "Captain, if you'll accompany me?" she said to Jessie.

Harbour stepped through the bridge hatch and walked a few meters down the corridor to a door labeled "Captain's Quarters." Once inside, she held a finger to her lips for Jessie and then answered the call on speaker.

"And to what do I owe the pleasure of this call?" Harbour asked.

"It's our duty, as leaders of the Pyrean society, to inform you that your arrival at Triton has reset the time period for the quarantine," Emerson said perfunctorily.

"As if I didn't know that," Harbour replied, with some heat. "Well, since we seem to be getting down to business without any preliminary niceties, let me ask you, Emerson. Has Lise returned the original *Honora Belle* files she discovered?"

"That's Governor Panoy to you, Harbour," Lise said, with her own brand of righteous indignation.

"And here I thought we were all being so chummy, Governor. Ah, well, then it's Captain Harbour to you."

"I've received them, Captain," Emerson said, trying to cool the conversation.

"But, have you received all the files that were taken from the colony ship?" Harbour asked.

"We sent the commandant every file we discovered," Lise said, in a huff.

"Commandant, I'm sending the file codes of three documents. Please check what you received from the governor against these three codes, and let me know if you have them."

"What are the files about, Captain?"

"Either you have them and can read them for yourself, or I'll inform you later of their contents, Commandant. Right now, I wish to test if you received a full set of the original files that were looted from the *Belle*'s library. I happen to have discovered the ship's log of all files that the library contained, and it appears that hundreds of files are missing. For now, I'm asking you to check on these three rather critical files."

Lise Panoy's next words were cut off by Harbour closing her comm.

Jessie stared at Harbour, surprise on his face. She wasn't the same woman he'd secretly met with on the station, who wouldn't risk her empaths and residents by hiding Aurelia.

"Sorry, Captain, my patience with this duplicitous pair is fast running out," Harbour said, reacting to Jessie's emotional misgivings. "Now, shall we take a small tour? And I hope you'll stay for dinner. Some of my people would like to give you a taste of what we're prepared to serve your crews."

"Fresh foods?" Jessie asked.

"For the most part, Captain. Shall we go?"

* * * *

"I assume you'll send me those three file codes, Commandant," Lise said. She was trying desperately to regain control of her temper. In her mind, she was throttling Harbour and completing the job that Corporal McKenzie failed to execute. Conveniently, her daydream didn't involve Harbour possessing empath power.

"I'm puzzled, Lise. If you discovered these original files by accident and turned them over to me, why would you want to know about the files that Harbour's checking on?"

"I don't pay you to be puzzled, Emerson. Send those codes when you receive them."

Emerson was staring at the codes on his comm unit and was busy searching for the first one. The files that Lise sent were being kept in a protected area, available only to Major Finian, the head of network security, and him. The search came up empty.

"Why do I have the feeling, Lise, that this is a repeat of the Aurelia case on your part? You keep me in the dark until circumstances force you to reveal more information."

"That's not my intent here, Emerson," Lise said, adopting a much more civil tone. Harbour's rudeness to her had colored her handling of Emerson, and she was regretting it.

"I'll tell you what's my intent, Lise. When I receive the file codes, I'll search the database for them, and then you and I can have another discussion about what is or isn't there. Good day, Lise," Emerson said, cutting the connection.

Lise swore up and down, as she stomped around her parlor. Rufus and Idrian, sitting on a couch, glanced at each other. Usually, Lise was the cool one of the group, but she was rivaling one of Pyre's geological eruptions.

"There is the possibility that Harbour is playing us, Lise," Idrian said, when Lise cooled down enough to stand still and stare out her window at the beautifully manicured grounds behind her home. "She might only have the log and picked out three file codes at random."

"For what reason?" Rufus asked. "She knows which original files were taken. It was the colony ship's protocol that copies could be made, but the original library was to remain intact. Did you hear the word she used during the conversation? She said looted."

"She isn't playing us. It isn't Harbour's style," Lise said, turning from the window. "I've known the woman for years. Before now, she would never be so rude as to cut me off in mid-sentence. No, something's changed. Let me rephrase that ... a great deal has changed. The question is what."

36: Dinner

"Hungry?" Harbour asked Jessie.

"After visiting the ship's hydroponics, I wouldn't miss the opportunity," Jessie replied, and Harbour detected his genuine enthusiasm.

They ended up taking a longer tour than she expected, but Jessie was intrigued by the vastness of the ship and its capabilities. Harbour had called on the help of Pete Jennings, one of her senior engineers, to answer many of Jessie's questions. The two men had walked and talked, while Jessie inspected the colony ship's main engines, environmental systems, hydroponic gardens, and many other infrastructure components.

Harbour admitted that before her election as captain, she would have been bored to tears, listening to the subjects discussed by Jessie and Pete. Not now. She paid close attention to the questions Jessie asked. In many regards, Jessie started with general questions that she might have asked, but then the men quickly delved into technological observations that lost her. Nonetheless, she made notes to follow-up on various subjects, much of which could be found in the ship's library. Apparently, the families who made their way downside saw no need to steal manuals on the specifications and maintenance of the ship's internal systems.

Harbour sent a quick message to Yasmin and Nadine, who said they were ready to serve food in the captain's quarters, and Harbour and Jessie made their way from deep at the aft end of the ship to the upper deck and forward to the bridge.

Jessie opened the door of the captain's quarters for Harbour with a polite, "Captain."

"Thank you, Captain." Harbour said, smiling. But inside the main salon, she stuttered to a stop, saying, "Uh-oh."

Yasmin and Nadine stood on either side of a table, which, a few hours ago, was bare. Now, it was covered in a decorative cloth. Plates, glasses, and tableware Harbour had never seen were tastefully laid out. A small, colorfully leafed plant was the centerpiece, and the two women were unabashedly grinning.

Jessie stood with a hand over his mouth. He wanted to laugh, but Harbour appeared to be thunderstruck, and he could feel her power leaking from her, as evidenced by the smiles fading from the women's faces.

"Absolutely delightful," Jessie crowed, hoping to shift the dynamics of the moment. "I get to taste fresh food in this charming environment. I can't wait." He quickly stepped to a chair, pulled it back, and swung an arm at it in a graceful gesture, saying, "Captain, your chair awaits."

Harbour was completely flustered. She was trying to evince a level of command, as the captain of the *Belle*, and Yasmin and Nadine had taken it into their heads to treat her as a woman enjoying a dinner date with a man. Worse, Jessie seemed to be electing to take their side. But it was discerning the crashing emotions of her friends, who were dismayed at her reaction, that made Harbour regret failing to appreciate their efforts. *That's not how a captain behaves,* Harbour thought.

"My apologies, friends," Harbour said, and she wrapped her words in the emotion she felt.

Both Nadine and Yasmin tipped their heads in acknowledgment and immediately bustled about with their preparations, while Harbour took the seat Jessie offered.

As Jessie crossed to the other side of the table, it occurred to him that empath sensitivity allowed communication on a second level, which augmented their spoken words and did much to eliminate the possibility of misunderstandings and preventing outright lies.

The women poured water and served small salads. Jessie took one look at the plate, and said incredulously, "Strawberries? You're serving me strawberries?"

"Are you allergic to them, Captain?" Nadine asked, with concern.

"No, they are usually too expensive aboard the JOS to enjoy. I don't remember seeing them on the tour," Jessie said, directing his last statement at Harbour.

"You only visited the one hydroponic garden, Captain. It's one of the smaller ones. There are two more of similar size, and three much larger ones."

Jessie shook his head at the incredible size of the colony ship. After several hours of touring, he hadn't begun to grasp its immense space.

Noticing Jessie was sorting through his salad, examining the bits and pieces, Yasmin explained, "The bed is spinach, Captain. The shavings you see are a bean plant that resembles the taste of almonds, and those are halved cherry tomatoes. The dressing is our own concoction made from many species of plants grown in the hydroponics. I hope you enjoy it."

Jessie stopped playing with his salad and dove into it. The three women hid their smiles, as Jessie made small appreciative sounds while he munched his way through to the last piece.

"I have to tell you," Jessie announced to the women, wiping his mouth, "if I was in the privacy of my cabin, I would be licking the plate by now."

Dinner proceeded to delight Jessie, and Harbour relaxed into the sensations from his enjoyment. When Nadine cleared the dessert plates, which had displayed collections of fresh berries covered in a concoction that cleverly imitated whipped cream, Yasmin held a bottle up and said, "Brandy, anyone?"

Jessie's head swiveled from the ancient-looking bottle with its amber liquid to Harbour and back to the bottle.

"You two have some explaining to do," Harbour said evenly.

"You had Dingles searching for something specific for you, Captain," Nadine explained, enigmatically. "And apparently, he's quite knowledgeable about the ways of captains, because he discovered what you might call a private larder behind a concealed panel. There's an extensive collection of items like this."

"It's been back there for what ... five hundred years ... trip time plus our time in this system?" Jessie replied. "It's probably gone bad."

Harbour picked up the flash of emotion from her two friends, and her tentative smile morphed into a grin, which she directed at Jessie. "I believe you'll find the brandy more than adequate. If I'm not mistaken, these two individuals put their health on the line to test taste it ... for the sake of our safety, mind you."

Jessie regarded Yasmin and Nadine, who blushed at his quiet stare. "Quite commendable of you," he allowed. "Well, now that we know it's safe, we might as well try it too."

Immediately, Nadine whisked out two delicate glasses that she'd concealed behind her back. "There's an entire collection of serving things like this back there too, Captain."

Yasmin poured the brandy and both women stood by, expectantly.

"Well done, my friends. Thank you for the lovely dinner," Harbour said. "I'll let you get to your beds."

Yasmin took a breath to object, but she caught Nadine's shake of her head.

"Certainly, Captain," Yasmin allowed graciously, and deposited the brandy bottle on the table. Then Nadine and she quietly left the cabin.

"Brandy," Jessie said, chuckling. He picked up the cut crystal glass, marveling at the light playing through it, and the deep amber color of the liquid.

Harbour inhaled hers and enjoyed the aroma. "A toast, Jessie," she said, holding up her glass. "To surviving the quarantine in style."

"And here I was being grateful to have some frozen meals delivered. My crews are going to fall in love with the *Belle*. I hope they don't start jumping ship to crew for you, Captain."

Harbour quirked an eyebrow at Jessie, who, after a moment of thought, realized his mistake.

"To surviving in style, Harbour," Jessie said, clinking his glass against hers.

After some appreciative sips of the brandy, Jessie, who had been observing how bare the salon appeared, except for furniture, said, "May I make a suggestion, Harbour?"

"Certainly, Jessie."

"You should move in here. Appearances for a captain are everything. Your people, crew, empaths, and residents, want to feel their captain is in firm control of their destiny. They expect you to be here. It demonstrates you know your place as their leader."

"I'll take it under advisement, Jessie. Thank you."

Jessie nodded and finished his brandy. Their glasses were, after all, not only delicate but small. Without a word, Harbour picked up the bottle and refilled his glass.

"What was the conversation you had about missing files when you spoke to ... what did Birdie call them ... their majesties?"

Harbour smiled and nodded, while she refilled her glass. During the next half hour, she brought Jessie up to date about the mysterious disappearance of the ship's library files, including the discovery by Dingles of the library log and copies of the missing files found in the first mate's cabin.

"I see. You were testing Lise Panoy to see if she turned over everything to Emerson," Jessie said, when Harbour finished her summary.

Harbour couldn't tell if it was the gleam in Jessie's eyes or the brandy that was exciting her. *Probably both,* she thought.

"Well done, Harbour," Jessie said, hoisting his glass, and Harbour felt a warm thrill work up from deep inside. It surprised her that she wanted Jessie's approval that much. "Don't keep me hanging, Harbour. I'm sure you've read the three files you're asking about. What's in them?"

Harbour set her glass down, thinking she'd consumed more than she should, and picked up her comm unit. After a few taps, she said, "There. You have copies too. It's best you read them for yourself."

Jessie checked his comm unit to ensure he'd received the documents and a yawn escaped his mouth. "Well, I hate to eat and run," he said, which received a polite chuckle from Harbour, considering dinner and their subsequent conversation had lasted more than three hours.

Harbour checked her crew log. There were four spacers on duty, and she contacted the first one on the list.

"Good evening, Captain," Birdie replied.

"You had day shift, Birdie. Why are you still on duty?"

"I slept too much the last bunch of years, Captain. I'm trying to make up for it."

"Pace yourself, Birdie," Harbour replied sternly.

"Aye, Captain. It won't happen again."

"What's the disposition of Captain Cinders' crew?"

"They've turned in for the night, Captain, and Ituau of the *Spryte* was notified. Dingles ordered a cabin prepared for Captain Cinders, and I can escort him there when he's ready."

"Since I've already had to lift the captain's face out of his plate to wake him, I think he's ready."

There was the slightest pause before Birdie replied, "Coming on the double, Captain."

"I think that poor, wizened woman is wondering if she's got to carry me to my cabin," Cinders said, chuckling. He rose and extended his hand, which Harbour took. "It's been a relaxing dinner, the likes of which I can't remember having, present company included."

Harbour thought Jessie might have said more, but a quick tap at the door caused him to drop her hand and Harbour called out, "Enter."

It was evident from the relief on Birdie's face that she found Jessie alert and standing. The captains curtailed their grins, as they glanced at each other.

"When you're ready, Captain Cinders," Birdie said.

"Lead on, Birdie," Jessie replied.

Jessie left without looking back, and Harbour turned to regard the table and the room. Dingles had urged her to move into the captain's quarters too, but she'd been reluctant, feeling she didn't deserve the extravagant quarters. "Appearances," she muttered to herself, turned out the lights, and closed the door behind her, as she left to return to her cabin.

In a short time, Jessie was lost. Birdie took so many twists and turns, he had no idea how to get to the bridge or the bay. So, he gave up trying to track their course and kept a tight hold on his comm unit. If worse came to worse, he could call for help.

The quarters Jessie was shown were comfortable, if small. The tiny kitchenette was stocked with drinks, but no food. He took a quick shower, made himself a hot drink, sat in a chair, and opened his comm unit. Curiosity demanded satisfaction, and he was dying to know what was in the three documents Harbour sent him.

Hours later, Jessie closed his device. He was stunned by the revelations. The room had taken on a chill, and he was tired. He glanced at the time, winced, and set a wakeup call for midmorning. Then, he crawled into the bed and was soon fast asleep.

* * * *

In the morning, Jessie dressed and exited his cabin, determined to test his ability to find his way to the bridge. He passed a few people, residents not spacers, said good morning, and kept moving. Jessie was about to call it quits when he heard a familiar voice.

"Good morning, Captain," Aurelia said brightly, when she spotted Jessie.

"Morning, Aurelia and Sasha," Jessie replied.

"Sasha, you're staring at the captain," Aurelia reprimanded.

"Why not? His emotional state is most confusing," Sasha replied, continuing to fixate on Jessie's head. "There's so many pieces all mixed up in there. Why's that, Captain Cinders?"

"That's because I worry about all the little people, like you," Jessie replied.

Rather than feel insulted, Sasha grinned. Contrary to Jessie's words and the tone of his voice, she hadn't felt any animosity from him.

When Jessie glanced the way Aurelia had come, she intuited what he needed from his brief instance of discomposure. "I was about to tell Sasha that we needed to end my tour for now and head back to the bridge, if you're going that way, Captain?"

"Happy to accompany the two of you," Jessie replied, with not a little bit of relief, which both girls discerned.

As the three of them headed back the way the empaths had come, Sasha hooked her arm into Jessie's.

"Sasha," Aurelia cautioned.

"What?" Sasha replied. "The captain doesn't mind if I study him, do you, Captain?"

"I never thought I'd say this, but I'm extremely grateful that of the two sisters, it was Aurelia who hid on my ship."

Jessie was frowning at Sasha, but the sisters were grinning at each other.

The threesome wound around the ship, guided by Sasha, until Jessie entered familiar territory. Then he eased out of Sasha's grip and hurried ahead. "You're on your own, spacer," he called back, as he disappeared around the corner.

"Well, what did I tell you?" Aurelia asked her sister.

"He's like Harbour. In most cases, there's little that leaks from her, but when it does there are so many different flavors of emotions that it's difficult to figure out what it means."

"I know what you mean ... complex, very complex," replied Aurelia, staring in the direction Jessie had taken.

Jessie located the bridge, but he was intrigued by a trail of empaths carrying personal goods in the direction of the captain's quarters. He fell in line and found Harbour supervising the disposition of her cabin's meager belongings. A worn chair sat in a corner with a reading light, which looked out of place with the sumptuous furniture, but somehow it felt right. It was as if it was announcing that the new captain had moved in, but it was Harbour who lived here.

"Good morning, Captain, did you sleep well?" Harbour asked.

"I did. I got a bit of reading done last night before I turned in," Jessie replied pointedly.

"Did you now? Would you like to take some time and discuss what you read?"

"Love to," Jessie replied, looking around at the activity.

"Have you eaten this morning?" Harbour asked.

"Not yet."

"Yasmin, please order some breakfast for Captain Cinders. I'll have a green. Have them brought to the study," Harbour requested, indicating a side door off the salon.

Jessie followed Harbour into a room obviously decorated for male tastes, and he winced at their forefathers' presumptions.

"I know," Harbour said, closing the door. "It makes you wonder at the attitudes of Earthers a half millennium ago. But to business ... did you get through all the files?" Harbour indicated a small table set with four padded chairs.

"Yes, I did. That's one set of disturbing documents."

"Can't argue with you there," Harbour replied.

"Harbour, if I read these documents right, they indicate our entire societal organization ... the governorship, the commandant, the Review Board, and our Captain's Articles ... they're all unfounded or, maybe more precisely said, they're illegal."

"That's my take, Jessie, but that's what the colonists agreed to, before they joined the expedition."

"But those people are gone," Jessie objected.

"True, but does it make their descendants any less responsible for the way it is today?"

"I've no idea, but I was wondering who would be put in charge of deciding this ... of adjudicating it?"

"Now, there's the question. We could always leave it up to Lise Panoy."

"Cheeky woman," Jessie replied, but he was grinning at the absurdity of Harbour's statement. "I understand now why you're setting a trap for Lise. You want to see if she'll hide these specific files and maybe others from the commandant. If she has them, I bet coin she will. They undermine the families' power. Are the other appropriated files as damaging as these three?"

"I haven't read through most of the ones that were taken ... the copies, I mean, that we found in the first mate's cabin. That would take weeks, if not months, and I've been too busy rescuing these lost spacers abandoned at Triton."

"Who greatly —" Jessie started to say, but was interrupted by a tapping at the door, which preceded the entry of two young women carrying dishes and juices to the table.

The smells of food tempted Jessie, but the red orange drink placed before him captured his attention. Sipping on the liquid, Jessie's eyes closed in ecstasy. "Now that's a breakfast juice. Okay, which one of you do I have to marry to be served this every morning?" Jessie joked.

"That would be Captain Harbour," one of the empaths quipped.

"And I'd make the proposal a good one, Captain Cinders. Our captain is particular about those things she possesses," the other added.

The two empaths exited, giggling, and Jessie's mouth hung open, the juice glass halfway to the table.

"Not used to bantering with people not of your crew, Jessie?" Harbour asked, when the door closed.

"That will teach me to come better prepared to breakfast aboard the *Belle*," Jessie replied, and Harbour and he shared a laugh.

It didn't take Jessie long to put aside the subject they'd been discussing and enjoy his meal. Harbour sat quietly observing him, while he consumed everything in sight.

"We're alone, Jessie," Harbour said, when he finished his breakfast. "You can lick the plate, if you wish."

"Don't encourage me," Jessie warned, draining the last of his juice glass and relishing its flavor. "How is it that you have these types of foods? And are they only for the likes of you and me?"

"There isn't that sort of hierarchy aboard the *Belle*. Your people probably had the same meal this morning. The downsiders eat this way regularly. They just don't share their best with the JOS. We learned long ago that they carefully control the types of food that are shipped topside. Over time, we've gained seeds and cuttings and started growing them in our hydroponic gardens."

"Speaking of downsiders, what do you intend to do with the discovered files?"

"How would I know, Jessie?" Harbour replied, throwing her hands up. "I'm still trying to figure out how to captain a colony ship of thousands of people who are depending on me for competent direction. And what am I doing? I'm exposing them to potential alien contamination and six months of quarantine."

"As I started to say, we greatly appreciate your efforts, Harbour. That reminds me, we need to discuss how you wish to be reimbursed for your efforts."

Harbour picked up her comm device, tapped on it for a few seconds, and pointed to Jessie's device, which sat at his left side.

Jessie opened his unit and examined the per diem schedule of services for Jessie's crew. The charges were divided into two major groups, services delivered to his ships or enjoyed aboard the *Belle*.

"Cantina charges with alcoholic drinks?" Jessie asked in amazement. He kept scrolling through the list, amazed at the detail and forethought that was put into it. "This is incredibly complete, Harbour. I had no idea you were such a detailed businesswoman."

"There are many things you don't know about me, Jessie Cinders," Harbour replied, and she stared at Jessie with a determined expression, before she broke into laughter. "Actually, Jessie, I had no idea how to define the services or the prices. This is all Maggie's doing."

"Ah, that explains it. Well, a good captain knows when to delegate responsibility," Jessie allowed. "You're rescuing us with wonderful food, drink, and accommodations. And we're here for six months. How can we help you, Harbour?"

"Dingles tells me that we can use some people, if you have crew to spare."

"Absolutely. I'll tell Captain Erring and Ituau to call Dingles and get him all the support he can use. I think once word spreads of the great food you're serving, it'll be a rush to sign up for duty. Anything else?"

"I was wondering about getting a look at the alien site. You know ... the one you and your people activated."

"Yeah," Jessie replied, rubbing his chin. "Not our finest moment ... technological newbies playing with an advanced alien site." He didn't want Harbour anywhere near the site and was furiously thinking of an excuse. "I presume you're vac suit qualified?"

"I bought one at the Latched On. Dingles recommended the place."

"Good advice. Quality goods for a fair price."

"Well, I intended to learn on the way out here, but I needed some personal time."

"Harbour, I don't know if anyone's told you, but if one spacer knows, every spacer will know as quickly as it's technically feasible."

"I heard something similar from Maggie. You're saying that your crews know what happened to me."

"Yes, and it's a good thing that Sasha took care of Terror. Otherwise, most of my crew would be locked in security confinement cells after they beat Terror within a centimeter of his life."

Harbour's eyes took on a distant look, and Jessie hurried to pull her back to the moment. He didn't want her thinking of the attack or the fact that the damage to her throat had nearly killed her. "I'm sorry to tell you, Harbour, that until you've passed basics on the vac suit, there's no way to see the alien site."

"What about some form of transport where you never leave its safety?" Harbour asked.

"That's not how our protocols work, Harbour."

"Ah, yes, Dingles mentioned that your people travel aboard shuttles with your vac suits on."

"Safety is paramount to spacers, Harbour. We live by our protocols, and there's no exception for anyone, not even me."

"Are you telling me that Aurelia learned these procedures?"

"According to the updates from Captain Erring, she's a born spacer, and Belinda and she formed a tight pair."

"Belinda had problems, didn't she?"

"How did you know that?"

"Conversations with Helena told me a great deal about her daughters. It became apparent that it was Aurelia's temperament that kept the family sane during their confinement. She would be drawn to someone emotionally troubled and would be hardwired to help. Did she?"

"Belinda hasn't had an episode of space dementia since about five days after she started Aurelia's training." Switching subjects, Jessie said, "Well, Harbour, I've got a lot to get started, as soon as I get back aboard the *Spryte*. I do have one favor to ask, even though it's me who is completely in your debt, and I mean that."

"Never be afraid to ask, Jessie," Harbour said.

Jessie stared into Harbour's cool gray eyes for several moments and had to focus to recall what he wanted to ask. "I've set up a long-lens cam at the alien site with a power supply to monitor the installation, but our ships haven't the capability to receive the weak signal, once we leave Triton's space. I think the *Belle* does."

"I'll inform Birdie that you need her assistance, and we'll provide around-the-clock monitoring of the cam."

"That's it? You don't want to know why?"

"It's fairly obvious, Jessie. The site's active, and you have no idea what that means, so you're taking precautions in case aliens arrive, thinking you called them." Harbour ended by raising her eyebrows, challenging Jessie to argue with her analysis.

"Yes, something like that. I hope I'm wrong. For the life of me, I hope I'm wrong."

This time when Jessie stood, it was Harbour who offered her hand. She led him out of the study and through the salon. When she opened the cabin's door, Aurelia stood there.

"Ready when you are, Captain." Aurelia announced. "I've got the *Belle's* layout on my comm unit and can get us back to our bay. The crew is standing by."

"Very efficient of you, Captain," Jessie acknowledged to Harbour. "Aurelia, you don't want to spend more time with your family?" Jessie asked.

Aurelia kept a polite smile on her face, but Harbour detected the young girl's severe disappointment at the offer.

"I believe your spacer has duties to perform, Captain Cinders, and I wouldn't want to keep her from them," Harbour said.

Jessie glanced between the women and was reminded of the secondary level of communication that the empaths enjoyed.

"Thank you again, Captain," Jessie said to Harbour, offering his hand. "Lead on, spacer," he said to Aurelia.

37: Slush

In the following weeks, spacers flowed from Jessie's ships to the *Belle* and back. Many had work duty, and some were enjoying downtime, but, truth be told, anyone assigned to duty on the colony ship thought they were on downtime, as they enjoyed an evening in the cantina and a daily diet served up by many of the residents, who harvested and prepared what the hydroponics produced.

One evening, Dingles and Ituau were sharing a drink and spacer stories, when Dingles turned the conversation to a serious subject.

"I don't think many people know this, and this isn't to go any further, Ituau," Dingles said. "I was in charge of outfitting of this ship ... crew, equipment, and parts ... and I can tell you that I just about emptied the ship's general fund."

"Well, sharing under the same constraints as yours, I know Jessie can't pay the per diem charges that are being racked up by our crew when you project it over six months."

"That means, if or when we make it to the JOS, coin is going to be terribly short. The principals will be broke."

"Seems that way, Dingles," Ituau acknowledged.

"The *Pearl's* still working," Dingles allowed.

"Oh, yeah, she'll produce enough slush to allow Jessie to cover about half of our time out here. I don't want to be in his deck shoes when he decides whether to use the *Pearl's* coin to pay the *Belle* or the crew."

"A lot of slush at Emperion?" Dingles asked.

"An enormous amount. Jessie's been trying to keep it quiet."

Dingles eyes drilled into Ituau's, which put the *Spryte's* first mate on alert. "Leave your drink and come with me." Dingles said, and abruptly left the cantina with Ituau hurrying to catch up.

* * * *

Jessie arrived at the *Belle* on the *Spryte*'s morning flight. His shuttle nestled next to that of the *Annie*'s, and when he exited the bay, crew waited to help him out of his vac suit.

"Lead on, Ituau," Jessie said, after greeting his first mate.

"Captain Erring and Darrin are waiting for us," Ituau said. She was fairly sure that she knew the way, but not wanting to get lost, while leading the captain, she constantly checked her comm unit to guide her. The size of the colony ship had Jessie's crew depending on a layout app, provided by Dingles, to find their way around.

Ituau tapped briefly at the door of the captain's quarters, and then opened it before standing aside. She followed Jessie inside, and she took a seat at the table with Harbour, Dingles, Yohlin, and Darrin.

"I called this meeting at the urging of my first mate," Harbour said. "Dingles, you have the floor."

"You'll forgive me for digging my nose into aggregate that isn't mine," Dingles said. "But I've been made aware through various sources that coin is short for both the *Belle* and your company, Captain Cinders." Dingles waited, but no one said anything. He did notice that Jessie's interlaced hands were tensing. "And Ituau shared with me some details about the amount of slush on Emperion."

Jessie glanced at Ituau, but she refused to meet his gaze, deliberately keeping her attention on Dingles.

As the only empath in the room, Harbour was fascinated by the tremendous ebb and flow of emotions. Obviously, things were being spoken about in mixed company that needed Jessie's permission before they were shared.

"Well, let me be the first to clear the air here. The *Belle*'s general fund is nearly depleted," Harbour announced. "How are you fixed for coin, Captain Cinders?"

Jessie's head snapped up, as if he'd been slapped, and his eyes narrowed, as he stared across the table at Harbour.

"Come, Captain, we're all in the same predicament out here. If we can't be forthright with each other, how are we going to find a way out of this situation?"

Jessie gazed around the table. Admittedly, they were some of his most trusted people, and Harbour had proven whose side she was on. Although he wasn't in the habit of sharing financial details about his company, he acquiesced to Harbour's request. "At the run rate of my crew, I can pay about fourteen weeks of the *Belle*'s bill, Captain."

"How about your crew? Does your coin cover your people?"

"No," Jessie admitted quietly, his hands tightening.

Harbour watched the faces of Jessie's people fall. As Jessie had said to her, crews wanted to believe in their captains, trust them, but, in these circumstances, the problem appeared insurmountable. Harbour summoned her power, dropped her gates, and broadcast with much strength. Around the table, heads tilted back, as if a strong wind had struck them in their faces.

"There," Harbour said, shutting down her sending. "Now we can focus on the issue, instead of lamenting how we got here. You were saying, Dingles."

The first mates were grinning, but the captains were frowning.

"Yes, well, if there's all this slush waiting on Emperion," Dingles continued. "Why don't we wait out the six months at that moon instead of this one?"

"Captain Cinders, if we helped fill the *Pearl*'s tanks, how much would that add to the company's books?" Yohlin asked.

"Excuse me, Captain Erring, that's only part of the idea," Ituau said, and she saw Dingles nod at her to continue. "I've learned from Dingles that the *Belle* has an extensive number of high-pressure tanks that are sitting empty. Admittedly, their connective lines need a little work, but the tanks are sound."

"Ituau, I'm sure Dingles informed you that my spacers are retired. They're not ready to be miners again, and we have an insufficient number of vac suits," Harbour said.

"How much storage space are we talking about?" Jessie asked. With that one question, he changed the dynamics in the room.

Dingles consulted his comm unit, tapping furiously for a minute, while Jessie waited. The captain was still frowning, but Harbour detected an entirely different blend of emotions from him.

"One of the *Belle*'s tanks has half the capacity of one of the *Pearl*'s," Dingles mumbled, as he worked. "The *Pearl* has a hex arrangement of tanks. That's twelve of our tanks to a full load of the *Pearl*. Our tanks are grouped four by four to the stack. They're six stacks wide and twelve stacks long, which equals ..."

"Ninety-six loads for the *Pearl*," Jessie said in awe.

"Dingles and I haven't figured out the most efficient way to get the slush into the *Belle*'s tanks, but we figure that's a problem for the engineers to solve," Ituau said.

"In six months, the *Pearl*'s crew could fill their tanks five or six times, but then that drops to three or four loads, when you add in trip time to and from the YIPS, plus unloading time," Yohlin calculated out loud.

Harbour smiled to herself. The people around the table were no longer feeling defeated by their predicament. They were focused on a way out of it.

"The *Pearl*," Darrin exclaimed. "We use the *Pearl* as the transfer mechanism. She has the equipment and capabilities to load the slush off the surface. Then we create a second transfer method to pump the slush from the *Pearl* into the *Belle*."

"It's going to be frozen in the *Pearl*'s tanks," Yohlin pointed out. "How are we going to get the slush to flow?"

"Heat pipes," Dingles said. "We have a load of them aboard. Power them up, push them into a tank, and suck up the melted slush like the YIPS does. Where do you think they got the idea?"

Jessie's hands unclenched. He crossed his arm, one hand stroking his chin, and he stared overhead. It was a few minutes before he spoke. "Captain Harbour, how long can you support all of us ... food, water, and operational fuels?"

"At the present rate of consumption, Captain Cinders, we can handle food, water, and any operational needs for about fourteen months, although, at the present rate, the alcohol might run dry in about nine months," Harbour said, grinning.

"Well, there you go. We only have nine months, at most," Ituau quipped.

"I think we're making the six-months quarantine an arbitrary timeline," Jessie said, speaking as if he was talking to himself. "Before, we were focused on surviving the time span. Now, we have the opportunity to turn the situation into a business opportunity. In a year, we could deliver the equivalent of about sixteen to eighteen loads of the *Pearl* at the YIPS. That would generate more than enough coin to cover everyone's expenses and generate a generous amount of profit."

Jessie continued to think, trying to see all the angles. It was a risk, betting everything on transporting one massive load aboard the *Belle*, but it answered the primary question of how to prevent going broke.

"Captain Harbour, how would you like to go into business with me?" Jessie asked.

"Let me make sure I understand this concept, Captain Cinders," Harbour replied. "We use my ship as the transport for Emperion slush. You use the *Pearl* and your crews to load the *Belle*, and we stay out here for a year. Then we haul the loads to the YIPS."

"That's the idea," Jessie replied.

"What's your offer?" Harbour asked.

"That's our cue," Yohlin said, looking around at the collection of first mates. Dingles glanced at Harbour, and she tipped her head toward the door. Once in the corridor, the five of them stood around, quietly discussing the idea. They had no intention of going anywhere and not being the first to find out if a bargain was struck.

"You do recognize, Jessie," Harbour said, when the door closed, "that we'll be exposing another crew to potential alien contamination."

"If you were to ask the *Pearl's* crew whether they'd risk exposure to a supposed and yet-to-manifest contamination to prevent losing their ship in six months when I declare bankruptcy, what do you think they would say?"

"Prior to this expedition, I wouldn't have had a clue, but, after spending time with my spacers, I believe that crew would do anything, short of breathing vacuum, to continue sailing."

"And you'd be right, Harbour."

"Question answered. Back to business, Jessie. What's your proposition?"

"I have the people and equipment, and you have the transport carrier. It sounds like an equal partnership."

"Agreed," Harbour said, taking the hand Jessie offered, but he didn't immediately let go.

"But, I'll still settle my bill with you for feeding and housing my people, and that includes any operational consumables," Jessie added.

"What about the work your crews are doing on my ship?" Harbour asked. "That's a fair exchange of services."

"We owe you for coming out to save our butts. That can never be repaid," Jessie said quietly.

"Well, business partner, we better set sail for Emperion. I can't wait to get the next call from the commandant and governor telling us the quarantine is another six months."

"But we keep the one-year plan to ourselves. Agreed?"

"Agreed," Harbour replied, and Jessie finally released her hand.

"Let's inform our people," Jessie said. "If I know spacers, they're waiting outside in the corridor to see if we struck a deal."

* * * *

The crews of Jessie's ships spent the next couple of days recovering the shelter, the equipment, and the rovers on Triton. At one point, Ituau caught up with Jessie for a private conversation.

"Captain, what about the alien site?" Ituau asked.

"What about it?"

"Well, for one thing, Captain, it's active."

"True ... and?"

"It's a hazard, sir!"

"To whom, Ituau? We're the first Pyreans out here, or are you concerned some unauthorized aliens might get trapped in the dome? Besides, it's not like we can shut it down. Maybe it'll become a tourist destination one day.

Right now, I'm more concerned about taking care of our people and the future of this company."

"Captain, I'm serious."

"I understand, Ituau. Having a little fun with you is all."

Ituau's mouth hung open for a minute, before her brain engaged. "And there it is... the first sign of alien infection. Captain Cinders has displayed a sense of humor."

"And who knows what'll come next?" Jessie replied, waggling his eyebrows.

"It's good to think we'll be coming out of this mess on top, isn't it, Captain?" Ituau said, hitting on the reason for Jessie's relaxed state of mind and his expansive sense of humor.

"More than I would have believed, Ituau. Regarding the alien site, I intend to make a Pyrean-wide announcement about what we've found and the state of the site."

"But you're not going to tell them how to enter it or anything like that?"

"No, definitely not that, but Pyreans, in general, have to know what's out here and the potential danger of an active site."

"You know they'll blame us for the site coming online, Captain."

"Yes, they will, and they'd be right. I thought about excluding that part, but it would come out one day, and that would be detrimental to our reputation. But, that's one of the reasons that I'm happy to have an alternative location outward of Pyre for longer than the next six months. When nothing else happens at the Triton installation, and we prove to be uncontaminated, it'll go a long way toward cooling opinions."

"Understood, Captain."

"What's the status of our monitor at the site?"

"Darrin planted a long-range cam that's far enough away from the site that the dome's energy isn't interfering with its software. The *Belle* lent us a more powerful solar power supply and transmitter. That's enabled us to upgrade the device's sensory programs, so that we can monitor full-time any ground or visual changes. However, once we reach Emperion, our ships won't be able to pick up the signal. The limitation is on our side, but Birdie told me the *Belle* won't have any problem receiving the transmissions from

Triton even at the YIPS or JOS, except when Pyre blocks line of sight with Triton."

"That's good news, Ituau. Let me know when we've recovered all our downside assets."

"Should that include any personnel aboard the *Belle*, Captain?"

"The *Spryte* and *Annie* have to recover any crew that's on downtime but no one who has a work assignment on the *Belle*. From now on, we treat the *Belle* as a sister ship. All general operations requested by Captain Harbour are to continue, but, most important, I need their tank system operational, as soon as possible. That's a priority! Am I clear on this?"

"Aye, Captain."

"I'll have a word with Captain Erring and ensure we're on the same page. When the crew transfers are complete for the *Belle,* notify Captain Harbour she's free to launch. Dingles estimates the *Belle* will take three more days than our ships to make the trip to Emperion."

38: Emperion

Jessie's quick estimates for the load rate of the *Belle* were significantly in error. The calculations he used were based on a single crew operating aboard the *Pearl*, but Jessie was supplying two more crews to support the recovery and transfer of slush.

But everything changed once the *Annie's* crew got hold of the pile of heat pipes aboard the *Belle*. The engineers were energized with new ideas, and they decided to bypass the *Pearl* as the transfer mechanism from downside to the colony ship. Instead, they planted the heat pipes into the fields of frozen gases, liquefied the material, and pumped it into some of the *Belle's* pressurized tanks, which kept the slush in a liquid state.

Crew repurposed the collar bases of Jessie's shuttles, enabling the ships to lift the tanks from Emperion's surface and transport them to the *Belle*. Two bays of the colony ship had originally been dedicated to filling the tanks with water and gases via Earth's shuttles. Now, Jessie's shuttles, which couldn't enter the bay with their dangling loads, released them 50 meters out from the *Belle* where crew, using the colony ship's small service vehicles, could maneuver the tanks into the bays.

The service vehicles matched velocity with the giant wheel of the *Belle*, before they could enter the bays. The tanks would touch the bay's deck, and the ship's centrifugal force would carry them along with the spinning wheel. Designers of the colony ship had provided for this process by providing lengths of flexible hose, which could manage the pressurized solutions. The slush tanks were pumped empty, transferring the load to the ship's internal tanks, and the service vehicles would return the tanks to the waiting shuttles.

It was two weeks after the ships had arrived at Emperion before the crews were ready to begin operations and deliver the first tank to the *Belle*; it was less than a week later before the delivery of the second tank; and it was two days after that for the third tank and every tank thereafter.

Captains, crew, and residents were delighted with the progress of the slush recovery, but, at a meeting aboard the *Belle*, Ituau burst the principals' bubbles.

"Captains," Ituau said, addressing the collection of captains, first mates, and key engineers, "has anyone considered the possibility that we're being too successful?"

"Explain," Jessie replied.

Harbour sensed Jessie's irritation at Ituau's suggestion, but she kept her power locked down. Ituau's opening statement had stirred emotions, and those around the table wouldn't appreciate being managed, at this time.

"Unless my calculations are wrong, we're delivering a tank to the *Belle* every two days, and each tank is the equivalent of half of the *Pearl*'s tank," Ituau said, glancing to the engineers for confirmations. When she received their agreement, she hurried on. "Then, by my calculations, we'll transfer eighty loads onboard the colony ship in the first six months and ninety-one tanks worth in the second six months."

"I don't understand the issue," Yohlin said.

"Me neither," Dingles added. "The *Belle* can hold three times what the crew might produce in the first year. We just can't feed everyone for that long."

"Oh, for the love of Pyre," Leonard lamented, smacking a hand to his forehead. "You're talking about the YIPS."

"Yes, Captain," Ituau replied.

"Okay, someone let me in on the secret," Harbour said.

"Following Ituau's calculations, we would arrive at the YIPS a year later with two ships holding the equivalent of fifteen ships the size of the *Pearl*," Jessie explained.

"But that's good, isn't it?" Harbour objected.

"The *Pearl* is designed to dock at the YIPS and be pumped dry. The *Belle* isn't. In addition, it takes the YIPS nearly a week to empty Captain Hastings' ship. How long do you think it would take the YIPS to figure out a means of transferring your slush and then emptying the equivalent of fourteen tanker ships?"

"Probably months, Captain," Dingles said.

"Which means that if we wanted to repeat our success," Yohlin added. "Jessie's ships would be loading the *Pearl* at Emperion and sailing to the YIPS several times, while we waited for this mother of a transport ship to return to the moon."

"And let's not forget that the YIPS will be receiving other deliveries," Leonard said, dampening expectations even further. "Who is it going to treat as priority?"

"And how much slush can the YIPS process in any one period of time?" Darrin added. "What if emptying the *Belle* becomes a low priority or a nonstarter because there is more supply than demand."

"It's simple. We don't stay the year," Jessie said, tapping the table. "We stay six months, and we deliver about seven-and-a-half tanker ships worth. I know that demand for slush is greater than supply, right now, and that gap is growing. I can strike a price for the *Belle*'s load that will have the YIPS manager eager to do business, especially if I offer the services of my people to expedite offload."

"Does that work financially in our favor to tie up your people at the YIPS, while the *Belle* is offloaded?" Harbour asked.

"We empty the *Pearl* first, and I'll send the *Annie* back with her to Emperion. With the crews of the *Spryte*, *Belle*, and YIPS, we can expedite the offload in ..." Jessie said, eyeing Darrin, who ducked his head into a conference with Dingles and Pete, a *Belle* senior engineer.

The captain's meeting went on, while the three men discussed and even argued the quickest means of offloading the colony ship so that they could determine the shortest time needed to strand the *Belle* at the processing station.

Jessie was intent on discussing a third subject when Dingles, Darrin, and Pete broke apart, and each man wore a broad smile.

"You don't need me to tell you about their emotional levels," Harbour said, laughing and indicating the men's self-satisfied expressions with a wave of her hand.

"Don't keep us waiting," Jessie ordered.

"Our idea, Captain Harbour and Captain Cinders," started Dingles, "depends on whether there will be a continuation of your agreement." He waited, while the two captains eyed each other.

"Oh, for the love of Pyre, shake on it, you two. You know it's a good deal," Leonard said, with exasperation, and the group erupted in laughter and applauded as Jessie and Harbour did just that.

"Okay, then, this is the idea," Dingles continued, and the three men outlined their plan to add an auxiliary pump station at the end of the YIPS longest terminal arm. The station's output would be joined to the YIPS delivery pipes, but it would require the *Belle* to position itself within 50 meters of the terminal arm, so that the crew could link a pressurized hose from the *Belle* to the pumping station.

"We can keep the *Belle* farther out," Darrin added, "if we're allowed to order more compression pipe of the specifications required. I'd estimate a week or so for every ten meters."

The captains eyed Dingles, and Jessie asked the first mate, "You want to bring the colony ship within fifty meters of the terminal?"

"We can do it, Captain," Dingles replied. "We've discovered this ship has positional lasers implanted every fifteen degrees around this ship's circumference. Danny and I can place this ship anywhere we want."

"With this plan, how long do you need to create this pumping station and then unload the ship?" Harbour asked.

"The setup would probably take about two weeks, and we estimate the unloading could be accomplished in three weeks. We won't have to spin the ship to shift the tanks around, like the *Pearl* does. Once we hook up the hose, we pump the ship dry," Darrin said.

"Dingles, Darrin, and Pete, I want a design with specifications and a materials list," Jessie requested. "I need it no later than a month before we launch for the YIPS. I want to send the information to the station manager and get his approval. I'll dangle the *Belle*'s load in front of him. That should get him salivating."

"Then we're counting six months from when we arrived at Emperion before we launch for the YIPS?" Yohlin asked.

"Affirmative," Jessie replied.

* * * *

In the days that followed, Harbour noticed Jessie's crew members waggling their fingers at one another as they passed. When the opportunity presented itself, she asked Jessie what the crew was doing, and she demonstrated, as best she could, what she had seen.

"They're practicing sign language," Jessie explained, laughing. "It was how Kasey and I managed to communicate when the dome cut off any standard means of communications. Without it, my crew and I might not have gotten out in time. Our water was dangerously close to running out, by the time we figured out how our rescuers could gain entry to the dome."

"Are you saying all spacers know this technique?"

"Hardly, Harbour. The crew realized that sign language is an asset, especially if their comms fail in vacuum. That drove them to start learning it. Spacers are like that. They'll collect any esoteric knowledge that increases their chance of survival."

"Say something in sign language," Harbour asked.

Jessie thought, for a moment, and then made a series of quick motions with his hand.

"Okay, what does it mean?" Harbour asked.

"Nothing of consequence," Jessie replied. "It was a simple greeting from me to you."

"If you say so," Harbour replied, and continued to the *Belle*'s bridge, where she'd been headed. She might never have given Jessie's demonstration of sign language another thought, except she perceived a spike of tension from him. It caused Harbour to carefully repeat the hand motions in her mind, and she made a mental note to find Kasey.

As serendipity would have it, Harbour passed Kasey in the corridor a couple of hours later, and she repeated the signs for him.

"You just told me I look beautiful today, Captain," Kasey replied, chuckling. "What crew member screwed up his sign language?"

When Harbour smiled, her eyes lighting up, Kasey regarded her for a moment, and his expression sobered. "Will there be anything else, Captain?" he asked politely.

"Negative, Kasey, thank you," Harbour replied.

When Kasey had enough distance from Harbour, he mumbled, "Captain Cinders, you old space dog, you," and he chuckled to himself.

* * * *

On the *Belle*'s bridge, Jessie requested Birdie set up a call with Commandant Strattleford. He intended to place a Pyre-wide call through the JOS, which would be received by every ship, stationer, and downsider.

"What would be the purpose of your call, Captain?" Emerson asked, when he heard Jessie's demand.

"That information would be delivered during my announcement, Commandant. This is my right per the Captain's Articles."

"Under normal circumstances, I would agree with you, but these aren't normal circumstances, Captain Cinders. I have no idea what strange manifestations you and your people have experienced, because of your exposure. I can't allow you to panic Pyreans with some sort of fantastical ramblings. I'm sorry, Captain, you'll have to wait until the six-month quarantine period has elapsed, which, as we've previously stated, was reset when you arrived at Emperion."

Jessie would have argued further, but Emerson abruptly terminated the call, and Jessie was left to swear at his comm unit.

Birdie whispered to Harbour, who laughed outright. "Captain Cinders, Birdie wants to know if you'd like to make your Pyre-wide call from here. Seems this ship has the communications gear, and she has the knowledge."

"I keep underestimating the capabilities of this ship," Jessie admitted. "If you would be so kind, Birdie, I wish to make my call now."

Birdie grinned and her thin, aged fingers flew over the comm panel. When Birdie was ready, she nodded to Harbour.

"This is Captain Harbour, broadcasting from the *Honora Belle*. I'm prefacing a Pyre-wide message of great importance. Please standby."

"This is Captain Cinders, with a message for every Pyrean citizen. It is my duty, as a ship's captain, to report any issue or obstacle that might be significant. I attempted to do this several minutes ago, but the commandant, in his infinite wisdom, saw fit to refuse me. Many of you are probably aware that six months of quarantine has been declared by the governor and the commandant against the *Spryte* and the *Annie* after we discovered an alien site on Triton. That six-month period has been reset twice. The first time was when we were joined by the *Belle,* when Captain Harbour graciously came to our rescue with sufficient resources to outfit us for the period."

Jessie could hear the shouts of the spacers and residents near the bridge, who whistled and applauded Harbour's decision. What he couldn't hear was the same loud celebration of spacers aboard ships and stations across Pyrean space, none louder than in the Miners' Pit.

"The quarantine was reset a second time, when my ships and the *Belle* joined the *Pearl* at Emperion. We'll wait out the time period here. The purpose of my message is to warn everyone away from Triton. We've discovered the alien site is active. There is an enormous power supply beneath it, and the energy dome that covers the installation precludes all normal communications methods near it. I can't stress this enough. We have no idea why this site exists, but the fact that it's active should be enough to warn away all captains. And, if this isn't enough, Darrin, known Pyre-wide as Nose, found nothing of value for my company on Triton ... no heavy metal deposits and no slush. So, if you're foolish enough to make the trip to this moon to visit the alien site, be sure that you're willing to make the trip at your expense."

"The aliens," Harbour whispered to Jessie. He frowned at her, thinking that it wasn't a good idea to mention the bodies, but she nodded firmly, encouraging him to speak up.

"I'm reminded by Captain Harbour of one other point about the site. Within the dome and on the deck of the installation are a group of alien bodies enclosed in vac suits. Two distinctly different body shapes are easily distinguishable. From our observations, we can tell that the aliens died fighting each other. Their vac suits are holed by a form of beam weapon that they're still carrying."

The bridge crew was eyeing Jessie, while he broadcast to the citizens of Pyre. When Birdie tipped her head up and gathered some wrinkled neck skin in her fingers, Jessie nodded his head in understanding.

"It's impossible to determine the age of this site," Jessie continued. "Its technological capabilities are far beyond ours, but we can see by the buildup of dust, surrounding the dome's outer edge, that the site has been abandoned for centuries. However, not wanting to be caught off guard in the future, we've set up a monitoring device. My ships can't receive the signal at any great distance, but the *Belle* has the equipment, and Captain Harbour has established a round-the-clock watch on the visuals and ground-monitoring signals."

Jessie glanced at Harbour and lifted his eyebrows, asking if she had anything to add.

"This is Captain Harbour, again. You might find this hard to believe, but Captain Cinders is too much of a gentleman to explain why we were refused the services of the JOS comm system. Apparently, the commandant thinks that we might be contaminated by visiting the alien site in such a way as to have our thinking fouled and incapacitating our speech. I can assure you that none of us show any untoward symptoms that would indicate an alien infection, although I can't speak for Captain Cinders, but I think he's always been an odd one."

The bridge crew's polite laughter was easily picked up and transmitted throughout Pyre, and Harbour lifted an eyebrow at Jessie, who grinned in reply.

* * * *

The combined ships' crews and residents worked at a fevered pitch. Calendars were marked with a countdown after Jessie set the launch date. The *Belle* would leave first, while Jessie's ships recovered their equipment.

For Jessie's crews, the mission to Triton, which had become a bust for valuable metal deposits, was replaced with a new and better opportunity. Filling the tanks of the *Belle* would go a long way toward banking a pile of coin toward comfortable retirements, and the thought of a continued relationship with Captain Harbour meant they could compete with any other tanker captain who ventured out to Emperion.

The residents of the *Belle* were invested in keeping the ships' crews well-fed and content, and the spacers found they never had it so good. The crew couldn't pass an empath without receiving a dose of appreciation, but most found reasons to avoid Sasha. Her power could have the spacers wearing loopy smiles for hours and forgetting what it was they had intended to do.

More of the *Belle*'s cabins were opened and decorated for downtime sleepovers by Jessie's crew. At the forefront of the residents' minds was the realization that their ship, and by extension themselves, was no longer the home of society's odd and disenfranchised. The spacers had transformed the *Belle* from a stationary hunk of metal to a sailing vessel once again. More important, their ship had performed an invaluable service by rescuing Jessie's people. The residents' steps were lively, their pride having been returned to them.

In addition, the future looked bright for the colony ship. The coin received for the impending huge load of slush would fill the general account and enable upgrades to the ship, and the residents had wasted no time submitting requisitions for items that they thought would benefit the *Belle*. But an uppermost thought, often shared by the residents, was of the day they voted for a captain. Repeated time and again in conversation was the comment about how lucky they were to be the ones who chose to support Harbour and stay aboard the ship.

39: The YIPS

Captains, crew, and residents awoke in the morning to be greeted by the all-important date. It had been six months since the mingling of the ships from Triton with the *Pearl*, which restarted the quarantine clock.

Crew followed their final orders, as to which ship they would accompany. Most were returning to their original positions, but Jessie had skimmed crew from each ship to reside on the *Belle* and ready the unloading process.

"You wanted to see me, Captain?" Aurelia asked, when she reported to Jessie's cabin aboard the *Spryte*.

"I'm transferring you to the *Belle*, Aurelia. Get your gear. The shuttle launches at thirteen hundred hours."

"Whatever you order, Captain," Aurelia said quietly.

Jessie could see Aurelia was crushed by the directive, but she was taking his order like a spacer.

"It's this way, Aurelia," Jessie said gently. "In the eyes of JOS security, you're still a fugitive. My ships will be returning to either the YIPS or the JOS for unloading, supplies, and downtime before returning to Emperion. You can be sure, one way or the other, the *Spryte*, *Annie*, and *Pearl* are going to be searched. If not boarded with a commandant's order in hand, security is going to be posted in the terminal arms, eyeballing every crew member who exits my ships. Do you want to take the chance of falling into security's clutches, after what you've heard from Captain Harbour about the collusion between the commandant and the governor?"

"No, sir," Aurelia replied.

"There's only one way we can make it tough for security to get to you. You stay aboard the *Belle*. That's one value of the pumping station. It's our installation, which means, technically, the colony ship isn't docked. If the *Belle* isn't docked and is capable of getting underway, security has no jurisdiction, no authorization to board her. You'll be safe."

"Am I done as a spacer, Captain?"

"Do you want to quit, Aurelia?"

"Not on your life, Captain, I want a position on your ships, preferably with the crew of the *Annie*."

"And here I thought you would request my ship," Jessie teased.

"I would, Captain, if your ship was the one doing the exploring. A girl's got to go where the excitement is," Aurelia replied, grinning.

"Spoken like a true spacer and explorer. Yes, Aurelia, when we get through this thing with security, you'll have a job on my ships. Wait," Jessie said, holding up his hands. "Don't get too excited. You'll have to interview with Captain Erring for a berth on her ship."

"Already have, sir. She says my position is waiting, once you clear me to return," Aurelia replied. She couldn't resist a smug expression.

"Cheeky, spacer," Jessie grumbled, but he was smiling. "Go get your gear and report to the shuttle for transfer with the others who are going to remain on the *Belle*."

* * * *

The *Annie* left Emperion days after the *Belle* sailed and headed for the JOS. The ship was greeted by a medical team with orders from the commandant to prevent the ship from docking at the terminal arm until the medics had an opportunity to conduct a blow out to vacuum and sweep the ship afterwards for any unidentifiable DNA formats.

Yohlin complied with every request, per Jessie's orders, and, three days later, the medical team gave the ship a clean bill of health. Yohlin insisted the commandant announce stationwide the procedures he'd implemented to check the *Annie* for alien contamination. She raised such a fuss that the commandant had Major Finian broadcast the message just to get her off his back.

When Yohlin led the first group of spacers off the ship, she noted that Jessie was right. Six security officers lined the terminal arm, checking their comm units and comparing an image of Aurelia to every crew member who passed.

Despite launching from Emperion's orbit days before Jessie's ships, the *Belle* arrived at the YIPS behind the *Spryte* and the *Pearl*. The YIPS crew had unloaded two of the *Pearl's* six tanks, when Dingles announced to Harbour that the *Belle* was stationary at 50 meters off the end of the terminal arm.

"Station manager calling, ma'am," Birdie announced to Harbour.

"Captain Harbour, here, Mr. Pendleton."

"Welcome, Captain Harbour. I don't mind telling you that you gave us some nervous moments, while we watched the *Belle* creep toward us. My compliments to your crew, especially your pilot. I was told you could position your ship fifty meters off the terminal arm, and my laser says you did just that."

"Nice to be appreciated, Mr. Pendleton."

"Please, Captain, I'm a working stiff. Call me Evan."

"Certainly, Evan. I understand the pumping station is already in place. We can begin laying the pressurized hose whenever you're ready."

"Give us one more day to complete the hookup of the station to our lines and check its integrity. I'll give you a call when we're ready."

"Understood, Evan. Do we get the same medical checkup as the *Spryte* and the *Pearl*?" Harbour heard Evan's chuckle.

"I told the medics they wouldn't find anything on Jessie's ships. Alien bugs are more likely to run screaming from Pyrean spacers than to seek them out as hosts."

"Why do I think there's a but coming, Evan?"

"Yes, ma'am, the medical team can't perform a blow out of the colony ship. I think they don't know how to conduct one, but that means I can't allow anyone off your ship."

"No problem, Evan. My crew prefers our cantina and hydroponic food over the limited resources offered by the YIPS."

"You have a cantina, ma'am?"

"Built and stocked by Maggie of the Miners' Pit."

"That tempts me to visit your ship except for ..."

"Except then you'd be breaking the newly added quarantine rules of the commandant," Harbour finished for Evan.

"Yes, ma'am," Evan replied quietly. "I'm awfully sorry about this, Captain."

"Not your fault, Evan. Let me know when you want us to begin building our pipe connection."

"Aye, Captain."

* * * *

"Birdie, time for that special call," Harbour ordered, after the crew had completed the linking of the *Belle* to the pumping station and the slush began flowing. Jessie had been right about the dearth of frozen gasses. Demand had far outstripped supply, and the YIPS processing tanks were nearly empty. The *Belle*'s delivery was desperately needed for station and downside systems operators.

"Aye, Captain," Birdie replied. She'd programmed the connections into her comm board and called the principals in advance to warn them of Harbour's call. Immediately, Jessie, Dingles, and Aurelia were connected, and Birdie set their connection to monitor only.

Harbour sat in her command chair, sipping on a green. When the connections were finalized, Birdie nodded to Harbour.

"Captain Stamerson, Commandant Strattleford, and Governor Panoy, I'm officially notifying you of the outcome of the Captain's Court held yesterday aboard the *Honora Belle*."

"There's no such thing as a Captain's Court," Lise objected vociferously.

"Quite the contrary, Governor," Harbour replied, warming to the conversation. Either she was broadcasting her pleasure, or the crew was pleased by the nature of the call. Either way, they were wearing smiles.

"I'll be sending a set of files to each of you that I imagine the governor failed to send you, Commandant, for whatever reason. You can read them at your leisure. However, I'll summarize them briefly for you."

Harbour took another swig of her green, realizing it was her initiating the smiles on the faces of her bridge crew, and, at this point, she didn't care. She wanted them to share in her pleasure.

"The *Honora Belle* predates our settlement, and, as such, is independent of the rules governing Pyre. According to the agreements signed by the original colonists, the *Belle*'s captain has the power to adjudicate any matter, concerning the colonists and descendants of this ship until such time as a formal election process of the new government is convened and completed. That process was never begun, which means my powers, as duly elected captain, remain in force over every descendant of this ship."

"This is preposterous," Lise said. It sounded as if she was spitting her words.

"Please understand this call wasn't to solicit your comments, Governor. Either let me complete my announcement or I'll end our conversation."

Jessie, listening on his private link, whistled softly. The woman he had greeted at Triton was different from the one he had met earlier in the storeroom aboard the JOS, and since Triton, she'd continued to adopt her role as ship's captain. His admiration for her efforts found a new level.

"I convened a Captain's Court to review the events surrounding the death of Dimitri Belosov. Standing before me was the complainant, Aurelia Garmenti."

"Complainant?" Lise shouted. She was apoplectic at hearing Dimitri's murderer was termed a complainant.

"Governor, if you wouldn't mind, I should like to hear the outcome of this process," Stamerson stated, with firmness.

"Thank you, Captain," Harbour said politely. "It was alleged by Aurelia Garmenti that following a lifetime of incarceration, she was required to spend time with Dimitri Belosov, who sexually assaulted her on multiple occasions. It was during one of these occasions that Aurelia chose to defend herself, and she chose to do so in the only manner available to her. She frightened him. Dimitri could have fled the room, but he chose to back onto the balcony and either toppled over the railing or threw himself over."

Lise was seething at this turn of events, but she needed to hear how Harbour proceeded, so she clamped her teeth shut with great difficulty.

"I heard from the complainant, her mother, and her sister, as to the nature of their enforced imprisonment. And, since the perpetrators of the kidnapping of Helena Garmenti and the subsequent incarceration of the family for seventeen years have already been convicted and sentenced for these crimes by the Review Board, I found substance for the complainant's claims of abuse by Dimitri Belosov. However, to ensure that fairness was observed, I secured multiple witnesses as to Dimitri Belosov's character."

"I'll need the name of those witnesses, Captain," Emerson stated officially.

"And you won't receive them, Commandant. You're not entitled to the Captain's Court records."

Aurelia, who was listening with Dingles on his comm unit, giggled, and the first mate smiled at her.

"Every witness detailed a personality that can only be described as sociopathic. In addition, the court has discovered that evidence procured at the Andropov home after the arrests was deemed unnecessary to present to the Review Board, prior to the hearing."

"What evidence, Captain Harbour?" Stamerson demanded.

"Found in the nightstand of a room that was reserved exclusively for Dimitri Belosov's meetings with Aurelia Garmenti were a collection of devices of the bondage type. Aurelia Garmenti testified to the nature and use of those items on her by Dimitri Belosov. In each and every encounter, Aurelia vocally protested Dimitri's use of his bondage devices and his subsequent molestations. The court found Aurelia Garmenti's testimony compelling, and the evidence points to a pattern of aggravated sexual assault by Dimitri Belosov on her person. In summary, it was the judgment of the Captain's Court that Aurelia Garmenti acted in self-defense, which resulted in the accidental death of Dimitri Belosov by his own hand. Therefore, the charge of murder laid against Aurelia Garmenti by the previous governor has been set aside."

"You won't get away with this, Harbour," Lise yelled, before throwing her comm unit across the salon, effectively ending her participation in the call.

"Captain, as commandant of the JOS, I can't abide by your decision. If Aurelia Garmenti sets foot on the JOS, she will be arrested and tried for murder."

"Aurelia Garmenti has no intention of visiting your foully governed station, Commandant, while you sit in that office, but I hope to remedy that one day, one day soon. And, while we're threatening each other, be advised that if you send your people to collect Aurelia, I intend to deny them entry to the *Belle*, and I don't care what orders they carry from you."

Harbour's comm unit indicated that Emerson had dropped off the call without replying, but Captain Stamerson remained online.

"For my part, Captain," Stamerson said, "I look forward to reading the documents that you've sent, and, may I say, well done, Captain, absolutely well done."

Harbour could hear the retired spacer captain chuckling, as he closed his end of the call.

* * * *

Aurelia visited Harbour in her quarters after dinner.

"I take it nothing's changed, Captain, regarding my freedom," Aurelia said.

"I'm sorry to say that it hasn't, Aurelia," Harbour replied. "On this ship, I can defend your freedom, but my announcement today was only the opening in a long fight to correct what's been done to our society. I'm afraid if you left this ship, you'd become a pawn in the struggle, and pawns are often sacrificed for the gains of those in power."

Aurelia was crestfallen, and Harbour sensed her descending darkness.

"But you're aware that Captain Cinders and I have decided to continue our agreement."

"Aye, Captain."

"Then there's nothing to stop you from joining up with one of Captain Cinder's ships when they leave the JOS for Emperion, but it will be incumbent on your part to rejoin the *Belle* before they make either station again. Understood?"

"Aye, Captain," Aurelia said, her smile and pleasure beaming at Harbour.

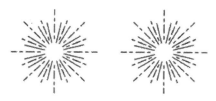

— The Pyreans will return in *Messinants* in mid-2018. —

— *BUT FIRST* —

— Watch for the return of Alex and company in *Vinium* in early 2018. —

Glossary

Colony Ship

Arlene – Artisan leader

Beatrice "Birdie" Andrews – Comm operator on the *Belle*

Bryan Forshaw – Propulsion engineer on the *Belle*

Celia O'Riley – Former name of the current Harbour

Danny Thompson – Pilot on the *Belle*

Dingles – Nickname for Mitch Bassiter, first mate on the *Belle*

Harbour – Protector of the empaths, captain of the *Belle*, originally known as Celia O'Riley

Herbert McKinley – Medical spacer aboard the *Belle*

Lindsey Jabrook – Previous Harbour

Makana – Artisan who decorated Harbour's skins

Nadine – Eldest active empath

Pete Jennings – Engineer and ex-spacer

Stacey Young – Medical spacer aboard the *Belle*

Yardley – Blind artisan, who works in metalcraft

Yasmin – Harbour's closest friend, empath

Downsiders

Andrei Andropov – Founder of the Andropov dynasty

Aurelia – Eldest daughter of Helena, also known as Rules

Dimitri Belosov – Son of Liana Belosov and the governor's nephew

Gerald – Tech at El landing pad

Giorgio Sestos – Governor's head of security

Helena Garmenti – Kidnapped by the governor, mother of Aurelia and Sasha

Idrian Tuttle – Dome family head

Liana Belosov – Sister of Markos Andropov

Lise Panoy – Dome family head, later governor of domes

Markos Andropov – Governor of Pyre's domes

Rufus Stewart – Dome family head

Sasha – Younger daughter of Helena, Aurelia's sister

Spacers

Angelina "Angie" Mendoza – First mate on the *Pearl*

Belinda Kilmer – Third mate on the *Pearl*, later second mate on the *Marianne*

Buttons – Crew member aboard the *Spryte*

Claudia Manning – *Spryte*'s shuttle pilot

Corbin Rose – Captain of the *Marianne*, bequeathed his ship to Cinders

Darrin "Nose" Fitzgibbon – First mate on the *Marianne*

Hamoi – Assay tech on the *Marianne*

Ituau Tulafono – First mate aboard the *Spryte*

Jeremy Kinsman – Navigator aboard the *Spryte*

Jessie Cinders – Owner of a mining company and captain of the *Spryte*

Kasey – Tech aboard the *Spryte*

Leonard Hastings – Captain of the *Pearl*

Mitch Bassiter – Known as Dingles, first mate on the *Belle*

Nate Mikado – Second mate aboard the *Spryte*

Orson – Shelter tech on the *Marianne*

Oscar – Assay engineer on the *Marianne*

Schaefer – Second mate on the *Marianne*, then traded to the *Pearl*

Sima Madigan – Mining captain on the *Dauntless*

Tobias Samuels – Lead excavation engineer on the *Marianne*

Tully – Survey engineer on the *Marianne*

Yohlin Erring – Captain of the *Marianne*

Stationers or Topsiders

Bondi – Member of the Review Board

Bowden – Officer in station security

Cecilia Lindstrom – Corporal in station security, later promoted to sergeant

Devon Higgins – Lieutenant in station security

Emerson Strattleford – Commandant of the JOS

Evan Pendleton – YIPS manager

Gabriel – Latched On store owner

Henry Stamerson – Head of the Review Board, retired mining captain

JD – El car freight crewman

Liam Finian – Major in station security

Maggie – Hostess of the Miners' Pit, ex-spacer

Miguel Rodriguez – Sergeant in station security

Nunez – Officer in station security

Pena – Young girl who Toby likes

Penelope – Terminal arm 2 manager

Phillip Borden – Groundskeeper employed by downsiders

Rules – Sasha's nickname for Aurelia

Sam – Terminal arm 4 manager

Stephen Jenkels – Engineer and architect of the orbital station, the JOS

Terrell "Terror" McKenzie – Corporal in station security, and Giorgio Sestos' asset

Toby – Boy in wheelchair awaiting BRC surgery

Vac Suits

Frances – Jeremy's suit name

Jessie – Aurelia's suit name

Spryte – Jessie's suit name

Objects, Terms, and Cantinas

Bender – Slang for empath

BNNT – Tiny, nanotubes made of carbon, boron, and nitrogen, interspersed with hydrogen for insulation

BRC – Bone replacement copy, pronounced "brick"

Caf drink – A mix of artificially grown coffee and cocoa with a mild stimulant

Cap – Transportation capsule

C-chip ring – Coin carrying/transfer system housed on a ring

Coin – Reference to electronic currency

Coin-kat or coin-kitty – Male or female sex service provider

Comm-dot – Communications ear-wig that relays to a comm unit or trans-stick

DAD – DNA analysis device

DBs – Refers to the people who live in the domes

Deck shoes – Shoes with patterned bottoms, which allow people's feet to adhere to decks

Downside – Refers to the domes on Pyre

E-cart – Electric cargo transport

El – Elevator car linked between the orbital station and Pyre's domes

Empath – Person capable of sensing and manipulating the emotional states of others

E-trans – Electric passenger transport

Green – Replenishing drink for the empaths

Latched On – Spacer supply house

Mag-boots – Boots that hold vac suited spacers to ship decks

Miners' Pit – Cantina owned by Jessie Cinders

Mist mask – Makeup mask

Mist wipe – Removes makeup

Normals – Individuals who have no empath capability

Ped-path – Walking and electric vehicle transport surface in the domes

Pull – Empaths term for reading the emotions of another

Push – Empath term for affecting the emotions of another

Review Board – Judicial body aboard the JOS

Rose's Reward – Used in the negative to mean an unsuccessful trip

Sensitives – Preferred alternate name for empaths

Shock stick – Weapon carried by JOS security personnel

Skins – Preferred clothing of stationers and spacers

Sleepholds – Places for people to temporarily bunk

Slip boots – Used to protect the feet inside mag-boots

Starlight – Expensive JOS cantina

Stationers – People who live on the Jenkels Orbital Station

Trans-stick – Pyrean fashion, which function as a transmitter

Vac suit – Spacer's vacuum work suit

Stars, Planets, and Moons

Crimsa – Star of the planet Pyre

Emperion – Pyre's second moon

Minist – Pyre's first and smallest moon

Pyre – New home world of Sol-NAC colonists

Triton – Pyre's third and largest moon

Ships and Stations

Dauntless – Mining ship, Sima Madigan captain

Honora Belle – Colony ship, also known as the *Belle*

Jenkels Orbital Station – Station above Pyre and anchors the El car to downside, nicknamed the JOS, pronounced "joss."

Marianne – Captain Jessie Cinders' first ship, referred to as the *Annie,* willed to him by Corbin Rose

Spryte – Captain Jessie Cinders' third ship

Unruly Pearl – Captain Jessie Cinders' second ship, referred to as the *Pearl,* willed to him by Corbin Rose

Yellen-Inglehart Processing Station – Mineral and gas processing platform called the YIPS, pronounced "yips."

My Books

Empath, the first novel in this new series, the Pyreans, is available in e-book and softcover editions. Please visit my website, http://scottjucha.com, for publication locations. You may register at my website to receive e-mail updates on the progress of my upcoming novels.

Pyrean Series
Empaths
Messinants
Jatouche (2018)

The Silver Ships Series
The Silver Ships
Libre
Méridien
Haraken
Sol
Espero
Allora
Celus-5
Omnia
Vinium
Nua'll
Artifice (2018)

The Author

From my early years to the present, books have been a refuge. They've fueled my imagination. I've traveled to faraway places and met aliens with Asimov, Heinlein, Clarke, Herbert, and Le Guin. I've explored historical events with Michener and Clavell, and I played spy with Ludlum and Fleming.

There's no doubt that the early sci-fi masters influenced the writing of my first two series, The Silver Ships and Pyreans. I crafted my stories to give readers intimate views of my characters, who wrestle with the challenges of living in space and inhabiting alien worlds.

Life is rarely easy for these characters, who encounter aliens and calamities, but they persist and flourish. I revel in examining humankind's will to survive. Not everyone plays fair or exhibits concern for other beings, but that's another aspect of humans and aliens that I investigate.

My stories offer hope for humans today about what they might accomplish tomorrow far from our home world. Throughout my books, humans exhibit a will to persevere, without detriment to the vast majority of others.

Readers have been generous with their comments, which they've left on Amazon and Goodreads for others to review. I truly enjoy what I do, and I'm pleased to read how my stories have positively affected many readers' lives.